THE
STEINBERG DIAMONDS

Marc Brosnan

HOBART BOOKS

HOBART BOOKS

THE STEINBERG DIAMONDS

COPYRIGHT © MARC BROSNAN 2022

ISBN 978-1-914322-10-5

First Published in 2022
by
Hobart Books, Oxfordshire, England
hobartbooks.com

Printed and bound in Great Britain.

The Steinberg Diamonds

By Marc Brosnan

Prologue

16thApril 1988, Sidi Bou Said, Tunisia

Despite the heat of midday in Sidi Bou Said, Wiener felt comfortable in his disguise. Under the canopy outside the small café, he stirred his coffee and studied the villa opposite. A sign on the gate gave details of a villa rental company, but this particular place would never see any holiday visitors. The other customers were locals who had chosen to sit in the air-conditioned interior. Passing traffic was light, consisting mainly of vans and trucks. One passing police car in an hour took no notice of the burka-covered customer taking a rest from the humidity of the day. In the early hours, he and a team of commandos had made a beach landing at Raoued near Tunis, under the direction of the Israeli intelligence service: Mossad.

Wiener had himself only recently joined the Sayeret Matkal special forces unit from the Israeli Defence Force a year earlier, and this was his first undercover operation. The target was a PLO leader who had allegedly assumed responsibility for a number of terrorist attacks that had shocked Israel, forcing the Prime Minister to sanction a Mossad assassination. The decision to end the man's life came after a bus full of workers, mainly women, were killed by a PLO raiding party whilst heading for their shift at Israel's Negev Nuclear Research Centre. Had Wiener known then that his own family would be lost in the same way he might have completed the job with greater efficiency.

i

The two men stood just inside the entrance gate and observed the vicinity through their mirrored sunglasses. Wiener could easily make out the weapons beneath their grey cotton jackets. He suspected they were carrying Glocks, the side arm of choice for PLO operatives. Wiener could not be sure if there were other PLO bodyguards inside his target's villa, but he would be prepared for anything. Under the blue burka he wore, Wiener ran his hand over the Uzi submachine gun. Not his usual weapon of choice but for this task he needed its fire power of 600 rounds per minute, chambered in 9mm Parabellum rounds. He also carried six spare box magazines in the pouch belt around his waist, each holding 30 rounds. The suppressor was fitted already but the noise of each shot would still be heard by anyone nearby.

Leaving a five Dinar note on the table, Wiener rose from his seat and crossed the street towards the villa. His loose-fitting burka billowed slightly in the soft breeze, and a well-trained thumb selected semi-auto on the safety selector by feel as he approached the gate. Single shots. That's all he needed. Calm. Precise.

One of the men inside the entrance nudged his partner as what he saw as a woman shuffled towards them. Wiener knew his next move would decide the success of the operation. As he reached the gate, he stumbled and held out his glove-covered right hand to steady himself on the railing. He let out a weak groan as he fell onto one knee. One of the men spoke in Arabic to ask if she was okay, whilst the other instinctively placed a hand on the Glock holster under his left arm. *'Da,'* Wiener groaned, the Arabic for water. Both men looked at each other as if unsure what to do. Help the woman, or simply ignore her? When the woman uttered *'Musaeida,'* or help, the first man started to unlock the gate. The second man kept a firm grip on his weapon, ready to pull it if necessary.

'What is wrong, old woman?' the gate opener asked. 'Are you okay?'

'*Shukranlak,*' Wiener muttered. 'Thank you.' He pushed the Uzi against the fabric of his burka and squeezed the trigger, dropping the first man dead before engaging the second and dropping him with the same, calm, precise single shot. Leaping to his feet, Wiener closed the gate and peered through the bars. No one was near enough to witness what had just happened. He removed the burka and threw it down at the base of the white-washed wall, laying on the ground to study the villa set back a hundred metres from the gate. There was no sign of movement but Wiener felt sure anyone inside would have heard the suppressed gun shots. Now things would be different.

Instinctively, his thumb once again found the safety selector and selected full-auto on the Uzi in expectation of the firefight to come. Slowly rising to a crouch, he made his way to the left side of the villa. At the rear of the two-storey building was a patio area and a large swimming pool. The water was an azure blue and shimmered in the sunshine, with loungers on one side and a small drinks table between them. Scanning the scene to his front, Wiener sensed a movement behind him. As one, his head, body and the barrel of the suppressed Uzi turned, just as a PLO man raised his AK and loosed off three poorly aimed rounds, fired more in panicked surprise than with any thought for the four marksmanship principles. The muzzle of the Uzi replied with a controlled plink-plink, discharging the remaining parabellum rounds into the PLO man.

Skilfully changing magazine with the speed and dexterity of a craftsman that knows his tools, he glimpsed the silhouette of a figure climbing the inside stairs leading to the upper level. Wiener followed, knowing he'd be an easy target on the patio from the first-floor balcony. As he reached the foot of the steps, a volley of shots from above.

'*Win the firefight.*' The drill flashed into his mind as he discharged a full magazine and forced the shooter back a landing. Purposefully, he scaled the stairs three at a time, reloading swiftly as he went. Scanning for threats, he detected movement as a door leading to a bathroom closed gently. He took a punt and fired a short burst through the flimsy plywood. Nothing. Had he imagined it? No... the crimson tide of fresh blood seeping under the door said otherwise. It was him, the target. He wasn't going anywhere.

Satisfied no one else was in the villa, Wiener left through a rear gate where a Volkswagen minibus was waiting, engine running and ready to go. Within minutes Wiener found himself back on Raoued beach, boarding a Zodiac RIB bound for the Israeli gunboat waiting offshore that would return them to Haifa.

July 2010, Bronx, NY City

Wiener sat at his favourite table in a corner next to the kitchen entrance in Lieberman's Deli, savouring a pastrami on rye with a side of coleslaw and Russian dressing. A waiter brought him his second lemon tea with his food. Since his family were murdered by the PLO in 1982 Wiener enjoyed mooching around the Bronx. He had planned to open a pastry shop of his own and name it after his daughter, but to date the fruits of this grand plan still eluded him. He preferred Liebman's Deli to the more well-known establishments like Katz.

Katz had become too much of a tourist attraction since featuring in *When Harry Met Sally*, so now he could never get a table. Subconsciously blending into his surroundings like any other lone diner, Wiener studied his iPhone whilst eating, looking up hotels in the UK in preparation for his forthcoming visit. Although an Israeli citizen, Wiener was Welsh by birth but had moved to a Kibbutz with his parents when he was a child. He swallowed the last of his pastrami and washed it down with the lemon tea. After tucking a fifty-dollar bill under his plate, he rose to leave. That left a large tip, but he figured the waiter hadn't eaten for a week

Outside, Wiener turned onto John's Road where his apartment was located. As he walked, he became aware of a person wearing a hooded top with his head bent down. The usual sort – a low-life punk. He rasped a remark as Wiener came upon him.

'Hey, Jew. You got the time?'

Wiener looked around him then faced the male. 'You talking to me, son?'

'Don't try to be smart, wise guy.' He pulled a hunting knife from his top. 'Let me have your wallet and no one gets hurt.'

'My wallet?' Wiener said.

'You deaf? Gimme your wallet or I stick you with this.' The punk raised the knife in line with Wiener's stomach. Slowly, menacingly, Wiener stepped in towards the knife. His six-two frame shadowed the sallow male's five-eight.

'Say please,' Wiener whispered.

'I fucking warned you...' In one slick movement, Wiener had grabbed the punk's knife hand and twisted so the knife fell to the ground, and then took him by the throat and almost lifted him from his feet, pushing him back into the parking lot.

'I have three questions for you,' Wiener hissed. 'Get one wrong and you're as good as dead. Understood?' The punk's fearful eyes stared back. A brief nod was all he could manage.

'Right,' Wiener said, 'First question. What city we in?'

'Noo... Noo York,' he stammered back.

'And what district is this?'

'Da Bronx, yeah, da Bronx.'

'Two from two,' Wiener said. 'Good so far. Now, what is the capital city of Australia?'

The punk grinned with his progress and anticipation. 'Sydney?' he said.

'Now, see,' Wiener said. 'I figured you'd say that. It's Canberra. Most punks like you think it's Sydney.' Wiener's grip around the man's neck tightened. His eyes bulged with the pressure. Then Wiener released his grip and stood back. The man spluttered and held his neck. Fearing a further attack, he took off down the street, coughing as he went. Wiener watched and shook his head. He then picked the knife from the ground and dropped it down a storm drain next to the sidewalk.

His mobile phone buzzed in his pocket, and seeing the name flash on the screen, Wiener answered. 'Mr Abraham Steinberg, to what do I owe the pleasure?' Wiener listened as his cousin from the UK spoke to him. 'You know what, Abe? I was considering a trip over some time. Guess your situation there has hastened my decision.' Wiener put his phone away and strolled thoughtfully towards his apartment.

One

Cardiff, January 1965

It was only a short run out from the GPO sorting office in the centre of the city across to Cardiff General Station. The night was cold, wet and miserable. The rain fell in heavy sheets, ice-cold droplets stinging the faces of the poor souls unfortunate enough to be outside, exposed to such abysmal weather. The small Austin J2 Post Office van pulled away from the loading platform carrying mailbags for the 10:05 pm Cardiff to Paddington train. For both driver and assistant it was a routine duty: get the mail onto a trolley at the station then up onto platform one to be loaded into the caged area of the guard carriage.

The men would then check that the all-important *final-bag*, the bag with the total number of the dispatch written on a buff label, went in last on the very top of the pile.

Among the contents of the final bag was a smaller green bag known in the GPO as a Remittance or Rem. This one carried the Registered Letter items. On this occasion, five of the registered letters inside the inner green bag contained fifty cut diamonds. A mix of size and shape but no one stone was less than a carat – some as much as five. High quality gems radiant with good colour and clarity in shapes of oval, pear, cushion, and heart. Some of the larger, five-carat stones were a brilliant cut, giving maximum scintillation, beauty and fire. The value of the diamonds neared £50,000.

Cardiff jeweller Maxwell Steinberg had addressed the packages to a dealer he traded with in Hatton Garden. During the month, he had bought precious stones from customers at his jewellery shop, as well as from other dealers or jewellers in the area. The previous December had been a good month for business. A number of individuals had looked to raise cash, probably for Christmas. A jewellery business in Gloucester had also gone into liquidation, providing him an opportunity for a good deal.

Steinberg bought a large number of cut diamonds as a way for the owner to minimise his losses before the liquidators stepped in. Steinberg always sent valuable stones by registered post as he believed it to be a safe, secure method of delivery. He retained complete faith in the postal system, despite the *Great Train Robbery* two years earlier. The jeweller believed it to be an economical method of dispatch when he considered the contents. It had never failed him yet.

However, on this occasion, despite the mailbags arriving safely, the diamonds failed to reach their London destination.

Two

Cardiff Bay, March 2010

Patrick Doyle stood at the railings outside of the Norwegian church, staring down at the water's edge, watching it gently lap onto the stonework. Looking up, he gazed out to Penarth Head, and the seaway to the world beyond. Pat, as he was commonly known, was disillusioned, unhappy, and in serious debt from his unsuccessful gambling. He'd taken the ill-advised step of borrowing money from a local 'loan shark' who now demanded instant repayment with an extortionate rate of interest. People passed, glancing curiously as he talked quietly to himself in his down-trodden solitude.

'How do I get out of this mess? My marriage is finished, well Christ, it never really started. The job's crap, and I'm in debt to a loan shark who wants to seriously hurt me.'

He looked solemnly at the lottery ticket in his hand. Seven lines, not even a bloody tenner.

Heading out to sea, bound for China, a bulk-carrier laden with a cargo of scrap metal. Just the one, unlike the flotilla of ships that filled Cardiff Docks when he sailed from there in the 1970's on the MV *Stella Maris* as a boy rating in the Merchant Navy.

'God, I wish I could sail away from this bloody misery.'

Pat turned his gaze towards the contrasting buildings that stood side by side, one from the 19th century – the red-brick

Pierhead building – and one from the 21st century – the ultra-modern *Senedd* building, home of the Welsh Government. With hands clutching the metal rail and head lifted skywards, he yelled out.

'Where the hell can I get some serious money?'

'Eh!'

This came from a passing man, a very dishevelled and worn looking individual, one of Cardiff's many street drinkers. The tell-tale bulge in his shabby coat from a half-consumed bottle of cheap white cider. Only eight in the morning, and the 'wino' was unsteady on his feet having already partaken of a skinful.

Maybe there are people worse off than me, he considered, half smiling.

Pat flicked his partly-smoked cigarette into the water, followed by the useless lottery ticket, before heading back to his flat in the Bay, shoulders hunched, not really paying any attention to his surroundings. As he reached James Street, a car screeched to a halt next to him. Two Asian men jumped out then stepped in front of him, blocking his progress.

'Mr Osman wants his money, Doyle,' said the larger of the two men. 'You have money to pay him, yes?' Thick set with crow-black hair and menacing eyes, he wore a light-brown cashmere overcoat despite the mild weather. The other, slightly smaller, but equally hard-looking man came closer, producing a knife from the inside of his leather jacket. He held it under Pat's chin.

'Mr Osman was kind enough to help you out when you needed him, but now you treat him with such disrespect.'

He pushed the knife slightly upwards, just enough to break the skin – drawing a crimson droplet of blood. Pat winced.

'We warned you this would happen if you held back, Doyle.'

'Look, guys, tell Mr Osman I'll have some cash for him later today. Honest, I will.'

The larger man shook his head.

'You told us this before, Doyle, but you did not keep your word. Mr Osman is not a patient man so now you must give us some money.'

'But I don't have any money, well not on me at least. Search me if you want.'

He spread out his arms. The men ignored his gesture.

'Then we have to take Mr Osman something else, a token.'

'Token. Like what?'

'Like a finger,' the knife man smirked.

'A finger!' Pat cried, stumbling back. The larger man stepped over, grabbing Pat from behind in a bear hug. The knife man took hold of Pat's left wrist while Pat struggled in desperation. The grip of the man holding him became tighter.

'For God's sake, guys. I'll get you some money. I will… please.'

Another car pulled up, this time a taxi. The driver jumped out then walked over to them.

'You okay, mate?' asked Elroy Blake, one of Pat's few close friends.

'None of your business, Blake.' The man flashed the blade for Elroy's benefit.

Elroy shook his head.

'How much d'you owe them, Pat?'

'Too much, well over a grand.'

Elroy leaned into his taxi and pulled out a coin bag.

'Give Ali Osman this,' Elroy said to the man with the knife. Elroy handed over a fistful of banknotes.

The money was snatched then quickly counted.

'Fifty pounds, huh.' He shoved the money into his pocket. 'But it is only enough for the time being; we'll be back for more, believe it.'

The two Asians returned to their car, and with a screech of tyres, they drove off in the direction of the city centre.

Pat looked at his friend, relief and gratitude etched onto his face.

'Thanks, Elroy. I'll pay you back as soon as I get paid.'

Elroy shook his head and grinned. 'Yeah, I'll join the queue behind those two.'

They both laughed. Elroy put his arm around his friend's shoulder. 'You've got to get this gambling sorted out, man, or those guys will very probably kill you.'

Pat nodded touching his finger to the spot where the knife had broken the skin, wincing before answering.

'I'm doing my best, mate. I really am. I even tried investing on the stock market. That's why I borrowed a grand from Osman. Trouble was, the markets took a dive. Lost the lot.'

'Stock markets are no different from the betting shop, man.' Elroy told him. 'Come on I'll give you a lift home – free ride.'

Pat welcomed the offer. He was truly grateful, relieved by his friend's timely intervention, but knew Osman's men would be back for him. Next time they might take a finger, possibly a lot more.

He shuddered as he sat in the front seat of the car. Clipping the seatbelt around him then leaning back against the headrest, he closed his eyes.

London, January 1965

A screech of brakes announced the arrival of the 1:15 am at platform three in Paddington. Just two minutes late. Standing ready on the platform were six bored-looking postal workers, shivering inside their winter issue greatcoats. They shuffled around, smoking cigarettes, stamping their feet to ward off the cold. One lay stretched out on the trolley. Half-asleep, he was roused by a colleague as the train made its noisy arrival along the platform.

After unloading the mail, they'd take it across to the Paddington District Sorting Office. A few disconsolate, tired-looking passengers left the train. Some showed the rumpled signs of having recently woken from an uncomfortable slumber, making their unhurried way to the exit barrier where a ticket collector stood ready to take the proffered tickets.

The postal workers converged on the mail carriage to remove the mailbags, loading them into the waiting vans. At the Paddington Sorting Office one particular bag was heaved onto a large table. Once cut, both label and seal were set aside. The postman who carried out this task took hold of the bottom of the bag, lifting it with a grunt, its contents spilling onto the table. He looked in baffled surprise at what fell out in front of him. Instead of the expected bundles of letters and the green Remittance bag, the contents were no more than a large number of old cut-up newspapers tied with string.

He ran to the office, looking for the duty Inspector.

'Sir, you'd better come and take a look at this,' the postman said, putting his head around the office door.

'What is it, lad?' asked the Inspector gruffly, resenting the intrusion. He put his rimless reading glasses into his breast pocket then followed the agitated postman across the sorting office.

'Right then, what you got?' he asked disinterestedly, wanting only to return to his coffee and crossword. A number of postal workers had gathered around the table, whispering, pointing at the bag's contents.

'See for yourself,' the postman said.

The Inspector growled at the assembled men, ordering them back to their duties before he looked at the piles of newspaper cuttings. The colour in his face drained as the realisation of what he saw dawned on him.

'Oh my God, get the drivers back here, NOW!' he shouted. 'Don't touch a thing. We need the police to stop the train from leaving. Where's the rest of the mail? I want all the other bags set aside then nobody go near them.'

He shook his head grimly with utter disbelief.

'I don't want to be the one to tell the police we've stomped all over any evidence if this turns out to be another bloody train robbery.'

Crossword and coffee forgotten, he hurried off to inform the night Chief Inspector.

Three

Cardiff Bay, March 2010

Pat Doyle had lived in his small flat near Cardiff Bay for the last four years. He'd bought, or rather over-stretched himself with a mortgage for one of the much sought-after waterfront apartments. The purchase was made twelve months earlier following the separation from his wife, Helen. A separation he'd got over. He'd never loved her, Pat often reminded himself, but he wasn't sure he really meant it deep down.

He'd bought the flat hastily when property demand in the Bay area exceeded supply, paying over the odds, and with little choice of location. The décor was simple yet elegant, the kitchen functional, the bathroom basic. One wall of the small, slightly cramped lounge was fitted entirely with shelves containing a large collection of books, CDs, and vinyl records ranging from classical to R&B, rock to easy listening. An eclectic taste, he told himself.

He pushed a disc, *Rumours,* by Fleetwood Mac, into a Bose music player before walking to the bathroom. He stood in front of the mirror to examine his face; a flannel, he dabbed at the cut from the knife.

'Pat,' he told his reflection, 'sort your life out or you're a dead man.'

He grimaced at the recollection of the previous day's encounter with Osman's heavies. He set the flannel down, arching his neck to get a better look at the cut. Little more he could do there. Returning to the kitchen, he finished off his cold breakfast toast before picking up a letter from the morning post. He reread the solemn warning from the bank about stopping his direct debits; they wanted funds paid into his account 'with immediate effect'. Another envelope contained a mail-shot from the same bank offering a loan. Complete irony: rob Peter – pay… well, Peter.

He finished the last of the toast, dropping the letter to the worktop with faint contempt.

At least they weren't threatening to slit his throat like some loan providers, he brooded, eyebrows knitted in frustration.

Pat arrived at the Child Protection Team office based within the County Hall building near his flat. After making himself a cup of coffee, he carried it over to his cluttered desk with the newspaper he'd bought on the way in. The open-plan design made it easy to speak with colleagues working at nearby desks but also exposed him when he needed some privacy. Sipping at his coffee, he read the front-page headline:

Turf Wars

Local drug gangs fighting it out on city streets.

'Jeez, it's getting like New York around here,' Pat commented to a female colleague sitting opposite. 'People are turning up dead, nearly two a week.'

'That's right,' the woman agreed. 'There was a programme on television last week about the Welsh drug barons. They claim Cardiff is controlled by one man in particular.'

Pat thought about Osman, wondering if he was in on the action. His thoughts veered off; he didn't really want to think about Ali Osman. He drained his coffee, considered a refill, but then thought better of it.

'Oh well, I'd better get off.' he announced. 'I'm visiting the Foley's place this morning.'

He set the cup down, folded the newspaper, put it under his arm, and made his way to the door.

'Rather you than me,' his colleague called after him.

'Or anyone else,' he muttered.

***

Pat dreaded home visits to see the Foley family, wishing he'd put on old clothes before he'd left for work that morning. No use wearing decent clothes because whatever he wore would reek of the ghastly smells that hung in the air all over their house, a mix of stale urine, excrement, and grease, overlaid with the sour odour of old tobacco smoke. The Foleys, happily oblivious to all of this, vigorously denied any problem in the way they lived.

Dennis Foley, an unkempt, grubby looking individual, rarely washed. His wife, Lila, was pretty much the same. On visits to the house, Pat politely refused offers of a cup of tea or coffee. He'd seen their mugs, chipped, heavily stained often with cigarette ends extinguished in the dregs. No way would he ever accept a drink from them.

He drove to the housing estate in his old battered Astra GTI. He'd bought the car second-hand thinking a GTI would help re-claim his youth, but he knew what he really looked like – a man who had simply borrowed his son's car for the day. The worn, unreliable engine seemed to break down more than it started, usually in the most awkward places. Due to the car's mechanical temperament, the garage bills had mounted up. Another debt he struggled to meet.

***

Pat pulled up outside the ramshackle property that stood forlorn in an obvious state of disrepair. Broken windows seemed to stare out at him, almost as if the front of the house was a face and the windows its sad eyes. Old paint peeled from the wooden frames. The sorry pile stood in contrast to the surrounding, better-kept houses with their neat gardens. The council had long given up on the place, along with the Foleys.

Groaning inwardly, Pat climbed out of the car. He could never fully prepare himself for the stench that would invade his nostrils, the nasal equivalent of a sledgehammer to the head. The children, Steven and Tanya, were playing in the front garden, an area littered with bits of old furniture, a redundant dog kennel, and a fridge with no door. Interspersed between all the detritus were empty cans, once containing either food or alcohol. Pat stared at the fridge, recalling how it never even had a door when it was used in the kitchen. He'd prevented their acquisition of a large dog three weeks earlier, much to the noisy dismay of the children. They were now using the kennel as a Wendy House despite the obvious signs of the previous occupant ingrained in the wooden floor and walls. The RSPCA would have condemned the kennel as unfit for canine habitation such was its state. He'd have to say something about the children he spotted sitting inside having some kind of picnic. Shuddering, he hoped it was just chocolate Tanya licked off her fingers.

'Hiya, Pat,' the girl greeted him as he almost fell over the loosely hanging gate. Dennis appeared at the door, stepping outside to confront Pat as he tried to compose himself after losing his balance. Dennis wore trousers that shone with age. A grimy vest sported a large hole at the back. He also wore a pair of odd slippers: one pink, the other brown.

'I've been a council tenant for fifteen years,' Dennis announced loudly as Pat moved slowly towards him. 'So I wanna exercise my right t' buy.'

'I'm sorry,' Pat responded. 'What do you mean?'

'Look, Pat, I knows my rights,' he continued. 'I voted Tory years ago 'cos they promised to sell us our houses. I knows I can have the place for cheap. I paid rent for all them years so now I wanna buy it.'

'Dennis, your rent was... is paid for you from housing benefit,' Pat reminded him as tactfully as possible. 'You've never actually parted with any money for the whole time you've been a tenant.'

'That's crap and you know it, Pat,' Dennis responded. Lila joined him at the door. 'You tell him, luv,' added the rotund Lila who now filled the door space. 'It's our right so we wanna get the council to sell it to us. You're our social worker so you 'ave to help us.'

Dennis looked up at Lila, nodding his agreement.

'Tha's right, luv,' Dennis said.

Pat glanced down at his feet, sighing inwardly.

'You do realise it would mean having to apply for a mortgage, don't you? How exactly would you repay a mortgage?' he asked wearily. 'You don't work, you claim benefit. You're better off with housing benefit as it covers the rent.'

Lila bellowed towards the house next door.

'Gaza, come 'ere now, I needs to talk to you.'

Oh God, Pat thought. Not bloody Gary Harris. That's all I need.

Harris had moved in twelve months earlier following his eviction from his council house in east Cardiff for anti-social behaviour. He appeared suddenly through a gap in the hedge, a tall, thin individual with close-cropped hair. Earrings covered his ear lobes, and tattooed fingers announced his love and hatred of who knew what. His badge of honour was the arachnid tattooed in the centre of his forehead. This had earned him the obvious nickname, 'Spider'.

'Go on, Spider,' Lila urged her neighbour. 'Tell Pat how you're buying yours with that loan you're getting.'

Pat grimaced when he realised she was referring to a spurious company, *OwnaHome*, who helped council tenants on benefits to buy their homes from the council at discounted prices. The company knew very well the new owners would likely default on their repayments. The properties would eventually be repossessed. A subsidiary company then stepped in buying the houses at auction for a fraction of their true value. Win-win for *OwnaHome*.

'Yeah, she's right like,' Gary Harris confirmed. 'This geezer said I qualified and I'll soon be an 'ome owner.'

His terrier-type dog, Rizla, joined Gary, sporting a studded collar that, in Pat's opinion, must be a lethal weapon. Time to leave. He could only take so much of this family.

'You know these children should be in school,' he informed them before walking down the path. Back in his car, Pat was relieved he'd had a lucky escape by not going inside the house on this occasion. As he started the car, listening to the alternator going through its painful screech when he turned the key, he could clearly hear the Foleys shout where they thought Pat should be at that particular moment. With their distasteful suggestions noted, he drove back into town.

Cardiff, January 1965

Reg Laine worked at the main GPO sorting office where he was responsible, with a colleague, for the registered letter locker, and that evening he prepared the dispatches for the

10:05 to London Paddington, making up the final bag with the registered items inside before a driver collected it, ready to take across to the railway station.

Being a Friday, he'd earlier signed for a number of registered envelopes, collected from the Westgate Street Crown Post Office that fronted the sorting office in the centre of Cardiff. He knew the envelopes came from a local jeweller. Often, he would wonder about what might be inside, more specifically, what he could do with whatever they contained.

'Jeez,' he muttered. 'How the other half live. There's me and Vi struggling to make ends meet while others have the life of Reilly.'

'What's that, Reg?' his colleague asked.

'Just thinking about me and the missus when I retire next year,' Reg replied.

'Hey, no looking back then, pal. You and Vi enjoying yourselves, eh?'

'Can't wait,' Reg muttered back, his colleague missing the overtone of sarcasm in his reply.

His wife Violet, an office cleaner, earned a pittance, so prospects for them in retirement were likely to be austere at best. This was in sharp contrast to his brother-in-law, Eddie Cross. Eddie lived the 'high life', or certainly high as Reg saw it. Reg owned a motor bike, an old Bantam D1 125cc he'd bought from the GPO when they'd upgraded to the newer D7 models for their telegram boys. Eddie drove a Ford Zephyr. Big, black, and shiny. Eddie was a regular gambler who frequented the town centre pubs and clubs, usually with some garishly dressed woman on his arm, out for a good time. Reg recalled how Eddie would buy him beer before asking questions about GPO work, seemingly interested in the contents of the mail bags. He knew the man to be a villain whose money came from diverse criminal activities.

That night after his shift ended, Reg went into *The York* publichouse for a couple of pints. He'd arranged to meet Eddie Cross in the back room. Tonight, Reg had decided he was going to put a proposition to Eddie that might – just might – ensure a comfortable retirement for Violet and himself.

Four

'Diamonds,' Pat shouted to the group around him.

'What?' exclaimed Elroy, 'Diamonds? Not again,' he said shaking his head. 'And I was going to go out with this.'

He held a card in the air but without revealing the suit. Pat placed a playing card down on the pile, smirking triumphantly as he announced, 'Last card.'

The others around the table looked at one another.

'Anyone got a Jack to change it?' asked Elroy.

Heads shook all around. Pat placed his last card, the seven of diamonds, on the table with a flourish.

'I do believe that's three straight games to me,' Pat announced smugly, scooping up the collection of coins from the table. 'Whose deal is it?'

Elroy pushed back his chair sinking the remains of his Red Bull.

'Count me out – I've got a taxi to run.' He slapped Pat on the back. 'And you look out for yourself, mate.'

Elroy Blake, the son of Afro-Caribbean parents, had been a close friend to Pat Doyle since their early school days. They often met up at lunchtimes in the dockland pub *The Windsor Hotel*. Pat frequented a few of the older pubs in the docks that remained. He remembered at least two from his childhood.

He did not particularly like the newer hostelries with their outlandish names, like *Turtle Bay*. Bloody hell. What were those brewery managers thinking when they arrived at the names for their public houses? Not content with turning perfectly good pubs into theme bars they also had to give them ridiculous names.

He liked the Docks with its two types of people, both the original residents of varied ethnicities, and the newcomers in the recently developed houses and high-rise apartment blocks. He recalled when the *Cardiff Bay Development Corporation* first came into being in the 1980s how he'd been totally opposed to it. It was at the height of Thatcherism, a period he remembered with severe distaste, having always voted Labour. He reflected on how he now embraced the area, with its restaurants, bars, cinemas, and the Millennium Centre, an opera house to rival the one in Sydney, the Welsh Government building, the *Senedd*, with its glass and timber interior and Welsh slate exterior. Pat rarely ventured out of this area except when work took him to 'the estates' or he needed to go into the city centre, usually to the library or bookshops. As an avid reader and historian, he was pleased to see the opening of a bookshop in the Bay that specialised in antiquarian as well as second-hand books. The proprietor – Tristan Rushby – referred to himself as an *antiquary* in rare books. Pat wasn't discriminatory in his own reading tastes; he read many books from the simple novel to the collected works of Dickens, although there were some authors he prized above others: Hemingway, Wells, Steinbeck, Defoe, Tolstoy, Darwin. All formed part of his collection. Pat's other passion was local history, particularly the Industrial Revolution following the onset of steam power, that elevated Cardiff to a wealthy city from the revenues of coal shipped through its once great docks. The enormous wealth created by a number of industrialists from the period helped shape the city into what it had become today. Their modern-day equivalents were the Arab oil sheiks in Saudi, propelled into wealth when oil became the new coal.

After leaving the pub, Pat made his way to collect a book from the shop based near the old Taff Vale Railway building when he decided to call into the charity shop to see how Demetra, or Demi, as she preferred to be known, was getting along.

Demi Boston, born in Cardiff to a Greek family, had striking features with dark eyes, olive coloured skin, and jet-black hair, usually pulled tightly back off her face, which did little to accentuate her beauty. Her family name was Karamanlis. Demi always charmed Pat with an infectious smile that lit up her face, like the sun rising on a new day. She was a single mother since separating from her former partner, Danny Boston, a violent drug dealer who'd often assaulted her when they were together. The abuse came to the attention of social services who took her two children into care, placing them with their maternal grandparents. The children returned to her care when she developed the courage to end the relationship and find her own home. Pat did a lot for the family as their social worker. He went the extra mile help her children, Chardonnay and Zak.

He had recently arranged for Demi to work as a volunteer in an animal sanctuary charity shop in order to help rebuild her lost confidence. The work was regarded as therapeutic, so it didn't affect her state benefit. As he approached the shop, he looked up at the hoarding above the window announcing the charity: Animal Rescue Centre or ARC, opened by a group of people in Cardiff who campaigned against scientists using laboratory rodents to find a cure for man's diseases. They kept rescued rats in a sanctuary; the shop helped to fund its running costs. He wondered if they released the rats back into the sewers the same way stranded seals were returned to the sea. Pat smiled as he pushed open the shop door.

'What's tickling your fancy?' Demi asked as he stepped into the shop grinning.

'Just an amusing thought,' he said. 'Nothing that funny.'

'No?' Demi said. 'Well, this might make you laugh. I was going through a box of stuff left outside, you know, books and that, mostly rubbish really. Well, right at the bottom of the box was a dildo.'

Pat looked puzzled,

'Oh come on, Pat. You know what I'm on about, a vibrator.'

'Yes, yes,' Pat replied. 'I do know what a dildo is.'

'Anyway,' she continued, 'I didn't know what to do with it so I put it out on the shelf over there.'

Demi pointed to a shelf near the door stacked with tacky looking ornaments, some cheap wine glasses, and a chipped Toby jug.

'So this old dear comes in looking for Mills and Boom books…'

'That's *Boon*, isn't it?' Pat interrupted.

'Yeah, yeah, whatever. So, she spots the dilly, asks how much. I said she could have it for a couple of quid. Well you should have seen her face, Pat. She chucked two quid at me then left. Shot out the door in a flash. Now here's the best bit,' Demi continued. 'The next day another old biddy comes in saying her friend bought a dildo the day before and will we be having any more in? I told her we only have stuff donated but I promised to keep my eye out for one and put it by for her.'

Pat's perplexed expression remained as he listened.

'She looked very disappointed so I told her there's a nice church candle on the shelf and with some Vaseline…'

'Demi,' he interrupted again. 'Tell me you're joking, please.'

'No,' she continued, 'it's true, and d'you know what? She bought the bloody candle. Honestly, Pat, I was in tears with laughter.'

'I'm sure there's a health and safety issue with things like that.'

'Get off,' she chimed. 'Who's ever going to know unless they find her dead with the candle jammed up her…'

'Okay, Demi. Let's not go there, shall we?' Pat said with raised hands, palms outwards, trying to avoid the mental image pushing its way to the surface. 'Anyway, how are you getting on here, – enjoying the experience?'

'Yeah, not bad. It'll do for my CV when I apply for a job in Tezzies.'

'I'm sure it will,' he agreed.

He looked around the shop that retained some of its original features such as the ornate plaster coving and ceiling rose. The doors were solid wood with wide architraves. Back over the years a number of businesses had taken on the premises but in the main the place had been empty. He made his way into a back room, where flicking the light switch did little to illuminate the space. The air smelt musky with a feeling of dampness in the atmosphere of the confined space. The room, filled with boxes of books, old clothes, and bric-a-brac, mostly donated to the shop, had no window to provide any natural light. He picked up a few of the paperbacks, the usual Jeffrey Archer, Tom Clancy and Catherine Cookson normally found in charity shops, nothing later than 1988. He dropped a much worn, yellow-paged copy of W*here Eagles Dare* back into one of the boxes.

In a corner under a pile of clothes laid out for sorting, Pat noticed a desk, an old piece of furniture made from light oak.

He pulled open the drawers, peering inside. One of the larger drawers refused to close properly. Pat pulled out the drawer to see what the obstruction might be. Putting his hand into the space, he felt something hard. He pulled out the object to examine it. It was an old book with a ridged spine, the subject being *Caskets and Coffins*. Flicking through the pages, he came across a carbon copy of a typewritten letter dated 1965. The letter was addressed to one Edward Cross Esq, in an area of Cardiff Pat knew had long since been demolished. Intrigued, he read the content.

Dear Mr Cross,

Following your instructions, I have placed the stones with a client for safe keeping. This person can be trusted to remain silent regarding your stated intentions. The stones may remain with my client for as long as required.

I have the details of my client's whereabouts so that the stones may be returned personally to you and Mr Laine at your request.

I await to hear from you in due course.

Yours sincerely,

A. Beers

'How cryptic,' Pat said to himself as he turned the flimsy sheet of paper over in his hand. Turning back to the book, he considered Tristan might be interested in it. He could trade it for another book, saving him some money. Looking once more at the letter, Pat folded it carefully before placing it in the top pocket of his jacket, deciding he would ask some of the older regulars at *The Windsor* about this place. Demi broke the moment when she put her head around the door and announced, 'Pat, cup of tea out here.' Welcoming the prospect, he stepped back into the front of the shop.

'I found this old book back there. How much d'you want for it?'

'Nothing, it's yours if you really want it.'

'No, I insist on paying. Anyway, it will be my contribution for the upkeep of a rat.'

After taking the money from his pocket, he reconsidered her offer, aware he was running out of cash.

'Well, if you insist. I'll call in again when I'm next passing.'

'Look forward to it,' Demi said, smiling.

Pat felt a wild urge to kiss her. So beautiful, he thought, aware that his feelings towards her had changed over the months, but hell, she was twenty-nine, he was old enough to be her – well – older brother. After draining his tea, he quickly left the shop.

Once outside, Pat decided to make his way back to the pub, but not before phoning his office to say he felt unwell and wouldn't return to work for the rest of the day. He looked nervously around the street in case Osman's men were out looking for him, then made his way to Singh's mini-market – Saturday promised a Lotto roll-over. A big win would guarantee an escape from all his troubles.

'Dream on, Doyle,' he told himself, stepping over the threshold, clutching the crumpled note he knew he should have used to pay for the book. The old Indian shopkeeper smiled in greeting as Pat entered.

'How are you today, Dr Doyle?'

Pat laughed before replying.

'Mr Singh, I'm not a medical doctor, you know. I have a PhD in history.'

The shopkeeper moved his turbaned head from shoulder to shoulder.

'Still makes you a doctor… you should not diminish your station. Now what can I get for you today?'

'Five lucky dips in tonight's draw,' he said holding out the £10 note. 'Mr Singh, you've been here for a long time. What can you tell me about the charity shop down the road?'

As he handed over the Lotto ticket, the elderly man said,

'Many years ago it was a funeral parlour, can't recall the owner's name. I didn't live here then. Strange goings on, a lot of people say. Ask some of the older residents, they are bound to know.'

'Yes, yes I will,' Pat said, thinking of just such a person he knew.

He left the small shop, unaware that the information he was to discover would significantly change forever his life, and the life of Demetra Karamanlis.

Five

Cardiff, January 1965

'Okay, I'm listening,' Eddie Cross said to Reg Laine. He put a fresh pint of Brains bitter on the table in front of his brother-in-law, before sitting down next to him. They were in the back room of *The York*, a small pub near the main railway line bridge that crossed what had once been the Glamorganshire canal. Reg often called in for a few pints after his late shifts before making his way home to the small terraced house situated between the prison and the British Rail goods depot. He'd lived with Violet in their house since their marriage in 1935. They had two daughters: Valerie and Veronica, both married with children and long since left home.

People who worked around the top of the West Dock area used *The York*. Not one of the places often patronised by Eddie Cross, but he'd agreed to meet Reg there, intrigued as to why Reg wanted to see him. He always had the impression Reg didn't really like him. Although the main bar was busy, the two men were the only occupants of the back room. Eddie listened as Reg explained how they could come by a lot of money, in cash and valuable items such as gold, precious stones, or both.

'So,' Eddie enquired, 'how do you know what the envelopes contain?'

'I don't,' Reg retorted, 'but given they're registered letters it can only mean one thing. Sometimes there's a large number of them in the dispatch, sometimes less. Now, once a month on a Friday, Steinberg the jeweller on the High Street, sends a load of envelopes to an address at Hatton Garden.'

Eddie's eyebrows rose with interest on hearing this, knowing it to be the diamond district of London.

'Bit risky, ain't it?' he asked, 'Valuables being sent in the post.'

'Not at all, it's very safe. Probably the cheapest way to do it.'

'And you say the mail bags are put on the train in a cage but the cage isn't locked?'

'Yes,' confirmed Reg, sipping on his beer, leaving a foam moustache on his upper lip. 'The bag with the registered letters will be easy to identify.'

'So, Reggie boy, you have an idea on how to nick this bag?'

'That's right. We, or rather you, swap the bag over on the train after it leaves Cardiff but before it arrives in Newport.'

Eddie frowned.

'So how do I get on the train?'

'You buy a bloody ticket like everyone else,' Reg snapped. 'It's a passenger train that carries mail in the guard carriage.'

Eddie gave this some thought then asked,

'Okay, so how do I get a full bag of mail off the train without being noticed? Ain't the ticket man at Newport going to be a bit suspicious when he sees a bloke carrying one of Her Majesty's letter sacks out of the bleedin' station? How d'you figure on that then, Reggie boy?'

Reg gritted his teeth. He hated it when Eddie called him that, as much as he hated the man himself with his slicked-back *Brylcreemed* hair, stripy suits, and black patent leather shoes. He lit another *Players* cigarette before looking around the room. Satisfied no one had joined them, he leaned towards Eddie.

'You don't walk off the bloody train with a mail bag, now that would be just plain stupid. No, you make the switch, chuck the bag out of the train window, then we go pick it up later.'

'Why do we need to swap 'em? Why don't I just chuck the mail bag out? Another thing,' he added, 'how'd I get this other bag onto the train in the first place?'

Reg raised his hands. 'Give me a chance, will you. I've thought all of this through.'

He took another sip from his pint.

'I'll get you an empty mail bag and a label from the sorting office. You take them onto the train. You'll also be carrying a suitcase, making you look like a proper traveller. Inside the suitcase will be the bag with a load of newspapers, all cut up and tied in bundles. When the guard's going through the train to check the tickets, you quickly fill the empty sack with the bundles, write the number of bags on the label, tie it, then swap them over.'

'Right, but why do we need to make a swap? That could get complicated. Or worse, me getting caught bang to bleedin' rights.'

Reg acknowledged his point.

'Look, the boys in Paddington will be expecting a final bag so the longer it takes before they find out it's gone missing the better.'

'Hey, bit like the great train robbery two years ago,' Eddie quipped.

'Yeah, except they got caught and this ain't anything like the same amount. We could end up with bugger all.'

Eddie lifted his scotch and water; he'd already started scheming. This, he considered, could be well worth the risk.

Reg left the pub, stepping out into a bitterly cold night. A County Class steam locomotive, one of the few remaining steam trains still running, crossed the bridge, pulling its heavy load of wagons filled with coal from the mining valleys in the Rhondda, making its laborious way to the docks at Barry. On the road, the lights of a small trolley bus stood out in the darkness of the evening as it made its final trip of the day from the Pier Head in Tiger Bay. Reg spat into the icy wind then shuddered. God, I hope I'm doing the right thing involving Eddie Cross, he thought. He hoped he was doing the right thing full stop. After turning up his collar, Reg lit another cigarette, pulling in a lungful of strong tobacco smoke before straddling his motorbike and heading home.

Six

Pat stepped into the warm atmosphere of *The Windsor*. The small pub bustled for a mid-week, with a number of regulars sitting at the bar and at tables around the room. Tonight, he looked out for one regular in particular: Desmond Taylor.

Desmond or Dezzie to his friends, originally from St Lucia in the West Indies, lived in one of the two blocks of flats built in the 1960s near Cardiff Docks. A former merchant seaman, Dezzie had worked below decks in the engine rooms of cargo vessels both steam and oil-fired. The experience of all those years in extremely hot, grimy, very loud conditions had left Dezzie partially deaf. Pat went to the bar to buy him his usual drinks, a bottle of Guinness with a double navy rum chaser. Sitting down beside Dezzie, Pat asked if he was okay. Dezzie nodded enthusiastically, his head of snow-white hair in sharp contrast to his ebony, wrinkled face.

'The landlady says she going to have a calypso night soon,' he grinned, showing at least three gold teeth. 'She goin' to get the *Jamaica All Stars* band with their pans.'

Dezzie laughed loudly, shoving Pat in the side. He felt the obvious strength still there in the old stoker's arm.

'Dez,' he asked. 'You ever remember an undertaker just up the road from here, back in the sixties?'

The old man screwed his face thinking then announced,

'Yeah, I remember. Beers,' he replied triumphantly, 'Arnold Beers. 'T'was a long time ago man. Why you want to know?'

'I was in the place that used to be his funeral parlour today. I wondered what happened to him. Did he move from the Dock?'

'Yeah, they moved Arnie, alright,' the old man recalled. 'In the back of his own hearse.'

'He died then?' Pat asked.

'Oh yeah, he sure died. Someone killed him, they say. Man, damn funny business. 'Twas in the paper for a while but I doubt anyone still gotta' copy lying about for you to look in.'

Grinning again, he sank the double rum with an almost fervent smack of his lips. Pat took the glass back to the bar for a refill, thinking to himself. That's right; no one *would* still have a copy. Except, I know where I can get my hands on one.

***

Monday morning found Pat Doyle sitting in the local history section of the library with a magnifying viewing screen in front of him, looking at microfiche copies of the South Wales Echo from 1965. After about an hour of scrolling, he eventually found the few stories about the death of Arnold Beers. The first story put out with a banner headline read:

Cardiff Undertaker Found Dead

Yesterday, Cardiff undertaker Arnold Beers, based in the docks area of the city, failed to arrive at Saint David's Cathedral for a funeral. The concerned relatives of the deceased, the Pesticios, a well-known Cardiff-Italian family, had to make their way to his premises where they found the coffin, placed in the back of a hearse, at the rear courtyard with no sign of the undertaker.

When the police arrived, they broke in only to discover the body of Mr Beers in his accommodation above the funeral parlour.

Chief Inspector John James of Cardiff Central CID announced, 'Foul play is suspected'. A member of the Pesticio family commented 'The whole affair came as a terrible shock to us. However, the funeral went ahead when another funeral firm stepped in'.

Whilst looking for more stories on the subject, Pat came across two other features in different editions of the paper, one in particular making him stare at the screen, his hand stroking his chin thoughtfully. Pat lifted the letter written by Mr Beers from the table to double check the date. It had been written only a few days *before* he was found dead by the police.

Seven

January 1965

Eddie Cross made his way awkwardly down the moving train towards the guard's carriage. He'd bought a return ticket to Newport from Cardiff General Station. He looked into the compartments at the other passengers too busy settling into their seats to notice him struggling with his heavy case and duffle bag. The train picked up speed as it headed east towards its London destination.

Reg Laine had earlier provided Eddie with a coarse, grey mail bag, the appropriate label, string, and seal, all placed inside the duffel bag. Eddie watched as the guard went down the train to start a ticket inspection. He figured he had about ten minutes to carry out the job before the man returned to his small area near the mail cage. Eddie entered the guard carriage; struggling past a couple of Raleigh pushbikes, he found the caged area with its sliding door. Eddie removed the empty mail sack from the duffel bag, filling it with the bundles of newspaper from the old leather suitcase. Once he'd secured the neck with the string and label, Eddie took a mailbag from the top of the pile. He checked the label ensuring it was the correct one denoting the *final bag* as Reg had explained. Noting the number, he wrote this on the new label then dragged the sack across to the door.

Eddie pulled down the window letting in a blast of frigid night air. He looked nervously towards the end of the carriage. The last thing he needed was the guard to return catching him *red-handed.* Eddie looked out, the wind full force in his face, straining his eyes as tears formed; he scanned the dark fields as they rushed by. He knew the exact spot, having travelled the route the previous day, checking for the landmarks indicating the precise location. The train approached a bridge that crossed the Rumney River.

Lifting the bag, he waited for the optimum moment. Suddenly, the sound of the vestibule door, dividing the carriages, opened as the guard came through.

With a grunt of effort, Eddie heaved the mailbag out into the night. The guard closed the dividing door before turning to give Eddie a suspicious look.

'Can I ask what you're doing in here, sir? Passengers shouldn't really be in this carriage. May I see your ticket, please?'

Eddie searched his pockets, patting them until he found the ticket, before handing it over.

'Just needed a bit of fresh air,' he told the guard. 'I'm okay now.'

The guard nodded.

'Arriving at Newport in about ten minutes, sir,' he said checking a pocket watch. 'Now I'll have to ask you to return to your seat.'

Eddie made his way back to find a seat where he remained until the train stopped at Newport. Stepping off with the case now holding just the duffel bag, he crossed to the opposite platform, smiling happily to himself.

He found a bench where he waited for the next train back to Cardiff.

***

Reg Laine sat nervously behind the wheel of Eddie's Ford Zephyr, parked in a side street near the General Station. The cold night air had steamed up the inside of the car windows. Reg watched blankly as rivulets of moisture collected before forming little runnels to the bottom of the windscreen. Sitting there alone, chain-smoking cigarettes, he turned over all the possible scenarios in his head. He knew the Post Office Investigation Branch, or IB, would conduct their own investigation as well as the police.

As one of the sorting office staff who would have handled the now missing bag, he would be under suspicion. However, many other postal workers would have the same knowledge as him so effectively anyone could be a suspect. He took another long pull on his cigarette trying to draw a modicum of comfort from this last thought, but a cold clammy sweat ran down his face and neck, his body betraying his mind.

Reg jerked suddenly when the passenger door opened, Eddie jumped into the seat next to him.

'All done,' he announced. 'Sweet as a nut. Now, Reggie, me old son, let's go and pick it up.'

Reg started the car, anxious someone may have noticed them at such a late hour, he slowly pulled away, heading for the east side of Cardiff. The night sky ahead took on a deep, hot orange colour, not a natural phenomenon but rather the glow from the opening of the blast furnaces at East Moors steel works.

'Listen, Eddie,' Reg said turning to his brother-in-law. 'Any valuables or money we get will have to be stashed away for a while. You know, until it all dies down. We can't just rush out and start spending.'

Reg lit another cigarette. 'I'll be under suspicion for a while,' he continued. 'So our houses are out of the question.'

Eddie nodded as Reg spoke.

'Got it all worked out, Reg,' he assured his anxious brother-in-law. 'I've thought about this on the train back to Cardiff and came up with a brilliant plan. I know this undertaker down the docks, Arnold Beers, you might have heard of him?'

'Yeah, I used to deliver to him many years ago when I was a delivery postman.'

'Well, I've had dealings with him over the years,' Eddie said.

Reg looked curiously at Eddie, wondering what kind of business he could possibly have had with an undertaker.

'Beers is a crooked, uncaring bastard,' Eddie continued. 'He steals from the bodies in his funeral parlour; anything from jewellery to gold teeth. He'll even take the shoes off the stiffs with the same shoe size as him.'

Eddie laughed aloud.

'Shit, Arnie hasn't bought himself new shoes in over twenty years.'

'That's despicable,' Reg blurted, morbidly offended.

'Oh, there's more,' Eddie continued. 'He has one coffin lined with pure white satin, it's in this coffin the families see their departed loved ones when they pay their last respects. But this isn't the same coffin that goes in the ground.'

'Why? What does he do?'

'Before moving it out, old Arnie puts the body into a similar coffin with no lining. The families know nothing about this. The expensive, satin lined coffin they'd paid for is still back at the parlour.'

Reg shook his head in disbelief.

'So what's your connection with him then?'

'I fence the stuff he takes from the bodies. I sell it on; take a cut of the proceeds, nice business, eh, Reg?'

'You're no better than he is,' Reg said quietly, feeling even more contempt for the man sitting next to him. 'It's the same as grave robbing, that is.'

'Yeah, that's right, Reg. Now you're part of the whole sorry business,' Eddie reminded him. 'So don't get too cut up about it.'

Reg knew the man was right.

'But can he be trusted? I don't like the sound of him at all.'

'Look, Reg. I've got so much dirt on the old bastard he'll do just as he's told.'

Eddie lifted his right hand in front of Reg.

'See this ring?'

On his little finger he wore a gold ring with a small ruby.

'Beers took this off a body last year for me to fence. I decided to keep it as insurance. It's engraved with the stiff's name. Any funny business from him, I show this to the family of the dead man he took it from.'

***

After pulling into a lay-by, Eddie and Reg scrambled over a wire fence into a field near the river Rumney and the South Wales to London main line. The ground, boggy from recent rainfall, made them slide most of the way towards the railway line embankment. As Eddie held a small torch, Reg followed him, trying to see in all directions at once, more nervous now than ever. On the road a car could be heard approaching, its headlights in the distance getting nearer. It slowed down as it came by the parked Zephyr.

'Eddie,' Reg whispered. 'What'd we do now? What if it's the police?' Eddie crouched in the wet mire, pulling Reg down with him.

'Shh,' he hissed, peering through the darkness at the car that passed his Zephyr. Picking up speed, it moved off, not a police car for sure or it would have most definitely stopped to investigate the lone vehicle. Feeling relieved, they continued searching. Eddie shone the torch, dimly illuminating the ground and nearby shrubs.

'There it is!' Eddie pointed towards a large, vicious looking hawthorn bush. On the ground lay the mailbag, wet with mud but intact. Eddie shone the torch over the bag as Reg retrieved it.

***

They stood shivering in the kitchen of Eddie's dingy little house, looking at the mud-stained bag on the table. Reg lit a cigarette whilst Eddie put water in a kettle to boil for tea. Opening a cupboard, he took out a bottle of *Johnnie Walker* whisky. After he'd poured two measures into the teacups, he quickly downed one before re-filling it. He offered one of the cups to Reg.

'Here, get this down you, Reggie boy. Do you good.'

Reg took the cup, gulping down its contents, the fiery spirit roaring its way down his throat. Thoroughly wet through, the drink did little to revive him. Reg still felt anxious, his hand holding the teacup shook as much with worry as cold, unlike Eddie who jumped about the place with excitement.

'What do we do with all this other stuff?' Eddie asked. 'There might be money in some of them.'

'We'll see,' Reg responded. 'Let's have a look at what's in the registered letters first.'

Eddie took a knife from a drawer containing his small collection of cutlery. Slipping the blade under the string at the neck, he cut the bag open. Reg put his hand inside, pulling out the green remittance bag that a few hours earlier he'd handled as part of a dispatch. They both stared at it for a few moments.

'Well,' Eddie said. 'Going to open it then?'

Reg took the small knife from Eddie, cut open the remittance bag then tipped its contents onto the kitchen table. There were five larger envelopes plus six regular sizes, all with their recognisable blue cross on a white background and sticker bearing the registration number. Reg recalled them from earlier, muttering quietly to himself.

'What's that, Reg?'

'Nothing,' he replied, not wanting to reveal his feelings of shear guilt, knowing this was all wrong. He'd been a loyal, honest post office worker since the day he joined aged fifteen, and now he stood there having committed a serious crime. Eddie, unable to contain himself any longer, grabbed a small, registered envelope.

'Here goes, let's see if it was all worth it.'

He shook the envelope over the table. A letter, with a £20 note tucked inside, fell out. After throwing both envelope and letter into the fire grate, he gleefully clutched the note.

'I'll light the fire in a minute so we can burn the rubbish.'

Reg nodded his agreement. After they'd opened the six smaller envelopes, they counted a total of £200.

'That's a hundred quid each,' Eddie announced, reverently touching the money.

Turning to the larger envelopes with their Hatton Garden address, Eddie opened the first of them. He pulled out a small velvet pouch with a string-pull neck. The soft bag felt heavy in his hand. The two men looked at each with wide eyes. Eddie carefully undid the string-pull before tipping ten, fine cut diamonds onto the table. Eddie whistled softly as the gems gleamed at him under the single forty-watt bulb struggling to illuminate the kitchen. Reg stared down at them, scarcely able to believe what he saw. One after the other they opened the remaining four envelopes containing similar velvet pouches – in each ten more brilliant stones.

'My God,' Eddie gasped. 'My dear God, will you look at that.'

They spread out the fifty stones of various shapes and sizes in front of them. Eddie picked up one the larger stones. 'What a beautiful little baby.'

'What d'you reckon they're worth then, Eddie?'

'Bloody hell, Reg. Stones like these gotta be worth a fucking mint I'd say. A fucking mint.'

'So, what do we do with them? How do we get rid of them, get the money for them?' Reg asked, unable to contain the exhilaration in his voice.

'Steady on, Reggie boy, steady on. We need to think this through a bit.' Eddie scratched his head. 'I can probably use someone I know up the Smoke. I'll make a few calls first, see who's about, who can handle something as big as this.'

The truth, unbeknown to Reg, Eddie Cross had no such contacts in London. He tried to impress Reg while working out how he could sell their prize on, taking a bigger share of the proceeds for himself.

'Right,' Eddie announced. 'Let's get a fire lit then burn the rubbish. You can open the other letters if you want, Reg, see what's inside. Some of them look like Christmas cards, never know, might be a ten bob note some kid was expecting from a weasel aunt. In the morning we'll take a trip down to Beer's place. He doesn't do funerals on a Saturday so he should be there.'

Eight

Arnold Beers looked like an undertaker straight out of a Dickens novel. Tall, and rake thin, his face a grey pallor with sunken eyes, and hawkish nose. A sombre appearance entirely in keeping with his profession. The man always wore a dark suit with a top hat originally belonging to his father. He'd worked for his father's funeral business since he'd left school at the age of fourteen.

Beers took over the business after his father had died in 1955. The premises were situated in the Docks area or *Tiger Bay* as it was commonly known. Beers lived above the parlour in a small flat. Across the middle of the large, front window, a black curtain hung from a brass rod. The upper glass panel had the words embossed in black lettering:

Beers & Son
Funeral Directors

Beers relaxed in a threadbare armchair, gently sipping tea from a bone China cup. On a nearby table stood a decanter of sweet sherry with a schooner glass alongside it. Only nine am, so far too early to partake of his first tipple of the day.

Startled by a loud knock, Beers lifted himself slowly out of his chair to make his way downstairs to the front door, expecting this to be someone announcing the death of a relative, or possibly the police, who would call if they needed the removal of a body. He did not expect to see Eddie Cross with another man standing behind him looking anxiously up and down the road.

'Mr Cross,' Beers said surprised. 'To what do I owe the honour of this early visitation?'

'Never mind all that crap,' replied Eddie. 'We need to speak to you about some urgent business.'

'Well, you had better come on in,' he invited.

The three made their way to the upstairs rooms. Eddie looked around the familiar accommodation, the living quarters of the undertaker. Dark, and sparsely furnished, he'd been here on many occasions to look at pieces of jewellery stolen from the dead. Eddie took the small pouches from his pocket, spilling the contents of one onto a table. Beers stared down at the table, visibly impressed by the diamonds spread out in front of him, his bony index finger pushing at the stones.

'Mr Cross, where did you come by such beautiful gems?'

'Where they came from is none of your damn business,' Eddie said.

'Then what service do you require from me?'

'What we need is a place of safe keeping until we're ready to collect them again.' Eddie pointed at the undertaker. 'You, my dear, Arnold, will keep them nice and safe; hold them here for a few weeks. Is that okay with you?'

'Shouldn't that be a few *months*?' Reg chipped in from behind him.

'Possibly,' responded Eddie.

'I will require a substantial fee for a service of this magnitude,' Beers said. 'You do understand, Mr Cross?'

'How bloody substantial?' Eddie snapped.

'This substantial,' Beers replied pointing to one of the larger, four carat diamonds on his table.

Eddie turned to face Reg who simply shrugged back at him. Eddie picked up a much smaller stone holding it up in front of the undertaker.

'This one will be your fee, Arnie. Take it or leave it.'

Beers hesitated but nodded his reluctant acceptance, not at all happy with the offer of the much smaller diamond.

After leaving the pouches with the undertaker, they made their way out onto the street, heading for the car parked nearby.

'Are you sure we can trust him, Eddie? He looks a bit shifty to me.'

'Look, if he tries any funny stuff, I'll wring his scrawny neck. Don't forget, I have this ring so he'll be fine, Reggie boy. Just you see.'

***

Later that day, after a few hours' sleep, Eddie Cross prepared to go out on the town. With his share of the stolen cash taken from the other registered envelopes to spend, he was going to celebrate in style. 'Yes,' he told himself, looking into a mirror whilst combing back his hair, 'it's Champagne and cigars tonight, Eddie boy.'

He gulped down a large measure of whisky then looked at the empty glass – the last of his *Johnnie Walker*.

'There'll be plenty more where that came from,' Eddie told himself. 'Plenty more.' Collecting his jacket, he looked around at the unkempt room. He tried to imagine a large house in the north of the city, a *gentleman's residence*.

'Fucking dump,' he muttered, the effects of the alcohol beginning to slur his speech. Outside, he slumped into the Ford Zephyr, fumbled with the ignition key then drove across the town centre to one of his usual haunts.

On the Monday evening following the theft of the diamonds, Reg sat at home with his wife. His eldest daughter, Val, had called in with her 6-year-old son, Barry. A feature in the evening paper ran the story of the mailbag stolen from the train. Just reading it made Reg feel anxious. Stories about the stolen diamonds were rife throughout the sorting office. Different versions of the theft ranged from 'dodgy train guards' to 'London gangsters' being responsible. The Post Office Investigation Branch had made the decision to call in the police due to the high value of the diamonds. Formal interviews of postal workers had begun as part of the ongoing investigation. The police had arranged to interview Reg the following day.

***

Later that evening came a knock on the door. Violet answered, returning to the living room followed by two uniformed police officers. Reg stared up at the two constables in their dark, trench coats, and helmets, the pair almost filling the small room. His heart sank. The game's up, he thought, it was obvious, how could he have been so bloody stupid. Before he could admit to his guilt, Violet let out a mournful cry.

'Oh, my dear God, when did this happen?'

She turned to her husband for consolation. Confused, Reg listened to one of the police constables explain how Eddie Cross had been involved in a tragic car accident.

'His car left the road and burst into flames. Mr Cross probably died almost instantly,' one officer said.

'I… I don't understand,' Reg stammered. 'How did this happen?'

The second officer removed his helmet.

'Someone reported an accident, sir. A car travelling at speed, driven by Mr Cross, swerved to avoid a pedestrian who'd stepped into the road. The pedestrian being the main witness.'

'When was this?' Reg quietly asked, folding his newspaper then crushing a cigarette into an ashtray on the small table next to him.

'It took place in the early hours of Monday, sir,' the officer continued. 'We believe that Mr Cross may have been drinking as reports say he was seen in a club about an hour prior to the accident taking place. Buying everyone drinks, clearly under the influence himself.'

'Is there anything we can do?' The first officer asked.

'No, no thank you, officers,' Violet said. She dabbed her eyes with the end of her pinafore.

Both constables offered their condolences before leaving the couple. Violet composed herself before telling her husband they would need to make the necessary arrangements as Eddie's only family.

'How will we manage to pay for the funeral? We only have a little money put aside for emergencies, nothing like enough for this.'

'Don't worry, my love,' Reg reassured his wife. 'We'll take care of everything, one way or another. 'He held Violet in his arms, hoping to God that Eddie never let anything slip out about the diamonds.

***

The following morning Reg and Violet walked the few hundred yards to Eddie's house. Violet had a spare key. Eddie, like most people in the area, had rented the small terraced house from a private landlord. Stepping through the front door, Reg bent down to pick up some letters lying on the mat.

'Anything important, love?' Violet asked.

'Nar, just a few bills by the look. One's a final demand.' He didn't mention the letter with a local postmark, the address written in black ink. 'I'll deal with them later,' he added.

Whilst she went about her brother's belongings, Reg opened the letter. Written by the undertaker, it told Eddie that he'd placed the stones with a client for safekeeping. The letter did not make a lot of sense but said enough to incriminate Reg should it fall into the hands of the police. He immediately tore it into pieces. Dropping them into a bin, he poured stale beer on the torn paper. He needed to visit Arnold Beers.

***

'Now then, Mr Laine,' droned Arnold Beers. 'This puts a different emphasis on the matter at hand.'

They stood together in the flat, just early evening and the room felt cold, the fire in the small grate needed building up. Reg had told Beers about the unfortunate accident involving Eddie Cross and that he would now collect the diamonds when the time was right. However, Beers, seizing the opportunity, was about to re-negotiate the deal heavily in his favour. With Eddie Cross out of the way he felt no threat whatsoever from the *postman* who stood before him.

'Yes, Mr Laine,' Beers continued, 'I do believe we are in an altogether different situation to Saturday morning when first we met. I was not entirely happy with Edward's measly offer, you see.'

Picking up a small glass, Beers took a sip of sherry.

'Far too small, Mr Laine, do you understand? Far too small, indeed.'

Reg looked suspiciously at the tall, gaunt man, sensing a stitch up. He knew from Eddie the man was an unscrupulous and deceitful character.

'Different? In what way?' Reg asked.

Beers drew a slender finger down the side of his face, looking down at the floor.

'Different in many ways, Mr Laine, in many ways. For a start, I have the stones in safe keeping so I will now dictate the terms of our new arrangement.'

'What do you mean?' Reg demanded. 'What new arrangement?'

'Well let us just say I will be taking far more than one diamond.'

Reg stared at the undertaker, his brow furrowed.

'How many do you want? Three? four?'

Beers laughed at this question.

'Mr Laine, you are clearly not *au fait* with the situation. Half is more what I have in mind.'

'Why, you cheating bastard'. He moved towards Beers. 'I'll…'

'Now, now, my good man,' Beers said. He held up the palm of his left hand. 'It won't do to be acting impetuous. After all, you need me to deliver the stones. No, Mr Laine, there will, rest assured, be something in this for you.' His mouth broke into grin revealing yellow, stained teeth. 'But considerably more for me, if you get my point. May I offer you a small sherry?'

Reg seethed inside, realising that the man was going to try to cheat him out of the diamonds he'd risked so much to come by. Grasping hold of the undertaker by the lapels, Reg pulled, his face almost touching the pointed nose of Arnold Beers.

'Now listen here, you lousy cheating swine,' he hissed in the undertaker's face, saliva spitting from his mouth. 'I want the diamonds now, and I'll decide what you get. D'you hear me?'

Beers tried pulling away from the grip Reg had on him. Struggling fiercely, Beers knocked the sherry decanter over as they grappled together. The fortified wine spread out on the thin rug beneath them. Exasperated, Reg pushed Beers away from him. The undertaker stumbled, lost his balance, and slipped in the spilt sherry. His head hit the corner of a desk as he fell backwards, the sharp corner split his head at the base of his skull. Beers lay motionless; blood oozing from the wound, mixing with the ruby liquid on the floor.

Reg gazed down in disbelief at the sight of the now unconscious, dying man at his feet, unable to comprehend what had happened. He looked around the room. The fire in the grate had burnt out. The slate-grey sky outside failed to lighten the room through the small window. Reg breathed heavily as panic set in.

'Be calm, Reggie boy,' he heard himself saying. *Reggie boy*, the name Eddie often used that he so despised. He paced the room, wondering where the undertaker may have put the diamonds. Reg opened the desk drawers, pulling out their contents. Nothing. He looked in other drawers and cupboards. Shit, they could be anywhere. Reg glanced down at the dying undertaker, fast realising the need to get out of the place. Taking a handkerchief from his pocket, he moved towards the door where he covered the brass knob before opening it. At the bottom of the stairs, Reg let himself out, relieved to find the street empty save for a mangy-looking mongrel who cocked his thin, rear leg on a lamp post, looking up at the man who stood on the pavement. Trying to compose a slightly shaking hand, Reg put a cigarette in his mouth, turned, and walked towards his motorbike parked at the end of the road. It quickly became apparent he had lost the diamonds for good. Only the undertaker knew where they were but he was now dead, killed by Reg Laine, a man who had now become a thief and a killer in the space of four days. He decided that after arriving home he'd tell his wife everything, then wait for the police to return; only this time it *would* be for him.

***

In the CID room at Cardiff Central, four jubilant detectives looked very pleased with themselves. They had, in a number of weeks, managed to solve two serious crimes committed in the city, and closed the cases. They had the person responsible for the theft of the mailbag and the killer of Arnold Beers, the undertaker from Tiger Bay. However, they didn't have the fifty, high-value diamonds belonging to the jeweller.

After the bereaved family had called the police to the undertaker's premises, they'd found Arnold Beers dead on his sitting room floor, with the obvious signs of a struggle and ransacking, as drawers were open, their contents pulled out. Suspecting foul play, they'd taken fingerprints, finding two sets: the undertaker's and another set that later matched with a known criminal: Edward Cross. The police had entered the home of Mr Cross, where they'd discovered, among other things, the charred and burned remains of letters including remnants of the registered envelopes in his fireplace. This satisfied the police that Eddie Cross had been responsible for the mail theft and the killing of Arnold Beers. However, Eddie Cross was also dead; killed they deduced, by his greed and drunkenness. Reg had been questioned as he worked for the GPO, part of the investigation concluded there had to have been an *inside* connection. Reg told the police how Eddie Cross had once asked him about the movements of mail but he'd told him nothing. He explained how Eddie knew other men in the sorting office, possibly paying them to help him steal a mailbag from the train. Reg also told the police that when he heard mail had been stolen, he was about to tip them off regarding his dishonest relative whom he suspected may have been involved. They accepted his story as plausible, and due to his long service and dedication to duty the matter ended there.

***

Reg Laine eventually retired from the GPO and thought constantly of what might have been. In many ways though, relieved it was all over. He could not bring himself to tell his wife the real story but one day he would. Lung cancer eventually took Reg, dying without ever knowing what had happened to the still missing diamonds.

Nine

Pat Doyle sat in the Cardiff library reading room rubbing tired eyes. Well known by the staff who generally referred to him as *Dr* Doyle, he'd carried out much research at the library given his interest in history. Looking through back copies of the evening papers from 1965, he made notes on a pad by his side. It proved to be a slow process as the microfiche wasn't indexed to enable specific stories to be easily located. Fortunately, on this occasion he'd found what he wanted. The stories were front-page news in different issues. One copy ran the story:

THEIVES STEAL MAIL FROM CARDIFF TO LONDON EXPRESS:

DIAMONDS INCLUDED IN HAUL

Brazen thieves stole cut diamonds with an estimated value of £50,000 from a Cardiff to London train last night. The diamonds belonged to Cardiff jeweller, Maxwell Steinberg, based in the city's High Street. Maxwell Steinberg had sent them by GPO registered post to a dealer in Hatton Garden. It remains unknown how the thieves knew about the gems.

Police suspect an 'insider' at the GPO may have been involved. The diamonds have yet to be recovered. A substantial reward has been offered by the jeweller for any information leading to their return.

Other follow-on stories reported the police had questioned the validity of Steinberg's alleged loss, as it would not be usual to send such high value merchandise by post, registered or otherwise. Further articles reported that the stones had yet to be recovered. Another, smaller column reported on a fatal car crash:

Police discovered the body of local man, Edward Cross, in the wreckage of his car yesterday. Police say the car, travelling at speed, 'left the road and burst into flames'. The family of the dead man have been informed.

A May 1965 edition of the South Wales Echo reported police investigations into the death of Arnold Beers, and the theft of mail from a London bound train had closed:

…conclusive evidence emerged linking the two incidents to a certain Edward Cross, a local man with a substantial criminal record, who had died when his car left the road then burst into flames in April of this year.

Police discovered evidence of the mail theft at his Adamsdown home, his fingerprints were also found at the murder scene.

Pat picked up his pad to read the notes he'd made, re-read the letter by Arnold Beers, then made his way to the exit, much to the relief of the library staff who were about to inform him they were due to close.

Back at his apartment, Pat listened to the morning news. He'd placed a cafetiere of strong coffee next to a large mug. The newsreader reported on how a body discovered in a car was another victim of the gang war that raged throughout the city. Pat shuddered; would he be the next victim? As he ate his toast, Pat also thought about his discovery. He read the notes from his research at the library the day before.

Death on the radio, on the streets, in his notes. Pat needed to get out and clear his head. Stepping over the morning post still lying unopened on the doormat, he walked outside into the cool morning air.

Demi worked most days at the charity shop, so he made his way there. As he turned the corner, Pat spotted Demi unlocking the door whilst talking to one of the men from the taxi office above the shop. He stopped to let her finish the conversation, gazing at the woman, captivated by her breath-taking beauty: a Greek goddess. Her parents, Khristos and Alexa Karamanlis owned a Fish & Chip shop on North Road. Her father, the middle of three brothers, emigrated from Greece in the early fifties and had prospered. Shame descended on the family when Demi became involved with Danny Boston. She'd met him when she was nineteen, becoming infatuated by him. Being older, he impressed her with his flashy lifestyle. Although Demi adopted his name, they'd never married. At the time, Demi did not realise his money came from drug dealing. He persuaded her to try some of the drugs starting with cannabis, eventually leading onto heroin to which she'd quickly became addicted. He'd even tried to get her to sell herself as another way to make easy money. When Demi refused, the violence started. When she became pregnant, the beatings eased off but after the birth of her second child, the abuse resumed. Following a number of police call-outs to their home when neighbours reported their concerns, social services became involved, hence Pat Doyle's involvement. Pat saw her as a strong, resilient woman who'd risked so much when she made the break from Boston, now serving a prison sentence for GBH and supplying heroin. He'd stabbed someone in a fight over drugs money landing him a nine-year sentence.

After the man had left, Pat sidled up to Demi as she unlocked the shop door. She looked surprised to see him so early.

'What's up, Pat, it's not the kids, is it?' she asked anxiously.

'No, the kids are fine,' he assured her. 'I just need to see you. Quick, in the shop.' He shoved her gently through the now open door.

'Oo-eer, and you haven't even bought me half a lager,' she mimicked. Demi crossed to a kitchenette at the rear of the shop. Pat gave a broad smile as he watched her go. Demi had a certain charm coupled with a sense of humour that enamoured her to him even more.

'Fancy a cuppa?' she called out from the little room. 'I'll pop the kettle on. Don't suppose you have any biscuits? I could kill a custard cream.'

He nearly offered to go out for some but stopped himself before replying.

'Sorry, I haven't but tea sounds good.'

Demi soon returned with two steaming mugs offering one to Pat.

She could see him eyeing the mug closely.

'Don't worry, they're not donated. I bought them from Supa-Value. Quid for four.'

He grinned as he took the mug from her. They stood sipping their tea.

'Well, if it isn't the children what is it then? Or are you just after my *gypsy creams*? Not that I have any of course.'

Pat put the mug down then removed the letter from his pocket.

'I've something I want to show you.'

He held the letter in front of her. Demi's face broke into a frown.

'Oh dear, is it a letter from a solicitor? Are you suing us for damages or something?'

'Seriously now, do you remember the book I took from here the other day? The one I found out the back.'

'I remember, seeing as we don't sell much, and only a sop would offer a tenner for a book from this place. No offence mind,' she added quickly.

'Well,' he continued, 'I think I may have stumbled across something.'

'You *are* suing us.'

'Demi, this is serious, and I'm not sure where to start.'

He carefully opened the letter before passing it to her.

'Yeah,' Demi said, after reading the letter, a puzzled look on her face.

He placed it down on the small counter smoothing it out.

'Look at the date, nineteen sixty-five.'

'So, it's an *old* letter,' she quipped.

'Yes, it's an old letter. But look at what's written *in* the letter.'

She took another glance, furrowed her brow then looked up at him. It meant nothing to her at all.

'It was written by an undertaker,' he explained. 'This place was his funeral parlour in the sixties.'

Pat told her about the mail theft from the train, about the diamonds, and Eddie Cross, pointing at his name in the letter. How Cross had died, and about the undertaker being killed upstairs, pointing above his head at the ceiling.

'Don't you see,' he continued, 'Cross stole the diamonds from the train, brought them here to Arnold Beers for safe keeping then Beers gets killed.' He looked at Demi with wide eyes.

'The diamonds were *never* recovered, within days the only two men who knew about them were dead.'

'What are you saying, Pat?' Demi asked slowly. 'The diamonds are here somewhere?' She started to look around the shop, swallowing hard. 'This place was a funeral parlour where they kept dead bodies?' She moved closer to him. 'I've been here all on my own in a funeral parlour? Oh my God.'

'I don't think they'll still be here somehow…'

'Jeez, I hope not,' she interrupted. 'I hope they buried them all.'

'No, not the bloody bodies,' Pat said. 'The diamonds. I don't think the diamonds are likely to still be here.'

Demi sighed. 'So what are you going to do then?'

'Well, there's the possibility they *might* still be hidden here, though I imagine the police must have searched this place from top to bottom. After all, they were conducting a murder enquiry so they probably turned the place upside down looking for any clues. Back then, they never thought too much about contaminating forensic evidence. It wouldn't hurt to take a look though, just in case.'

'Look where?'

'Let's start in here,' he replied, making his way towards the back room. Demi followed closely behind.

'We could lift some floor boards; then see if there are any false walls. I noticed some rusty tools in a box out front with an old wooden handled claw hammer.'

'I'll go and get it.' Demi walked off, returning moments later with the hammer. 'This'll do nicely,' Pat said admiring the solid-steel claw.

After prying up a floorboard, he peered underneath.

'We're going to need a good torch. It's dark under here.'

'What about upstairs?' she asked. 'Didn't you say the undertaker lived upstairs?'

'That's right,' Pat confirmed. 'He did. What's up there now?'

'The owner of the whole building runs a taxi business from up there. He rents this part to the charity. Word is it helps his conscience.'

Pat looked up at her from his kneeling position.

'His conscience, what d'you mean?'

'The owner is a well-known gangster. He feels he's giving something back by letting us have this shop for a cheap rent. Load of crap if you ask me,' she added with indifference. 'Especially from the stories I've heard about him. Get on his wrong side they say, and you're as good as dead.'

'Sound like a charming individual. So, who is this generous benefactor?'

'His name's Barry Laine.'

'Barry Laine?' Pat said with a note of surprise. 'That's a name I haven't heard in a long time. I've seen it in the papers though, usually related to some incident or criminal activity.'

Pat recalled the earlier conversation with his colleague about serious crime in the city; he made the connection to Laine.

'D'you know him?' Demi asked.

'I did once, a long time ago.'

Pat returned to the shop front to look for any other tools he could use, pondering the name he'd just heard. Suddenly, the door opened, a heavyset man of West Indian origin walked in. Pat recognised him as the man Demi had had spoken with earlier. He stood about six foot four, wearing a leather jacket and denims. Under the jacket, a red tee shirt clung to his muscular torso. His bald head shone like glass.

'Rent man!' he announced. A grin spread across his face. Pat went to call Demi but before he had the chance to utter a word, she burst into the front of the shop shouting:

'How much would these diamonds be worth then...?' She stopped dead.

'Oh, Hi Lennie,' Demi called, recognising the man almost filling the doorway. Pat considered very few people would try to fare dodge if Lennie was indeed a taxi driver. The man now looked a little curious before asking,

'What diamonds? Don't tell me some fool has donated diamonds to *this* worthy cause?' the big man said looking around the shop with distaste at its well-worn stock of clothes, books and general tack.

'Yeah, we had the Crown Jewels dropped off earlier by some woman who looked a bit like the Queen,' Demi joked. 'Claimed she had no further use for them. Want to have a look, Len?'

'Just remember the *Man's* deal. We get first refusal on anything which looks like it might be worth something, Okay?'

He looked suspiciously towards Pat.

'What's with the hammer, dude, doing a spot of DIY? Thought I heard banging on my way down.'

'That's right,' Pat replied. 'There's some loose boards back there.'

He indicated towards the door behind him. 'Demi complained about tripping over them.'

Standing behind him, Demi nodded her agreement.

'Yeah, they're in a terrible state,' she added. 'Whole place needs doing up to be honest. 'It can be quite dangerous walking around in the dark.'

'I'll tell the boss,' Lennie laughed. 'I'm sure he'll send in the builders. 'He walked towards her with his open hand outstretched.

'So, let's have the rent. I ain't got time to stand here all day listening to this shit.'

Demi opened the till then handed over some notes. The big man grabbed at them and grunted.

'Hardly worth the fucking bother.'

After leaving the shop, his footsteps could be heard sounding his way back upstairs to the taxi office. Demi glanced back at the till.

'Well, there goes my float. I hope the first customer's got the right money.'

Pat smiled, looking at her standing there almost desolate.

'How low is the rent exactly?' he asked.

'Twenty quid a week but it clears the till if we haven't sold a great deal, like most days.'

Pat put his hand in his pocket, taking out a tenner that he was going to put on a horse he'd seen tipped in the morning paper.

'Pop this in the till and I'll keep the hammer.'

Demi grinned back at him.

'Tell you what; I'll throw in a chipped Charles and Di mug. Would, *sir* like a bag for them? Be another five pence.'

Laughing, they picked up their mugs of now lukewarm tea, and continued drinking.

***

By lunchtime, Pat had made a thorough search of the place, concluding there were no hidden gems in the shop. He checked his watch. 'Okay, that'll do for now. You close up, I'll go get us something to eat.'

Pat returned with baguettes, doughnuts, and lattés from a nearby coffee shop. As they sat eating their food, Pat mulled over the letter he'd discovered in the back room. With a mouthful of bread, he suddenly splurted, 'My God, I think I know what he did with the diamonds.'

Demi was about to bite into her doughnut.

'What?'

Taking the letter over to her, he read out '…*I have placed the stones with a client… can be trusted to remain silent… details of my client's whereabouts...* Don't you see?'

'See what, Pat?'

'See what he did with the diamonds.' Pat slapped the piece of paper with a back of his hand. 'He'd put them with a body, in a coffin. It's obvious.' Pat grinned as he shook his head. 'Why didn't I see it before now? It's why they were never found. Why they're still out there somewhere. The sneaky old git.'

Demi took the letter reading it for a second time.

'Brilliant, Pat. You're right. It must mean that. *Doesn't it?*'

'Of course the letter's somewhat cryptic but it's what old Beers meant by his clients. His *dead* clients and they would be silent.'

Demi nodded her head. 'Yeah, I suppose, except you've overlooked one minor detail. 'What body, and where was it buried? What if it was cremated?'

'Cremated? Shit, I never thought about that,' Pat said as he rubbed his chin. 'Nar, too risky. Cremation wouldn't destroy the diamonds though, just the body. Still, I'm sure we can find out from somewhere, there has to be records. He couldn't have carried out that many funerals at the time, surely?'

Pat stood there pinching the bridge of his nose.

'Got it,' he said after a few moments. 'The papers said Beers was supposed to have conducted a funeral on the day they found him dead. I bet he hid the diamonds with that body. There was a name mentioned in one of the papers. Bloody hell, what was it?'

'Hang on, hang on,' Demi cut in. 'What if we do find out where the body's buried. Are you suggesting we simply go and dig it up? I think they still have the death penalty for grave robbers, don't they?'

Pat looked deflated when he considered this. Once again, Demi had a valid point. He had to admit it didn't look good.

'By the way,' she said bringing him back from his malaise. 'You didn't say how much the diamonds were worth, did you?'

He looked at the sugar from the doughnut still on her mouth, the speck of jam below her bottom lip. He wanted to remove it with a kiss. Instead, he simply responded to her question.

'Well, I used the internet at the library and Googled a cost-of-living index calculator. I put in the value reported in ninety sixty-five – fifty thousand pounds – it calculated that by today's value the diamonds are worth approximately half a million pounds.'

Demi stared at him, the coffee in her cup slowly pouring out onto the floor.

Ten

Wednesday evenings were often quiet in the city centre with mostly students taking advantage of the mid-week drinks offers in the bars. The castle end of Westgate Street attracted few people with just a group of smokers outside the Angel hotel. Above an antique and reproduction furniture store a light shone in a room occupied by three men, one tethered to a wooden chair looking very anxious.

'Well, my little Turkish friend. Going to kill my cousin, I hear. Cut him up into little pieces then feed him to the dogs. Did I hear right?'

Barry Laine asked the questions. With hands behind his back, he paced the room above the furniture store, one of the many businesses he owned throughout the city. A powerful desk-lamp pointed directly at the poor soul bound to the chair illuminated his olive-coloured skin glistening with sweat caused by fear.

The furniture business acted as one of Barry Laine's 'fronts'. He also owned bars, nightclubs, massage parlours plus a fleet of taxis. As well as his legitimate enterprises the police knew he dealt in drugs, smuggled alcohol and tobacco, ran prostitutes from the *massage parlours*, a protection racket targeting small businesses, and sold counterfeit antiques, and fake, branded high-end merchandise. A successful, powerful man feared by the many of his like throughout Cardiff and beyond.

Ali Osman's wide, terror-stricken eyes stared up at Barry Laine, and his henchman. Osman owned a number of kebab take-aways, dealt in drugs, and money lending – Laine would have indirectly supplied him with the drugs he sold. Although not an immediate threat to Laine, Osman had established himself as a rival gang leader who could eventually consolidate enough muscle to take him on.

Osman had lent money to Laine's cousin, Frankie Galdini. Frankie's gambling problem meant he was unable to repay Osman the £500 he'd borrowed plus interest. Interest that now increased the initial loan to £750.

'I hear two of your guys held a knife to my cousin's throat yesterday. Is this correct?'

Osman shook his head.

'They demanded repayment in five days, or else.' Laine paused. 'Or else what, my little friend?'

'Please, Mr Laine,' Osman pleaded. 'I didn't know that Frankie's related to you, this is all a terrible mistake.'

'You see, Ali,' Laine continued, 'when I found this out, I had you brought here so you could explain your actions to me personally.'

Lennie grinned from behind Laine in the shadow of the barely lit room; when Lennie had collected the rent money from Demi the previous day, Pat Doyle thought he was just a taxi driver. But, known as *Hatchet Lennie,* from his reputation for carrying an axe about his person with the propensity to use it if necessary – to inflict injury, to extract information, though often, to just simply inflict pain for the sheer pleasure it gave him. Lennie was Barry Laine's enforcer.

Laine showed Osman a mobile phone video clip of a man with his feet in a large tub of wet cement.

'Recognise him?' Osman peered at the grainy image on the small screen.

'I'll help you. It's your friend, Abdul, who's heading for a watery grave as we speak.'

The impact on Osman had the desired effect.

'Mr Laine, please, I beg of you. Frankie will owe nothing. I can promise you.'

Laine glanced at Lennie.

'It has been a grave misunderstanding,' the stricken man continued. 'If I'd known he was your cousin I would have *given* him the money. Please, Mr Laine. You have my solemn word this will never happen again, *never*.'

Once more Laine looked towards Lennie as if seeking acquiescence. Lennie simply shrugged his wide shoulders. Laine turned back towards Osman.

'Just this once, Ali, I'm prepared to let this go.' Osman showed obvious signs of relief. 'But,' he continued, 'Abdul *will* sleep with the fishes.'

Laine had picked up the phrase from *The Godfather*, liking himself in the role as the head of a crime outfit. He'd often thought of his great-uncle Eddie, an old Cardiff villain back in the 1960's. He recalled the stories told by his grandmother, Violet, and by his mother and her sister about the time his granddad had pulled off a *great train robbery* with Uncle Eddie, getting away with a fortune in diamonds only to be cheated out of them by a nefarious undertaker who'd kept the stones for himself. This followed by the mystery surrounding their disappearance after the undertaker turned up dead.

Laine considered the story dubious given the amount of exaggeration and embellishment about the whole affair, making his two male relatives sound like *big-time* villains in their day.

Laine, however, *was* a successful businessman, albeit a dishonest one, having built up a considerable empire in the city using violence and fear to consolidate his position among the Cardiff criminal fraternity. He could rely on his men to carry out his bidding; men like Lennie Randall who had dismembered many of those unfortunate persons who saw fit to cross Laine or interfere in his affairs.

Laine nodded his head.

Lennie responded immediately to Laine's non-verbal instruction, walking across the room towards the tightly bound man. As he approached, his hand reached into his jacket pocket from where he withdrew a closed flick knife. Lennie extended his arm, the knife just inches from Osman's face. With the slightest movement of his thumb, a metallic click filled the room. A long silver blade sprang from the body of the knife. Lennie laughed and ran the razor-sharp blade along Osman's exposed neck, lightly touching the skin but delivering sufficient pressure for Osman to appreciate how easily it could slice his throat, something he almost expected.

Warm liquid ran down the terrified man's trouser leg, forming a pool on the floor. Squeezing his eyes together, Osman began to pray audibly through his tears. He recognised the sound of the knife slicing through sinew, his body tensed as he prepared for the imminent pain. His legs could hardly support him as Lennie lifted him to his feet. Osman realised he was still alive and in one piece. He even managed a smile when Lennie signalled to another man standing outside the door to take him away. Lennie closed the door and turned.

'You want this Abdul dude taken out in a boat tonight, boss?'

'Yes, I do. Get it over with quick. I have to show Osman and the others I mean business. Then tell Frankie everything's okay. Tell him if he's ever in any kind of trouble in future to come and see me.'

'Sure, boss,' Lennie responded, 'you know Frankie, he probably didn't want you to know he'd goofed up.' Putting the knife away, he removed money from another pocket. 'I called in at the charity shop yesterday.' He offered it to Laine. 'Why don't we take some serious cash from those bloody geeks, this is hardly worth the effort.'

Laine knew this but would not let on he had desires for the woman. Demi was nothing like the woman he'd married, a woman who acted more like a WAG, always demanding more from him in terms of material possessions so she could be seen to live the celebrity *wife and girlfriend* lifestyle. Laine didn't want to cause the charity financial difficulties by demanding an extortionate rent. He wanted to keep the shop going so Demi remained working there.

'Keep the notes, Len; just make sure you only ask for that amount, okay? No upping the cost because *you* want more.'

'Sure thing, boss. But today I thought they were going to offer me diamonds,' he said grinning.

Laine stopped in his tracks, turning slowly towards his henchman.

'What's that about diamonds?'

Lennie told him about how Demi had come into the front of the shop earlier asking some geeky friend of hers what he thought some diamonds were worth.

'Geeky friend,' Laine said. 'Who's that then?'

'Dunno. Some dude was there doing repairs to the floorboards, least that's what he said. Made a hell of a row with his banging about. He had a hammer when I saw him.'

'The woman mentioned diamonds and their worth, you say? Anything else, did she say any more?'

'Look, boss. All she said was the friggin' Queen dropped them off so I guess she's taking the piss. I took the dough and left.'

'This geek, describe him to me. Who is he? You know him?'

'I just figured he's a friend. I ain't never seen him before. Probably some guy who's got the hots for the chick, hoping to get his hand in her knickers.'

Laine was about to dismiss the matter, accepting the explanation as plausible. Yet it seemed all too much of a coincidence – the shop, the mention of diamonds. Why mention diamonds? Laine needed to find out more. He'd bought the property years previously with the intention of ripping it apart to look for the gems his grandfather had lost. Now, in the same place that had been the undertaker's shop, the last known whereabouts of the gems, someone mentions diamonds.

'Lennie, find out what you can about this geek. I want to know who he is, where he's from. Soon as you have something, get back here.'

***

The Cardiff library had just opened its doors. Pat and Demi made their way to the reading rooms on the second floor.

'There should be something in the obituary columns about the recent deaths around that time,' Pat said. 'Then we could try another possible angle.'

'What angle would that be?' Demi tried to keep up with Pat as he hurried towards the reading room.

'The register office at Park Place, it should contain the records of deaths from that year, possibly who had conducted the funeral instead of Beers.'

The library assistant recognised Pat Doyle from his earlier visit, happy to locate the requested microfiche with the 1964/65 editions of the South Wales Echo. Demi became more excited now she knew the missing diamonds were worth a fortune. Picking up a copy of the morning's paper she started to browse while they waited, slowly turning the pages. She read the horoscope page.

'Look,' she said, pointing, 'what my stars say.' She read aloud. *'You should put all your efforts into an oncoming challenge, do not be swayed by doubters. A trip over water is looming, and love blossoms. Lucky colour Indigo.'*

'That's spooky, don't you think? You know, the challenge bit. What's your star sign, Pat?'

'I don't go in for all that nonsense myself,' he told her.

'Oh I do. I'm really into *astronomy*.'

'It's *astrology*, 'Pat corrected.

'What is?'

'Star signs. It's called astrology.'

'Eh?'

'Astronomy is the science of the movement of the stars, and the measurement of the universe. Whereas astrology is more about the movement of the planets, about how they impact on people and events.'

'You sure?'

'Trust me, I'm a doctor.'

Demi looked back down at the paper.

'What colour's indigo?' she whispered.

'Blue.'

'Yep,' Demi said nodding. 'I do like blue.'

**

As they waited, Pat recalled the time from when he knew Barry Laine. He'd lived near the Laine family up until the age of fourteen. Barry Laine lived with his mother. No one really knew what happened to his father. There also an Aunt, who had a son, Frankie, who was a lot younger than Laine. The area was eventually demolished, the whole community dispersed to different parts of the city's periphery. After that, they never saw each other again.

'Penny for them.'

Pat looked up from his reverie.

'I'm sorry. What'd you say?'

'Your thoughts, you looked miles away.'

'I was,' he admitted. 'Thinking about the time when I knew Barry Laine. We were kids who lived not far from here. I seem to remember Barry was a bit of a *wide-boy* even at a young age. Always scheming, looking for ways to make easy money. Stealing lead from roofs, stealing from shops, that sort of thing.' Pat smiled at a particular memory. 'I remember one scam he used to pull. Barry would take his grandfather's racing pigeons from the loft in the garden. Then he would approach unsuspecting kids in the street and offer to sell them a bird for a couple of bob each, telling them how the birds make great pets. He usually managed to sell a number of them before heading home.'

Demi looked at him inquisitively.

'How's that a scam?'

'Because by the evening all the birds he'd sold were back at the loft waiting to go inside for food. His grandfather never knew his fancy homing pigeons had gone missing for a few hours.'

'Wow. And you were involved?'

'Not quite. Barry never gave me anything, not money anyway.'

'So what did you get?'

'Well,' he continued, 'there was a time he took me to the railway goods depot near where we lived. Barry wanted to break into the box vans in the sidings. On that occasion we came away with about two dozen boxes of bubble gum.'

'You're joking? You stole chewing gum from a train?'

Demi laughed aloud, other library users looked over towards her, disapproval etched on their faces.

'Not a brilliant haul, I admit, but Barry knew the sweets were saleable. Every kid in the neighbourhood was chewing gum for weeks. My jaw ached from constant chewing.'

Demi's head shook as she tried to stifle her laugh.

'You robbed a train and got paid in bubble-gum? That's the funniest story I've ever heard.'

'It's true,' Pat assured her.

'It must be. Who'd make up something like that?'

Pat picked up a photography magazine, dropping it in her lap.

'Just read this and try to keep quiet.'

'Yes, Mr Biggs. Or should I say, *Mr Spearmint.*'

Pat doubted Laine would remember him.

He looked at Demi, who'd become engrossed in the magazine, wondering why he'd let her get involved. This was stepping over professional boundaries by involving a *client* in his personal life. Perhaps he should simply tell the police what he'd found out. After all, how would he recover valuable gems from a grave?

The thought of half a million pounds motivated him. He'd work something out.

'Jeez, what a way to try to solve your problems,' Pat said quietly to himself.

Demi looked up from her reading.

'What was that?'

'Nothing.' Pat rose from his seat. 'Come on, let's go.'

They crossed over to the reading room after the library assistant had returned with the microfiche.

'So, where'd we start, Doc?' Demi said, smiling.

'The first thing we do is try and find out who was in the coffin at the undertaker's back in nineteen sixty-five,' he told her as he operated the machine. 'Then find out where the coffin's buried. We should also see if there were any reports of the stones ever being recovered.'

He moved through the scrolls of the microfiche.

'Right, here we are.' Pat located a particular headline about the mail theft, and the death of the undertaker. He moved the fiche to the sections with the births, deaths, and marriages: *hatch, match, and dispatch* as they were colloquially known, he found a few death notices that stated Arnold Beers had carried out the deceased's funeral arrangements.

'Look,' Demi said pointing at the screen. 'There. *Goosep* Pesticio.'

'It's Giuseppe,' Pat corrected as he read the detail.

The funeral date coincided with the day of Beer's death. The notice confirmed a Requiem Mass at Saint David's Cathedral in Charles Street followed by interment.

'That's him,' Pat confirmed. 'I'm sure they mentioned a Pesticio in the first article I'd read. It has to be him.'

'So now all we've got to do is dig him up, Demi said. 'Got a shovel?' she added turning to Pat, a sassy grin on her face.

'Yes,' he acknowledged. 'That's the tricky part. Anyway, before we worry about that we need to find out which cemetery, it just says interment.'

She nudged him with her elbow. 'Look on the bright side. At least we know he wasn't cremated.'

***

Queen Street teemed with its usual mix of shoppers, office workers, and visitors, all hurrying in different directions. At the bottom of Park Place, a large fairground ride radiating a synthesis of colour and light carried shrieking children who sat astride galloping horses, waving at parents as they sped around.

Pat hated coming into the centre of Cardiff, the hurly-burly of the crowd, street buskers singing songs alongside college students playing popular tunes on violins, street vendors selling soap-bubble guns, sunglasses, neck scarves known as snoods. Weary shoppers sat on the few available bench spaces. Pat pushed his way through, heading for one of the many coffee shops which seemed to equal in number to the mobile phone shops.

'Come on, let's go in here,' Pat said pushing open the door of a *Starbucks*. 'We'll get a coffee and think a few things over then decide what we'll do next.'

'Fine by me,' Demi agreed. 'But this time let me pay for the coffee.'

Once seated with their flat-whites, Pat took a small writing pad from his jacket, placing it in front of him. Demi leaned on the table waiting in anticipation for his ideas to flow. He looked at the blank sheet of paper then started to doodle. Becoming impatient, Demi pointed at the pad.

'What's this? Is it our plan, in some kind of code?'

He looked, smiling at the sweet face peering back at him.

'Sorry, just thinking.' He tapped the pencil on the pad. 'Right, it's like this. First, we have to locate the cemetery. Then we have to figure a way to get to his remains. If we succeed, and it's a bloody big if, I hope the diamonds are still with him, if they are, bingo, but then what?'

'But then what,' Demi repeated back at him. 'Then you're rich.'

'Theoretically, yes. Though we can hardly stroll into a jewellery store asking *how much will you pay us for this lot?* No, we have to figure out a way to sell them. To sell, what are in fact, stolen diamonds.'

Pat tapped a pencil on the pad again.

'This is all getting a little too complicated and out of our depth.'

'Pat, this is over half a million we're talking about,' Demi said excitedly. 'Think about it. You'll be set up with that kind of money. Set up for life.'

Pat had thought about little else.

'Yes,' he agreed. 'But only if we can sell them, I mean, what do we know about that anyway. Then there's the problem of actually getting to them. Can you see us digging up a grave at midnight, like Burke and Hare?'

'Yeah, you got the Burke part right,' she quipped. 'You'll think of something.'

He smiled back thinking it was all quite surreal. He decided on a refill, only this time a double espresso. His thoughts were clearer with caffeine coursing through his veins. The kernel of an idea had begun to formulate.

Eleven

The deep, rich aroma of freshly brewed coffee made from *Old Brown Java* beans brewing in a percolating machine, mingled with thick cigar smoke, filled the air of the city-centre office of Barry Laine. He sipped his coffee from a bone China cup, taking in his surroundings. The room's furniture included a desk, a low table, a sideboard adorned with silverware. On one of the walls hung a large painting, a seascape with a schooner making for port before the onset of a storm, an original work by an American artist who specialised in ships under sail. Worth at least £5000, Laine had paid far less for it when he had persuaded the previous owner into parting with it when the person developed a heroin habit. Sitting on an executive, English hide leather chair, Laine felt its texture under his hand as he drummed his fingers on the wide arm.

Laine needed to satisfy himself that the mention of diamonds at the old funeral parlour was no more than mere coincidence. How could anyone, particularly the young woman with her geeky friend, know of what took place there many years previously? He'd summoned Lennie to his office who stood waiting for Laine to speak.

'Right, Len. Did you do what I asked – talk to the woman and her friend?'

'Sorry, boss. When I got there, the place had closed. I did go in to take a look around though.'

'And?' Laine asked, impatiently. He needed to know what they knew, if they knew anything at all.

'All I could see was someone had carried out a search,' Lennie continued.

'How so?'

'The obvious signs, floorboards lifted, that kind of thing.'

'Anything else?' Laine pushed.

'Yeah, I asked some questions around the area. See if the geek's known.'

'And is he?'

'Yeah, he is. Name's Patrick Doyle, some kind of social worker. That's about it.'

Laine pondered the information; it had to be more than coincidence. First, the woman asked what the diamonds were worth, followed by the man ripping the place apart, the man being none other than Patrick Doyle, a name from his past.

'Lennie, I'd like you to tell our friends I'd appreciate a chat with them. No rough stuff, mind.' Laine considered the beautiful young woman. 'Gentle persuasion only,' he added. 'D'you understand?'

'No probs. Shall I bring them here?'

'No, I'll see them at the house. My wife's away so we'll have a cosy little reunion there.'

***

At the Register Office, Pat introduced himself to the woman behind the reception desk as Dr Doyle. He explained about his research into the history of Cardiff Italian families for a book he was writing.

'I need to know the details of any records you may have in order to trace some of the families with no living relatives. Is this something you can help me with?'

Demi stood next to him smiling; she looked Italian given her Greek features. Pat provided the names of some of the families, having compiled a list at the coffee shop, adding the name Pesticio to other Italian names to make it appear like a genuine request.

The Assistant Registrar checked the database on a computer.

'Yes, Dr Doyle, there are records under the names on your list. What exactly do you need to know?'

'Maybe if I concentrate on one family at a time,' he suggested. 'Let me see.' He pretended to study the list. 'How about Pesticio?'

The woman tapped at her keyboard then waited for the information to upload.

'We have that name,' she confirmed. 'Anything else?'

'Well, the period I'm researching is the nineteen sixties,' he told her.

The woman looked up from the screen.

'Births or deaths?'

'Mmm, deaths,' he said nonchalantly.

They eventually narrowed the names recorded to a certain Giuseppe who had died in 1965. However, the registrar felt certain this family still lived in Cardiff, as Giuseppe Pesticio was the founder of an ice cream company still trading with many outlets around the city.

'Where did the funeral take place? I'd like to take some photos of the gravestone for my book.'

The woman returned to the computer, tapping the keys.

'Not sure you'll have much luck with that,' she informed him.

'Why not?' he asked.

The woman's next statement made his heart race. He tried to disguise his excitement, thinking of the fortune possibly within his reach.

'Giuseppe Pesticio wasn't buried in the ground the way most people would be,' she informed. 'They placed his coffin in the family mausoleum at Cathays cemetery. That should make a far more interesting picture, Dr Doyle.'

'Cathays cemetery,' Pat explained to Demi as they left the Register Office, 'is the oldest cemetery in the city. It's divided into different sections for different religious denominations. 'Church of England or Wales, Roman Catholic, Jewish. There's even a Chinese section, though it's quite small. The Pesticios should be in the Catholic section.'

Pat had been surprised to learn of the family's mausoleum. He knew they were popular in the Victorian era as he had seen many of them at Highgate cemetery in London. Mausoleums were status symbols for the upper class. The Pesticios were no doubt a rich, Italian family, and after all, mausoleums originated from ancient Rome.

They arrived at the cemetery, parking as near as possible to the former chapel that now housed the cemetery office.

They walked over to the stone building. The official inside looked up from his newspaper at the two damp individuals standing before him. They both shuffled their feet, looking somewhat awkward. He picked up his mug of tea, took a loud slurp then asked:

'How may I help you?'

Pat indicated towards Demi.

'We're looking for the resting place of my friend's relative, a certain Giuseppe Pesticio laid to rest in this consecrated ground. We'd like to pay the gentleman our respects.'

Pat ushered Demi forward where she produced a small posy of flowers she'd bought in a petrol station on their way to the cemetery. The man stood up, walked over to a steel locker then opened the door.

'What name did you say?' he asked looking back at them.

'Giuseppe,' Demi replied. 'Uncle Giuseppe.'

'Need another name, luv. First name's no good. They're all in alphabetical order of last names, you see.'

'That'll be Pesticio,' Pat said spelling it out. 'P.E.S.T.I.C.I.O.'

The man went back to his cabinet. He ran a finger along the volumes selecting a large dossier he pulled from the shelf. Placing the large book on the counter he started to flick through the pages.

'*M, N, O, P, PES*, hah, here we are – Pesticio you said? Mmm, gotta few of 'em in here, we have. Who exactly are you looking for?'

'Giuseppe,' they said in unison.

The man located the details of the resting ground in the ledger.

'It's a mausoleum,' he announced. 'Not many of them in here. You related then?' Demi nodded slowly.

'I miss him dreadfully,' she lamented.

'Ruddy 'ell,' the man responded. 'He's been dead for bleedin' years. Close, were you?'

As they walked out of the office with the location of the tomb scribbled on a piece of paper, Pat turned to Demi.

'Let's not be too emotional, shall we?'

She turned to look into his face wiping an imaginary tear from the corner of her eye.

'Uncle Joe meant so much to me.'

'Yeah, except he actually died long before you were born.'

'Oh right,' Demi said. 'Never thought about that.'

The soggy, wet ground made their feet sink into the mud as they made their way towards a large stone-built edifice surrounded by steel railings.

'This must be it,' Pat announced. He looked around. 'No other tombs as far as I can see.'

Peering through the railings, Demi read out an inscription on the last resting place of the Pesticios:

'Mary Mother of Jesus, weep for the *port holes* of the dearly departed.'

'Weep for the what?' Pat asked looking at the inscription above the door.

'*Poor souls,*' he corrected her.

Demi pointed out that the words were fading, making them difficult to read. Pat then read out an inscription in Latin: *Media vita in mortesumas:*

'In the midst of life we are in death'.

He walked slowly around the grey building, its railings about six feet high, the tops tipped liked spears. Arriving back at the entrance, he shook the securely locked gates.

'So that's why he chose this one,' Pat whispered.

'Yeah, it's like a little church,' Demi commented. 'How many d'you reckon are in there?'

'No, I meant why Beers chose Giuseppe's coffin to hide the diamonds. He knew he wouldn't have to dig them up. He could have come here anytime. Who would notice an undertaker? Who'd be suspicious if he'd been seen going in there?' he said pointing at the stone building. 'After a time he makes an excuse to go in, something to do with the coffin, he claims. Opens the lid then retrieves the stones. Now all we need to figure out is how do *we* get in there?'

'I know,' Demi replied, 'we come back at night and break in.'

Pat snapped his fingers. 'Brilliant idea! We scramble over the cemetery wall in the dark, force this lock, kick in that door, prise open the coffin lid, grab the diamonds, then run like hell back to the main road to catch a bus into town.'

'Yep,' Demi confirmed, 'except I didn't figure on us catching the bus.'

Looking up at him, she sensed his incredulity. 'You gotta better plan then?'

Pat shook his head. 'Nope, but I'm sure I'll think of something.'

They walked away from the tomb, Demi still clutching the flowers.

'No way I'm leaving these here,' she said holding up the bouquet. 'They cost you four and a half quid in that garage. 'Anyway,' she added, 'I don't even know the bloke.'

Pat waved at the attendant in the office as they approached the exit who gave them a perplexed look as they went by. The man had discovered something else about the Pesticio family in the records but decided it wasn't worth mentioning.

The rain had stopped, making the return journey less eventful.

'Are you doing anything in particular this evening?' Pat asked.

'No, why?'

'Well I thought we could meet up, you know; try to work out how we can get to the diamonds.'

'Good idea,' Demi agreed without hesitation. 'Mum will look after the kids for me. I could do with a night out. Where're we going then, somewhere glamorous?'

'It's a little pub down the Bay,' he told her.'

'Not glamorous then,' she sighed. 'Okay, give me the directions, and I'll be there.'

'Great. I've booked a fortnight's leave as well. I need to get away from the job for a while. I've been working on a history project about the seamen of Tiger Bay.'

He could tell by the expression on Demi's face he needed to explain the subject in more detail.

'Oh, right, sailors,' she said nodding.

Twelve

Pat sat at his kitchen table working out how they could get into the tomb of the Pesticio family. This wasn't going to be easy. Whatever plan he could think up would not involve Demi, not the breaking in part anyway. He considered telling Elroy. Maybe seek his help. Elroy had a reliable car, and being a taxi, it wouldn't look out of place any time, day or night. The hardest part would be getting into the mausoleum. The lock on the outer gate, then the lock on the tomb door itself. He thought about coffins, about decomposed bodies, he shuddered. This isn't right, he told himself then shoved it to the back of his mind. He needed the money. With over half a million pounds worth of diamonds just lying there he'd make it work, somehow.

Pat stepped into the Lamb & Flag at eight pm. He had arranged for Elroy to collect Demi. The *Lamb*, busy as usual, with most of the regulars in. He waved at Dezzie who sat in the corner playing dominos with three other West Indian men. Dezzie lifted his empty glass, winking towards him. Pat nodded, paying for a double rum. He ordered himself a pint of *Brains bitter*. Turning from the bar, he spotted Demi entering the pub with Elroy behind her. She looked stunning. Her long, black hair was hanging loose over her shoulders, not fiercely pulled back in a ponytail. Her face showed a hint of make-up, accentuating her Greek beauty. Breathless, he crossed over to greet her.

'You look lovely.'

'Thank you,' Demi replied coyly. Her face slightly reddened.

'Can I get you a drink?'

'Just a coke for me, thanks. It's all I ever drink now.' She scanned the bar. 'This is nice. Do you come in here often?'

He wasn't sure how to respond to the question.

'I like to think of it as my local,' he indicated with a sweep of his hand. 'I only live about half a mile away as you know.' He took a sip of his beer, thought about rolling a cigarette but didn't want to stand alone in the street. Elroy joined them saying he was 'between fares.'

'I know most of them in here quite well,' Pat told her.

Demi looked around the small bar again, taking in the mix of customers.

'They seem like a nice bunch of people,' she told him. Pat glanced around at the regulars: Dezzie with his three friends, the tenant, Mr Nooks, who stood behind the pumps taking sips from a glass of whisky under the bar. Mr Singh, who owned the small shop, sat with a friend, drinking orange juice. The rest of the clientele consisted of people whose names were unknown to him but familiar faces all the same. The pub boasted an old jukebox, playing a song by Diana Ross: *Love Child*.

Pat bought a glass of coke, then after they found a table he leaned towards Demi to whisper he was going to let Elroy in on their plan. Before he could tell Elroy, the bar door opened. Hatchet Lennie stood there looking in. He strode across to them. Lennie threw a quick smile at Demi, a nod at Elroy.

'Sorry to break up the party, dudes, but I have a car waiting outside. The boss wants a chat with you.'

The man looked menacing with his gleaming bald head, large muscular frame, and a neck almost the width of his head. The trio around the table looked up at him; wondering what he meant. Pat asked the question.

'A chat about what, exactly?'

'You'll find out when you see him,' Lennie sneered. He moved sidewards, arm extended towards the door.

'Now's not convenient. I'm with friends.'

Pat indicated towards Demi.

'She's invited as well,' Lennie said.

'Elroy?' Pat asked.

'Nope. Just you two.'

None of them moved.

'Mr Laine doesn't like to be kept waiting,' Lennie snapped. 'The car's outside; laid on special.'

'Can I have another drink please, Pat?' Demi asked offering her now empty glass.

'I believe my friend isn't ready to leave just yet for the congenial company of your employer,' Pat said.

The man towered above him.

'I'm also reluctant to do so,' Pat continued. 'As I have no idea what this is all about.'

Lennie Randall sat down next to him, leaned over to speak softly in his ear. Pat's face drained of colour as he stood up.

'On second thoughts, I think maybe we should go and see Mr Laine.'

***

The black BMW made its way towards the opulent home of Barry Laine. In the back, Pat and Demi sat in the luxury of the leather interior, customised with added refinements. Music played from the speakers. Pat recognised the voice of the Jamaican singer, Jimmy Cliff, singing a Ska version of *Many Rivers to Cross.* Pat hummed to the tune. Demi spoke first since leaving the pub.

'Now this is what you should get yourself.' She looked impressively around the sumptuous interior.

'On my salary? I could just about afford the dust caps on one of these. Anyway, never mind the bloody car; what do you think he wants with us?'

'Maybe he wants to re-negotiate the terms of the rent on the shop. Or serve us an eviction notice.'

'I somehow doubt it. No, this is serious. I can feel it.'

Demi took him lightly by the hand.

'What did Lennie say to you in the pub that made you change your mind about this?'

'Oh, nothing,' Pat sheepishly replied.

He looked through the black, tinted windows shuddering at the thought of his penis being stretched across a *butcher's block* with a steel axe poised above it, about to be brought down to sever him from his manhood. He quickly dismissed the gruesome thought from his mind's eye.

The car pulled into the grounds of the house through electronic gates then made its way up a long drive to the double doors set within a four-pillar porch. An expanse of lawns, shrubs, and hedgerows surrounded the house. In the middle of one lawn, a fountain, with a statue of a woman holding a vessel above her shoulder, spouted water that cascaded around her. The naked statue's voluptuous form with pronounced breasts glistened under spotlights from the surrounding pool.

As she stepped out of the car Demi caught sight of the figure.

'Will you look at that! It's like Roath Park.'

Pat took in the opulence surrounding the home of Barry Laine.

'All a bit ostentatious, if you ask me'

'A bit what?' Demi said frowning.

'You know, gaudy, showy, that sort of thing.'

'Well, I like *that* sort of thing. Jeez, it's like a palace. I bet he's got a swimming pool and everything.'

'I bet,' Pat responded in a derisory tone.

Lennie walked on after telling them to follow him, his feet making a pronounced crunching in the gravel as he went. Demi and Pat obediently fell in behind. Once at the door Lennie pressed the bell then returned to his car leaving them waiting alone. A melody of chimes could be heard somewhere from within. Pat recognised the tune as the opening to Beethoven's fifth symphony: *Da Da Da Daaa*.

As if on cue the door opened where they were greeted by a thick set man of West Indian origin, who appeared as equally as menacing as Lennie but half his height. The man wore an evening suit with a bow tie. He motioned for them to step inside. Once across the threshold they stood in a vast hall with its central feature – a crystal chandelier – hanging from the ceiling. Its light shone through the individual pieces of cut glass appearing almost like diamonds. A man made his way down the staircase drawing their attention from the grandiose light fitting.

'Ah, do come in, my friends,' Barry Laine invited. 'Preston, please offer our guests drinks.'

Preston acknowledged with a nod of the head.

'What can I get you, miss?'

'Coke for me, please.'

'Sir?'

'I'll have Perrier water please.'

'Ice and lemon in both?'

'Just the water for me,' Pat replied.

The man made his way to another room to prepare the drinks. Barry Laine had reached the bottom of the stairs then walked across the polished wood floor towards them. As he approached, Pat sensed a mix of expensive cologne, and cigar smoke. It wasn't an entirely unpleasant combination. Laine stopped to face him, hand outstretched.

'Pat. Nice to see you again. It's been a long while since we last met.'

This recognition took Pat by surprise. He'd have walked past Barry Laine in the street, unrecognised since their school days.

'Or should I call you, *Dr* Doyle?' Laine added.

'Pat will be fine.'

'But I hear you're a doctor, now. I'm impressed.'

'Not the medical type. I have a PhD.'

'Hey, still a doctor all the same. Who'd have thought two scruffy urchins from way back would have done so well, eh?'

Pat looked around the hall at its furniture, *objets' d'art,* Impressionist paintings, antiques, and fine porcelain.

'I haven't done *this* well.'

'True enough. I have become rather successful,' Laine boasted. 'You know, cut a few deals along the way.'

A few throats more like, Pat thought.

Laine turned towards Demi.

'And you must be the lady who works at the charity shop. A pleasure to make your acquaintance. Demi, right?'

'It is, but I'm only a volunteer, I'm not…'

'Volunteers are very important,' he interrupted, a wide smile revealing cosmetically whitened teeth.

'Thank you,' Demi giggled slightly.

'Please. Let's go through to the drawing room.'

He indicated towards the door Preston had gone through earlier.

'Drawing room,' Pat muttered quietly. He felt like blasting this out but held back the temptation. *Listen to the pretentious bastard. I bet he doesn't even know what a bloody drawing room is, and what's with the plummy accent?*

They stepped into another luxuriously furnished room. Barry Laine showed them to a couple of deep-padded, finely upholstered armchairs. As they sat, Preston approached them holding a salver with three drinks.

'Your Perrier, sir. Cola, miss.'

He handed a glass to Laine containing an amber liquid.

'Your usual. Will that be all, sir?'

'Thank you, Preston. You can leave us now.'

Laine raised his glass towards them.

'Cheers.'

'Cheers,' Demi replied doing likewise in return.

'Now then, I'm sure you'll want to know why I've asked you to join me this evening.' Laine said.

'Asked?' Pat blurted, regretting the outburst immediately. 'Asked,' he repeated quietly. 'Like we had a choice? Your minder threatened me with menace. To refuse would have resulted in me parting company with certain vital organs.'

'He said what?' Demi spluttered as she swallowed a mouthful of cola.

'Oh you mustn't take Lennie too seriously,' Laine said. 'I really must speak to him about that. He does tend to be a bit theatrical at times.'

Yeah, Pat thought, *a right little Macbeth.*

'Anyway,' Laine continued, 'back to why you're both here. I understand that during a recent conversation between you both at the shop you mentioned something about diamonds, about their value. Am I correct?'

Silently, they looked over towards Laine. Pat's mind raced. How did Laine know about the diamonds? He'd formulated an answer to the question.

'Whilst doing some research at the library for a project I'm working on, I came across some reports about a mail theft back in nineteen sixty-five. It said that some diamonds went missing. I merely told Demi here about the story so she asked me what they might be worth.'

'That's right,' Demi added then quickly took another sip of coke.

'So tell me, what were you looking for in the shop?'

'Looking for?' Pat feigned surprise.

'Yes, with a hammer, tearing up boards. Lennie told me all about it.'

'No. I wasn't *looking* for anything,' Pat insisted. 'I was just doing some repairs. I tacked down a few loose boards. What would I be looking for?'

'You tell me,' Laine replied.

'He's right,' Demi interrupted. 'I kept tripping over the bloody things all the time. I asked Pat if he could sort them out for me. Sorry, should I have asked for your permission first?'

Go, girl, Pat thought. Good response.

Laine sipped his cognac, studying them over the rim of the glass. He rose from his chair, crossed the room to a table where he opened a cherry-wood box, took out a Cuban cigar, rolling it between his fingers. Putting the cigar under his nose, he inhaled before moving it to his mouth. He picked up a box of matches, struck one then held it to the end of the cigar. He drew smoke in rapid puffs before turning back towards them, holding out the cherry-wood box.

'Forgive me. Can I offer you a cigar?

'No thank you,' Pat said.

'Me neither,' Demi smiled.

Laine collected a large ashtray then returned to his chair. He examined the glowing end of the cigar before speaking.

'I'm going to tell you both a story. Some of this you may have heard from when we were nippers, Pat. You know, local gossip.'

Pat raised his eyebrows not knowing what to expect.

Laine told them how his grandfather had come up with the idea to make some serious money. How he'd involved another family member. Between them, they'd stolen a mailbag containing a large number of valuable diamonds. Unfortunately, he revealed, his one relative died in a car crash, and another man with whom they entrusted the safekeeping of the gems had died under different circumstances.

'So you see my grandfather had been cheated out of the diamonds. Diamonds I believe may still be out there,' Laine said pointing towards the large windows.

'Now,' he continued, learning slightly forward, 'this is where it gets interesting. This other man was an undertaker who worked from his funeral parlour in the docks.' He turned to face Demi. 'The charity shop where you work as a volunteer, the building I now own.'

Sitting back in his chair, Laine took another long draw on his cigar; the end glowed between the grey ash and dark brown of the tobacco. 'Unfortunately, my granddad killed the undertaker. He'd gone to see him to get his diamonds back. They got into a fight, but the undertaker died before telling granddad where they were.'

Demi looked surprised. 'Your grandfather *killed* the undertaker? Wow.'

Pat looked down between his feet then spoke.

'Hardly a clever move on his part given that Beers had the diamonds?'

Laine looked over at Pat.

'Now who said anything about Beers?'

'You did, didn't you?' Pat's face immediately reddened as he inwardly cursed his error.

94

'Never mentioned his name once,' Laine said. 'I think you're holding back on me, Pat. Now how did you know the name of the undertaker?'

Pat began to panic, annoyed having let the name slip out.

'I must've seen it in the papers during my research. Yes, of course. It happened around the same time so I must've have read the article.'

Pat considered this a plausible response. Laine pretended to give the explanation some thought.

'Of course, Pat. How else would you know the name? No doubt it would've been reported in the papers.'

Laine knew of the link between the death of Arnold Beers and the missing diamonds. It became obvious to him that his old friend knew a lot more than he'd let on. Now he needed to find out what he knew, and how.

Thirteen

Back in his flat, Pat and Demi sat drinking coffee. Freshly ground Columbian beans he'd purchased from a supplier in the Bay. Demi struggled with the nutty flavour, more used to *Nescafe*. Music came from the *Bose* player, a Joni Mitchell album: *Ladies of the Canyon.*

The room filled with lyrics about the Woodstock music festival. Throughout the return journey, Pat had kept a hand over his crutch. Demi spent the ride looking through the tinted glass into the night watching the indistinct shapes of traffic as it flashed by. Now they were safely back, Pat felt more than a little relieved. He pondered on their involuntary visit to the palatial home of Barry Laine.

'Did you hear all that *successful man* crap?' Pat scoffed. '*That'll be all, Preston.* If he's a butler then I'm Lord bloody Lucan. Laine's nothing but a gangster. I always knew he would turn out to be a bad 'un.'

'He's certainly come a long way from pigeons and chewing gum, and whatever else he was involved in,' Demi mused.

'He was involved in everything and getting steadily more sophisticated as he grew older. One night, when we were kids, he had us break into the Catholic Truth Society shop next to the Cathedral in Charles Street.'

Demi shook her head in mock disbelief.

'To steal little statues of Jesus and Mary then sell them around the houses of the mainly Irish families. We'd knock on doors saying two shillings for Jesus, a shilling for Mary or two and six for both.'

'Wow! Sounds sophisticated,' she said feigning awe. 'Stealing religious icons from the church then selling them for shillings. How bad does it get?'

'Okay, okay, most gangsters start out small. Anyway, how's your coffee, want a refill?'

Demi shook her head, looking at the bottom of her mug with its dark dregs. Pat cleared the table before carrying a notepad from the kitchen. 'Okay, we need a plan. We need to work out how to get into the tomb, what we can expect to find once we're inside. Identify the right coffin, open it…'

'Wait a sec,' Demi interrupted. 'Find coffins? Open them up? This all sounds a bit scary when you put it like that. Will there still be a body inside? Will we… will you rather, have to touch it?'

Pat looked over, trying to sound encouraging.

'There's well over half a million pounds worth of diamonds inside that little stone building. Just think of what we could do with all that money.'

'Buy you a decent car for a start,' Demi suggested.

'Yes, well. That had crossed my mind. You and the kids would also be set up. Buy a small house maybe.'

Demi frowned. 'Are you saying you plan to share some of this with me?'

'Fifty-fifty. We do this together so you'll get half.'

'Pat, that's really kind of you, but honestly, I don't expect you to…'

Pat waved his hand to silence her protest. 'Partners,' he added.

They sat in the quiet of the kitchen. The sound of a police helicopter buzzing past broke the moment.

'To be honest, I don't expect you to actually be there. You know, with the coffins. Though we may need some additional help, possibly Elroy, for instance.'

'How many diamonds will you give him?'

Pat hadn't thought about this.

'I don't know. Maybe I'll just pay him for any help he provides. I also think we could use someone who has experience in this sort of thing, breaking into places, I mean.'

'Who've you got in mind for that, anyone in particular?'

'Someone I'll ask as a last resort,' Pat said thinking about the only person he knew with burglary skills. 'If I can figure a way to do this myself, I will. We need to keep this on a need-to-know basis, get too many people involved, the whole thing could go...'

'Tits up?' she butted in.

'I was going to say pear-shaped, but yes, that's pretty much what I meant.'

Pat began to pace the room. Something bothered him. He stopped to peer out of the window. The helicopter still scanned the area; its searchlight sweeping the ground below.

'I'm not entirely sure the delightful Mr Laine is convinced with the explanation we gave him earlier. I think he's worked out we know more than we've told him. He's not stupid. That's why he's where he is today.' He turned to face Demi. 'Barry Laine's nobody's fool. I don't think we've seen or heard the last of him.' He returned to his seat.

'We have to be very careful from now on,' he continued. 'That man is dangerous, he'll stop at nothing to get what he wants. I'm not prepared to see you get hurt.' He paused. 'Or me for that matter.'

'My hero,' Demi cooed. He smiled at her knowing Laine had desires for the woman he had become besotted with. He would do everything he could to prevent Laine ever cheating him again.

Fourteen

Barry Laine summoned Lennie back to his place to tell him he wanted Doyle and the girl watched.

'I want to know their every move. Where they go, who they see, what they do.'

Lennie listened, dutifully nodding.

'Keep me fully informed, day or night.'

'No probs, boss, I'll stick like glue,' he said pushing the palms of his hands together.

'Not too close, Len. Don't let them know we're keeping tabs on them. This I can't stress enough, they're to come to no harm either unless I say otherwise. Got that?'

Lennie nodded again feeling a pang of disappointment. He liked harming people.

After Lennie had left, Laine returned to his study; taking his drink he sat at a large desk situated in a bay window. Picking up his iPhone he scrolled through the music selecting Bach's *Jesu, Joy Of Man's Desiring* that filled the room from four concealed speakers. He sat contemplating, thought about what Pat Doyle had told him, not persuaded by his explanation, convinced Doyle knew about his grandfather's diamonds. Was this a potential breakthrough? At last, an opportunity to finish what his grandfather had started back in 1965, and his old school friend would be responsible for re-uniting the Laine family, or Barry Laine at least, with the long-lost diamonds.

'Why do I listen to this shit?' he asked himself. Picking up his iPhone he switched from Bach to the sound of *Queen*: *Fat Bottomed Girls*.

'Now that's more like it,' Laine told himself, increasing the volume to almost maximum.

***

Pat returned to the house in the Ely district of Cardiff where he hoped to find the only person he knew who could help him gain access to the crypt. He knocked the door and waited. He heard the sound of a dog barking from within, a deep bark suggesting a large breed. Tanya opened the door.

'It's Pat Doyle,' she shouted behind her. Pat stepped inside trying not to breathe through his nose but the rancid smell of the place still struck him. He was met by Dennis Foley still sporting his grubby attire.

'Hi Dennis,' Pat said in as jovial a voice as he could muster. 'Don't suppose you know where Gary is by any chance? I've knocked his door but got no answer.'

'What d'you want him for'? Dennis asked. 'He ain't got any sprogs.'

'Oh, I just need a word with him. It's nothing important.'

Dennis produced an iPhone from a pocket in his tracksuit bottoms and tapped the screen.

'That you, Gaz?' Dennis said into the phone. 'Look, I got our social worker wiv us, he wants to see you. Yeah, right, he's 'ere now. Okay, see you in a bit.'

He ended the call returning the phone to his pocket 'He's on his way.'

Pat decided to wait outside. The stink of the house got to him plus he needed to speak with the man in private.

As Pat reached the front gate, Harris had already arrived. He eyed Pat warily, wondering why he was suddenly in demand. Residents in the area were very distrustful of people in authority, especially social workers. Pat simply told Harris he needed his help with 'something' and would willingly pay him £50.

'Wha' kinda help we talkin' about then?'

'I just need to get into someplace. I thought you may be able to assist with the locks.'

'Break into somewhere, you mean?' Harris quizzed.

'Yes, something like that.' Pat began to wonder if this was such a good idea. Harris might tell people on the estate he was helping a social worker commit a crime. He reminded himself if this went as planned, he wouldn't be a social worker any longer. He'd be sipping cocktails by a pool on some exotic, distant sun-kissed island. Pat could almost feel the sun on his face as he ruminated. Harris did not take long making up his mind.

'Okay, I'll do it.'

'Great,' Pat said. 'I'll pick you up at around seven this evening.'

Pat headed back to collect Demi. She had insisted on being involved despite the location of the diamonds. Demi found it exciting, and even though Pat told her he didn't want her to be there she'd pleaded to go along.

Pat reluctantly decided she could, agreeing to collect her enroute. Having made the visit to enlist Gary Harris, he now needed to persuade Elroy. He'd let Elroy know a little more about his plans. They'd arranged to meet up at the Merchant Seaman's War Memorial outside of the Senedd building in Cardiff Bay.

***

'Diamonds?' Elroy exclaimed, 'A fortune in stolen diamonds? And you know where they are?'

'Indeed I do, Elroy. Indeed I do. Now are you willing to help us out?'

'Us?' he asked, 'who's *us* exactly?'

'Just Demi and me. Oh, and I've asked someone to lend their expertise, but he knows nothing about the diamonds. His role is a one-off for fifty quid.'

'What kind of *'expertise'* are we talking about here? Anyway, what about the fifty notes you owe me, seeing as you're splashing it about.'

Pat looked across the harbour towards the wooden replica Norwegian church.

'Oh, you know, breaking into places and the like.'

'Breaking into places? What places, and where are these diamonds, exactly?'

'In a mausoleum at Cathays cemetery, but don't panic, it'll be easy. I've cased the joint, so there should be no problems as I see it.'

'Mausoleum? Cased the joint? Will you listen to yourself? You can't go breaking into a mausoleum, that's sacri… that's bloody grave robbing. Have you gone completely gaga?'

He leant on the wall in front of him shaking his head in disbelief.

'Elroy, Elroy,' Pat said trying to mollify his friend. 'All you have to do is drop us off in your taxi near the cemetery then wait until we come back, hopefully with the diamonds.'

Elroy turned to face Pat, snapping his fingers

'Simple as that, eh? Look, my friend. Aren't you forgetting something? Your subject is history, not archaeology. You can't go around like some *Indiana Jones* breaking into tombs. A social worker and a woman from a charity shop. Jeez, you couldn't make it up.'

'Okay, okay, I understand,' Pat relented. 'I guess I'll need to ask someone else for help.'

Pat turned to walk towards the red brick Pier head building. Elroy remained where he stood, watching him, still unable to believe what he'd been told.

***

'What's he got in the duffel bag?' Elroy asked Pat as Gary Harris climbed into the back of the taxi, dog in tow on a length of cord. Demi sat up front dressed in black denim pants with a black roll neck sweater. Pat had explained his plan earlier saying she would need to wear something dark. He wasn't expecting her to look like a professional cat-burglar but decided to let it go.

'It's me gear, innit?' Harris responded.

'It's his gear,' Pat repeated. 'He told me he'd need to get tooled up for this kind of job.'

Elroy groaned inwardly. He looked in his rear-view mirror at the spider tattooed on Harris's forehead. 'I don't think the police will have too much trouble fitting a description if this goes wrong.'

'Elroy may have a point there,' Demi said. 'Maybe we should wear a stocking.'

'I ain't wearing no feckin' stockings like some tranny,' Harris proclaimed.

Pat tutted. 'I think she meant over our heads.'

Shaking his head, Elroy started the car, pulling away from the kerbside.

Fifteen

About a hundred metres behind them, a black BMW pulled out to follow the taxi.

'Okay,' Pat said, 'this is what we do. First, we go into the cemetery where we'll take cover out of sight somewhere. The gatekeeper will probably think we've left by another exit. Then, after he's locked up and gone, under the cover of darkness we'll make our way to the mausoleum, then we'll break in.'

Demi nodded. Gary Harris frowned. Pat was deliberately vague about the rest, no way had he wanted Harris to know what they were likely to discover once inside the tomb. He looked at Gary Harris.

'Once you open the mausoleum, I'll pay you the agreed fifty pounds and you can make your way back home.'

Harris readily agreed to this, saying he didn't want to spend any more time in what he'd described as a 'bone yard' than necessary. After entering the tomb, Pat knew he would first need to identify the coffin with the body of Giuseppe Pesticio inside, then open the lid. He had his own toolkit for this part of the plan, a screwdriver. Coffins lids, he believed, were mainly screwed, not nailed down.

Elroy wiped his hand across his brow beginning to feel apprehensive as they approached the cemetery.

'Was it necessary to bring that bloody dog?' he asked looking back at Harris with the small terrier on his lap.

'Where I goes, Rizla goes. Innit, fella?'

Harris tickled the dog behind the ear. Pat looked nervously down at the animal fearing it would bite him just for the sheer hell of it. He didn't like dogs, especially terrier types bred to kill rabbits.

The car pulled over about fifty yards from the cemetery entrance.

'Okay,' Elroy said, 'I'll drive around the streets; you call my mobile when you want picking up.'

Pat, Demi and Gary climbed out of the car, making their way towards the gates. Demi carried the same but now wilted bunch of flowers. The attendant in the gate office saw them approach, recognising them from their earlier visit only this time noticing the strange looking man with a dog.

'Come to pay our respects, again,' Pat said putting his head around the office door. 'Remember? Mr Pesticio?' He put his hand on Harris's shoulder 'Our friend here is going to do a spot of weeding for us.'

'Top o' the mornin' ta yer,' Harris said.

They made their way to the Pesticio tomb, Pat still unable to believe Gary Harris's attempt to pass himself off as some kind of Irish handyman. The attendant watched, wondering if the woman would leave the flowers this time.

Outside the gates, the BMW pulled to a halt. Lennie Randall reported the events back to Barry Laine.

'That's right,' he confirmed into his mobile. 'They've gone into a cemetery. Get this, there's some dude with them who's got a dog on a length of string.'

'The girl with them?' Laine asked.

'Yeah, carrying some shitty looking flowers.'

'Okay, Len, sit tight and keep me informed. But on no account do you go in after them.'

Inside the cemetery, the trio were at the site of the mausoleum. They stood side by side looking at the structure. As darkness loomed, a light rain began to fall.

'We need to find somewhere out of sight,' Pat told them.

Cold and damp, Demi rubbed her hands.

'I feel like shit,' she said to Pat. 'How long will this take?'

'Weather's pretty bad, but hopefully we'll be away from here as soon as we can.'

Pat took hold of the metal gate, giving it a light shake. It rattled noisily. He immediately regretted his action. Gary Harris sat on the ground smoking a roll-up cigarette as he played with the dog. Pat decided to join him taking out his own tobacco pouch from an inside pocket.

Demi glanced at the soggy ground with distaste, deciding to remain standing. She busied herself by pulling petals from one of the wilted flowers.

Pat looked around before pointing to a large headstone away from the mausoleum.

'Come on. Let's get out of sight behind there. If we stay here the attendant might see us.'

They trudged in single file towards the headstone, Harris coaxing the dog on the end of the length of the string.

'I hope its warmer behind there,' Demi said, 'coz I'm starting to freeze.' Pat looked back at her.

'Well, I doubt there'll be a blazing log fire but it will offer some shelter from the wind.'

Demi grunted. 'Sounds lovely,'

The attendant checked his watch – eight pm. Time to lock the gates. After a walk around the cemetery locking the other gates, he returned to the main entrance ready to secure it before leaving for home. He thought about the three people who'd passed him earlier but had not left through the main entrance. He gave a quick scan of the area to make sure they were not still in the cemetery. It wouldn't be the first time he'd locked up leaving some unfortunate people inside. Satisfied the place was empty; he pulled the large iron gates together, securing them with a heavy chain and padlock.

Pat heard the loud clang carry across the cemetery, guessing the place had closed up for the evening. The rain eased off but the temperature had dropped even further. He pushed his hands deep inside his pockets, contemplating another cigarette. All three of them started to shiver.

'Another hour should do it,' Pat told them looking at his watch.

'I'll be dead by then,' Demi uttered through chattering teeth.

Harris grinned at her. 'You're in the right place then, luv.'

For a few moments they just stood in cold silence, the eeriness of the place surrounded them like a shroud. Suddenly, Pat turned, putting his head around the stone. He'd heard a sound. *What the hell was that?*

Lennie watched the man secure the gates, puzzled why Doyle and the others hadn't left at the same time. The attendant walked down the road towards a bus stop. Lennie looked over his shoulder; a bus had crossed the traffic lights heading towards them. The attendant put his hand out for the bus to stop.

Lennie jumped out of the car and ran towards the man before the bus arrived.

'Hey, mate, I'm looking for some friends who went into the cemetery earlier, one of them had a dog.'

'Yeah, I saw them but they weren't in there when I closed up,' the man said shaking his head. 'Must've left by one of the other exits.'

'What other exits?' Lennie asked.

'There's two other gates y'know. Lots of people leave by them, depends where they're going.'

When the bus stopped the attendant boarded without a glance back at Lennie. As it pulled away, Lennie took out his mobile to contact Laine. 'There's no sign of Doyle or the others. Some dude in charge reckons they went out another way. What d'you want me to do? Take a drive around?'

Laine agreed with the suggestion.

'Yeah, do that, if there's no sign of them make your way to Doyle's flat. They'll probably show up there at some point.'

Glad to be back in the comfort of his car, Lennie drove round the nearby streets. Satisfied they weren't still in the area, he made his way back to the Bay.

***

In the distance, the sound of the City Hall clock chimed. With the drop in temperature, a low mist clung to the ground, drifting around the headstones. The cemetery took on the appearance of a set from a Hammer Horror film. The very thought made Pat shudder as he took in the eerie landscape. He checked his watch when he heard the clock start to strike the hour – ten pm – dark enough to emerge from their hiding place. He moved back towards the small building where he looked at the door through the gates, wondering what the inside of the tomb contained. Probably a room with shelves – on the shelves, coffins. Pat hoped the coffins weren't stacked on top of each other with old Giuseppe at the bottom. He didn't relish doing any heavy lifting, especially with only Demi to help him. Pat decided he would check this out before dismissing Harris – though he really did not want him staying around any longer than necessary. Demi had become restless as well as cold. She wandered around trying to keep warm then suddenly stopped in her tracks.

'What's that noise?' she whispered.

'What noise?' Pat asked. He strained to listen, recalling a sound he'd heard earlier.

'Listen, it's coming from over there,' Demi said pointing towards some gravestones about twenty metres away. Pat took a step forward. He could now hear a low rasping sound.

'You're right,' he confirmed. 'Let's take a look.'

Demi looked up at Pat. 'You sure? It could be anything.'

Harris did not attempt to join them as they edged their way nearer to where the reverberation became louder. Demi held tightly onto Pat's arm as they tread forward. He shone the torch down to the point where the sound was loudest. It came from behind a gravestone. Demi quietly read the inscription:

Here lies Emanuel Lewis who fell asleep on the 12th day of December 1902. 'Jeez,' Demi announced, clinging even tighter to Pat's arm. 'I didn't know dead people snored.'

Pat glanced down at her, a look of bewilderment on his face.

'Eh? Of course they don't.'

He peered over the top of the stone, a man lay propped against the other side, snoring inside a sleeping bag; clutching a plastic three litre cider bottle like a sleeping child clutches a teddy.

'It's a bloody wino,' he revealed quietly so as not to wake the man. 'Shit girl, you had me worried then.'

'What happens if he wakes up?' Demi whispered.

'Somehow, I don't think that's likely. He's well out of it. Right, let's go back and get Harris to do his stuff. It's dark enough now; we don't want to be here all night.'

'Bloody right,' Demi agreed. 'Let's do it.'

Harris was about to roll himself another cigarette when they got back to him. The dog, curled up at his feet, snored almost as loud as the comatose wino.

'He's dead to the world. Just like all of 'em in here, eh?' Harris gave his dozing pet a foot tap causing the terrier to wake, suddenly look around, and wonder what had interrupted his slumber.

'Right,' Pat said, 'we're going in.'

They moved across to the metal gates. Harris bent forward examining the lock making an *mmm* sound as he did so. Opening his duffel bag, Harris removed a heavy crowbar.

'What the hell are you going to do with that?' Pat asked. 'I thought you were going to pick the lock using some fancy instruments.'

'I am,' Harris assured.

'Well. Where are they?'

'Here.' Harris held up the metal bar before him. 'I pick locks with this.' After forcing the bar between the gates, Harris yanked it towards him. The gates sprang open with a clatter that echoed around the cemetery. Pat quickly looked about then back to Harris.

'Can't you be a little quieter?' he hissed. 'Someone might hear us making a row like that.' Harris simply grinned, pleased with the result.

'I could have done that,' Demi announced. 'We're paying him fifty quid for this?'

'I 'aven't seen a note yet,' Harris reminded them. 'When do I get my money anyway?'

'I have it right here,' Pat said tapping the side of his jacket. Once we're inside I'll hand it over.'

They stepped through the now open gate and stood in front of the doors to the tomb. Harris inserted the iron bar near the lock and heaved on it, grunting as he did. It took some pulling and shoving before the doors relented. Harris pushed open the one door then put his head inside.

'Feckin' dark in here, where's the light?'

Pat stood behind him, shining the torch through the opening. What he saw surprised him. The beam of pale light illuminated the bare walls. There were no shelves with coffins as he'd expected. He stepped inside to take a closer look. Empty.

'Shit' he shouted. 'Shit, shit. Now what?'

Demi, who had hesitantly held back, stepped gingerly inside the structure.

'What's wrong? What's the problem?'

'It's empty,' he told her, shining the torch around the bare interior. That's what's wrong.'

'It can't be,' she said following the beam of the torch. 'Why would it be? What've they done with them?'

'Right,' Harris interrupted. 'Let's 'ave me money, I've done my bit and got you in, though why you wanted to get in 'ere is a bleedin' mystery.' His hand stretched towards Pat.

'Wait a minute, wait a minute.' Demi reached over, taking the torch from Pat, then shone it down at her feet. 'Down there. They must be down there.' The torch lit a patch of stone beneath them. Pat looked down, reading the inscription engraved in the stone. *Nel mane di dio.* "In the hands of God." 'It's a vault, a bloody vault,' he said. 'I should have known there wouldn't be coffins in this part.'

'S'cuse me,' Harris interrupted, 'it's pay me time. Now hand over the fifty smackers so I can get on home.'

'No,' Pat said quickly. 'No, you can't go just yet. We need you to pick another lock.'

Harris looked around the dark, empty space, a perplexed expression on his face.

'What lock would that be then?'

'You're standing on it,' Pat said.

Harris looked down at the floor, even more confused.

'That stone is a movable slab,' Pat told him. 'It lifts away where below is a vault.' He put his arm around the man's shoulder whispering, 'Help us lift it and I'll pay you an extra twenty. Deal?'

Harris grunted his agreement.

Using the crowbar, they managed to prize the stone away. It revealed an opening in the ground. The two men sat on the floor, perspiration visible on their faces, breathing heavily from the exertion of lifting the heavy slab. Picking up the torch, Pat crawled over to the rectangular opening. The beam of light revealed a flight of stone steps descending into the darkness of the space below. The three of them stared through the wide aperture trying to make out what was at the bottom. Harris looked back towards Rizla, the dog stood outside the door, making a pitiful whining sound.

'Cum 'ere, boy,' he called slapping the top of his leg. Rizla remained statue-like at the entrance.

Harris returned his gaze back to the steps feeling a cold chill down his back. He shuddered as he pointed to the vault.

'No feckin' way I'm goin' down there. Give me the feckin' money, then I'm outta here.'

Pat agreed. They stepped back outside into the night air. The mist rose higher as did the sound of the sleeping wino behind the headstone, oblivious to all that happened nearby. Pat took the money from his pocket, counted seventy pounds before handing it over to the eagerly waiting man who shoved it in his pocket. Harris turned, walking towards the nearest wall. As he went, he whistled, Rizla dutifully followed behind. Pat watched them as they made their way between the gravestones reminding him of Bill Sykes and Bullseye.

Demi emerged from the vault, a frightened look on her face.

'Don't ever leave me in a place like that on my own again.'

'Sorry, I thought you came out with us.'

He indicated for them to return inside. They hesitated momentarily before stepping over the threshold of the door.

'I'm scared, Pat,' Demi said as they stood together in the darkened space of the mausoleum. 'Surely you don't want to go down there, do you? You don't know what's down there.' She retraced her steps back outside. Pat followed.

'Look, it'll be okay. It's no different to what we'd expected if the coffins were just inside the tomb. They'll simply be in a space at the bottom of those steps.' He shone the torch beam through the door.

Demi shrugged. 'I don't know. It's not what I expected at all. Do we have to do this? I know there's a lot of money involved but I'm not so sure now.'

'Okay, if you don't want to go through with this, that's fine by me,' he said. 'You wait out here, I'll go in alone. Honestly, I don't mind at all.'

Demi stood in front of him nodding her head, hands folded as she shivered slightly. The mist had increased, swirling around their feet, the doors of the mausoleum swinging gently in the light breeze. Pat returned inside to the top of the steps. A nagging doubt held him back, unable to take the next step to descend into the vault. As he stood there, the City Hall clock chimed, this time striking midnight. *The witching hour.* He hadn't realised how long they'd been there. Extending his foot, he placed it on the first step. 'Oh Well, here goes,' he muttered quietly. 'It's now or never.'

Suddenly, he felt a hand on his shoulder, he gave out a shriek, nearly falling headfirst down the steps. In response to his sudden reaction, Demi also screamed. They clung on to each other in the darkness, the torch fell from his hand and down into the vault.

'Shit. What are you doing?' he said. 'I thought you were going to wait outside.'

'Like hell. I'm not staying out there on my own. I'd rather take my chances with you.'

Pat sighed inwardly on hearing this, pleased not to be going down there on his own. They both gazed down at the dim light of the fallen torch in the vault below.

'Well at least it still works,' he said relieved. 'There's no way we could've carried on without any form of light.'

'What about your ciggy lighter,' she suggested.

'And what do we burn exactly? Anyway, we don't want to end up cremating them by setting fire to the place.'

'Good point,' she whispered.

'Okay, after three,' he said.

'Three,' she immediately responded giving him a slight push towards the steps. Pat turned to resume his descent with Demi close behind. They reached the bottom where they stood in the dim, shadowy vault. Pat retrieved the torch from where it had landed then swept the cone of light around the confined space. There were coffins placed in recesses, five in total. At least two appeared new in light oak veneer with shiny brass handles. Pat dismissed them from the search. Of the five coffins one was more of a casket, much larger than the others. Pat approached, shining the light across the lid where he noticed a brass crucifix, mottled with age. Below the cross lay a plaque with an inscription written in Latin. *Requiescat in pace – Rest in peace,* but the name was unmistakable: *Giuseppe Alfonso Pesticio.*

'Bingo, this is him. Old Joe's in this one,' he said looking over his shoulder towards Demi. 'Here, give me a hand.'

Between them, they managed to drag the casket to the middle of the floor space.

'This is the bit I'm dreading,' Demi said.'

'Well, I'm not exactly over the moon with joy myself.'

Pat scanned the lid to see how it had been fastened down; there were screws about every twelve inches. He commended his foresight, taking a screwdriver from his trouser pocket. He turned to Demi.

'I'll need you to hold the torch and shine it on the head of the screws, Okay? 'He directed the driver onto the first screw.

'Oh shit. That's all we need.'

'Now what's wrong?' Demi tried to look down at the lid of the coffin.

'The screws are flat heads, and I've only brought a bloody posidrive, look.' He showed her the driver with its star head.

'Not much use then?'

'About as useful as an ashtray on the back of a motorbike,' he retorted.

Demi looked back at the lid. 'So how do we get in there? Can we force it open?'

'With what?' Pat said with a hint of tetchiness to his voice. 'There's hardly going to be a selection of tools down here.'

'Yes, I know that, Mr Grumpy, but the man with the spider tattoo didn't take his iron bar when he left. It's still up there by the entrance.'

'He did. Uh, he didn't? It's still up there? I'll go and fetch it,' Pat said beginning to climb the steps.

'Wait for me. I'm not bloody staying down here on my lonesome.'

Pat found the iron bar lying on the grass. Lifting it, it felt heavy in his hand. He conjured up images of the places where the man used it to gain entry, to steal, to violate other people's lives. Now he would use it to violate the dead, to invade a sanctuary of peace and rest. The one place one would not expect such an intrusion. Taking the bar, they made their way back down into the vault.

'I don't like this,' he said when they reached the bottom step. 'Unscrewing the lid is one thing but forcing it open with a crowbar has to be sheer sacrilege.'

'I know, I know,' Demi agreed. 'But when you consider our options there's not likely to be another chance, is there? So it's now or never.'

'I guess you're right. We'll just have to do our best to put things back in good order before we leave.'

'Sure, and I'll run around with a duster so it'll look as good as new.'

'Okay, little miss sarcasm. You know what I mean.'

'Well, what are people going to think when they see what's happened? Two broken locks and a coffin with its lid ripped off? Mice?'

Pat stared at her in the dim torchlight, held back by doubt.

'Okay. Let's do it,' he said.

Together, they approached the large casket. Demi shone the beam of the torch onto the lid. Despite the coldness of the outside, the small space began to feel warm and clammy. He pushed the bar into the space just under the lid then pressed down, the sound of splitting wood from the casket reverberated around them giving the impression it could be heard all over, that people would show up to see what had happened. Outside, however, the cemetery remained in its stillness. The wino lay undisturbed clutching onto what little remained of his cider, oblivious to the endeavours taking place below.

They took hold of the casket lid at each end, lifting it clear before carefully placing it on the floor. Turning back to the now exposed casket, Pat looked inside, hoping the diamonds would be there in full view so he could pick them up without touching the corpse within. This wasn't to be. Inside the coffin lay a man's skeleton covered with the remnants of the suit in which he'd been laid to rest. What remained of the late Giuseppe hardly filled the space. Pat put a hand in another of his pockets taking out a pair of yellow household gloves.

'What are they for?' Demi whispered watching behind.

Pat glanced back at her, pulling on one of the rubber gloves.

'I'm doing the dishes – what do you think there for? I'm not putting my bare hands in there.'

After pulling on the second glove, Pat placed a hand inside the casket, feeling around, desperate to avoid looking at the skeleton. The back of his hand touched the interior of the casket, sweat dripped from his brow. Please don't sit up to ask what's going on, he willed the decomposed remains.

On the first exploration of the coffin, Pat did not locate any diamonds. Would they be loose or placed in some kind of container? Following further attempts, Pat decided there was nothing inside the casket but the bony remains of the late *Signor* Pesticio. He staggered back in disbelief. There were no diamonds, no treasure trove worth a fortune. Nothing but the skeleton of an old ice cream seller. Turning to face Demi, he shook his head.

'There's no diamonds in there,' he told her. 'Whatever the undertaker did with them; he didn't put them in with *this* body which means he must have hid them somewhere else.'

Demi looked back at him, thinking before she spoke.

'Like where?'

'Who knows, Demi? Who knows?'

They'd have to start again, he thought. If at all.

Sixteen

Barry Laine took the call from Lennie, thinking about what he'd been told. What were they doing in a cemetery? The woman carried flowers so maybe they were visiting some family member of hers. Nothing untoward about that at all, he considered. Yet the more he thought about it, the more he felt something didn't sit right. If they were there to pay their respect to a dead relative then who was the person with the dog? A dog tethered to a length of string, surely not a friend of Doyle's. Doyle was a bit of a woolly-headed liberal, a do-gooder but not that bloody good. No, there was something dubious about their behaviour. What were they up to? He took a sip from the glass of the single malt in his hand as he pondered. Slowly he started to make the connections: diamonds…undertaker… bodies… cemetery.

Realisation hitting him like a thunderbolt, he leapt from his chair. How could he have been so blind? All those years he'd never realised what was now so very obvious. Laine snatched up the phone to call Lennie.

'Where the hell are you?' he shouted into the phone.

'Uh? I'm parked outside Doyle's place. Been here for hours but there's no sign of them. Why? What's the problem?'

'Go back. NOW! Get yourself back to the cemetery.'

'But the place is closed up. What's this all about?'

'Never mind, just go back and get in there. They're in the place somewhere. When you find them; bring them straight back here, you got that? Back here.'

Lennie raced back the way he'd came, tyres screaming as he pulled away, headed back towards the cemetery.

'How the hell do I get in the place at this time of night?' he asked himself. 'And what the fuck is all this about?'

***

Pat almost felt like crying. Breaking into tombs at the dead of night, in the spurious belief he would discover a long-lost treasure. That seemed to him as ridiculous as having a parchment map of some desert island. *X marks the spot – Long John Doyle.* As far-fetched as believing he would become rich, retiring to the good life. Some hope. Demi helped him replace the casket lid, ready to return it to the shelf space. With a bit of luck no one would ever know about the intrusion, though he doubted it very much.

He bent to lift the coffin. Facing him on the lid, he again noticed the blackened crucifix with the scripted plate below – Giuseppe Alfonso Pesticio – Alfonso? He didn't recall seeing the name Alfonso printed in the obituary notice of the paper.

'Pass me the light,' Pat shouted, excited at the sudden revelation. Demi handed over the torch, sensing a change in his attitude. He moved swiftly about the vault shining the torch over the lids of the other coffins.

'Yes, yes', he blurted. 'It's this one. It has to be this one.'

The brass plate on the lid bore another inscription but this one had only the name Giuseppe Pesticio.

'There's two Giuseppe's. We opened the wrong coffin. This is our Giuseppe, in here.'

'Are you sure?'

'Only one way to find out.'

Together they moved the coffin of the second Giuseppe Pesticio onto the floor. Pat used the iron bar to prise off the lid. The body inside looked far less decomposed than the first, though it had collapsed in on itself and skeletonised, a suit still intact. Using the light, he shone it the full length of the corpse. At the bottom end he noticed the body lacked shoes; revealing near skeletal feet. Pat moved his still gloved hand inside, feeling gently along the side of the body. About halfway, his fingers touched something. Pat decided to peek inside. Placed next to the bony hand of the corpse were five small, velvet pouches. Cringing, he lifted one of the pouches. It felt heavy from the contents inside. Raising the small bag, he illuminated it for Demi to see.

'Are they the diamonds?' she whispered.

Pat placed it on the floor before returning to the inside of the coffin from where he removed the remaining four pouches. Looking again at Demi, Pat tipped the contents of one of the pouches into his hand. Under the light of the torch, they saw ten gemstones of various sizes. Moving to a corner, Pat tipped then spread all fives pouches onto the floor, revealing the fifty diamonds that had been lying next to Giuseppe Pesticio since 1965.

'We've done it,' he said in hushed tones as they knelt over the gems. 'We've only bloody well done it.'

After replacing the jewels back into the little pouches, they returned the coffins back to their spaces. Taking a last look around, Pat whispered a quiet apology to the late Pesticio family. He aimed the now fading torchlight at the steps as they started to make their way out. Halfway up, Pat stopped. Something made its way towards him; he felt a tremor of fear run through his body. Demi, right behind him, sensed something was wrong. She tried to push him onwards but Pat refused to move.

'Pat, what's wrong? I really would like to get out of this place. Why have you stopped?'

'Can't you see it?' he said almost inaudible.

'What? See what?' Demi panicked wondering what he could see that made him rigid in front of her.

'On the steps,' he whispered, 'coming towards us.'

Demi looked cautiously over his shoulder fearing the worst.

'That?' she said, pointing towards the step. He nodded.

'It's just a bloody spider. Shit, you had me going there. I thought…Oh let me pass. Demi brushed away the spider sending it to the bottom of the steps where it scurried into a corner. At the top, Pat raced out into the cool night air, starting to take deep, steady breaths.

'I'm sorry, it's just I don't like spiders, never have.'

'It was only a little 'un.'

'Size doesn't matter.'

'Speak for yourself,' she laughed.

Pat recovered himself enough before trying to close the mausoleum gates that just kept swinging open. 'Sod it,' he said then turned towards Demi. 'Come on, we need to get out of here. I'll phone Elroy and tell him to collect us.'

They left the gates open.

'D'you think you can climb the wall?' Pat tasked.

'Right now,' Demi replied, 'I'd jump over the bloody thing just to get out of here.'

A light shrill from his mobile stirred Elroy from a gentle slumber. 'I'll be outside the main gates in a few minutes,' he told Pat, rubbing his tired eyes before heading off.

Along the road next to the perimeter wall, he saw them both scramble over the top before dropping to the pavement, relieved that the man with his mangy dog wasn't with them.

Elroy drew the car to a halt. Unlocking the doors he mouthed, 'it's open. 'Pat and Demi scrambled into the car welcoming the warmth of the interior that enveloped them as they sank into the upholstery.

'Well, did you find them?' Pat opened a velvet pouch to remove one of the stones. Elroy gave out a low whistle as he stared at the pear-shaped diamond in Pat's hand.

'Wow,' Elroy uttered. Pat dropped it back with the others. Elroy drove on. 'Now where're we going?'

'Head into town, I'll think about what we do next on the way.'

Elroy made a U-turn back towards the city centre.

***

Lennie pulled up near the gates, jumping out, he peered through the iron railings. He could just make out the shapes of the monuments and gravestones as the mist swirled around them covering the area with a grey, gossamer-like blanket. Taking out his phone, he called Laine.

'I can't see anyone in the place. The mist is like pea soup in there,' he said still peering through the gate. 'What d'you want me to do now, leave it?'

'No, 'Laine snapped his reply. 'I don't want you to leave it. Get inside and see if you can find them.'

Lennie took a high-power flashlight from his car before scrambling over a section of the stone wall. The beam helped illuminate the ground through the mist. Taking careful steps, he looked around at the headstones, convinced the place was deserted. His foot caught in something soft. He shone the beam on the ground, illuminating a dew-soaked duffel bag. A kick told him it was empty.

Lennie lifted the beam of the torch continuing with his search. In the distance, barely visible through the thickening mist he noticed the entrance to the mausoleum with its open gates swinging gently back and forth, squeaking on their rusty hinges. Another sound stopped him dead. A rasping carried through the darkness. The noise reverberated, rising and falling. Lennie's heart beat faster as he remained motionless. A cold fear gripped him.

'What the fuck's that?' he whispered. 'Keep going, Lennie, boy. Keep going.' Inching towards the door of the tomb, he nudged it slightly open, tilting his head to one side trying to pick out any sounds from within. Silent as the grave, he thought then quickly regretted it. He moved again when this time his foot connected with something hard.

Lennie picked up the crowbar discarded earlier by Pat. Frowning, he quickly realised what it had been used for. He gingerly stepped forward to enter the mausoleum. Instinctively, he maintained his grasp on the crowbar for added protection should he need it. The power of the lamp illuminated the space below, empty apart from the coffins.

'That'll do for me,' he said. Before he turned back, the beam of light reflected something colourful down in a far corner of the vault. Curious, he made his way below then picked up what he took to be a crystal. Clutching the stone in his hand, Lennie retraced his steps to the outside. The sight that met him almost made him collapse.

'I'll take that, thank you, sir,' said one of two police officers pointing to the crowbar.

'Hey, it's not what you think,' Lennie protested. 'I... I was looking for someone.'

'Yeah, yeah,' the second officer droned. 'Tell it to the judge. Residents nearby complained they'd seen torchlight and movement in the cemetery since it closed.'

A third police officer walked through the mist holding onto a confused and bleary-eyed man.

'Your lookout fell asleep,' the officer quipped. 'Found him spark out behind a gravestone. Hell, he was snoring so loud I thought someone was sawing wood.'

'Eh? He ain't with me. Shit man, you got this all wrong.'

The first officer shone his torch at the doors of the mausoleum. 'Anyone else hiding inside?'

'Go take a fucking look,' Lennie scowled. The officer made a quick examination of the vault, shuddered then returned to his colleagues.

'All clear in there. Come on, let's go.'

Neither man struggled as the police officers put them both in handcuffs.

'You're being arrested on suspicion of committing criminal damage,' the first officer told them followed with a barely audible caution. The three officers escorted Lennie and the wino to their vehicle parked out on the roadside. In their haste to get out of the cold cemetery, the arresting officers failed to notice Lennie discreetly dropping the stone from his hand and pushing it into the soft, muddy ground with his foot.

***

Given the light traffic on the road, the taxi soon arrived in the centre of Cardiff. Elroy pulled over near the Hilton Hotel. Pat looked across at him.

'Why have we stopped here?'

Demi glanced through the window at the castle opposite wondering the same.

'I still can't believe what you two just did. Show me those diamonds again.' Pat took a pouch from his pocket, tipping the contents into his hand. He stared at the mix of different shaped stones, hardly believing it himself. Elroy selected a pillow-shaped stone to hold in front of the interior light.

'How d'you know if they're real? I mean they certainly look real, but I ain't no expert.' Demi leant between the front seats.

'Elroy! Who goes to the trouble of hiding fake diamonds in a coffin with a dead body? Of course they're real.' She turned to Pat. 'Aren't they?' They both looked at Pat in expectation.

'Oh, for God's sake,' he said. 'Of course they're real. It was in the papers at the time. Remember?'

'He's right,' Demi agreed. 'I saw it myself in the library.' Elroy handed back the stone.

'Decided where we're going then?

'Drive down to the station.'

'The station?' Demi asked. 'We're catching a train?'

Pat smiled at her. 'No, we're not catching a train; as if.'

She flopped back in the seat.

'I like trains,' Demi said. 'They remind me of holidays when I was young.'

Pat spotted Elroy's cloth cash bag in the taxi, he asked if he might borrow it. When Elroy agreed, Pat placed the velvet pouches inside the bag then rolled it up.

Elroy stopped on the station's taxi bay, drawing looks of disapproval from the taxi drivers could officially use the area. Pat got out, making his way to the left luggage lockers. The announcement system inside informed an empty concourse of morning train times, reminding passengers that the whole station area operated a 'no smoking zone'. He heard the quickness of footsteps approach. A man wearing a full-length overcoat carrying a briefcase made his way towards the platforms, disappearing up the steps.

Selecting a small locker, Pat placed the bag inside. He removed the key then made his way back to the car.

They'd agreed Demi would need to go home first. Pat relished the thought of a long, hot shower followed by his bed where he would sleep for at least eight hours. With a look of contentment on his face, he buzzed down the window of the car to gaze at the reddish sky. Dawn. He listened to the sound of a multitude of birds singing their morning chorus. Gulls wheeled in the sky like war planes in a dog-fight, in search of rubbish bags or discarded food from the previous evening. One gull, perched on a litterbin, savoured the delights of a half-eaten kebab. A refuse truck made its way towards the city's business premises – a race to the rubbish: refuse collectors versus the sea birds. Traffic on the road increased as people who worked early shifts made their way to work. A normal start to a normal day. In a few hours, Cardiff would be fully awake, a thriving city going about its business. The experience of the last twelve hours all seemed a little surreal to Pat Doyle but surreal didn't come close to what lay ahead.

***

Barry Laine took Lennie's phone call from the police station.

'They've arrested you for what?' he asked. He listened as Lennie explained his predicament. 'Okay, I'll arrange for a solicitor to be with you. Say nothing until the brief arrives then only tell him the bare minimum. In the meantime, start thinking up some plausible story.'

'Boss,' Lennie said, 'this doesn't look good.'

'Don't worry,' Laine assured his henchman. 'The brief will get you out in no time.'

Laine ended the call. Musing, he took a small, black book from his desk, flicking through the pages until he found the number of a firm of solicitors he used and trusted given his type of business. Laine had a direct number for one of the senior partners. He punched in the numbers waiting while it rang. Eventually, a voice groggy with sleep answered.

'Yes.'

'Hello, Guy. It's Barry Laine. Sorry to call on you so early but I need a favour.'

Laine outlined the situation to Guy Hilton, the senior partner in the firm of Hilton, Burns, and Blakemore. Laine told him he needed a lawyer at the central police station right away. Guy Hilton agreed to arrange it personally. He immediately contacted a junior member of the firm to go into the city centre police station. Guy Hilton wasn't going to delay acting on the instructions of his most valued client but then neither was he getting out of bed at such an unholy hour. The unfortunate young lawyer he called was Rebekah Rosen – Rosen, since her marriage to Isaac Rosen, a barrister who worked for an established firm of lawyers near the Law Courts – before their marriage, her name was Steinberg.

Seventeen

At the police station, Lennie was cautioned a second time before being interviewed in the presence of his solicitor. The drunk found sleeping was let off with a 'simple caution'. During the interview, Lennie had tried to tell the police he'd been looking for a friend who often slept in the cemetery when he came across the open vault.

'I'm sorry, Mr Randall,' the interviewing officer said to him, 'but the man we brought in with you insists he's never seen you before in his life.'

'Yeah, well he's a liar then, ain't he?' Lennie snapped. 'Like I said, I went in to look for him, saw the open vault, and out of curiosity took a peek inside. When I came out you lot were standing there.'

'Then how do you explain the crowbar?' the officer asked.

'I'm sorry,' the solicitor interrupted. 'My client's already answered that question. He found it on the ground.'

The officer smirked and wrote something in his notepad.

'So you maintain you had nothing to do with this offence?'

Lennie slowly nodded his head.

'Please answer the question for the benefit of the tape, Mr Randall,' the officer said.

Lennie pushed back in his chair placing his hands behind his head.

'Yes, I had nothing to do with it. What would I want in a fucking crypt? It's not exactly an Egyptian tomb now, is it? It may have escaped your attention, Sherlock, but it was empty.'

When the interview concluded they'd charged and bailed him to appear before the Magistrate's Court.

***

Rebekah Rosen gave Lennie a lift back to Laine's house, given the police had impounded his BMW as part of their investigation. 'What a fucking mess this has turned out to be,' Lennie said to his solicitor as she drove along the Barry road towards Sully.

'What d'you reckon on my chances in court. Should I plead not guilty?'

'I don't really know just yet,' she told him. 'You'll need to call at my office so we can go through your case in detail. We'll need to construct it properly. By the way though, what were you doing in the cemetery when the police arrived?'

Lennie thought before replying, guessing he could trust the solicitor who worked for Guy Hilton.

'How well d'you know Barry Laine?'

'Well enough. I know he's not exactly a man of noble repute, shall we say, but he is a valuable client of our firm.'

Lennie smiled at her response before he continued. 'Barry wanted me to watch this geeky dude, had me follow him. Why? I'm not really sure. A few days ago I mentioned diamonds to him, from then on he starts acting all strange, gets me to bring these two dudes to his house.'

Rebekah frowned as she looked across at him. 'Two?'

'Yes. There was a woman as well. Tasty little piece, I think Baz fancies her.'

'Okay, okay, then what?'

'Well, apparently he knew the man from his school days. Don't know what they spoke about together but now I have to follow them. Baz reckons they were still in the boneyard earlier so he told me to go in after them, and now this.'

Rebekah steered the car through the gates leading to Laine's house, stopping on the gravel drive. Stepping out she looked around, visibly impressed with the place. Together they walked up to the door. Rebekah pressed the bell. Again, the sound of Beethoven peeled from within.

How tacky, she mused.

Laine, rather than Preston, opened the door before inviting her in. The solicitor, although further impressed with the interior décor, reminded herself of the owner's real enterprises.

'This way,' Laine beckoned. He admired the shapely, and attractive lawyer who brushed by him. The fragrance of expensive cologne lingered as Rebekah entered his study. She refused the offer of a drink but Lennie gladly sank a large whisky, a cheaper brand he noticed, not the good stuff his boss usually kept for guests. Rebekah outlined the situation repeating what she'd told Lennie during the drive to the house. Laine looked towards his minder.

'Well?' he said, waiting for an explanation.

'Look, I did what you asked, I went over the wall. They must have gone by then or else I missed them. It was fucking dark, man, and foggy.'

'Language, Leonard. We have a lady present.'

Lennie continued, not in any way bothered by the presence of the woman.

'Anyway, I came across this vault surrounded by railings. I could see it had been forced open, the jemmy still there on the ground. So I went inside but they weren't in there, but someone had been in there. Fucking scary stuff, man. Oh yeah, nearly forgot. I did find a stone down there. T'was in a corner, it looked like a crystal or possibly even a diamond...'

Laine leapt from his seat, startling the solicitor.

'What? Where is it? Do the police have it?'

'Hey, boss, what d' you take me for? Of course they don't have it. I dropped it before they hauled me off in cuffs.'

'Dropped it where? Where is it now?'

'Excuse me,' Rebekah interrupted. 'What exactly is this all about?'

'It's about diamonds belonging to my family, Laine said in response. 'Stolen in nineteen sixty-five and hidden away.'

'Stolen? Stolen by whom?' she asked.

'Not by,' Laine said, 'from. From my grandfather, they were his but he'd been cheated out of them, and I believe the man we're watching might now have them.'

Laine's voice became more excited. 'I figured they were placed in one of the coffins. I think Lennie found one of the missing stones earlier in the cemetery, which means they were there all along.'

The lawyer watched an animated Laine as he paced the room.

'Look, I'm sorry, it's been a long night,' Rebekah said closing her briefcase. 'I still don't see what this is all about. How does this help the case against your employee?'

Laine turned to face her.

'Hey, stuff the court case. Lennie can plead guilty; I'll pay the fine. There are far more important things to sort out now.'

'I'm not sure you appreciate the gravity of the matter,' Rebekah continued, 'Mr Randall here, if found guilty, could be sent to prison given the serious nature of the offences.'

'It would only be for a few months,' Laine responded. 'It's not exactly in the crown court. He'll do it standing on his head, won't you, Len.'

Lennie wasn't too happy with this prospect but dutifully nodded.

'See. What'd I tell you,' Laine confirmed. As Rebekah made her way to the hall, she said she'd arrange an appointment, possibly tomorrow. Laine thanked her before showing her out before returning to the study.

'So, where'd you hide the stone?' Laine asked his minder. 'Will you be able to find it?'

'Sure, I pressed it into the ground with my foot, just outside the vault, shouldn't be too difficult to find.'

'Right, I want you to go back there and find it. Then we'll sort out Doyle when you return.'

'To the cemetery?' Lennie said. 'I think that might be a breach of my bail conditions, boss.'

'To hell with bail conditions,' he shouted. 'Just get me that fucking stone.'

***

A light drizzle started to fall as Rebekah and her husband Isaac Rosen left their house the following evening, walking the half mile to her parent's home. Already at the house was

Abraham Steinberg, his wife Judith, Rebekah's two brothers: Michael and Israel, and their respective wives.

The family never discussed business around the table but Rebekah was eager to tell them of her recent experience with her client. She outlined the events about the man's arrest at the cemetery. His employer, a renowned 'city gangster' whose family had lost diamonds in 1965, that had been stolen then somehow went missing. Her mother frowned disapprovingly at her daughter.

'Rebekah, must you raise such unpleasant things at dinner? You know we do not discuss work matters at this table.' She looked to her husband for support. However, her father took a different view.

'No, my dear,' he said to his wife. 'Let her finish.'

After dinner, Abraham, picking up his glass of wine, rose from his chair.

'Please, let us all retire to the lounge. I want to tell you another similar story about missing diamonds.'

When he'd finished his story, the family sat around the spacious lounge in total silence. Israel, the youngest son, spoke first.

'Your grandfather sent diamonds to London in the post? Was he mad?'

'These diamonds,' Michael, the eldest son said, 'they belong to us then? Why didn't I know about this before, father?'

'Why didn't any of us know?' Rebekah added. 'This gangster is trying to claim them as his property. We should go to the police; tell them we know where they are. That this Doyle person and some woman have them.'

Abraham looked into his wine glass as he slowly shook his head.

'I'm afraid it's not that simple. Your great-grandfather made a claim against his insurance company, they contested it so he went to court. They tried to argue his only entitlement to compensation should be the value covered by registered post. A lawyer in the family agreed to represent him but the case dragged on for years. It took its toll on Max's health, and nearly ruined the business. My father struggled to keep the business going. However, the court eventually found in our favour, and the insurance company paid out in full.'

'Then the diamonds belong to that insurance company, not to us,' Rebekah said.

'Legally yes, but…'

'But what, father?' she interrupted. 'No, we must hand this over to the police.'

'Please let me finish, my child. Back in nineteen sixty-five, the family business put up a reward for their return – just in case the insurance company failed to pay out.'

'But they did pay out.'

'I know,' he continued. 'The reward money was put on deposit, ten thousand pounds. It's still there, never been touched. Now if we were to honour that reward, increasing it to say, fifty thousand, then this Mr Doyle may return them to us.'

'Father, this is quite illegal,' Rebekah scoffed. 'You should not even contemplate such a thing.'

'Hold on a minute,' Michael said. 'This Doyle chap won't know about the insurance pay-out so he might be very willing to take the reward money.'

Rebekah threw her arms up. 'Not you as well, Mike, I'm surrounded by villains.'

'No,' added Israel. 'It makes good business sense. Doyle gets the reward, we get the diamonds, everybody's happy.'

'No, Izzy,' she retorted, using her pet name for her younger brother. 'Not *our* diamonds, the insurance company's diamonds. You'll all go to prison.'

Rebekah turned to her husband who sat quietly sipping his wine. 'Isaac, will you make them see sense or will you think it's good business as well by having to represent them all in court?'

Isaac commented that whilst he could not condone this suggestion, it wasn't his affair, he was not, after all, a Steinberg. 'It's Steinberg family business,' he said.

'You are *part* of this family,' Rebekah reminded him. He didn't respond

'Oh, this is futile.' She turned to her mother. 'Please make them see sense, or are you reverting back to a Cohen on this one?' referring to her mother's maiden name.

'Rebekah, let's go and make the coffee. The men can sort this out between them. I'm sure they'll do what is right in the end.'

Rebekah threw a stern look at her husband then made her way to the door. Her mother and sisters'-in-law followed.

Eighteen

Pat and Demi sat around a kitchen table in Pat's apartment drinking coffee and eating biscuits.

'We need to figure out what to do next, what to do if Barry Laine sends that big guy to look for us again.'

'Lennie's nice enough,' Demi said, 'he'll be okay.'

'Demi,' Pat blurted. 'He's a thug, an enforcer. He'll do whatever Laine orders, and if it includes breaking our bones then believe me, he'll do it.'

'Yeah, I suppose you're right,' she said lowering her head.

'He can be a bit scary. Anyway, exactly how long do we leave the diamonds in the station locker? Will they be safe?'

'They're safe for now but we'll need to get them soon. Thing is, then what do we do?'

'Sell 'em on eBay,' Demi quipped, a sassy look on her face. Pat smiled, wishing it were that simple.

'Tomorrow we'll go and get them and take them to the charity shop,' he told her. 'I'll hide them in that old desk where I found the letter.'

He considered the irony of his suggestion, the diamonds back in the former funeral parlour.

'Once we have a better plan we'll go from there,' Pat said.

Demi lightly stirred her coffee. 'All sounds a bit airy fairy to me.'

'Are any of your family in the jewellery business?'

She gave this some careful thought.

'Don't think so. Though I could always ask my father, but as far as I'm aware it's all hair and chips.'

'Sounds appetizing, remind me never to eat at the *Nissaki by Night*,' Pat said referring to a restaurant owned by one of her relatives in the city. 'Seriously though,' he continued, 'don't mention any of this to your family. We keep it on a need-to-know basis.' He pulled the cellophane wrap off a pepperoni pizza he'd found in the freezer. 'Now, let's eat something.'

'Mmm, looks delicious,' Demi said. 'I do like a frozen pizza with a dubious sell-by date.'

After they'd eaten their food, Demi checked her watch. 'I'd better be off, only it's getting late.'

Pat desperately wanted to ask her to stay the night; instead he went to find her coat.

'Can you meet me in town tomorrow at eleven o'clock, at the front of the station?' he asked, handing over her coat.

'Sure, I'll be the one wearing a giant leek,' she joked.

'Okay, nice and inconspicuous then.' He opened the front door. 'Are you sure I can't give you a lift home? I really don't mind.'

Demi re-checked her watch. 'Better not, only I do need to get home tonight, not next week. I'll get a taxi.' He closed the door, laughing at the dig at his car.

The cemetery in daylight made it easier for Lennie to locate the Pesticio mausoleum. With only a cursory glance at

140

the shiny new padlock that now secured its tightly closed gates, he walked on, stopping occasionally, pretending to read the epitaphs on several headstones, but really taking the opportunity to check no one had followed him. Satisfied, he made his way back to the mausoleum.

Bending forward, Lennie began to search for the spot where he'd imbedded the gemstone in the soil. He considered the possibility that the police may have found it when they returned to photograph the scene as part of their prosecution case against him. When he eventually spotted it, glinting in the sunlight, he gave out a low whistle. Just slightly visible in the ground, he used his flick-knife to dig it out. He picked it up and stared down at the stone sitting in the palm of his hand.

'Must be worth a few grand,' he said to himself. 'Now I could go back saying it wasn't here, keep it for myself.' Lennie quickly dismissed the notion as foolish. Laine would have him killed if he ever found out he'd been cheated.

Lennie shrugged off the idea as he returned to his car with the diamond still clutched in his hand.

***

The car refused to go into gear despite pushing hard on the gear stick.

'Bloody clutch, go in, damn you,' Pat cursed, forcing the stick. He knew it would never make it up the ramps of the multi-storey to the higher levels.

'Stupid bloody car,' he shouted at the windscreen.

He parked in one of the vacant 'Disabled Drivers Only' spaces. A notice that threatened unauthorised vehicles would be towed away appealed to him. Maybe they'll scrap the bloody thing if I refuse to collect it, he thought. After removing a slim attaché case from the front passenger seat, Pat made his way to the nearby railway. He considered calling Elroy to take them down to the Bay but knew he'd called on him too many times for lifts. By a quick mental calculation, Pat reckoned he owed his friend about £30 in fares plus the £50 Elroy gave to Osman's men when he'd rescued him from the two thugs. Pat cringed, thinking of a knife hacking off his finger. Elroy always refused the money but it was his friend's livelihood. 'I'll insist he takes it as soon as I can pay him,' he told himself as he walked through the entrance of the station concourse.

Pat withdrew £200 from an ATM in the concourse that further increased his overdraft. Overdraft, credit cards, mortgage, car loan. The black cloud of financial misery cast its dark shadow around him. On a positive note, Pat thought of the prospect of more money than he'd ever dreamt of, possibly within a matter of days. He scanned the area, doing a double-take when he spotted Demi near the ticket booths, wearing a yellow fluorescent jacket. She waved at him, standing out like a human Belisha beacon. Acknowledging her wave, Pat walked towards her.

'Good morning, Demetra. No leek then? I might have missed you.'

'What, in this coat?' With outstretched arms, she twirled around.

'You look like you're about to start work on the railway line in that get-up,' Pat quipped.

'It's chucking it down; this is all I could find that's waterproof. I can take it off if you don't like it.'

Despite sky-high levels of anxiety, Demi managed, as always, to raise his spirits.

'The coat's fine, honestly. Now come on, let's have a coffee in the coffee shop.'

They carried their cups of frothy cappuccino to a corner table out of the way of anyone who might overhear his plan to hide the diamonds. Pat glanced at the coffee shop's only other customer, a female who looked like one of the city's many students, who frantically stirred a latté with a wooden stick. He noticed she wore earplugs connected to an iPhone. Satisfied they wouldn't be overheard, he started to explain their next move.

'Right,' he whispered. 'This is what I think we should do.'

Demi leaned across the table, her head slightly tilted.

'Why are you whispering?' she asked.

'Because I am, now listen. I'll get the diamonds from the locker, then I'll call Elroy. We'll go straight to your shop where I'll put them in the old desk in the back room.'

'Good plan,' she whispered back. 'Then what?'

'Then I'll need to figure a way to dispose of them for as much as I can get.'

'Got any ideas who you can contact?'

Pat shook his head. 'Not yet, but I'll think of someone.'

Demi picked up her cup smiling at him.

'As I see it, there's one major flaw with this great plan of yours.'

Pat furrowed his brow at her. 'What flaw would that be?'

'You don't actually know anyone, do you?'

'No, I don't,' he conceded.

'Thought so. Not much of a plan then, is it?'

'Have you got a better one?'

'Might have,' Demi responded with a hint of a smile. 'Last night when I went to collect the kids, I was talking to my dad. Without giving anything away, I simply asked about what other members of our family do for a living. He told me some of them are in Greece where they own small businesses. Others are in this country working in various occupations. A few who did well here, returned home prosperous to retire. Now here's the interesting bit.'

Demi quickly glanced over each shoulder then leaned back across the table.

'One relative is in the jewellery business, but not in this country. He owns a large shop on the island of Rhodes. So maybe this person could help us. What d'you think?'

'I'm not sure,' Pat mused. 'It's an option, but I'd like to consider some others as well. I mean, this relative of yours lives in Greece. Not exactly local, is he?'

Demi shrugged. 'Fine, consider away. Just as a matter of interest though, how many relatives do you have in the jewellery business?'

'Let me see.' Pat pretended to count his fingers. 'None.'

Pat removed the locker key from his pocket turning it between his fingers; finishing his coffee he stood up.

'Ready?' he asked.

Demi took hold of the attaché case. 'As I'll ever be.'

They made their way over to the left-luggage lockers. Pat fleetingly scanned the area before inserting the key then opened the door. He lifted out the coin bag containing the velvet pouches. It felt heavier than he remembered. Pat glanced over his shoulder, convinced everyone in the station knew what he was doing. Demi handed him the attaché case so he could place the bag inside.

'Right, now can I use your mobile to call Elroy?'

Pat cupped the phone in his hand as he spoke. After saying a few words, he listened then ended the call.

'He said he'll be here as soon as he's dropped off the fare he's with. How about another coffee while we wait?'

The hectic concourse bustled with people going about their business, using the shops and cafes, catching or leaving trains. A woman walked into the station from the street carrying a large selection of worn carrier bags, her wizened face ingrained with the dirt of her down-trodden life. Pat's nose twitched as she passed him – a tang of damp clothes and body odour. The Ralph McTell song – *Streets of London* – came into his head, he started to hum it quietly. Demi glanced at the woman then at Pat.

'Jeez,' she whispered to him. 'You're both *humming.*'

He nudged her gently on her arm. Making their way back to the coffee shop, he caught sight of a familiar figure heading towards the station from the multi-storey car park – Hatchet Lennie.

Leaning into Demi, Pat told her to head for the platforms.

'Why? I thought you said Elroy's picking us up.'

'Just keep moving,' he insisted, steering her towards the steps leading up to the platforms. 'Don't turn around,' he whispered over her shoulder. 'Lennie's headed this way.'

'Oh shit. Now what?' Demi asked as she quickened her pace. They made it to Platform One where a high-speed train was just about to move off; the engine noise increased its high pitch scream, a station official stood next to an open door. Pat ran towards him.

'Wait,' he shouted. Glancing up at the information monitor, Pat saw it was the midday service: Cardiff to London-Paddington. The man ushered them on board the train.

'You timed that right, mate, she's just pulling out.'

'Can we pay on the train?' Pat asked.

'See the conductor,' the man replied then slammed the door behind them. The train picked up speed as it headed out of the station. Through the window, they saw Lennie reach the top of the platform steps. He glanced towards the departing train, spotting them inside. After an attempt to run after the train, Lennie gave up the chase standing helplessly on the platform glaring, not relishing having to explain this to Barry Laine.

Nineteen

Barry Laine leaned on his desk with clenched fists, not believing Lennie had been so close to the diamonds only to let them slip away.

'A train? On a train? I don't fucking believe this. You let them catch a train?'

'I didn't exactly *let* them catch it, boss. They were ahead of me jumping on just as it was leaving.'

'London,' Laine said tersely

'That's what the rail dude told me, Paddington to be exact. Want me to head up there?'

Laine knotted his brow.

'Why. D'you know where they're heading for in London?'

'No.'

'Then don't ask stupid questions. They could get off at Newport and head back here.' Laine rubbed his forehead, contemplating the situation. 'Right, I want men watching both their places. The minute they show, you pick them up. Use reliable men, not jerks who'll lose them by letting them hop on a bus. And watch that Elroy guy as well; he might be called to pick them up somewhere.'

He looked at Lennie who stood in front of him.

'What the hell are you waiting for? Get on with it.'

Laine picked up the diamond Lennie had handed over to him earlier. Turning it slowly, he stared in awe at the beauty and clarity of the small, pear-shaped three carat stone, kissing it lightly.

'Soon,' he whispered, 'I'll have the rest of the little beauties we were cheated out of by that undertaker.' Grasping the stone, Laine smiled at the thought of a whole lot more soon to be in his possession.

***

Pat and Demi found two vacant seats on the train. Other passengers, many of whom were working on laptop computers, surrounded them, machines plugged into power points under the tables. Some were holding mobile phones to their ears to conduct business as the train sped through the countryside. Pat feared that Lennie might be racing over to Newport to meet them as the train pulled in. They were able to relax a little when it moved on with no sign of him. Pat had decided they wouldn't get off at Newport for the same reason. The conductor entered their carriage.

'Tickets from Newport.' The man stopped next to Pat, hand outstretched.

'Two returns to Paddington, please,' Pat said.

The man tapped his hand-held machine with a pen.

'That's three hundred and fifty pounds, sir.'

Pat's eyebrows shot upward. 'How much?' he shrieked. 'You should be wearing a mask, mate.'

He handed over a credit card praying the little machine wouldn't spit it back in disgust. The transaction went through. The other passengers who'd reacted to the sudden outburst returned to their business.

'What are we going to do in London?' Demi asked. Pat still looked exasperated sitting opposite her.

'Phone your parents, ask them to collect your children from school.'

'Oh stop being the bloody social worker, I'd already arranged that. But I'll need to tell them where I am and when I'll be back. I mean, I'm only supposed to be down the Bay.'

Demi sensed something from the look Pat gave her.

'When will we be back?' she asked, tentatively.

'I really don't know.' Pat slid one of the tickets across the table between them. 'You should be okay to stay on the train and return this evening. Phone Laine when you get back, tell him I've got the diamonds and left the country. Tell him I took a plane to New York, but whatever you do, stay away from him.'

'What will you do there?' D'you know anyone in New York? Anyway,' she added. 'I'm not going back without you.'

Reaching over, Demi took him by the hand.

'We're in this together, mate.'

'Demi,' he said softly. 'You have to go back. You've two children to look after, parents who will be worried sick. If you stay with me, you might get hurt. Laine is dangerous, you understand. He'll stop at nothing to get his hands on these,' Pat said rubbing the case beside him. 'He'll kill for them if he has to.'

Demi sat back in her seat. *Make your mind up time.* After considering her options, she decided to contact her mother as soon as they arrived in London. To tell her she would be staying away for a while, a short holiday. She'd miss the children, but surely it wouldn't be for long, would it? Pat could run forever, she couldn't. Demi turned towards the window, pressing her forehead against the glass. Her mind was made up.

Pat contemplated his limited options. There was no way he could let Demi stay involved any further. He'd persuade her to return to Cardiff, to her family. He didn't need enraged Greeks gunning for him as well as gangsters. He'd continue with this alone. There was however, one small issue, Pat could not head for New York or anywhere else outside of the country. His passport was back at his flat.

***

Abraham Steinberg had arranged to meet his two sons at their city centre store. Being after six pm, the shop had closed for the day.

Steinberg explained his strategy to them.

'We'll get in touch with this Doyle and the woman,' Steinberg told his sons. 'Offer them thirty-five thousand pounds as a reward for the return of the diamonds.'

'Why not the full fifty you increased it to, father?' Michael asked.

Steinberg swivelled in his chair, wagging a finger at them.

'I want to hold back on fifteen thousand in case they refuse. It gives us something to barter with.'

'Good idea,' Israel added. 'Who knows, they may even accept the thirty-five K, then we keep the difference.'

'Possibly,' Michael said, 'Nice one, Izzy.'

'Have you given any thought to what we do about this Laine?' Michael continued. 'He also wants the diamonds. How do we take care of a ruthless gangster?'

Steinberg nodded. Israel shook his head.

Steinberg rose from his seat and leant on his desk.

'This is what I suggest we do. We offer Laine twenty-five per cent of the diamonds' current value. I'm sure he's a reasonable man who will do business with us.'

Michael wasn't so sure.

'Father, he might possibly wonder why we're trying to negotiate a deal on property that already belongs to us. Surely, he'll soon realise we have no legal claim to the diamonds?'

'Mike's right,' Israel said. 'Anyhow, I don't altogether share your view about his reasonable nature.'

'I quite understand your concern, boys. However, I do have another idea, one I won't share with you unless I need to.

Steinberg returned to his seat. Michael glanced over to his younger brother who simply shrugged back at him.

'What I am prepared to share with you both is this. My idea will ensure the return of the diamonds to us. It may even take care of this Laine fellow at the same time.'

After the brothers had left the office, Steinberg opened a drawer, taking out a small book, the pages divided by letters of the alphabet. He checked his watch. *Too early to call New York,* he thought, not wanting to wake his cousin in the early hours and then have to ask him for a favour. You really didn't want to upset a man such as Ben Wiener.

Twenty

The train arrived at London's Paddington station twenty minutes late due to signal failure outside Reading. They stepped onto the platform, joining the throng of other people hastily making their way towards the exits, probably now late for meetings or missing other train connections.

Now what? Pat Doyle didn't know anyone in London. He rarely came to the place other than for the occasional training course. Pat looked around the expanse of the cathedral-like station; a flock of pigeons flew over him heading for the open skies. A whistle shrilled loudly announcing the departure of a train on the opposite platform. He gripped the attaché case with the realisation of what might be a hopeless predicament ahead of them. He now had to tell Demi to get back on the train and return to Cardiff.

Taking her by the hand, he looked into her delicious brown eyes. Eyes you could fall into.

'This is where it ends, Demi. It's getting too dangerous. I want you to get back on the train.'

The danger and excitement appealed to her. Demi looked up at him, those dark brown eyes reflecting the overhead light. Smiling, she shook her head.

'You've got to be kidding.'

'Nope, I'm serious. You have to go back.'

'Where are you going?'

'I'll think of something.'

'*We'll* think of something,' Demi announced, pulling on his arm. 'Now, come on.'

Realising she wasn't going to take no for an answer, Pat relented. They walked towards the ticket barrier together.

'I haven't been to London since I was a kid,' Demi told him. 'We'd come here to visit relatives of my father, at a place called Hammersmith.'

'Do you still have family living here?' Pat asked.

'I think so. Why? Should we try to contact them, see if they'll put us up?'

'Mightn't be a bad idea. It could buy us some time to plan what we do next.'

'Another plan, eh?' Demi said. 'Okay, when I phone home, I'll ask for an address. Dad could contact them, tell them we're on our way.'

Pat thought about this for a moment before nodding his agreement.

'Just tell your parents you're here for a few days. You can mention visiting relatives then.'

After inserting their tickets into the automatic barrier, they made their way towards the road exit running alongside the large hotel.

As they stepped out onto Praed Street, Pat glanced back nervously into the busy station, half expecting a huge, angry man to come bursting through the crowd after them, waving steel, keen-sharp hatchets like some demented circus act. He pointed down the road then walked towards the entrance of *The Hilton Hotel.*

'Come on, in here.'

153

Demi looked up at the imposing Victorian building once owned by the former Great Western Railway. A commissionaire stood ready to open the door for them. Demi followed Pat inside, looking out of place crossing the checkerboard marble floor in the yellow fluorescent coat that she still wore. The palatial interior boasted a sweeping staircase, art-deco revival panels, and murals. Soft jazz music drifted from concealed speakers adding to the hotel's relaxed ambiance. Standing before the reception desk, they both knew they appeared out of place amongst such grandeur. The man at the reception desk wearing a dark pinstripe suit and pink shirt with matching tie looked them over, nose twitching as they both approached the counter.

'Do you have any rooms?' Pat asked.

'Simply hundreds, sir,' the man said in a soft, effeminate voice. 'This is a hotel, after all.' he continued with a small sweep of his perfectly manicured hand, an insincere smile on his face.

Demi returned his oily grin. 'You don't say. And there's me thinking we're in Westminster Abbey. He meant available rooms.'

'Madam?'

'Okay, okay,' Pat whispered. 'Let's not start a scene shall we, Demetra.'

'Well, he bloody started it.'

The man tapped at a keyboard.

'Just the one room, sir?'

'No, we'd like two singles if you have them,' Pat replied.

'How many nights, sir?'

'Just the one for now.'

'Will you require dinner, sir? We have a number of restaurants including the brasserie grillroom.'

The man pointed towards the entrance to the restaurant.

'Nah,' Demi said. 'I saw a pizza place out there. We'll get a takeaway.'

'The hotel disapproves of guests taking outside food to the rooms,' the man informed flicking his carefully groomed hair with his hand.

'Disapproves or disallows?' Demi asked.

'Disapproves.'

'Then we'll get a takeaway.'

'As you wish,' he said pushing two plastic swipe key cards across the marble counter, along with a form to complete.

'Is that all your luggage?' He pointed to the attaché case. 'Do you want me to summon the bellboy?'

'No thanks,' Pat responded.

'Rooms 285 and 286, on the second floor,' he said pointing towards the lifts.

'Why have you wasted money on two rooms when one would have been fine?' Demi asked as they stood waiting for the lift to arrive. 'Separate beds, of course.'

'I snore like a pig in labour,' he joked.

They stepped into a modestly furnished room with its two single beds, chairs, and writing desk. A fully stocked minibar was located under the desk. The flat screen TV, attached to a wall over the desk, welcomed them to the Hilton Hotel. Demi grinned at the screen message.

'Hey, Pat, we're on the telly.'

Pat peered out of the window on to the busy street below. Taking a deep breath, he moved over to face Demi who was drinking a coke she'd taken from the minibar.

'God, what a mess,' he sighed. 'I can't believe we've just booked into a bloody Hilton hotel, in London of all places. Now, I wish I'd brought my passport instead of leaving it in the flat.'

Demi gave him a perplexed look.

'Don't get me wrong,' he added. 'I'm not planning on leaving the country. Well, not unless it's absolutely necessary. I think I'll phone Elroy… get him to go to the flat and fetch it.'

Pat checked his watch.

'He can *FedEx* it – should arrive by the morning. Elroy keeps a spare key to my place. Where I live, leaving one under the doormat isn't a safe option.'

'Then I'll need mine as well,' Demi said. Finishing the last of her drink, she flopped into a large chair. 'Don't think I'll bother with another one, not at two quid each.'

'How much?' Pat shouted snatching up the tariff card. 'Right, I'll buy a replacement from a local shop and put it back in the fridge. Two pounds for a lousy can of coke.'

'Well it is the Hilton,' Demi responded with a sweep of her arm.

'Do I look like Bill Gates? Only everyone seems to want to charge me extortionate prices…' Pat stopped suddenly. Demi's comment had registered with him.

'Then you'll need your what?' he asked.

'My passport, I do have one, you know.'

Pat crossed over to her, shaking his head.

'No, Demi. No, no, no. It's bad enough you being here in London, but no way will I let you leave the country with me. Anyway, it probably won't come to that so you won't need a passport.'

She stood up from her chair.

'Pat, it's not about running away. It's about how we get rid of these diamonds,' she said pointing at the attaché case on the bed. 'We can't wander around London with half a million quid's worth of gemstones. What if we were mugged? Can you imagine the face of the mugger seeing this lot when all he was expecting was a…' Demi hesitated, 'well, something worth a bloody lot less?'

Pat gave her a knowing glance; he had to admit she was right. He was getting way out of his depth without the slightest idea about what to do or where to go next. It had been a panic decision to come to London based entirely on the sudden appearance of Hatchet Lennie, and anyway, where would he get the money to pay for air fares? Pat opened the case, taking the coin bag from inside. He tipped it onto the bed, revealing the small velvet pouches, then emptied one pouch into the palm of his hand. Ten radiant stones twinkled at him under the overhead light of the room. Demi did the same with another pouch; between them they emptied all five pouches spreading the stones across an area of the duvet.

'Fifty little beauties,' Demi said. 'Such lovely shapes.'

Picking a stone, she held it in front of Pat. 'Look, it's shaped like a pear. And this one's like a little pillow.' One of the larger stones caught her eye. 'Not sure about this one, though. It's a funny colour.'

Pat took it from her, examining it closely.

'You're right,' he agreed. 'It's got a pink tinge to it whereas the others are dazzling white. Probably a flaw.' He said this with an air of knowledge he didn't possess. 'Okay, let's put them back into the pouches. We'll divide them into piles of ten.'

'Hang on,' Demi announced when they'd finished. 'I've only got nine in this pile. One of the other piles must have eleven.'

After recounting them twice they realised there were only forty-nine stones in total. They went through each pouch again, plus the coin bag searching for the missing stone.

'Maybe there were never fifty in the first place,' Pat said. 'It was only the papers that said there were fifty. They could've been wrong.'

'Typical,' Demi snorted. 'Never trust the papers, I say.'

'Or,' he recalled thinking back, 'I could have dropped one of them in the vault.'

'Oh well,' Demi said with a shrug of her shoulders, 'Just try not to lose any more, eh, clumsy.'

Pat placed the case in the safe he'd discovered in the room's wardrobe. He read the instruction on how to set the combination lock, feeling a pang of relief once he'd secured the door. 'Okay, let's make our phone calls then we'll get something to eat.'

***

Elroy sat in his taxi reading a newspaper when his phone rang. Pat explained their predicament to his close friend.

'You're in London with Demi? You dirty old sod. Hang on,' he continued, 'you're her social worker, that's professional misconduct, surely?'

'I'm the *children's* social worker,' he reminded his friend. 'Anyway, it's not what you think, not by a long shot. Anyway, I need you to go to my place and get my passport.'

'Your passport? Where the hell you going, man?'

'Please, Elroy, no questions. Just do me this one favour.'

'Okay, okay,' he agreed. 'Where will I find it?'

'Should be in one of the kitchen drawers.'

'Anything else?' Elroy said, sardonically.

'There is one other thing,' Pat said.

'Hey, I was only kidding.'

'I know, but I also need you to go to Demi's house to collect her passport. She'll let her parents know you're calling so they'll have it ready for you. Then send them here by courier.'

'Pat, d'you know what you're doing, man? I mean, seriously?'

Pat hesitated before replying.

'Not really.' He gave Elroy details of the hotel's address in Paddington.

***

Demi's mother frowned, equally as shocked when her daughter told her what she'd planned.

'Your passport for a holiday?' her mother said. 'At such short notice...where do you intend to travel? What about the children? Who are you going with?' She listened to Demi before responding. 'A friend, what friend? Khristos, please speak to Demetra.' She handed the phone to her husband. 'She's not making any sense.'

'Hi, Dad. Look, I'm fine. I'm with Pat Doyle. We're in London and we need to sort out some business.'

'But, Demetra,' he interrupted. 'We're worried about you.'

159

'Dad, there's no need to worry, honestly. Pat's taking care of everything.'

'What do you need?' he asked.

'The address of our relatives in London, they still live here, don't they?'

'Yes. Andreas and Aella,' he replied. He gave his daughter the address in Ravenscourt Park, near Hammersmith.

With the phone calls out of the way, they decided they would eat at the pizza restaurant nearby rather than in the room. Before leaving, Pat had an idea.

'Okay, there should be another safe like this one in the other room we booked.'

He opened the safe removing the attaché case.

'I'll put this in the other room's safe, and we'll stay in here.'

'So we'll both sleep in this one?' Demi asked.

'Why not, it has two beds, we'll take one each. It'll only be for tonight, tomorrow night at a push. Wait here a minute while I take this next door.'

As soon as he returned, they left the hotel. Hungry, Pat looked forward to his favourite food. They ordered two large pepperoni pizzas with two beers. Demi went across to the 'help yourself' salad bar. Pat remained in his seat, biting on a bread stick. The first free thing all day, he thought. A muffled ring tone of a mobile phone startled him.

At first, he looked around thinking it came from elsewhere before realising it was his own. He rarely carried a phone unless it was unavoidable.

'Hello,' Pat said cautiously.

'Hello, Pat,' a voice replied, almost in a rasp. 'I believe you have something that belongs to me.'

Pat's appetite evaporated almost immediately when he recognised the voice of Barry Laine.

'How did you get my number?' he asked politely. Looking across the restaurant he noticed Demi, dish in hand, deciding on what to select. He didn't want her to know about this call.

'I tend to get whatever I want,' the voice continued.

'So what do you want?'

'Don't play games with me, Doyle,' Laine snapped. 'You know exactly what I want. I know you're probably in London with the woman. By the way, how is the lovely Demi?'

Pat listened but did not respond.

'Just return the stones to me and that'll be the end of it. Mess with me, Doyle, and you'll end up getting seriously hurt.'

Pat's mind raced.

'What if I don't have them anymore?'

'Don't jest with me either, Doyle,' Laine growled. 'We both know you have them. Give me the stones, nobody gets hurt. Okay?' After a pause, Laine continued. 'By the way, Lennie's itching to get his hands on you. Boy, you really pissed him off when you jumped on that train. Get back on another train and I'll be at this end. Do that, and I'll call him off.'

'I'll need to think about this. Can I get back to you?'

'Think? What's there to think about?' Laine demanded, fast losing his patience. 'You really don't have a choice in this, my friend. Okay, you think and I'll call you back in exactly one hour.'

The phone went dead. Pat switched it off, shoving it back into his pocket.

Demi returned, sitting down opposite him with her dish.

'Nothing much left but bleeding beetroot, lettuce, and olives,' she groaned. 'I hate olives.'

'I'm sure they'll refill them,' Pat said. 'Did you ask?'

'I tried one guy but I think he's Polish.'

'Having Greek heritage, I thought you'd like olives,' Pat said trying to change the subject.

'I'm not a born Greek,' she protested. 'I was born in Cardiff. I'm Welsh.'

'No, what I meant was by having Greek parents you would have eaten olives from a young age. Didn't you?'

'Oh yeah, olives, vine leaves, peppers. Yuk! It's why I hate them now.'

Pat gazed across the table, admiring her Greek features, thinking her facial expressions were pure magic.

'Your name, Demetra,' he asked. 'What does it mean?'

'It means Mother Earth,' according to my parents. Sounds daft, doesn't it?' she said picking at her lettuce, wondering whether to eat it.

'Not at all,' he insisted. 'It's lovely in fact.'

'I prefer Demi. You know, like Demi Moore, the actress?' she said giving up on the lettuce. 'So, what about Patrick, what's that mean then?'

'Named after a saint, but I prefer Pat. Like Pat St Clements, the actress,' he joked.

Demi screwed her face at him. 'D'you mean the one from *Eastenders?*'

Pat Nodded.

'It's Pam, not Pat.'

They laughed until their food order arrived. The Polish waiter informed them, in flawless English, that they'd replenished the salad bar.

Twenty-One

Elroy searched the glove compartment of his car for Pat's spare door key. He knew it had to be in there. He kept it as a spare for Pat who'd often leave his jacket in the pub. He'd already been to Demi's parents to pick up her passport ready to send on. He eventually found the key and let himself into the flat.

'Bloody hell,' he said aloud. He looked around the unusually tidy flat. No clutter of books, old vinyl record sleeves, the odd dirty plate with a half-finished pizza, the usual detritus that greeted him whenever he visited.

He pulled open a kitchen drawer, tightly stuffed with papers, envelopes, and credit card statements.

'Jeez, what a mess. 'He opened another drawer, glancing inside at the selection of cutlery and cooking implements. Satisfied it would be in the first one, he lifted out the pile of papers, glancing at a few of the statements. Money owed on all of them. Near the bottom, he spotted the familiar royal crest on a burgundy cover.

Sitting at the small kitchen table Elroy placed both passports in the Jiffy envelope he'd purchased at a local shop. Checking the piece of paper with the address of the hotel, he wrote it on the front of the padded envelope, then sealed it and let himself out.

As Elroy stepped into the passage, Hatchet Lennie greeted him.

'Hey, Bro,' Lennie said. The two men faced each other on the stairwell. Lennie towered above the much smaller man in front of him.

'Shit,' Elroy caught his breath as he took a step back. 'You fucking scared me.'

'Did I? Oh well. What have we here then?' He pointed to the package in Elroy's hand.

'This? Just a letter I'm posting, nothing really.' He swallowed hard.

'Then you won't mind if I take a look,' Lennie said snatching the packet from Elroy's hand. He studied the address label. Ripping open the bag, Lennie removed the passports and flicked through the pages.

'Tell you what,' he held up the two passports, 'I'll deliver these personally.'

He grinned at Elroy.

'You, my little friend, you're coming with me.' He almost pushed Elroy down the stone steps of the stairwell. Outside, Lennie opened the door of his BMW, nodding for Elroy to get in. He called Barry Laine.

'I know exactly where they are, boss,' Lennie said into the phone. 'I'll be with you shortly.'

***

The following morning Lennie Randall left the M4 motorway in London, heading east along Holland Park Avenue towards Paddington. Laine had given him strict orders. First, get the diamonds, and then return to Cardiff with the minimum of damage caused. In other words, don't break any bones but break them if you must. Lennie hoped he'd be breaking bones.

He drove along Praed Street passing the Hilton. He needed a place to park. Lennie didn't want a repeat of the Cardiff fiasco; he knew they would instantly recognise him and take flight. The last thing he needed would be to tell Laine he'd screwed up a second time. No, he assured himself, this time no mistakes. He parked his car in a side street, ignoring the 'residents only' notice, then made his way to the main road, standing opposite the Hilton where he could watch the entrance. Lennie could feel the weight of his steel axe in the inside pocket of his leather jacket and the flick-knife in the pocket of his trousers. He checked his watch: ten am. Pressing himself into a doorway, he studied the front of the hotel entrance, ignoring the glances some passers-by gave him. He eventually spotted them as they stepped out of the hotel, walking towards the entrance to Paddington station. Lennie noticed the absence of the case – the one Pat Doyle was carrying when he followed them the day before. Deciding not to go after them, Lennie entered the hotel. He'd wait for them to return, then confront them in their room. Rubbing the outside of his jacket, Lennie felt the outline of his axe, its cold steel pressed against his chest. He smiled. 'Got ya,' he muttered.

Lennie spotted the concierge standing behind a lectern. He approached, giving a friendly smile, all the while checking the large foyer, making sure that Doyle and the woman hadn't returned. Lennie glanced at the man's name badge: Maurice.

'Hi, *Morris*,' he said, hand outstretched towards the concierge who came forward, dressed in a suit with tails, stylish waistcoat and cravat. 'I'm here to meet some friends. Can you tell me what room they're in?' He held a £20 note between his fingers. 'I can then go on up and see them in their room.' Lowering his voice he added, 'You could also get me a bottle of champagne, none of your fancy stuff, mind. A surprise for the woman, it's her birthday.'

The concierge took the money plus an additional £50 for the wine, before making his way to reception then over to the bar. He returned with a bottle of *Oudinot* rosé.

'Your two friends are actually out right now but Mr Doyle is staying in room two-five-eight.' The concierge never mentioned the second room.

'Not a problem,' Lennie smiled, 'I'll wait in the bar.'

'Can I order you a drink, sir? While you wait.'

'Yeah,' Lennie replied. 'Tell you what, open this.'

He handed back the pink champagne, not about to waste it, particularly as he didn't see any change from the £50 note.

Lennie found a corner of the dimly lit bar where they would not easily spot him on their return. As he sat sipping his drink, he gave thought to his initial idea about confronting them but decided on another way. He waited for an opportunity. The moment presented itself when the concierge was called away to assist with an enquiry from another guest. Lennie downed his drink then made his way to the lifts.

Another £20 and he'd persuaded a cleaner to open the room door by saying he'd lost his entry card. Once inside, he began a thorough search, and with very little in the room he soon found the safe at the bottom of the wardrobe. He examined the steel box; gaining entry would not be possible. Lennie decided to sit and wait for their return. Dropping into the armchair, he wished he'd brought the champagne with him.

∗∗∗

Demi checked the Underground map at Paddington station, working out the route to Ravenscourt Park. They'd eaten at a McDonald's, a much cheaper option than the hotel as breakfast wasn't included in the price of the room. She ran a finger along the green line.

'We take the District Line from here to Ravenscourt Park,' she explained. Pat nodded his agreement. 'It's nearer than I thought. I had visions of spending the day on the bloody Underground getting lost.'

'You can't get lost on the Underground.'

'I can, believe you me. I once went to a conference on drug abuse. The conference venue was in Westminster but I got off at South Kensington, don't ask me why. Anyway, I ended up at a place called Cockfosters.'

'Trust you,' she giggled. 'Cockfosters! Where's that?'

'Exactly.'

Demi phoned her father's cousin, Andreas, on a mobile number, explaining they were in London and would like to visit. She ended the call then looked for Pat who stood nearby, gazing at the architecture of the station roof. Demi went over to him.

'No problem. Andreas even offered to collect us on his way home from work. He told me his office is near the Kings Mall shopping centre, wherever that is.'

'So what's Andreas's business?'

'Dad said he's an accountant or something. I dunno really. Anyway, I told him we'd make our own way to his house.'

Pat nodded, quietly wishing she'd accepted the offer of a lift.

'Andreas and his wife will let us stay with them, cheaper than that bloody hotel. Can you believe breakfast wasn't included?'

'How long will they let us stay? To be honest, I'd really prefer that you went back home. I can stay here and try to sell the diamonds.'

Demi poked him in the chest. 'Look, we've already had this discussion. I'm staying with you. Okay?'

'Okay, okay,' he agreed. 'Now, let's go back to the hotel and wait for the delivery of the passports from Elroy. I've tried phoning him but there's no answer.'

'I'm sure he'd have been in touch if there's a problem,' Demi said, hopefully. 'They probably arrived while we've been out.'

***

The multitude of people at Paddington Station increased in number. Trains arrived and left regularly, and nothing ever seemed to stand still. A young couple argued over lost train tickets while another nearby couple passionately kissed each other. Pat wondered if they would be separated for long. Once more, he turned his attention upwards to the glazed roof supported by iron girders, impressed by the architecture of the station designed by Brunel.

'Come on, dreamer,' Demi said, pulling at his arm.

They moved through the crowd towards the hotel. Given the time of day, they expected the package from Elroy to be waiting for them at the front desk.

A young female receptionist greeted them.

'Can I help you, please?' she asked.

'Yes,' Pat replied. 'Is there a package for me? Patrick Doyle, room 285.'

She looked down at a computer scanning the screen.

'No, sir, nothing has arrived today. Are you expecting something?'

Pat looked at Demi who simply shrugged.

'I'll try Elroy again. He may not have posted it in time.'

As they turned from the desk, the receptionist told them they did have a visitor looking for them. Pat felt his stomach drop, hardly able to speak. 'When did this person call?' Demi asked. 'We're not expecting anyone.'

'About an hour ago,' she replied. 'Ordered champagne from Maurice, then he took it into the lounge.' She pointed in the direction of the bar.

'W... what did this person look like?' Pat stammered. He cringed in expectation of the answer.

'A large gentleman, possibly of African origin.'

'You mean he's black?' Demi asked.

'Yes, madam.'

'Oh shit,' Demi uttered.

'Is there a problem, madam?'

'Do you know if he's still here?'

'Doesn't appear to be, madam,' the receptionist glanced around the foyer. 'Shall I inform you if he returns?'

'Straight away,' Demi spurted. Pat managed to calm his nerves enough to ask for their bill and settled up. He pulled Demi to one side.

'We'll get the case then make our way to your relative's house. If we jump in a cab, it should be quicker.'

'What if he's in our room, waiting for us?'

This did nothing to reduce Pat's already critical anxiety level.

'We've got to get out of here now,' he told her almost shaking.

'Not without the bloody diamonds, we don't. C'mon,' Demi pulled on his arm. 'The diamonds are in the other room, remember?'

The corridor was empty as they almost crept along to the second room. They stopped outside the door to listen.

'Shall we go in?' Demi whispered.

'What if he's in there?' Pat whispered back. 'We're done for if he catches us.'

'Don't be such a wimp; if he is, we simply tell him we no longer have the diamonds.'

'If he is, we simply hand them over and run you mean.'

'Wha'ever,' Demi shrugged.

The room was empty with no sign of any disturbance. They both gently pressed their heads against the wall dividing the rooms. At first, they heard nothing, then after a moment the sound of a flushing toilet followed by a door closing.

'Shit,' Pat said, 'he's in our room waiting for us.'

Pat entered the combination numbers on the safe door then removed the attaché case. Demi went to open the door.

'Okay, let's go.'

'Wait a sec.' Pat moved across to the desk where he started to write on a sheet of hotel notepaper.

'Jeez, Pat,' Demi hissed. 'We don't have time for this.'

Within minutes, they were heading back down the stairs into the foyer. Pat stopped at the desk. The same receptionist smiled at him.

'Please can you pass this to our friend should he return.'

'Of course, sir.' She took the hotel's courtesy envelope from him with the note inside. Pat began to feel a little intrepid as they stepped onto the busy London street, heading for the underground inside the main station. Demi stopped on the pavement when she noticed something across the road. 'Come on,' she said, 'over here.'

'Why? What's over there? We need to get away from this place.'

'There, look.' Demi pointed across the road.

Within twenty minutes, they were back in the station. The underground teemed with commuters with standing room only when they squeezed themselves onto the crowded tube train. It rattled through the tunnels at speed, heading for their destination.

***

Lennie stood outside the Hilton reading the note handed to him by the receptionist. After reading it through twice, he screwed it into a ball and threw it to the ground, shouting expletives that attracted the attention of passers-by.

Lennie,

Sorry we missed you. We would like to have shared that champagne with you but we had a train to catch and could not wait. Hope you enjoyed your brief stay in London. We promise not to tell Mr Laine you sneaked a ride on the London Eye. Regards

He darted across to his car, deciding to phone Laine during the drive back down the M4. As he approached the BMW, he noticed something very wrong – all four of the car's tyres were flat. The burst of expletives was louder and longer.

Twenty-Two

Abraham Steinberg sat in the large, red leather chair dominating the space behind the grandiose oak desk of his office. His chin rested lightly on the point of a silver novelty letter opener in the shape of a scimitar sword, its dulled point digging into his skin, focusing his mind on the problem in hand. Slowly, he twisted it between his fingers in an attempt to stimulate further ideas.

His daughter sat on the other side of the desk with a disapproving look on her face.

'Father, there's no reason why you should want these diamonds. You're now being just as dishonest as Barry Laine.'

He turned his head to avert her look of condemnation.

'The stones belong to an insurance company,' she continued, 'not to you.'

'Rebekah, I know. I fully understand what you are saying but try to see it from another perspective.'

Steinberg gently placed the letter opener in its presentation box. On a sideboard opposite sat two crystal decanters upon a silver salver. He poured a measure of rare brandy into a matching crystal brandy bowl, swirling the dark, amber liquid around the bottom before taking a sip.

'That man your firm represents is, as well you know, a serious villain. I've made enquiries at my lodge, where I was reliably informed he has had people killed.'

He waited for a reaction but his daughter sat unmoved.

'I take it from your silence you already know this much?'

'What difference does it make to you? Doesn't it also tell you something else? That he's dangerous perhaps.'

'Oh, I am very aware of his parlous activities,' he agreed. 'So I have taken steps. No, let's say precautions, to counter any threat he may pose.'

After swallowing the last of his drink, Steinberg returned to his desk.

'If *we* do not take possession of the diamonds then *he* will.' He leaned on the desk, both hands spread in front of him. 'His family stole them from *our* family, and I intend to get them back regardless of what the law says. If the Steinberg family are not to have them, I cannot countenance the alternative, and certainly not an insurance company.'

Rebekah sensed her father's determination. Looking him in the face, she asked, 'What is it you want me to do?'

***

Back on the M4, Lennie sped towards Cardiff, gripping the steering wheel with such intensity it turned his knuckles white.

'No more Mr Nice Guy,' he kept repeating. As soon as they had the stones, he would tear the bastard's head off. He had carnal thoughts of what he would do to the woman but knew his boss had plans for her.

Barry Laine could not believe Lennie's version of events.

'Idiots. That's who I employ. Absolute, first-grade idiots.'

Lennie simply shrugged at his boss then glanced at the four men sat around Laine's office.

'Let me get this right,' Laine said. 'First you let them catch a train, then not only do they get away from you in London, they let your fucking tyres down.'

One of the four men sniggered. Laine turned glaring at him. 'Sorry, boss,' the now stone-faced man murmured.

'Then it's four hours before the RAC arrive to inflate the tyres,' Laine continued. He brought his fist down on the desk.

'Idiots.'

Laine lowered his voice to a whisper.

'I don't suppose you know where they went with my diamonds?'

'No, boss.'

'Thought not. I mean, that would be too much to expect.'

'Listen, boss, give me a few days, I swear I'll find them.'

'You think so?'

'Sure, boss. No problem.'

'Don't talk shit,' Laine hissed. 'What? You simply going to stroll around London hoping to bump into them. Is that it?'

'Well, I…'

'No, just listen, Leonard,' Laine cut in. 'We'll use a more persuasive method. One I guarantee will have both Doyle and the woman back here within twelve hours.'

Lennie frowned, his mind working overtime. Laine put his face almost nose to nose with Lennie's face.

'Doyle's taxi driver friend down in the basement. Drag him up here.'

***

Rebekah Rosen left the magistrate's court, returning to the small office she occupied on the top floor of the firm's premises in central Cardiff. She looked out of the small window, thinking that, in the bigger law firms, the more senior your position, the higher the floor you occupied. Not this firm. Here, the non-partners and juniors occupied the little rooms in the attic. She'd considered her father's request, appreciating his reasoning. Her dilemma was: she would breach client confidentially and abet a criminal act.

Should she help her father? The consequences could be dire. Rebekah knew she'd lose her job, never be able to practise law again. She picked up the slim file from her desk with the name *Leonard Randall* written in the top right-hand corner. Rebekah reminded herself who employed the man. Another dilemma troubled her: Isaac. He'd never forgive her if this went bad. She thought of her husband, of his position in chambers.

'I have to do it,' she said, staring through the small window.

Rebekah watched a group of people opposite, chatting together outside the Premier Inn hotel, smoking cigarettes.

'I promised father I would do this for him,' she told herself.

Despite the risks, she didn't want Barry Laine to obtain the diamonds either. Criminal law could be a dirty business; it often made her consider a career change. Rebekah put Lennie's file down to study a letter she'd received in that day's post, touching it lightly with her finger. Rebekah reread an offer from a friend of Isaac's to join a high-powered firm specialising in contract law. An offer she'd seriously consider. Folding the letter, she placed it in her briefcase, then picking up the phone, she called Barry Laine.

'Hi, Mr Laine, it's Rebekah Rosen. I'm looking for Leonard, only he failed to show up in court this morning.' She listened to his response. 'The magistrates issued an arrest warrant,' she told him, then listened again.

'Well, when you do see him tell him to contact me immediately.'

'As soon as I see him, I'll pass that on,' Laine said.

'Thank you,' she responded. 'I'm obliged.'

Laine pocketed his iPhone, grinning as he turned to face Lennie who was with him in the warehouse of his antique furniture business. They both looked down at Elroy gagged and bound to an old chair. Elroy stared back at them with a terrified look. He knew what they were capable of doing.

'That was your brief, Lennie boy, seems you should have been before the beak this morning.'

'Oh dear, Mr Laine, I clean forgot.' They both smirked at Elroy.

'Now then, Leonard,' Laine said. He slowly lit a large cigar with a match, blowing a plume of thick, pungent smoke at Elroy. 'What are we to do with our Mr Blake here?'

'Removing fingers with a bolt-cropper usually does the trick,' Lennie suggested. He reached down behind a *chaise longue* to lift a bolt-cutter, holding it in front of him. Elroy gave a muffled gasp on seeing the instrument, his breathing labouring through the gag.

'Shall I start with the little pinkie?' Lennie said as he moved towards the chair, opening and closing the steel jaws, 'or maybe a thumb?'

He'd done this sort of thing before, getting a great deal of sadistic pleasure from watching his victims writhe in agony. He also liked to hear them scream and beg. He wasn't particularly fond of the quick kills, like slitting throats. He much preferred the slower methods of torture.

'Steady on, Lennie boy,' Laine said putting his hand on Lennie's arm. 'Let's see what the good Dr Doyle has to say first.'

Laine took out his phone, selecting a contact. A recorded message spoke to him.

'*Hi, sorry I can't take your call right now...*' Laine didn't wait to hear the whole message.

'Shit, why doesn't the bastard answer? 'He crossed to his office, Lennie in tow. 'I need to consider the situation carefully, Len,' he told his minder. 'Why would they want to remain in London? Does Doyle know anyone there?'

Lennie sat near the door, bolt croppers on his lap.

'Maybe the woman does,' he suggested.

'Maybe you're right, Len. Maybe she does. But we've got the ace card by holding Doyle's little friend out there. I don't want to resort to violence if it can be avoided, Len. Too many people in this game had pasts that caught up with them. Once the police get their claws in you, they never let go. They already think I'm responsible for a number of missing rivals in the drug trade – missing presumed dead.'

Lennie smiled at a particular thought.

'They'd be right there, boss. I cut their fucking throats, remember?'

'Yes, well, least said the better on that one, Leonard. We'll give it another hour then try Doyle again. The problem as I see it, Len, is this. If we can't get through to Doyle, how can we use our trump card who's tied up out there?'

'What about the woman's family?' Lennie suggested. 'They might know something.'

'Yeah, Len, they just might. Okay, I need to do a few things first so we'll come back later. If we don't get through you can visit her family.'

A malevolent grin spread across Lennie's face.

***

Elroy Blake sat bound to the chair with strong nylon cord and watched his captors as they left, wondering how long it would be before they returned. He pondered the situation. Lennie had brought him here with the passports, so they knew the location of Pat and Demi, given he'd written the address on the package. Yet somehow they'd given Lennie the slip as he'd arrived back from London without them. From Laine's reaction, Elroy guessed he was not a happy man. Now they'd threatened him with one of Lennie's manicures as a way to get to Pat and the woman. Things had become far too complicated for him. His favour for a friend – collecting the passports – had resulted in threats to remove his fingers. Who's to say they'd stop there?

Elroy felt the tightness of the nylon line cut into him every time he moved. The gag around his mouth made breathing difficult. *Elroy, you need to get out of here, man, so think.* His eyes scanned the room they'd left him in – a warehouse, full of old-looking furniture. Boxes and packing cases were spread around the area. Leaning against the wall next to Laine's office were the bolt croppers. Elroy heard a door slam somewhere in the building followed by footsteps. His eyes fixed on the door, waiting for the return of the two men intent on cutting him up. Beads of sweat ran down his forehead, stinging his eyes. He pushed his head back, staring up at the high ceiling. He tried to slow his breathing. Eyes closed, he slowly counted to ten. The footsteps he'd heard became faint. Another door closed, this time further away.

With another scan of the room, Elroy spotted a small table, on top of which sat a cigar case with a box of matches.

Elroy's mind raced; he needed to act quickly. By summoning all his remaining strength, and employing some odd shuffling and jumping movements, he managed to manoeuvre the chair over to the table. He tried not to make much noise just in case there might be someone else in the building. Newspapers spilled out of packing cases lying about the floor. Elroy felt quietly confident when he noticed smoke alarms on the ceiling. He decided to go for it. He reached the table, giving the legs a kick – it hardly moved. He tried again. The nylon cut into his shin as he did.

Resting, he let the pain ease then closed his eyes to concentrate. After a moment, he pushed the table with both feet. This time the pain increased but it went over. The matches and cigar case were now on the floor. Again, with his feet, he pushed the matchbox towards a pile of newspapers. Placing his foot on the box, Elroy pushed down hard. The matches inside pressed together, igniting some of the newspaper. Flickering yellow flames spread as the discarded paper began to burn. Elroy could feel the heat from the growing fire as more paper was set alight. The smoke reached his nostrils as the material continued to burn. Finally, it drifted towards the smoke detectors. The loud clang of bells from the alarm system rang out around the building. Elroy tried to shuffle backwards away from the inferno; thoughts of burning alive panicked him as flames spread all around.

Elroy didn't expect the fire to rage as it did. At this rate, the whole warehouse would become a furnace, fire engulfing everything in the place. He felt his feet beginning to get hot and he could smell burning rubber from the soles of his boots. Elroy hoped that the gag would prevent him becoming unconscious through smoke inhalation, although that might mean remaining conscious whilst being burned alive.

Elroy squeezed his stinging, watering eyes, waiting for his agonising end. Bound to the chair, he suddenly felt a spray of coldness on his face. Water? A sprinkler system he hadn't noticed sent water cascading down from small jets along the ceiling, soaking everything in the room as it doused the flames. The alarm continued to sound followed within minutes by the unmistakable wail of fast approaching sirens. With his head on his chest, Elroy gave out a sigh, praying this would not upset his captors too much. The doors crashed open, Elroy lifted his head, and squinting though stinging eyes, he saw the two of them standing in front of him, one brandishing a large axe.

***

The two fire fighters spotted Elroy in the corner of the room. They made their way over, looking surprised to see him tied to the chair.

'Thank you, thank you,' Elroy gasped when they removed the gag from his mouth. Between them they untied him, guiding him out of the building onto the street.

A senior fire-fighter approached to speak with his colleagues. He then turned his attention to Elroy. 'Are you responsible for the fire?' the officer asked. Elroy nodded sheepishly. The man waved a police officer over to join them.

'They found this one inside tied to a chair. He's lucky to be alive.'

'We'll need to speak with you about this,' the policeman informed him, 'but first we'll get the paramedics to examine you as soon as they arrive.'

'We'll *also* be speaking to you about this incident,' the senior fire officer said to Elroy. 'Do you know the owner of this building by any chance?'

Elroy nodded, relieved to be out of the place alive, not receiving attention for burns of any degree. The relief quickly evaporated when a black BMW pulled up. Barry Laine and Lennie stepped out.

'They own it,' Elroy whispered to the senior officer whilst trying his best to hide behind the man.

Twenty-Three

The tube train thundered from Paddington to Ravenscourt Park. Demi's relative, Andreas Dranias, lived with his wife just off a road near the station, only a few minutes' walk to the house. Pat noticed most of the driveways of the properties had either Mercedes, Lexus or Range Rovers parked on them. As they ambled along, Pat became aware of peeking residents not used to seeing strangers walk along their road, particularly one wearing a hi-vis coat. Pat wondered what such people did during the day; probably whist drives or coffee mornings, organising events for charity and the like, he presumed.

'Here it is,' Demi announced, checking the address she'd written earlier on a piece of paper. She glanced around nervously before pressing the highly polished brass doorbell, trying to remember the last occasion she'd met her relatives, and wondering what kind of reception they could expect. A smartly dressed woman in a black two-piece suit of light material opened the door. Her hair was black with streaks of silver grey, tied back tightly into a bun. Around her neck, she wore a heavy gold chain in the Greek key design. Demi looked at her then smiled.

'Aella?' she said almost in a whisper. The woman returned a huge smile, her arms outstretched.

'Demetra,' she blurted. They hugged each other on the doorstep. Aella looked towards Pat. 'Is this your friend?'

'Yes, this is Pat Doyle. He's my… my very good friend,' she said, not wanting to admit that he was her social worker.

'Do come in,' Aella invited. 'Your father phoned to say you would call. It's so nice of you to visit. I wish your cousins were here to see you.'

As they stepped into the spacious hall, Pat looked around, taking in the décor. 'Nice home you have here,' he commented.

The furniture was mainly in dark oak. Pictures of Greek scenes adorned the walls. Numerous framed pictures of white, sugar-cube houses with ochre-tiled roofs and fishing boats with wizened men repairing fishing nets. Family photographs surrounded the living room. Andreas and Aella Dranias had two sons, Pavlos and Spiros. Graduation photographs of two smiling boys holding scrolls sat on a sideboard.

'I'll make coffee,' Aella said. 'Please, relax, make yourselves comfortable.'

'Oh, yes please,' Pat said clutching the attaché case. 'Coffee would be great.'

'There is so much to talk about,' Aella said. 'Let me take your…your coat, Demetra.'

'Thank you,' Demi replied. She handed over her hi-vis jacket.

For over an hour Demi and Aella reminisced about family get-togethers, holidays, weddings, and funerals. Andreas eventually arrived home, also greeting Demi affectionately.

The closeness of a family who only came together on special but infrequent occasions impressed Pat. He thought about his own family. Pat was the only child of his parents, who were also only children. No cousins, aunts or uncles. He knew of distant relatives but had no idea where they might be, or whether they were still alive. Even his wife had left him. Aella later prepared a dinner of lamb with vegetables. They made light conversation around the meal. Aella recalled a family wedding that made Demi laugh.

'You must have been about eight at the time,' Aella mused. 'Old Spiro had you standing on his feet dancing you around the floor. Everyone clapped and shouted. You looked so beautiful in your white dress with a blue satin sash and a matching bow in your hair.'

Aella reached across to stroke Demi's face. 'So beautiful,' she repeated.

'Aella, don't,' Andreas said. 'Can't you see you're embarrassing Demi in front of her boyfriend?'

Pat felt the heat rise in his face. 'This is fantastic lamb,' he said hoping to change the subject. 'What's it called?'

'Kleftiko,' Aella told him. 'I hope you like garlic, only I tend to use more than most people prefer.'

'Oh, I love garlic,' Pat assured her.

After the meal, they returned to the lounge. Pat and Demi sat together on the large sofa. Andreas and Aella took the armchairs. Pat placed the small case on the coffee table between them.

'I'm afraid we're in a spot of bother, Mr Dranias…'

'Please, call me Andreas,' he said smiling. 'What kind of bother, nothing too serious I hope?' He glanced over to Demi, 'Are you…'

'No, nothing like that,' Pat cut in. *If only,* he thought.

'We're being chased by some dangerous people,' Pat continued. 'They want what we have in this case. That's how we came to be in London. I did try persuading Demi to return home but she wouldn't listen.'

'That's right,' Demi said defiantly, 'I refused and I'm still refusing.'

'What exactly is in the case, Pat?' Andreas asked.

'Diamonds,' Pat said. 'Worth a small fortune, and the reason a Cardiff villain named Barry Laine wants them.'

'What?' Andreas exclaimed. 'I'm sorry but you'd better explain this in more detail.'

Pat relayed the story of how they discovered the diamonds, followed by Barry Laine's involvement.

Aella moved over to sit next to Demi, placing a hand on her niece's shoulder.

'Maybe you should listen to Pat, my chicken. You don't want to get hurt.'

'Aella's right,' added Andreas. 'You should return home. I'll take you myself if you wish.'

Pat hoped she'd take up the offer but expected to hear what she said next.

'No, I'm not going home. I'm staying with him,' she thumbed at Pat, 'and that's final.'

'I seem to remember you were always a stubborn little girl,' Aella commented. 'Stubborn just like your father. So, where do you plan to go?'

Pat placed his empty coffee cup on the table.

'I did consider going abroad for a short while. I'd asked a friend to FedEx our passports to London, but Barry Laine's man turned up at the hotel. I guess he must now have our passports. He probably managed to somehow get to my friend. Now I'm not sure what we'll do.'

'Do you still want to go abroad?' Andreas asked.

'I think so,' Pat replied. 'Let the dust settle a bit then maybe sell the diamonds.'

'Ah yes, the diamonds,' Andreas said. He crossed over to the large bay window and closed the curtains. Taking a bottle from a cabinet, he poured four small glasses of ouzo. After handing each of them a drink he told them how he may be able to help.

'As you may know, I'm an accountant. I have a substantial client base with the majority being small businesses in the west of London. However, I'm very aware that some conduct less-than-lawful practices. That's none of my business, and I don't get involved.

Tomorrow, we'll get passport photos of you both. Then I'll contact an Egyptian businessman whom I happen to know provides fake passports for any nation. The only problem will be the cost. Since new passports are checked electronically, he will need to make them about eight or nine years old.'

Pat looked somewhat apprehensive on hearing this. Dodgy businessmen reminded him too much of Barry Laine. Could they be trusted? Could Demi's uncle be trusted? Talk about a rock and a hard place.

'I don't have a great deal of money,' Pat said. 'I certainly have no access to any large amounts of cash. I'm assuming this man doesn't take credit cards?'

Andreas laughed at Pat's comments.

'May I see the diamonds?' he asked.

'Yes, of course, they're all in here.'

Pat opened the case, removing the contents and spreading the stones on the coffee table. Andreas picked up one of the smaller gems, examining it closely.

'They're beautiful. How many are there?'

'Forty-nine,' Pat replied.

'Then perhaps we can offer to pay with a diamond. I'm sure my client will agree to accept such a payment.'

'Does he deal in diamonds then?' Demi asked.

'He deals in any currency, my dear.'

'Can we trust him?' Pat asked then regretted the question. 'No, I'm sorry. I shouldn't have said that.'

'No, my friend, you are right to be concerned. After all, we are all strangers to you. If it helps to reassure you, I saved him fifty thousand pounds in taxes last year. Of course, he paid me for my services but he also values my knowledge in finance. I think we can trust him.'

Aella stood, gathering up the now empty glasses.

'It's getting late so let's continue this tomorrow, shall we? I'll make up the beds in the boy's rooms; you can take a room each.' After Pat returned the diamonds to the case, they followed Aella upstairs.

***

The following day Andreas drove them to a post office in the Kings Mall shopping centre to use the photo booth. With photos obtained, they returned to the house where they'd arranged to meet the Egyptian businessman, Nadir Mohamed, who was there waiting for them. Nadir stood over six feet tall with the distinguishing features often seen in people of wealth. His eyes sparkled as he looked around. He wore a well-tailored silk suit with a chalk-grey pinstripe. His shoes were hand-stitched soft Italian leather.

'Pat. Demetra,' Andreas said. 'May I introduce Mr Nadir Mohamed.'

'So very pleased to make your acquaintance, Pat,' Nadir said shaking him by the hand. Turning to Demi, he lightly took her hand, bending forward to kiss it, dark eyes glancing up to meet hers.

'Miss Demetra, the pleasure is all mine.'

Demi smiled back. She felt her cheeks tingle as she admired his handsome features.

'Thank you, Mr Mohamed.'

'Please, call me Nadir. We are all friends here.'

Pat coughed lightly. 'Andreas says you may be able to help us. Is that so?'

'Let us all sit then you can tell me exactly what you require. I will promise to do my best.' Nadir indicated towards Andreas. 'After all, I am indebted to my friend here.'

'We'd like to travel to Europe but our passports have been taken from us,' Pat explained.

Nadir nodded as he listened.

'So without passports we can't travel.'

'I will not ask what your business is, Pat. That is none of my concern.' Nadir placed his right palm on his chest saying, 'But rest assured, I will get what you need.'

'Can you get us passports?' Demi asked.

Nadir gave out a slight laugh.

'But of course, Miss Demetra. You shall have them in less than twenty-four hours.'

'That's very reassuring, Nadir,' Pat said guessing the man had done this sort of thing before. 'Now there's the question of money.'

Nadir raised his hands.

'Please, Pat. We can discuss money some other time. I know I can trust you, after all you are…'

'I think you should hear him out,' Andreas interrupted. 'It's fair to say Pat hasn't any money as such but he is prepared to make you an alternative offer. One I personally believe you will find as attractive as cash.'

Nadir's eyes widened towards Pat.

'Is that so? What would this offer be?'

Pat had previously selected a medium size diamond. He handed it to the Egyptian who made a careful examination of it. 'This is an extraordinarily beautiful diamond,' Nadir said. He removed a jeweller's loup from his jacket pocket so he could study the stone in detail. He paused briefly for thought, replaced the loup in his pocket before returning his attention to Pat.

'You are prepared to offer this as payment for my services?' Nadir said holding up the diamond.

'It's all I have,' Pat said quietly.

'Then we have a deal.' Nadir rose from his seat with an extended hand. Pat shook it confirming the deal.

***

Andreas showed Nadir out. Pat looked down at the diamond Nadir had returned to him, pleased he'd accepted it as payment. Aella joined them, carrying a tray of refreshments. The smell of fresh coffee filled the room. On a salver were small baklava. Andreas sat with them explaining what he'd planned next. He held a small notebook in his hand. Pat finished his coffee and cake, wiping his hands on a linen napkin. Demi chose simply to lick the syrup from her fingers.

'I have contacted a close family friend who lives on the island of Rhodes,' Andreas told them holding up the book. 'His name is Stefanos. He owns a jewellery business.'

'My father's mentioned him,' Demi said. 'Is he a relative?'

'I think he may be a distant cousin. Anyway, I spoke with him earlier so if you can get out to Rhodes, he may be able to help.'

'Will this Stefanos buy the stones?' Pat asked, 'for a reasonable price?'

'Hey,' Andreas said hands outstretched. 'He's a jeweller, of course he'll buy them. Now, we have to get you out to Rhodes.'

***

Within the hour a flight was booked, two seats for the following day with Olympic Airways, flying from Heathrow to Athens. After considering a transfer flight from Athens to Rhodes they decided on a ferry from Piraeus harbour – longer, but a lot cheaper. Pat became concerned about the amount of debt on his credit card account, fearing he would reach his limit, making the cards useless. Andreas was aware of this so he offered a temporary solution.

'Do not concern yourself about money, my friend. It is likely you both will soon be very rich.'

Pat thought about this. He liked the sound of 'very rich'.

'I will give you some cash. A thousand pounds should help you.'

'That's a lot of money,' Pat said. 'I don't know when I can repay you. I mean, a thousand pounds. No, I can't accept that amount of money but thank you all the same.'

Andreas stood up.

'Wait here, my friend.' He returned from his house safe carrying ten thousand pounds in twenty-pound notes. Pat's jaw dropped on seeing the cash. He had no further qualms about falling on the largesse of Andreas Dranias.

***

Nadir Mohamed arrived at seven pm the next day, producing two passports. The documents looked worn and well used. Pat flicked through to his picture.

'I haven't aged much, seeing as this is supposed to be nine years ago.' Demi looked at her photo.

'Nor me,' she added. 'Won't the officials at the airport be a bit suspicious?'

Nadir shrugged.

'There is little I can do about photos so recently taken.'

Taking Pat's passport, he opened it for them to see.

'The pictures have been made to look as worn as the books. I can assure you on European flights, especially to the popular holiday destinations, you should have little to worry about from the immigration officials as they will pass scrutiny.'

Pat took the diamond from his pocket then handed it to Nadir.

'As we agreed,' Pat said. Nadir took the stone, bidding them farewell

'I will take you to the airport,' Andreas insisted. 'Your flight leaves at five so we'll be in good time if we leave around two o'clock.'

Demi hugged her cousin.

'You have been so kind to us,' Demi said, wiping a tear from her cheek. Aella walked over to Demi to hold her.

'My dear Demetra, please take care of yourself.'

'I'll be alright. Pat will look after me,' Demi said looking over, winking at him.

Aella faced Pat, placing her hands on his arms.

'Please, Pat, take good care of our niece.'

'I intend to,' Pat assured her.

***

The Mercedes sped west along the M4, arriving in time for them to check in. Andreas went with them to the departure gate, reminding them of the details of his friend in Rhodes. He shook Pat by the hand then hugged Demi. As he watched them go through to the departure lounge, he took out his phone. Andreas had agreed to phone Demi's parents to let them know they went off safely.

After returning to his house, Andreas noticed a BMW parked outside. He went into the lounge to find Lennie sat in an armchair cleaning out a fingernail with his flick-knife. Andreas looked across to his wife who wiped tears from her eyes with a shaking hand. Lennie smiled at Andreas, pointing to a chair with his knife.

'Please, sit down. I've been speaking with your good lady but she doesn't want to tell me anything. Now that won't do at all.'

'You see, I've come a long way, so I expect answers to my questions.' Lennie made a point of opening and closing his knife. Aella pushed her right hand against her mouth, her face ashen.

This was the second Greek family Lennie had visited in twelve hours. After Elroy had managed to make his escape

193

from the clutches of Barry Laine, courtesy of the fire service, Lennie had made his way to the home of Demi's parents. He told them he needed to find Pat whose dying mother was asking for him. They did not hesitate in providing the address in London especially when Lennie said he would also bring Demi home. Lennie suggested they did not contact them as this sad news was not best conveyed over the phone. Demi's parents agreed.

Now sitting with Andreas and Aella, the knife in his hand, he applied a different approach altogether.

'Well, where are they?'

Andreas managed a weak smile. 'I'll tell you where they are,' he said checking his watch, 'they're probably just taking off from Heathrow heading for the US as we speak.'

Lennie rose from his chair, removing the notebook belonging to Andreas from his own pocket.

'I found this on the table when I arrived.' Lennie waved the notebook. 'And inside, this little business card. Rodos Gold. Is that where they're heading?'

Andreas shrugged. Enraged, Lennie grabbed hold of him, pulling him to his feet as he screamed in his face.

'Enough of the lies. Now, where are they?'

'Leave him alone,' Aella cried out. Lennie turned to face the woman. Andreas seized the moment by attempting a grab for the knife. He started to struggle with the stronger man. Stepping back, Lennie stumbled across the coffee table. They fell to the floor. Andreas made a feeble attempt to punch him in the face, but Lennie just laughed. A well-placed knee made contact with Andreas's groin, the dull pain nauseating him. Lennie stood and grabbed Andreas by the hair, pulling back his head. He held the knife to Andreas's throat.

'Where in Rhodes?' he demanded. 'Tell me or I'll slit your fucking throat. Right here, right now.'

'The address on the card,' Aella sobbed. 'Please, leave my husband. I beg you.'

'Are they meeting anyone?'

He pulled harder on Andreas's hair and he gave out a piercing cry. Aella told him all she knew about the arrangement to meet their friend at his jewellery shop in the main town. Lennie smiled at her.

'Thank you.' He lightly drew the blade across Andreas's throat. Blood dripped onto the Persian rug. He let Andreas go, pushing him to the floor. Aella screamed as she rushed to her husband.

'Don't worry, it's not a deep cut,' Lennie told her, 'just a warning. If you go to the police someone else will call and finish him off.' Aella sobbed louder as she applied her scarf onto the wound.

'That's no idle threat, lady. Go to the cops then hubby dies. Got that?'

Lennie made his way out, already on the phone to Barry Laine as he walked through the door.

Twenty-Four

Ben Wiener stepped out of Lieberman's Deli in the Bronx district of New York where he'd eaten a late lunch. Wiener had lived in this part of the city for many years. He'd moved there from Tel Aviv after leaving Israel's secret intelligence service, Mossad. Based mainly overseas, Wiener had become one of the agency's top assassins and he'd been involved in covert operations for the State of Israel until an attack on a bus by a Hamas raiding party had killed his wife and young daughter. Despite a distinguished career with Mossad, Wiener never got over the loss of his family so decided to 'retire'. Since moving to New York, he had helped with various Jewish charities within the mainly lower east side area of Manhattan.

Six foot three with a muscular frame, Wiener continued to look after himself in terms of physical strength. His dark brown eyes took in every detail around him. He could commit to memory details of any person he'd watched or met: what they looked like, what they wore, how they spoke. He could instantly recall a car registration or phone number noted months previously.

He wore the traditional dress of the Hasidic Jews: a long black coat with a large, wide-rimmed fedora hat. Despite this attire, he was not Hasidic; his heritage was from Ashkenazi Jews of central Europe. After years of working covert operations, often in some form of disguise, he felt less recognisable dressed like this – less likely to be a 'hit' from some past enemy. He easily blended in with the Orthodox community that still lived in the area.

Wiener was heading home from Lieberman's when his mobile phone vibrated in his pocket. He answered the phone as he walked along Johnson Avenue listening to a request from his cousin, Abraham Steinberg.

Wiener had promised himself a vacation, so the prospect of a trip to the UK appealed to him. Abraham Steinberg lived in Wales – a pleasant change from London, the only place he'd returned to since leaving Cardiff as a child to live on a Kibbutz with his parents. That one visit to London had been work related with the British Secret Intelligence Service – better known as MI6.

Wiener made a call of his own, booking himself onto a BA flight to London the following day.

***

The plane landed at Athens Venizelos airport then taxied to the arrivals area – it was eleven pm Greek time. Pat adjusted his watch then waited until all the passengers had left the plane before giving Demi a gentle nudge to wake her. She looked at him with a puzzled frown before remembering where they were.

'Have we landed?' Demi asked with a bleary voice that matched her look.

'Yep,' he replied. 'We need to get off. I think the cabin crew want to sort things out.' Pat took hold of the attaché case pressed between them. He'd been surprised at Heathrow when it went through the x-ray machine as the security staff showed no interest in its contents. A bottle of water would have caused consternation, but diamond smuggling seemed to be okay.

They made their way to the vast, state-of-the-art concourse where they'd decide what to do next. There were no ferries running at night so a stay in a hotel seemed the best idea. Spotting a tourist office, Demi made her way across to ask about local hotels. She returned, telling Pat the Hotel Apollo had vacancies.

Impressed, Pat asked, 'Can you speak Greek?'

'*Nai'* she replied.

'No?' Pat said.

'*Nai* means yes, now come on, there's a taxi rank outside.' They made their way to the exit. Outside the sultry evening air struck them as they left the air-conditioned lounge. A row of taxis stood on the rank, and Demi headed for the first in line. The driver leant against the side of his car smoking a cigarette. He smiled when he saw them approach.

'*Kalispera,'* Demi greeted. '*Xenodhohio Apollo, parakalo*,' she continued, asking for the hotel. The driver opened the rear door for them to get in. As they headed into the bustling city of Athens, Demi spoke with the driver. The inflection in her voice lacked any trace of her pronounced Cardiff accent. Pat could not help but smile.

'The Rhodes ferry leaves early from Piraeus harbour,' she told Pat. 'So the driver says it would be better if we went there instead, spend the night at one of the hotels near the port.'

'I'm impressed,' Pat told her. 'Your Greek is excellent.'

'It's all we spoke when I was a kid at home.'

'What else did he tell you?' Pat asked pointing to the driver.

'He said it's a fast ferry, wanted to know if we're on holiday. I said we were.'

'Okay, tell him to take us to a hotel near the harbour then.'

Pat looked out at the busy city with its shops, bars and Tavernas, watching a host of people strolling along the pavements, some hand in hand. Locals and tourists were mixing, enjoying the balmy evening. He smiled at the tourists as they avoided the calls of the restaurant waiters trying to entice them in to eat.

Athens, he thought, *a city with a most glorious history, worshipped by gods and mortals, the birthplace of democracy.* Most of the wise men of ancient times were from this place alone. He'd be happy just to visit the Acropolis, the 'sacred rock' of Athens, promising himself he'd return one day to study the history of this magnificent place.

'Here we are,' Demi said as the car pulled up at a hotel. Not a fancy building by its appearance, and Pat hoped it would be inexpensive. He gave the driver €20. 'Keep the change,' he told him with an air of affluence. As they walked into the hotel, Demi turned to him.

'The fare came to twenty euros exactly,' Demi said. 'So I imagine he appreciated the tip.'

'I didn't know. Why didn't you say something?'

'Live with it,' Demi said as she strolled over to the man behind the reception desk. *'Ehetekenathomatia?'* – do you have a vacancy? They booked in, paying for one night's stay, and flopped almost exhausted onto the single beds. There was little in the way of furniture: a table under the window and two wicker chairs. The single beds looked comfortable with crisp white sheets. They had eaten on the plane, so decided sleep as the best thing given their early start in the morning. Pat hid the attaché case under his mattress for safekeeping, then climbed into bed. He listened to the sounds of Piraeus harbour drifting in through the window: gulls screeching, horns blasting, the chug, chug of small fishing boats heading out to sink lobster pots. With no air conditioning, the room felt stifling, perspiration appearing on his face. Heavy, tired eyes soon closed and he drifted off into a deep sleep.

The following morning Pat and Demi made their way to the harbour. As the third largest port in Europe in terms of passenger traffic, the place was a hive of activity. The motor traffic barely crawled along. Ahead of them, they spied the large ferry moored to the quayside, resembling an ocean liner. At the shipping office, they bought two tickets for the sailing to the Dodecanese islands in the Aegean Sea. Pat read the leaflet that came with the tickets.

'I thought you said this was a fast ferry,' he waved the leaflet under her face. 'It's a fifteen-hour trip. I've been on shorter cruises.'

'I didn't say it was fast, the taxi driver did. Maybe fifteen hours *is* fast to them. Who knows, maybe they had to row it before.' Pat glimpsed at Demi with a curl to his mouth.

They made themselves comfortable in one of the ship's cafés and Pat ordered them coffee with cakes for breakfast. The sun radiated its heat in the clear, azure blue sky. Within an hour of being on board, the ship gave a long blast on its horn then slowly headed out to sea.

***

Abraham Steinberg met with Rebekah in the office of his Cardiff jewellery store. Rebekah had wanted to speak with her father about the diamonds, about how they'd been stolen from a train in 1965.

'Do you realise it was Laine's grandfather who was partially responsible for the theft of the stones, along with his uncle?' Rebekah said. Steinberg shook his head. 'Incredible. They were train robbers?'

'Yes, almost. Well, legally theft, not robbery. Therefore, Laine feels his relatives were cheated out of the diamonds as they were meant to provide his grandparents with a happy retirement.' Rebekah then explained about the involvement of the undertaker, Arnold Beers.

'What happened to him?'

'Well,' Rebekah continued, 'he was apparently killed by Laine's grandfather.'

'My God! Murderers as well as thieves. No wonder Laine's the thug he is today.' Steinberg rose from his chair, and pacing the room he said, 'The audacity of this man to think he can now claim them as his own because his grandfather stole them in the first place.'

Rebekah watched her father, tempted to remind him the diamonds were the property of an insurance company, so not legally his. She knew she could never persuade him to see sense of, so she chose instead to explain to him the dangers of crossing a man like Barry Laine.

'Father, if this man wants the diamonds, then I don't think anyone will stand in his way. He's a dangerous individual with people on his payroll who'll carry out his dirty work with no trace back to him. Laine's far too smart to ever allow the finger of blame to be pointed at him.' Rebekah paused to let this sink in before continuing.

'The police have never succeeded in charging him with crimes they know he's responsible for, directly or indirectly, including murder. He's a ruthless gangster.'

Steinberg listened to his daughter's concerns, fully aware of the type of man he was up against. He had two options: one he would share with his daughter, the other he would keep to himself. He stood behind her, placing his hands on the back of her chair.

'Rebekah, I would like you to arrange a meeting with this Mr Laine. Tell him I would like to negotiate a deal with him.'

'Deal?' Rebekah said, turning quickly. 'What kind of deal?'

Steinberg returned to his desk and opened a drawer, retrieving a bundle of banknotes.

'This kind of deal,' he said dropping the notes onto the desk. 'It's the only kind of language people like Laine understands.'

Rebekah noticed the top note was a fifty.

'I want to offer him a payment that will hopefully buy him off.'

'How much is there?' Rebekah asked anxiously, looking at the large bundle of cash in front of her.

'Fifty thousand pounds,' Steinberg said lifting the bundle, waving it lightly in his hand. 'All used notes and tax free.' He smiled back at her, pleased with his plan.

'Father, I get the impression Laine isn't in this for the money. Fuck! He's probably far richer than you.'

Steinberg flinched at the unexpected profanity from his daughter.

'He's in this to finish something his grandfather started many years ago,' she added.

Steinberg shook his head. 'Rebekah, I think you may be underestimating this villain. He's in it for the money. Everything this man does is for money – money, power, and greed. His grandfather is long dead so it's not as if he's going to hand the diamonds over to him.'

He leaned forward, crossing his hands before resting his chin on them.

'I am prepared to go to a hundred thousand should he want to negotiate a better offer,' Steinberg said. Rebekah sighed, knowing she was not going to discourage her father.

'How would you like me to set up this meeting?' Rebekah asked beginning to feel uneasy with the whole idea. 'Do I invite him here or will you go to his place? Please, don't tell me you'll meet him alone. I'll go with you to any meeting – if I'm with you he's unlikely to do anything foolish.'

'I do not intend seeing this man on my own,' Steinberg assured. 'So your presence won't be necessary when I do. Tell him I'll meet him on his terms, wherever he wants, so long as it's in public.'

Rebekah looked at her father with an expression of concern. 'Who'll go with you? Izzy or Michael?'

'I have someone very reliable in mind,' Steinberg replied as he sat back in his red leather chair.

Rebekah left the dimly lit office and called Laine, saying someone wanted to meet with him to discuss the matter of the diamonds and asking him to trust her regarding the meeting.

***

'Trust a fucking solicitor?' Laine said, waving his phone at Lennie. 'When did anyone trust solicitors?'

Lennie was preparing to leave for Rhodes. He had returned from London with the information they needed on the whereabouts of Pat Doyle and the woman. Laine had told him to arrange to leave for the Greek island immediately as they may try to dispose of the gems in Rhodes.

'I don't get this at all,' Laine said. 'These diamonds go missing in nineteen sixty-five. They show up now and every motherfucker knows about them and wants a piece of the action. What the hell's going on?'

'So what's with the brief?' Lennie asked. 'What's she after?' He checked his passport and money before placing them in an inside pocket of his jacket. 'Anything I need to know about?'

'She wants to set up a meeting; someone wants to discuss the diamonds with me. That's all she'd say. Any idea who this might be?'

'Not a clue, boss. You want me to try and find out?'

He stared at Lennie, trying to decide the best course of action to take. He preferred to have his minder with him when he went into unknown situations. He considered not sending him to Greece until after this meeting, if he decided to go along with it. On the other hand, he needed to ensure the return of the diamonds before Doyle had a chance to dispose of them. He made his decision.

'I want you back here by Saturday, Leonard, with the stones. That's two days. It's not a fucking holiday, d'you hear? If I decide on the meet, I'll take some of the boys with me.'

Laine slapped his man on the back then went to join his wife for a pre-arranged lunch at a nearby restaurant he owned. He only felt safe in his own establishments. He recalled an attempt on his life a few years back. A rival crime gang had burst into a city centre bar where he'd been drinking, shooting him in the shoulder in what should have been a head shot. A lucky escape. Since then, Laine only frequented his own places with the safety of his armed minders around him.

Lennie had arranged a flight out to Rhodes. The jeweller's address was on the business card he'd taken from the man whose throat he'd cut. Finding the shop would be simple. Knowing the restrictions on flying, he'd travel unarmed, but would buy a decent knife as soon as he landed on the island. A knife he planned to leave behind before his return home, planted firmly between the shoulder blades of Dr Patrick Doyle.

Twenty-Five

The ferry docked at the harbour side in the port of Rhodes. Pat and Demi stood on the upper deck watching as the majority of the passengers prepared to disembark. Pat pointed out the two statues of the deer each side of the entrance to Mandraki harbour, telling Demi that the famous Colossus of Rhodes was reputed to have stood there in ancient times.

'It was one of the Seven Wonders of the World, a statue of the God Helios, over a hundred feet high.'

'What, and it stood there?' Demi pointed at the gap in the harbour wall.

'According to the legend but I don't think so. It was probably inland. There's no way the ancient Rhodians could have built it there.'

'So where is it now?'

'Well,' Pat continued, 'it supposedly fell after an earthquake. Given it was made mainly from bronze it probably disappeared bit by bit over the next few hundred years, no doubt put to other uses.'

'Wow!' Demi said leaning on the ship's rail, staring back at the two columns trying to imagine the huge statue.

'Demi,' Pat called to her. 'We need to go.'

They headed for the gangway to leave the ferry. Demi made a few enquiries with some locals. 'Come on,' Demi said pulling on his sleeve, 'the old town's just a few minutes away.' A fierce sun beat down on them from a cloudless sky as they headed towards Mandraki.

'The shop's called *Rodos Gold,'* Pat said reading the details from a business card Andreas had given him.

As they walked, he looked towards the Palace of the Grand Masters in the distance. He knew some of its history; it was built by the Knights of St John in the 14th century. Demi walked over to a restaurant to ask a young Greek waiter where they could find *Rodos Gold.* Just a few minutes away, he said, smiling after her as she walked back towards Pat.

'There it is,' Demi said excitedly, pointing to a sign with the shop's name in large, gold letters. The shop had two windows each side of the door. The displays showed off a mix of gold and silver jewellery. One section boasted a collection of luxury watches with names such as TAG Heuer, Omega and Cartier.

They pushed open the heavy glass door, stepping inside the cool, air-conditioned interior. A man serving an American tourist looked up smiling. Pat wandered around the shop with its glass cases displaying more jewellery: wedding rings, engagement rings, and bracelets inlaid with gemstones such as ruby, sapphire and diamond.

The American tourist left.

'Can I help you, please?' the owner asked in accented English. He stood small in stature, with a dark-skinned face and jet-black hair. A black moustache hid the top of his mouth. Demi greeted him in Greek. Pat raised one hand saying, 'Hello.'

'Demetra,' the man almost shouted. 'Come in, come in. I am Stefanos.' He beckoned them to come by the counter into a back room. He gave Demi a kiss then shook Pat by the hand.

'Andreas told me to expect you. I thought you were not coming. That something happen to you, like Andreas.'

'Happen to Andreas? What happen… I mean *happened* to Andreas?' Demi stammered. After sitting down, Stefanos told them about the man who'd used a knife to cut Andreas after she and Pat had left for Athens.

'Oh, my God,' Demi said slowly. 'Is he… is he alright?'

'Yes,' Pat added, fearing the worst. 'Is he okay?' They both knew who'd been responsible for the attack on Andreas.

'Yes, yes,' Stefanos said, 'He is fine but still in shock. Aella is worse, so frightened. What is this all about?' he continued. 'Why he do this to my friend?'

'Poor Aella,' Demi said wiping tears from her eyes. 'She must have been terrified. This is all my fault. We should never have gone to their home.' Looking into Pat's face she asked, 'What should we do?'

Pat turned to Stefanos. 'You say he's okay and that's good. But are there any messages for us?'

'No. Only that I must help you as best I can, this man will not get away with the harm he cause to Andreas. There is more bad news, I'm afraid.'

'More?' Demi said, 'Has anyone else been hurt?' A noticeable panic rose in her voice as she thought of her parents and children.

'No. No one else hurt,' Stefanos assured them. 'But this man is maybe coming here. Aella told him you come here to Rhodes. Is not her fault, you understand?'

'We understand perfectly well,' Pat said. He looked back into the shop front almost expecting to see the sinister face of Hatchet Lennie grinning at them through the window.

'Is the front door locked?' he asked almost sheepishly.

'Look, we go to your hotel and plan,' Stefanos told them. 'I already give this much thought. I have a suggestion for you. First, I make quick phone call.'

They made their way back into the shop. Pat placed his hand on Demi's shoulder. 'I'm sure everything will be fine.'

Biting her bottom lip, she nodded, hoping he was right.

Once Stefanos had secured his shop, they made their way to a small hotel on a street corner just outside the old town. Stefanos greeted the owner, telling him his guests had arrived, indicating Pat and Demi standing behind him. Once inside their room they sat around a small table. Pat placed the attaché case on one of the two beds. The heat of the day had raised the temperature in the room to oven-like levels. Pat opened the French doors. A cool breeze fluttered the net curtains into the room. Stefanos indicated for him to return to his seat.

'Please, Pat, come sit,' he patted the chair next to his. 'I know about the diamonds. I will do my best to help. If I can buy them I will, if not, I will advise you where to get the best price.'

Stefanos rubbed his face with his hands. 'But first I want you to listen to my plan.' Pat sat next to him as he reached out to hold Demi's hand.

'Your plan?' he said.

Stefanos nodded. 'It seems this man will stop at nothing to get your diamonds. He will hurt many people in trying, yes?' They nodded their agreement. 'So let him have them,' Stefanos said.

'I agree,' Demi announced pointing to the attaché case on the bed. 'These bloody things have caused too much trouble for all of us. Yeah, let the bastard have them, I say.'

'No, no. I do not mean the gems you carry in that bag,' Stefanos said shaking his head. 'No. I mean let him have *other* diamonds.'

'Other diamonds?' Pat said frowning. 'What *other* diamonds?'

'Ah, you see, this is my plan. Stefanos wagged a finger at them. 'I have made a call to a man I know. A Turkish diamond dealer named Fazil. He will meet us here later with other stones for you to see. I called him before we left my shop.'

Stefanos approached the bed, pointing down at the attaché case.

'Now, please, can I look at the stones you have in your bag?'

'Why, yes of course.' Pat opened the small case removing the pouches. He gently picked up each pouch, tipping the diamonds onto a table next to a reading lamp. The eyebrows of the Greek jeweller rose on seeing them.

'When Andreas said you had some diamonds, I never think this many.' Stefanos took a magnifying glass from his pocket then picked up a round-shaped stone, peering at it closely, turning it slowly between his fingers. Replacing the stone, he picked up another, this one shaped like a pear, but again, meticulously examining it. Stefanos placed it with the others then faced the couple sat opposite him.

'My friends, how much do you know about diamonds?'

'Not as much as you do, I'll wager,' Pat said with a grin.

'I know they cost a lot,' Demi added. 'If you go by the prices in the Clive Ranger diamond shop. So what can you tell us?'

Stefanos spread the stones over the table.

'What you have here are real beauties, all of them. Please, I show you.' Selecting a round shape, he held it up to the light. 'A diamond has four parts,' he explained holding up his hand showing four fingers: 'cut, colour, clarity, and carat. This one is most expensive type – the round. It reflects light, it sparkles more than any other shape. Please, see,' he said handing the stone to Pat.

'Also, they are far more expensive as less is lost when cutting the rough stone, much less than when other shapes are cut. See this.' He selected a pear shape to hand to Demi.

'When you examine a stone, you must look for any flaw,' he continued. 'This could be outside or more so, inside. A flaw such as a dark spot or a cloud. I see no such flaws here. In English they are called *inclusions*,' Stefanos informed. Pat returned his stone to the table.

'Does that mean they're more valuable then?'

Stefanos nodded as he picked up a cushion shape for examination.

'I will need to see them all, then I will tell you a value,' the old Greek said. They watched the jeweller as he carefully studied each stone in turn. Stefanos took a small notebook and pen from an inside pocket of his jacket. He jotted down figures as he examined each one. A note of excitement entered his voice as he examined a larger round shaped stone.

'This cannot be,' Stefanos said. 'I have never seen one like this. Incredible. Very much incredible.' Demi stood up.

'What is it, Stefanos? What cannot be?' The man started to mutter in Greek. Pat looked across the table with a puzzled expression.

'What did he say?'

'He said something about a miracle diamond, rarely seen. I'll ask him.'

Demi spoke in Greek to Stefanos who looked up at her. The man responded to the question that Demi translated.

'Stefanos says it's a rare pink diamond. So rare that in all his years as a jeweller he's never seen one. Apparently, it's worth more than all the rest combined.'

'Wow,' Pat declared. 'Does he know how much exactly?' Pat became more excited at the prospect. 'Ask him if he knows how much.' Stefanos replied to her question shaking his head as he spoke.

'He cannot say for sure. We'll have to take it to a dealer who specialises in such stones, possibly in Antwerp or London.'

Pat looked over towards Stefanos.

'These diamonds are worth nearly half a million pounds by my calculation,' he told the jeweller. 'Are you saying this one stone is worth as much?'

Stefanos nodded his agreement.

'This is what I think,' he confirmed. 'Experts say there is only one coloured diamond for every ten thousand colourless diamond. In 2002, the average cost per carat of a pink diamond stood at thirteen thousand pounds. This year it topped seventy-eight thousand. This rare pink is easy a five-carat stone, so three hundred and ninety thousand pounds.'

'Shit,' Demi said almost falling back into her chair.

'I will be honest, I never expected so many diamonds, and now this one.' Stefanos held the pink stone, gazing at it in admiration. 'I cannot possibly buy all these from you. I suggest you take them to Antwerp. There, you should obtain best price.'

They sat silently in the warm and stuffy room, the light fading as the sun slowly set. Outside, the sound of crickets mingled with the traffic noises on the street below. A knock at the door startled them.

'Jeez,' Demi hissed. 'Who's this?' The jeweller waved his hands in a frantic motion.

'Be still. It will be my friend, Fazil.' Stefanos opened the door to a rotund man wearing an over-sized white linen suit, a case in one hand, a handkerchief in the other. Although bald on top, he also sported a large black moustache the same as Stefanos. Using the handkerchief, Fazil mopped his brow and head, both glistening with perspiration.

Pat stood. 'Mr Fazil, so pleased to meet you.'

Stefanos showed the Turk to a chair then poured him a glass of water. The Turk slowly whistled as his eyes fell on the diamonds. 'Allah be praised! I am seeing a fortune here.'

Stefanos nodded, 'A fortune indeed.' Pat decided against revealing the pink diamond that he'd placed out of sight under a pillow.

'I have brought what you asked of me, my friend,' Fazil said to Stefanos. Opening the case, he removed a box. Lifting the lid, Fazil showed them a large quantity of clear stones. Pat looked over at the two men. 'I don't understand. *More* diamonds?'

'All is not what it seems, my friend,' Fazil said. 'Here, take this, compare it with one of the stones you have.' Pat took a cushion shaped stone from the Turk then picked up a similar stone from the table. He peered at them closely. Shaking his head he announced, 'I don't get it – they look the same to me.' As he handed them across to Demi, Stefanos leapt from his seat.

'Please, do not mix them,' he said. 'What Fazil has brought here are not genuine diamonds. They are fake diamonds.'

Fazil nodded in agreement. 'Simulants,' he said.

Demi lowered her head towards the large pile of stones in the box, gently pushing at them with her index finger.

'Stimulants? You mean they're not real?'

'No,' Fazil corrected her. 'Simulants. Synthetic stones made in Russia. They contain many of the same properties of natural diamonds. Even jewellers such as Stefanos here will have difficulty telling them apart from the real thing.'

Stefanos nodded excitedly. 'This is so, my friends, they are very convincing, yes?'

Stefanos selected a stone from the box, holding it between them. 'These stones are the best fakes in the world. They are hand cut and flawless. Take them, let the black man have them. He will think they are real and take them back to his boss. Who is to know any different?'

'What happens when they discover the stones really are fake?' Demi said. 'They'll come after us again.'

'Has this man ever seen your diamonds?' Stefanos asked.

'No, no, he's never seen them,' Pat confirmed.

'So you give him these diamonds, he won't know any different. Believe it; if they can fool me, then the others who want them can also be fooled, for sure. They may even think your diamonds were always fake.'

Demi nodded her head, smiling.

'Brilliant. I think they would fall for that. Pat, d'you think they will?'

Pat could feel himself perspiring in the humidity. He considered it a risk worth taking. He looked at the Turk who grinned back at him, beads of sweat dripping from his dark face.

'Are they pricey?' he asked.

Stefanos frowned. 'What is pricey?'

'*Posokani*?' Demi translated. 'How much?'

'Ah yes, how much.' Stefanos understood. 'They are not costing much,' he assured them. 'You will need the same amount as you have here.' He looked across towards Demi for clarification.

'Forty-eight,' she told him. Stefanos turned towards Fazil.

The Turk slowly rubbed his chin for a moment then announced, 'One thousand euros. This is good price; much less than my usual cost for such quality stones.'

'Pat shook his head. 'We don't have that kind of money. We only have what is left from the loan Andreas kindly gave us.'

Stefanos waved his hands at them.

'No, no, my friends, I will settle with Fazil. You will pay me again. Do not worry about this.' Pat felt quite humbled by this second act of generosity from Greek people willing to help them. He hoped he would be in a position to settle his debt with them when the diamonds eventually sold. Stefanos turned to the Turk and spoke about the arrangement between them. Fazil smiled, nodding enthusiastically; between them, they selected forty-eight synthetic stones and put them in a brown envelope, before handing it over to Pat. Both men stood, shook hands, then crossed to the door. Pat leaned into Demi to whisper.

'I thought Greeks and Turks disliked each other.'

'Only in Cyprus,' she told him. 'Anyway, they're businessmen. Money bridges many divides or something like that.' He nodded his understanding before Stefanos returned to the centre of the room.

'Now, my friends,' he beckoned to them. 'You must leave tomorrow. The man on his way here will arrive soon, and then you will be in great danger. I must go now, please take care.'

They thanked him, bidding him farewell at the room door. Pat locked the door then pushed a chair against it – just in case. He felt tired and worn. Noticing his reflection in a mirror, he could see the tension in his face. Demi came up behind him, holding him around his waist.

'Don't worry,' he assured her. 'This will all be over soon, even if we end up giving in to Barry Laine.'

'We've bloody well come this far so I'm not giving up yet,' she responded. 'You heard what Stefanos said, one of the diamonds is worth a fortune on its own. We could give the others to Laine then sell the pink one for ourselves. What'd you think?'

Pat turned to face her. 'It's an idea worth considering.' He paused before continuing, 'Except I want to beat that bastard, not let him have the satisfaction of getting his grubby hands on any of the diamonds thinking he's beaten us. We'll return to Athens in the morning for the first available flight to anywhere.'

He slumped into the small chair where he thought about their next move. Demi lay on one of the beds. Nightfall dimmed the room. He sat in the encroaching darkness thinking about his life so far. He could hear the sound of disco music playing in a nearby bar. A buzzing Tuk Tuk passed below the window. Pat felt he had changed over the last number of days, no longer prepared to let things pass him by. No longer would he tolerate the demands of others, least of all Barry Laine. His ex-wife had always tried to dictate his life for him. Do this, go there, do that. He thought of Demi. The last week had brought them so much closer together. Whatever happens from here on, he thought, life will never be the same.

***

Hatchet Lennie arrived in Rhodes on an island hopper flight from Athens the following afternoon. He found conditions on the flight cramped due to his bulk, whilst also enduring two noisy children travelling with a family who sat in front of him. With no baggage, he left the airport quickly and headed straight for the address printed on the card in his pocket. Within an hour of landing, he was outside the jewellery shop owned by Stefanos. Before he entered, he looked around the area, spotting just what he needed. The shop he chose sold gifts and souvenirs as well as a range of medieval knives, daggers, and swords. He selected a 12-inch dagger plus an imitation Browning semi-automatic ball-bearing pistol that looked convincingly real to the untrained eye.

Making his way back to the jewellery shop, Lennie entered and locked the door behind himself. There was no one inside except the owner standing behind the counter. Stefanos had been waiting for Lennie's arrival and had a story prepared that would hopefully send the man down a blind alley.

Lennie wasted no time with meaningless introductions. He would get the information he needed and leave. Lennie stepped behind the counter and pushed Stefanos into the back room, sat him on a chair then shoved the gun hard against the man's head. Through clenched teeth, Lennie rasped a question at him,

'Where's the man who came to see you earlier with the diamonds?'

'Diamonds? Man?' I…I don't…'

'Don't fuck with me, old man,' Lennie cut in, 'I've already sliced one Greek.'

Lennie took the knife from his waistband, pushing the tip into the man's neck. 'Right, I'll ask you one more time. Did

216

the man and his woman friend come to see you with a stash of diamonds?'

Stefanos made the mistake of hesitating. Lennie hit him hard across the face; the man fell heavily to the floor from the force of the blow, lying foetus-like as kicks drove into his stomach. He cried out. 'Please, please! I tell you what you want.'

Lennie grabbed the man's throat, squeezing hard. Stefanos began to choke, tongue protruding from his open mouth, as he gagged for air. Tears streamed from Stefano's eyes, as blood dripped from a split lip. Lennie lifted him to his feet with considerable ease, holding the gun to the man's head, wishing it was real so he could pull the trigger, wishing he could watch the old Greek's brain cover the wall behind him.

'Yes, yes,' Stefanos cried out as Lennie loosened his grip. 'They were here but now they have left, gone to Venice.' He gasped for breath. The room began to spin as a wave of nausea came over him.

Lennie pulled him closer.

'How'd I know you ain't a lying little bastard, and they're still here somewhere? How'd I know they're not heading somewhere else just so you can send me on a fucking wild goose chase, eh?'

Spittle formed on Lennie's mouth as he raged with anger at the helpless Stefano.

'Tell me where they are or you're fucking dead, got that?'

Lennie swapped the gun for the knife. The blade glistened under the fluorescent light. Although not sharp, it looked menacing as he slashed the air in front of Stefanos face.

Stefanos nodded. 'I have the name of the hotel, booked it myself. I also paid for the flight. Look, here is the receipt.' He leant over, opened a drawer, and produced the receipt Pat had given him in anticipation of this event. Lennie snatched it from the man's hand. After a glance he appeared satisfied with it. A hard push sent the old man across the room. Stefanos fell badly to the floor.

Lennie snarled, 'Bollocks!' He knew he had to break this news to Barry Laine. He looked down at Stefanos. 'How did they get to Venice?'

'They went from here to Athens, there onto Venice.'

'When did they leave? What flight?'

'This morning, an early flight, I took them myself.'

Moving closer, Lennie pointed the knife at the old man still cowering over his counter.

'And the diamonds?'

'They have them. They will sell them in Venice.'

'So why didn't you buy them? You're a jeweller.'

'I don't have the kind of money they are worth. I did offer to buy some,' Stefanos lied, 'but they wanted to keep them together. Worth more that way, you understand?'

Lennie's eyebrows rose. Intrigued, he pondered a golden opportunity for his own benefit.

'So how much are they worth exactly?'

'Well over half a million Euros,' Stefanos told him, 'Likely more.'

'Half a million,' Lennie whispered to himself.

He considered what he could do with that kind of money – move to the Caribbean, live the highlife. Jamaica maybe. Laine would never reach him there. Lennie made a decision: he'd follow Doyle to Venice, and to hell with Barry Laine. For once, Lennie decided, he was going to be his own man. He looked down at the jeweller who'd slid back to the floor.

'Hey, dude, it's your lucky day.'

Lennie's fist struck the man's face, smiling as he heard the satisfying crunch of breaking bone. After dropping the dagger on the table next to the gun, Lennie walked back onto the street looking for a taxi to take him to the airport.

Twenty-Six

Barry Laine had agreed to meet Steinberg at the Café Royal on the High Street. As this was not an establishment owned by Laine, he had three of his men in the place, one sat with him whilst two sat on a near-by table. Heavy set men with shaved heads, one wore sunglasses despite the dimness of the restaurant.

Abraham Steinberg arrived, accompanied by Ben Wiener.

Wiener wore a long black overcoat that disguised his physique. On his head, he wore a wide-brimmed black fedora. He also wore glasses with heavy black frames but the lenses were clear. This was another element of his disguise – an attempt to mask the strength of his face, to appear weak. Wiener was anything but weak. As he entered the restaurant with Steinberg, Wiener took in everything around him, becoming immediately aware of the two men sat at a table drinking only water; he surmised they were with Laine, who rose from his seat as Steinberg and Wiener approached.

'Ah, Mr Steinberg,' Laine said. 'So glad to make your acquaintance.'

Laine raised a hand to attract a waiter who placed menus on their table.

'I'm delighted you have agreed to meet me today,' Steinberg said. 'Allow me to introduce my associate, Mr Wiener.' Wiener simply nodded an acknowledgment. Laine smiled back at the imposing man sitting opposite who had not even removed his hat. Laine did not bother to introduce the man sitting next to him.

'Mr Laine,' Steinberg continued, 'I understand you are interested in acquiring items that once belonged to my family, that *still* belong to my family. Am I correct?'

Laine drummed his fingers on the table as he considered what Steinberg had said. Aware that Wiener was staring at him, he felt uneasy.

'Mr Steinberg, I'm also *delighted* we're having this meeting. I hope we can come to a satisfactory arrangement today.'

Steinberg looked down at the table then back to Laine before replying.

'The only arrangement, as I see it, is you telling me when you will return…' he hesitated, thinking carefully about his next words, 'the diamonds that were stolen from my family business many years ago.'

After a few moments of silence between them Steinberg continued.

'I am led to believe it was your grandfather who was responsible for the theft. I am prepared to overlook this. I bear no grudge against you personally, Mr Laine. The sins of the fathers shall *not* be visited upon the sons,' he quoted. 'Do you understand?'

Laine wanted to slap the man opposite. *Do I understand,* he reflected?

'Mr Steinberg, you do realise that I know where the diamonds are right now, and therefore I'll decide if you should have them or not. We are both businessmen,' he said raising his hands, 'so let's do business.'

'What do you have in mind, Mr Laine?'

Laine tapped the side of his forehead twice with his index finger.

'I have money in mind, Mr Steinberg, and lots of it.'

Wiener now spoke. He pointed a finger directly at Laine. 'Why should we pay *you* money for what rightfully belongs to us?'

Who the hell is this man? Laine wondered again. He's not a minder. Minders don't get involved. Laine smiled at them both.

'You are paying, shall we say, for my services. Without me, you may never see the diamonds. I can arrange for them to be with you in a number of days, at a favourable price, of course.'

Steinberg nodded. 'Of course. So, what kind of price? There will be a limit on how much I'm prepared to pay for them.'

'Sure,' Laine said. 'So what are you prepared to pay?'

'Thirty thousand pounds – cash.'

'Nothing like enough,' Laine responded quickly. Steinberg hesitated.

'Okay, Mr Laine. Fifty thousand and that's stretching it.'

Wiener leant over to whisper in Steinberg's ear. Steinberg listened and nodded.

'What did he just say?' Laine demanded.

'Only that I stay at fifty, not a penny more,' Steinberg said.

Laine rose from his chair.

'Sorry, Mr *S*. If you want the stones, you'll have to do better than that. Good day to you both.'

He turned to walk away, his minders in tow.

'Mr Laine,' Steinberg called after him. 'One hundred thousand.'

Laine turned to face the two men, slowly walking back to their table where he placed his hands on the back of a chair.

'A hundred grand?' Laine said nodding. A very generous offer, Mr *S*.' He paused. 'I'll consider it.'

Wiener removed his glasses. His dark eyes locked on Laine's eyes.

'When exactly will we get the diamonds if you agree to accept Mr Steinberg's *more* than generous offer?'

Laine tore his eyes away to look at Steinberg. 'I'm expecting one of my men to deliver them within the next twenty-four hours,' Laine said. 'As soon as he does, I'll be in touch.'

Barry Laine then left the restaurant without turning back.

***

Laine stormed back into his city centre premises. 'Where the hell is Lennie?'

One of the men at the back of the showroom made his way over.

'Sorry, guv, no word yet.'

'Give me a phone,' Laine demanded.

The man took his mobile from a pocket and passed it over. After a few moments, Laine threw it back.

'Fucking answering machine,' he spat.

'You want me to try again, maybe leave a message, guv?'

'Yeah,' Laine agreed. 'You tell him I want him back here with those fucking stones.'

'I'm sure he'll be here soon, boss,' his driver reassured. 'You know Lennie. Could be there's no signal.'

'Well go on, try his number again,' Laine ordered. 'He'll never answer if you just stand there gawping.'

Laine began to wonder if his minder would try to double cross him. Once Lennie had the diamonds, he could easily take off, never to return. If he were to do this, he'd be dead. Laine also thought about the girl. He wanted her as well as the diamonds. She would be a big pull in one of his many massage parlours. He needed more women like her as the competition was fierce. Massage parlours were opening everywhere with mostly east European girls, forcing prices down. The driver redialled but received the same prompt telling him to leave a message. He did.

He looked back towards Laine and shrugged his shoulders.

***

Steinberg and Wiener watched as Laine left the restaurant with his minder. The other men sitting at another table followed him out. Wiener took in their every detail, noticing the bulges in their jackets, their height and build. They were amateurs who probably carried pop guns. Wiener's gun wasn't so obvious: a 9mm Sig Sauer P226R, one of the best handguns on the market. He preferred the 226R as it not only accepted a suppressor, it also carried fifteen rounds in its magazine. He'd collected the handgun from a safety deposit box in London when he'd arrived from New York, left there after his one and only visit. He kept similar weapons in various cities around the world for this very reason. He also carried a Fairbairn Sykes 'fighting knife' in a leather sheath with leg straps. He'd calculated if he'd needed to act, he would have first taken out the man sat next to Laine. He doubted Laine carried any kind of weapon; he paid others to do that for him. He would then have put a bullet in the head of each of the men opposite before they had the chance to stand up. It would have been over very quickly.

He turned to Steinberg. 'Abe, why'd you offer him that much? He'd have taken less. I figure he'll ask for more now. Then what you gonna do?'

'Sure,' Steinberg replied. 'But that's my final offer, like I said, not a penny more.'

'D'you know something, Abe, I get the feeling he ain't got those rocks. There was something in his eyes that told me he was bullshitting.'

'He doesn't have them *yet*,' Steinberg agreed. 'But he says he will have them soon. We just have to wait until he gets back to us.'

Wiener began to think. 'Okay,' he said. 'So who does have them? If we can figure that out, we could by-pass that *putz* then do a deal with this other guy, maybe a better deal. Ask Rebekah, she seems to know who this other person is.'

'I'll get in touch with her,' Steinberg agreed. A waiter handed them menus recommending the dish of the day. 'Honey roast ham with seasonal vegetables,' he said, pen and pad ready.

The two men smiled at each other. 'We've changed our minds,' Steinberg said handing back the menus.

***

Pat and Demi flew from Athens to Venice, then on to the *Antony* hotel situated close to the airport. The large hotel would be ideal for their plan. Pat left details of their scheme with Stefanos back in Rhodes. When Lennie turned up at his shop, Stefanos would tell him whatever he wanted to know so that he'd follow them to Venice.

Once checked in they made their way to a room on the eighth floor with a magnificent view of the Venetian lagoon. Demi took the pouches out of the attaché case, handing them to Pat who put them in his pockets. The fake stones he placed inside the case then put the case in a drawer.

Demi stared out of the window towards the ancient buildings of Venice. The structure of Saint Mark's Campanile – the bell tower that stood in front of the Basilica of San Marco – reared prominently in the distance. Without saying a word, Pat joined her at the window. He stopped just close enough for her to feel the warmth of his breath in her hair. She closed her eyes, thinking how much better it would be if he would just wrap his arms around her. It had been a long time since a man had held her affectionately.

'Great view, isn't it?' Pat said. 'See that,' he pointed towards the bell tower. 'The original tower collapsed in nineteen hundred and two. The Venetians built a second tower almost immediately. How about we go across? Maybe visit St Mark's?'

'How long do we have before Lennie gets here?' she asked refocusing her mind on the matter in hand.

Pat checked his watch.

'Six hours, eight at the most. We could check the flights out of Athens to give us a better idea. So, d'you fancy that ride over to Venice?'

'I'd love to. Is this where they have the Leaning Tower?'

Pat smiled at her.

'No, that's Pisa, a different part of Italy altogether.'

'Yeah, I tend to get them mixed up,' Demi said laughing. 'I never knew about you being a doctor,' she said, changing the subject. 'I think Pat Doyle's a bit of a dark horse.' She tilted her head. 'So how come you're a social worker?'

'I studied history many years ago,' Pat explained. 'My particular area of interest is South Wales following the

226

industrial revolution. I did my PhD at Swansea University… I wanted to lecture but it didn't pay the bills after my marriage ended. I went into social work for a regular salary.'

'After your marriage ended?' Demi said surprised. 'You were married? D'you have any children?'

'Fortunately, no,' Pat said. 'Both too busy with work. Might have been nice though,' he added.

Demi stared at him, making him feel uncomfortable. Walking away from the window he picked up his phone. Taking a piece of paper from his pocket, he punched in the number for Stefanos, waiting for the ring tone at the other end. Stefanos answered. Pat was relieved to hear he was okay. Stefanos didn't tell him how he'd been beaten and needed hospital treatment.

'The man left for the airport once I'd told him you had gone to Venice. He will be there very soon. You must take care of yourself, my friend. Please, take care of little Demetra. He is dangerous. A monster.'

Pat thanked him before ending the call, feeling decidedly uncomfortable about the monster reference. He turned to Demi.

'I think Stefanos is okay. He did sound a bit shaky though.'

Demi looked at him with concern.

'Lennie is heading for Venice,' Pat told her. 'We'll leave the fakes in the drawer then go out. We can keep an eye on the hotel around the time his flight lands. He'll easily locate this hotel room, I'm sure.'

Opening a drawer, Pat checked the attaché case inside then turned back to Demi. 'Right, let's go see the sights.'

They took a water taxi near to Saint Mark's Square. Demi marvelled at the architecture as they strolled amongst the imposing medieval buildings. The place teemed with tourists, many taking photographs. When they'd seen enough of the city, Pat took Demi's arm.

'Come on,' he said, 'let's make a move back to the hotel. If the flight is on time from Athens, Lennie should arrive fairly soon.'

Given the quiet reception area, they decided to wait at a nearby bar across from the hotel's entrance.

It was no time before Demi spotted Lennie making his way towards the hotel.

'Look, he's here,' Demi hissed.

Pat, who was reading a menu, wincing at the prices, looked up.

'Shit,' Demi added. 'What if he's seen us.'

Taking her hand, he gave it a light squeeze.

'Don't worry, he didn't.'

'D'you think he'll find them?' she asked. 'What if he can't get into the room?'

'Oh, he'll find no difficulty with that,' Pat said. 'Even if it means kicking down the door. As soon as he comes out, we should know if he has them. He'll go straight to the airport and take the first flight to London.'

***

Inside the hotel, Lennie Randall made his way to the check-in desk, holding a €50 note in his hand ready to pay for the information he needed. He had little trouble finding out the room number. On the eighth floor, he spotted a hotel cleaner with a trolley. He told her he'd lost his entry card for his room. She overcame her initial reluctance to open the door when he produced another €50 note. As there was little in the way of furniture in the small room, Lennie soon discovered the diamonds in one of the drawers. Satisfied with the ease of his search, he helped himself to two miniature bottles of Jack Daniels from the minibar then left.

***

Pat and Demi peered over their menu cards, continuing to survey the hotel entrance.

'Lennie's coming out,' Demi said. 'He's got the case with him. Jeez, he didn't waste any time.'

Pat moved from his seat when he noticed Lennie wave his hand.

'He's stopped a taxi. Quick, let's go.'

The pair walked out of the bar and hailed another taxi. Jumping in the back they asked the driver to follow the taxi not far in front. Keeping a safe distance, they followed it into Marco Polo airport.

Once inside the concourse they kept Lennie in sight as he headed for the flight desks.

'Hey, now that's interesting,' Pat observed.

'What is?' Demi asked.

'He's at the KLM Dutch airline desk.'

'So?'

'So he's not going to London. But why fly to the Netherlands?' Pat paused, then turned to Demi excitedly. 'Antwerp!'

***

After Lennie had gone through the departure gate, they immediately returned to the hotel in order to plan their next move. Once back in the room, Pat took the diamonds from his pockets, tipping them onto the bed. Now they were aware of the pink diamond's potential value it seemed to stand out from the others. Picking it up, Demi softly kissed it before placing it back down.

'So how come Lennie didn't catch a plane for London?' she asked.

'I really do believe our friend may be pulling a fast one on Barry. He's going to try and sell those fake stones in Antwerp. Why else would he go there of all places?'

'What happens when he finds out they're almost worthless?' Demi said. 'I'd like to be a fly on the wall when that happens.'

Pat nodded. 'I don't think we're held in high esteem as it is. When he's thrown out of some swanky diamond shop, he's going to like us even less.'

They both laughed at the thought of Lennie's reaction as he was shown the door at some exclusive premises in the diamond district of Antwerp.

Later, as they made their way out of their room, Pat's phone rang. They looked down at the device on the table. It vibrated along with the ring tone. Pat decided to answer the call. As the screen displayed a number he didn't recognise, he tentatively raised the phone to his ear.

'Hello.'

A female voice responded.

'Patrick Doyle?'

'Yes, who is this, please?'

'You don't know me,' the voice said. 'My name's Rebekah Rosen. I'm a solicitor in Cardiff. Are you free to speak?'

Pat waved towards Demi, indicating for her to return. She crossed the room and mouthed, *who is it?*

'Yes, I can speak,' Pat said. 'What's this about?' he asked.

'It's about how I might be able to help you. Rosen is my marriage name. It *was* Steinberg. Does that name mean anything to you?'

'Yes, I know the name Steinberg. Why?'

'Diamonds, Mr Doyle, though I think you already knew that,' Rebekah told him. 'I would like to meet up with you, to discuss this further. Where are you now?'

'Wait, hold on a minute, you could be anyone. How did you get my number?'

'Of course, my apologies. I'll give you the number for my office. Better still *Google* it then call me back. The firm is Hilton, Burns and Blakemore on Churchill Way. Our website has me listed as an associate. I'm here right now if you want to call back. Ask to be put through to me direct, I'll tell the receptionist to expect your call.

He turned towards Demi. A look of dread covered her face as she asked,

'Who was that? Barry Laine?'

'No. A solicitor, or so she claimed. I'm to call her back. She wants to talk about the diamonds.'

'How does she know about the diamonds? I don't like this, Pat. She probably works for Laine.'

'You could be right,' Pat agreed. 'Just because she says she's a solicitor means nothing. She may well be working for Laine.' He saved the number then switched off the phone.

'That's all we need,' Pat said, 'another person after the diamonds. Come on, let's go.'

Twenty-Seven

On the plane, Lennie chewed over his options. His huge frame just about fitted into the seat of the Fokker 70 City Hopper aircraft, but at least there were no children sat near him. He didn't feel comfortable with his actions. Barry Laine wouldn't think twice about having him wasted for this double cross. For Lennie, the alternative was a life on a West Indian island. Jamaica, Trinidad, or Tobago, lying in the sunshine sipping rum cocktails. Screw Laine and his orders. This would be his time to live the good life. Hell, these diamonds had to be worth close to half a million, he reminded himself. What he could do with that kind of money. Laine would never find him, nor did he give a shit about never returning to Cardiff.

The aircraft started to make its descent, dropping through the clouds until the ground below became visible. Lennie's ample frame jolted in his seat as they hit the tarmac with a bump, the sound of reverse thrust slowing it down with plenty of runway to spare. He peered through the window as the KLM flight taxied to the terminal at Antwerp airport. Within the hour, he would be in the centre of the city where over a thousand of the world's leading diamond retailers would compete for the chance to pay him big bucks for his merchandise. All he had to do now was seize the best deal on offer.

He made his way through customs and immigration to an outside taxi rank, where he settled in the back of the car at the head of the line.

'You speak English?' he asked the driver.

'Yes, I lived in London for many years. Where can I take you?'

'Okay,' Lennie continued, 'I need the diamond district, and a top-notch dealer.'

The car pulled away, heading along a tree-lined avenue for the centre of Antwerp: to *Diamondland*. The driver suggested *Orsini* on the *Avenue De Keyserlei*.

As they travelled, Lennie removed some of the stones from the bag he'd put them in. He'd thrown away the attaché case, preferring to carry the diamonds in his pocket. He smiled to himself as he thought about Doyle and the woman returning to the room only to discover their precious little cache had gone. He wished he'd been able to inflict serious harm upon Doyle, though having the stones more than compensated for that lost opportunity.

The taxi stopped outside the *Orsini* store – one of the best-known jewellers in the city.

'Hey, dude,' Lennie said studying the premises. 'This is a shop. I want to sell, not buy.'

'Yes, sir. This establishment will carry out valuations as well as purchases,' the driver assured him. 'If they're not interested in something they will recommend another dealer in the area who might be.'

Lennie paid off the taxi and stepped inside the plush interior of the store, where his jaw dropped. *Fuck, imagine knocking this place over*, he thought. A young male assistant looked across at the large man who had just entered, walking over to greet Lennie with a courteous smile.

'Good day, sir. My name is Daan. Is there anything in particular I can show you?'

Lennie looked down at the smartly dressed assistant with the smile still fixed to his face.

'Yeah, maybe. D'you buy diamonds?' he asked.

'To be honest, sir, we are a retail business, but we certainly purchase quality stones. Do you have a diamond to sell?'

'More than one,' Lennie said, returning the man's smile. 'Can I show you?' Daan indicated towards a table with cream leather chairs on each side. Lennie tipped the diamonds from the bag onto a black velvet mat. The assistant's eyebrows rose when he saw the large number of stones in front of him, their brilliance accentuated by the blackness of the velvet beneath them. He selected a stone before adjusting a lamp to examine it.

'Are these your diamonds, sir?'

'They certainly are. You interested? 'Cos if you are, how much we looking at?'

Daan looked across at Lennie as he gestured towards the stones sitting between them.

'We would need to establish their authenticity first,' he said. 'But please, with all due respect, sir, we would also need to ensure they are not stolen property. Purely routine, you understand.'

Lennie grinned at the assistant.

'Yeah, I can dig that, so how long will it take?'

'I will need to inform Mr De Groot,' Daan said. 'He's the manager. I will only be a moment. May I take some of the stones to show him?'

'Be my guest,' Lennie agreed. 'I'll take a look around the shop while you're gone.'

Daan selected a number of stones to place in an envelope he'd taken from a small drawer in front of him.

Lennie strolled around the shop, smiling at a young, red-headed female assistant who stood behind one of the counters. He gazed into some of the display cabinets, admiring the fine selection of jewellery, particularly a diamond-studded bracelet. Lennie wondered why there were no price tags when Daan came up behind him.

'A very nice piece, sir. It's from the Leo Pizzo house. You clearly recognise excellence. Would you like to try it?'

'Yeah, maybe later.' He returned to his seat at the table.

'So, the valuation. How long?'

'About twenty-four hours, possibly less,' Daan said. 'We have our own valuators who can calculate the most accurate price. Now, if you'll follow me over to the desk, sir, I'll prepare a receipt. Do you have the name of your hotel?'

'Not yet,' Lennie replied. 'I've only just arrived and I don't plan on staying long.'

'I can recommend the Golden Tulip Hotel,' Daan said. 'It's nearby, where we'll be able to reach you as soon as we receive the valuation. There is of course normally a fee for this service. However, should we decide to purchase then any fee will be waived.'

Daan took a Faber Castell fountain pen from his inside pocket.

'Can I take your name, sir?'

'Smith,' Lennie lied. 'Mr Smith.'

He accepted the receipt from the assistant before handing over the bag with the remainder of the diamonds inside.

'There you go, *Dan,*' Lennie said, mispronouncing his name. 'I'll see you tomorrow.'

Grinning like a child in a toyshop, he left. Once outside, Lennie looked up and down the road, deciding what to do next. A young woman walked past him. Lennie followed her with his eyes, deciding he'd visit the fleshpots of Antwerp and really enjoy his brief stay.

'Tomorrow, Lennie boy,' he told himself. 'If all goes well, I'll buy that diamond bracelet by *Pizza,* maybe a gold Rolex as well.'

***

The patrons in the bar of the Golden Tulip Hotel eyed the man who constantly checked his watch as he downed glasses of beer, muttering to himself. He'd left *Orsini's* about five pm the previous day. It was now mid-afternoon with still no word from them. He pushed his empty glass away then walked out of the hotel, making his way to the jewellery shop. As soon as Lennie entered the shop, Daan went into the back office, returning with another man.

'Good day, sir,' the man said, studying Lennie very carefully. 'My name is Mr De Groot. I'm the manager here at Orsini's.'

'Yeah, nice one,' Lennie grunted. 'I thought you were going to call me. I'm a busy man, I have other business to deal with elsewhere.'

'Indeed,' De Groot said. 'Please, will you join me in my office?'

Lennie followed, sitting in the proffered seat at a large desk where he noticed the diamonds spread out on a green baize cloth. Lennie assumed the stones had only just been returned, that they were about to call him. De Groot, a slight man of about sixty with coiffed, snow-white hair, sat himself down opposite. He wore an impeccably tailored suit befitting his position. On his left wrist, he sported the kind of watch Lennie would like to own, or steal. De Groot's steely blue eyes peered through a pair of frameless glasses.

'It's *Mr Smith*, I believe?'

Lennie nodded, still unsure of the situation.

'May I enquire where you obtained these stones?' De Groot asked.

'Enquire away, Mr Groot, but I ain't telling. All I'll say is they're completely legit, if that's what you're worried about.'

'Not exactly, Mr *Smith*. You see these stones are not what they appear to be.'

De Groot eased back in his chair, placing both hands on the arms.

Lennie furrowed his brow. He looked at the stones then back to De Groot.

'What are you saying, exactly? Where's this going?'

Lennie began to feel a little uneasy. He'd wondered why the little scrotum he saw yesterday didn't deal with him today. Unless the diamonds are worth so much it could only be the manager who handles such transactions?

'You see, Mr *Smith*,' De Groot waved a hand over the stones spread out on the desk. 'These are fakes, not actually diamonds at all…'

'What?' Lennie spat. 'Fakes? What d'you mean, fakes?'

Lennie's screwed face glared at De Groot.

'Please, Mr *Smith*, allow me to finish,' De Groot said calmly. 'There are two points I wish to raise. Firstly, did you buy these believing them to be genuine? If you did, you may be seriously out of pocket. Secondly, if you do know these are fakes, were you going to try and defraud us?'

Lennie could barely speak. His mind raced in all directions, bewildered as he tried to work out what had gone wrong.

'Fakes, as in not real?' Lennie said swallowing hard.

'Precisely,' De Groot confirmed. 'They are known as Russian Brilliants, in other words synthetic diamonds. Quite beautiful to look at, they often pass as the genuine article to many people in my trade.'

De Groot picked up a stone to hold under his desk lamp.

'They have no internal fogging like poorer imitations. They are so good that I, Daan and others also took them to be genuine at first glance.'

De Groot lifted a small black instrument from his desk.

'This is a diamond tester, Mr Smith, extremely reliable, and used throughout the industry. However, we always send larger quantities of precious stones to our nearby laboratory for thorough testing. Sadly for you, Mr Smith, these stones here were revealed as *simulants*.'

'I… I don't understand.' Lennie pushed back his chair and stood. Grabbing a handful of stones, he stared down at them. 'So what are they worth then?'

'Well, as Daan will have told you yesterday, we charge for a valuation.'

'Not if you're buying. *Dan* told me you drop the fee.'

'Mr, umm, *Smith,* we certainly will not be making an offer for these,' De Groot assured him, again waving his hand over the fake stones. 'However, given your predicament I suppose I can make a – how would you say – *ball park figure*?'

'So shoot,' Lennie said.

'About two thousand Euros maximum, depending on the buyer,' De Groot informed him. 'They are indeed used to make good quality jewellery, not that we would ever sell such jewellery, you understand.'

Lennie slumped back down into the chair, his dreams evaporated before him along with the Pizzo bracelet, and Rolex watch. *Oh shit,* he thought*, how do I explain this one to* Barry? De Groot interrupted his ruminating.

'Shall I have these put in a box for you?'

Lennie could barely muster a nod. De Groot pressed a button on his phone,

'Daan, will you arrange a presentation case for Mr Smith's merchandise, please.'

De Groot made his way over to the door. Outside Daan stood with a box that Lennie considered to be worth more than the stones he would place inside it.

***

On his way to the airport Lennie fabricated a story he'd hoped Laine would swallow. From the departure lounge, he phoned his boss to break the news. If this didn't work, he was as good as dead.

'Baz, its Lennie. Jeez, you'll never believe the shit I've had. Anyway, I got the ice. Wow, man.'

'Just where the hell are you? I've been trying to contact you for days.'

'Yeah, yeah. My phone went flat so I bought a new battery. I followed the dudes to fucking Venice from Greece…'

'Venice?' Laine interrupted.

'Yeah. Anyway, I managed to get the rocks from them and booked a flight back to London. I had time on my hands so I had them valued. You know, out of curiosity like.'

'Did you?' 'Why'd d'you do that then, Len?' Laine said quietly, a pent-up fury held back.

'Like I said, curiosity, that's all. Anyway, here's the low down. Turns out the diamonds are phoney.'

Laine listened, even more convinced regarding his earlier theory about Lennie's disloyalty. He didn't want to scare him off with a fit of rage though.

'Leonard, you just get back here with the diamonds, okay?'

'Sure, Baz, I'll be there tomorrow, first thing.'

Laine dropped the phone onto the desk. He pulled open a drawer removing the one diamond Lennie had found at the cemetery. He peered at its radiance, wondering what game Lennie might be playing. Dialling a number, he called one of his men and issued instructions.

***

Climbing out of his Jacuzzi, Laine donned a white towelling robe. He looked longingly at his swimming pool, regretting not having had lessons. The pool cost him over forty grand but only his wife used it, usually with her friends. Now she was at their place in Majorca, spending his money, probably getting laid by Spanish waiters.

Checking the time, he figured Lennie should be arriving about now. This was going to be interesting.

He strolled over to the changing area where he carefully dried himself. Image being everything, the last thing he needed was to look rushed when he confronted Lennie. Fully dressed, he went into the main house. Lennie was at the door with two of his other men. Together they all moved into the semi-darkness of the office. The two men sat on a sofa against the back wall. This left only one chair in front of Laine's desk. Lennie checked the room before sitting opposite his boss. He felt a sense of *déjà vu* recalling his meeting with De Groot less than twelve hours previously. He felt uncomfortable with the two men sitting behind him. He knew them well, between them, they had killed and maimed for Laine on more than one occasion. Lennie began to twitch; at least he had his axe again. He would take out at least one of the bastards if things started to get heavy. He placed the box provided by De Groot on the desk.

'Are these my diamonds?' Laine asked quietly.

'Yeah, boss, but like I said...' Laine raised his hand.

'Quiet,' he ordered. Lifting the box, Laine turned out the contents, spreading the stones around with the palm of his hand.

'So, you say these are phoney? Want to enlighten me a little more, Leonard?'

'Sure, boss. Like I said, I had some spare time so I went into this jewellery shop in Venice. I mean, you'd want to know their value, wouldn't you?'

'Yeah, sure I would, Len, nice of you to go to the trouble,' Laine said glibly.

'No probs. Cost me a hundred euros, then they told me they're fake. Jeez, can you believe that?'

Beads of sweat appeared on his brow. Lennie turned to the men behind him and shrugged. He turned back to face Laine.

'Fake,' he repeated.

Laine lifted a piece of paper to reveal a single diamond underneath. Picking up the stone, he examined it for a moment, turning it slowly between his fingers. Laine felt the unease of the man sitting opposite.

'Len, let's just say I have an itch that I can't scratch.'

Lennie frowned.

'You remember this diamond, Len? The one you found at the cemetery?' Lennie nodded his head once.

'Well, this morning I had it checked out, and guess what?'

Lennie shook his head slowly as more beads of perspiration ran down his face.

'It's the real fucking McCoy, Len. Twenty-four carat – top of the range diamond. Well, three carats to be precise.'

Laine leaned forward, resting his arms on the desk.

'So, tell me, Leonard, how come this little beauty is real, yet according to you and your one hundred Euro check, this pile of glass is shit?'

Lennie thought for a few seconds, knowing he'd been caught out. He used the other part of his story, a part he considered to be possibly nearer the truth.

'Okay, okay. After following Doyle and the woman to Venice, I found their hotel where I managed to get into their room, but they weren't there. After a quick search I found the diamonds in a drawer. Now, thinking back, I asked myself, why didn't Doyle have the diamonds with him, and if he didn't, why weren't they put somewhere safe? Then it dawns on me. They *wanted* me to find the fake stones. So I figured Doyle had got these fakes from somewhere, knowing I was on to them. Stands to reason, eh?'

Laine's facial expression exuded suspicion.

'And you worked this out all by yourself?'

'Sure, boss, on the plane.'

Laine considered the possibilities, along with the plausibility of Lennie's new version, but was still unconvinced. He lifted the box, examining the inside and the underneath before replacing it gently on the desk.

'Okay, Leonard, let's do a quick summary of your achievements so far, shall we? First, you follow Doyle and the woman to London where they manage to give you the slip. Then they take off for Greece. You go after them but they give you the slip, again. Then it's fucking Venice where they fob you off with this crystal chandelier repair kit.'

Laine picked up a few of the stones letting them fall from his hand back onto the desk.

'Then you decide to have a valuation carried out for curiosity?'

Laine reached over, placing his hand on the lid of the box, opening and closing it softly.

'Tell me, Len, did this jeweller take the stones away by any chance?'

Lennie became more anxious as his boss interrogated him from across the desk. He stammered a reply.

'W… well, yes. He took them out back to study them in detail. Apparently, they're so good you need a machine to test them,' Lennie explained.

'Could it be then, the jeweller made the switch, gave you this heap of shit, keeping the real stones for himself?'

'No way, Boss, this was a top-notch establishment. One of the best in Antwerp.'

Laine's eyes widened feigning surprise. 'But I thought you had them valued in Venice? Now you say it's Antwerp.' Laine stood straight, throwing the box across the desk.

'It says Orsini's of Antwerp inside the lid. Do you take me for a fucking fool, Len?' Laine screamed. 'Do you?'

Laine slammed his fist onto the desktop, making the fake diamonds jump, an intensified rage aimed at the man in front of him.

'What the fuck's going on, Len? Does Doyle still have my diamonds? If so, where is he now? Or are you trying to tuck me up? Which is it? The truth, Leonard, *now!*'

Lennie tried to formulate a more plausible explanation. Standing with raised hands, he became aware of the two heavies behind him also on their feet.

'You gotta believe me on this one, Barry,' Lennie pleaded. 'Would I be dumb enough to come back here if I'd tried to pull a fast one? Would I? I came back so you could tell me what to do next. The real stones are still with Doyle, they must be. He can't run forever.'

Laine glared at his number one henchman, a man he trusted with his life. He nodded slowly.

'Okay, Len,' Laine said pointing at him. 'Just this once I'll give you the benefit of the doubt. But, if I ever find you trying to rip me off,' looking across to the other two men, he added, 'this goes for all of you… I'll kill you myself. Now, get out.'

As the three men left the room, Laine sat back in his chair and was about to sweep the false stones off his desk in anger when an idea came to him. Picking up his iPhone, he flicked through the screen.

'Hello, Mr Steinberg? It's Barry Laine. I'm calling to say I've given serious consideration to your offer of a hundred grand for the diamonds, and I accept. One condition however, I only take cash.'

Laine paused, listening.

'So when can we meet?' He listened again then ended the call. Laine put down the phone and gathered up the fake stones before dropping them into the presentation box. A smile widened across his face.

'Now that's what I call a good deal.'

Twenty-Eight

In the hotel restaurant, Pat and Demi ordered *baccalà* with polenta, a seafood dish recommended by the waiter. as 'dish of the day'. Placing the food in front of them, he wished them *buon appetito.*

Before leaving their room earlier, Pat had located the number he'd saved for Hilton, Burns and Blakemore in Cardiff, and immediately called the firm. A receptionist answered, confirming Mrs Rosen did indeed work for the firm, and was in her office expecting his call. The receptionist put the call through to Rebekah Rosen. Their discussion lasted nearly an hour as Rebekah explained how her father wanted the return of the diamonds, that a considerable reward was on offer, and that she would act as an intermediary between him and her father.

'This sounds fine,' Pat said, 'except for one thing.'

'What's that?' Rebekah Rosen asked.

'A man named Barry Laine, a Cardiff gangster. He also knows about the diamonds. Needless to say, this is a man who usually gets what he wants, a man not shy in the use of gratuitous violence.'

'Yes, I'm aware of Mr Laine,' Rebekah Rosen disclosed. 'It was through him, in fact, that I learned of the diamonds in the first place. He's a client of our firm, though not me personally. I can assure you, Mr Doyle, I have no interest in his affairs whatsoever. I am doing this for my father. I have no other reason or motive.'

'A very noble reason, indeed, Mrs Rosen. However, my concern is for the personal safety of my friend and me.'

He threw Demi a smile that she reciprocated.

'I have no intention of upsetting Barry Laine,' Pat continued. 'Maybe the best way would be if I dealt with him directly. If I let Laine have the diamonds then your father could negotiate with him for their return.'

'I fully appreciate your concern, Mr Doyle,' Rosen said. 'All I can say is my father's not without influence. He will do his utmost to protect you.'

She paused before adding, 'As his daughter, I personally guarantee this.'

Pat considered her offer before replying.

'I'll need to think about this. Right now I'm not so sure, you do understand where I'm coming from?'

'Of course,' Rosen agreed. 'Let me give you my direct number so you can get straight through to me.'

***

The now full hotel restaurant resonated with the sound of diners enjoying themselves: light chatter interspersed with laughter. Pat looked up nervously as people arrived, half expecting Lennie to reappear. If Lennie had gone to Antwerp, he would soon discover he'd been duped, then head back here to try to find them. Pat concluded they'd outstayed their time in Venice. If Lennie did return, they needed to be long gone by the time he arrived.

Pat watched as Demi picked at her food, deeply regretting getting her involved in all this stupid mess. Between them, a small candle flickered; in the soft light she looked more beautiful than ever. Had he been married to her and not Helen, he would have jumped out of aeroplanes, abseiled over cliffs, run with bulls in Pamplona. Even stood up to Barry Laine and his mob. He wanted to tell Demi the way he felt about her, the way their life could be together, not as her social worker, but as her lover, a father to her children. Demi looked up, aware of Pat staring at her.

'What?' she asked.

He smiled back.

'Nothing, I just get the impression you're not exactly enjoying your baccalà.'

'I'm not too keen on fish and yes, before you say anything, I was persuaded by the waiter. He made it sound nice but hey, fish is fish. Anyway, I'm not that hungry.'

Twenty-Nine

Abraham Steinberg put down his phone then turned to Wiener.

'Mr Laine accepts our offer. However, he said he wants the money in cash. He has the diamonds with him now so we're to take the money to his office over on Westgate Street.'

Wiener crossed the room, rubbing his chin, eyes closed while he spoke.

'I still don't like it, Abe. Something isn't right here. I can sense it and I'm rarely mistaken.'

Steinberg nodded at his cousin. 'Okay, you may be right, but what else can we do?'

Wiener turned. His dark eyes bore into those of his cousin.

'Against my intuition, we'll go make the deal. But rest assured, I'll take care of that *schmuck* if he tries to pull any tricks.'

***

They arranged for the transaction to take place at Laine's antique furniture business in the centre of Cardiff. A large building consisting of a showroom, warehouse space and offices, the furniture business made a healthy profit in itself but it was just a front for Laine's criminal activities.

Lennie rapped on the door of Laine's office then went in.

'The jeweller's here with that other guy.'

'Okay, Len, bring them up, and keep a close watch on the other guy, something about him bugs me.'

Steinberg, with Wiener alongside him, followed Lennie through the first-floor warehouse area. Laine stepped out of his office to greet them.

'Mr Steinberg,' Laine said, hand outstretched, 'so pleased to make your acquaintance again.'

The two men shook hands. Wiener kept his hands by his sides.

'Please, join me in here.' Laine indicated towards his office. Lennie followed close behind.

'Thank you, Mr Laine,' Steinberg said. 'You remember my associate, Mr Benjamin Wiener?' Wiener nodded his head towards Laine as he entered the room carrying a briefcase.

'I see you've recently had the misfortune of a fire,' Steinberg commented. 'I noticed the damage to your warehouse as we came through. Nothing too serious, I hope.'

Laine winced at the reminder of Doyle's taxi driver friend who'd managed to escape from him by starting the fire. His men were out looking for him but so far he'd managed to evade them.

'A minor accident, all covered by insurance,' he lied. 'Can I offer you gentlemen a drink?'

Laine picked up a bottle of whisky from a period cabinet.

'It's one of the better malts, fifteen years old.'

'Not for us, thank you all the same.'

Laine put the bottle back on the cabinet.

'Me neither then. I never drink alone.'

Wiener studied the room, calculating the distance between him and Lennie who stood next to the door. They had passed at least three other men in the building on their way to the office. All three stared intently as he'd walked by in his full-length black coat and black hat; standing well over six feet, he appeared truly menacing. As they sat together in Laine's office it was Wiener who spoke next.

'Well, Mr Laine, do you now have the diamonds? We're too busy to be wasting time here. I mean, this is hardly a social call.'

Laine looked over to Lennie, surprised that Steinberg had not opened the discussion.

'The diamonds, please, Leonard.' He held out his hand. Lennie passed him the small box that Laine placed it in front of him on the desk.

'Gentleman: the Steinberg diamonds.'

Steinberg glanced over the desk at him.

'Yes, very droll, Mr Laine. May I?' Steinberg said pointing at the box.

'Please, be my guest,' Laine agreed.

He watched as the jeweller lifted the lid, turning the contents out in front of him. Taking a small magnifier from his pocket, Steinberg selected a stone, closely examining it through the eye glass. He did this with about ten stones in all before passing the magnifier to Wiener who did likewise. As Laine watched the two men, he could feel his palms becoming clammy, expecting Steinberg to announce they were fake diamonds. He felt relieved when he heard him say,

'They appear good quality to me.'

Laine decided to play along.

'Yes. I agree. They are of a high quality, not that I'm anything of an expert so I bow to your superior knowledge. Now, about the money.' Laine said as he gathered the stones towards him. 'Do you have the cash?'

Wiener placed the briefcase on the desk and flicked open the catches before turning it to face Laine.

'One hundred thousand as we agreed, Mr Laine,' Steinberg said.

'Thank you,' Laine replied. 'You have my utmost trust so I won't bother to count it.'

Laine reached across, closed the lid then pushed the case towards Lennie.

'Pop this in the safe, Len.'

Laine stood, handing over the box that Wiener took from him.

'A pleasure to do business with you, gentlemen. Now, how about a celebratory drink to close the deal?'

Wiener put the box in his coat pocket before responding. 'Alcohol's not to my liking, Mr Laine.' Steinberg simply shook his head.

'As you wish. Leonard, do see our friends out, please.' He watched them leave with a smile spread across his face. Pleased he had just sold a pile of glass for a cool hundred grand but still irritated that the real diamonds were not yet in his possession. Lennie returned to the office.

'How long before they come back knocking on the door, boss?'

'Not long, I'm sure, but that's the least of my concerns. I want the real stones from Doyle. Can I trust you, Len? That's what I need to know right now.'

Laine peered into the eyes of his henchman without flinching, waiting for a response.

'Yes, boss,' Lennie assured him. 'You *can* trust me. I'll get the diamonds and take care of Doyle at the same time.'

Holding up both hands, palms facing outwards, he repeated,

'Trust me.'

'The girl, Len, I want her as well, so you don't harm her in any way. Understand?'

'No problem,' he confirmed. 'Do I bring her here or take her to one of the dives?'

'Bring her here. There'll be plenty of time before she meets the rest of the girls.'

Grinning, Lennie left the room. Laine picked up a glass. Half filling it with whisky, he tipped his head back, feeling the warmth of the liquid roll down his throat. Smacking his lips, he toasted the doorway. 'Here's to the next hundred grand.'

***

Pat gazed down from the hotel room window. He'd considered their options: Plan A – return to Cardiff; Plan B – sell the diamonds in Antwerp and to hell with going back.

'Shit,' he thought to himself 'Plan B isn't really an option for her though.' He turned to face Demi as she sat on the bed and considered his next words carefully before speaking.

'Demi, I really don't know what to do for the best. In that little case we have a fortune in diamonds. However, there's a very irate and dangerous man determined to get his hands on them.'

Doyle turned back towards the window.

'We also have an opportunity to return them to their rightful owner and take whatever amounts to a substantial reward.'

Demi walked across the room to join him at the window. He turned to face her, looking down at her dark eyes and full mouth.

'You decide, Demi said. 'I'll go along with whatever you think is for the best. We hold the cards; we can name our price in terms of this substantial reward. Offer to go fifty-fifty maybe. Who knows? He might agree.'

Pat pondered the suggestion. Demi was a lot brighter than he gave her credit for. 'Pat,' Demi whispered.

'Yes?'

'Kiss me.'

Pat hesitated before responding. 'I… I'm not sure,' he stammered.

'Oh, come here,' Demi put her hands behind his head to pull his face to hers. Their mouths met and pressed together. As they kissed, they moved towards the bed where they fell onto it, fumbling with each other's clothes in their haste to remove them. Their kissing intensified, their passion heightened. It had been a long time for both of them, a long time since they'd both experienced such intimacy.

***

The following morning brought glorious Italian sunshine. Pat lay on the bed listening to Demi in the shower. He was tempted to join her, but he still suffered some inhibitions. He felt slightly apprehensive that last night may just have been a one off, something she may now regret, never likely to repeat. He took a bite from a croissant, part of the breakfast tray he'd ordered.

'Hey, save some for me, greedy.' Demi stepped back into the room, a towel wrapped around her. Taking the croissant from him she bit into it before handing it back. Smiling at her, Pat held out his hand. She took hold of it, sitting down beside him, and she leant over to kiss him gently on the lips.

'What's it to be, lover boy, home or Antwerp?'

He had given this a lot of thought.

'I'll arrange to meet the solicitor and go from there,' he told her. 'Let's see how much money we can squeeze from them, eh?'

'Why not? sounds good to me.' Demi stood up, letting the towel fall slowly to the floor. Pat's inhibitions evaporated and moving over he let Demi climb into the bed next to him.

***

Their plane lifted easily from the runway at Marco Polo heading for Heathrow airport. Pat clutched the attaché case whilst Demi read the in-flight magazine that detailed the history and benefits of the budget airline.

'I suggest we phone this Rosen woman from the airport as soon as we land,' Pat said. 'Arrange to meet her somewhere.'

Demi looked up from her magazine.

'Sure,' she agreed. 'But where should we meet? Her office? Or somewhere more public?'

'Her office sounds okay to me, what d'you think?'

'Why not. Do we take these?' Demi said as she touched the case. Pat pondered the question.

'No, we can leave them at the station in the secure locker we used before. Then we go across to her office, see what's on offer. If we don't like it, we walk away.'

'What if it's some kind of set up? What if she has people who won't let us simply *walk away*? What then?'

Pat took hold of her hand, with a weak smile he said,

'I can't see there being any trouble in a city centre solicitor's office, can you?'

'Maybe not,' Demi agreed. 'Maybe we should case the joint before we go in. Look out for Lennie Randall or Barry Laine.'

'Case the joint?' Pat said with mock surprise. 'What films have you been watching?'

'You know what I mean,' she elbowed him in his side. 'We don't want to go rushing in only to find it's some kind of a trap.'

He thought about this for a few moments.

'Maybe I should just go on my own. You stay back and…'

She cut him off.

'No, we go together, Pat. Together.'

'Okay, okay. Together it is then.' He leant across to gently kiss her. 'Always together.'

Thirty

The look on her father's face surprised Rebekah Rosen. She'd arrived at her parent's home to speak with him, to explain about the telephone conversation she'd had with Patrick Doyle. Sitting in his study with Ben Wiener they listened to what she had to say. Wiener sat holding the stones in front of him.

'Hold on, Rebekah,' Steinberg said interrupting his daughter. 'Are you telling me Doyle has my diamonds and he wants to discuss a deal with us?' He looked over to Wiener. 'I don't understand.'

'That's right, father, I'm waiting for him to get back to me so we can arrange a meeting.'

She looked over to the desk at the stones Wiener had now placed there.

'What's this? Are they the diamonds? Now *I* don't understand. Can someone please tell me what's going on?'

'These, my child, are what I bought from Laine earlier today.'

'How much did you pay him?' she asked. Wiener responded before Steinberg.

'Too bloody much. Your father is a fool, and now he may be an even bigger fool.'

Steinberg looked at him.

'Please, Ben, let's take this one step at a time. I examined the stones and they appeared genuine to me. You also examined them.'

'So now I'm a jeweller?' Wiener said.

'Yes, I mean, no. Anyway, we know different since I tested them with this,' he said picking up a small diamond-testing machine. Steinberg placed the instrument down on the desk. 'Let's return to Laine and get my money.'

'My, my,' Wiener stood with raised hands. 'A naïve fool as well. You think Laine is going to simply hand back a hundred grand? He's sold you trash, my friend, and he knew it. We'll get the money back, that I guarantee, but not by asking.'

Wiener picked up his handgun and cocked it.

'Father,' Rebekah shrieked. 'He's got a gun.'

'Ignore him, child. Ben, put that away,' he ordered. 'Listen to what Rebekah is telling us. It looks as though Laine doesn't have the diamonds either, at least not just yet.'

He turned back to his daughter.

'We need to meet this Doyle, find out exactly what's what. Can you arrange this as soon as possible?'

Rebekah nodded her agreement. 'Probably tomorrow.'

'Then tomorrow, we will visit Mr Laine once more.' Wiener said.

Rebekah stared back at Wiener who was now pushing a magazine into the Sig's handgrip.

***

The following day at his warehouse, Laine carefully examined a mahogany writing bureau, an original antique piece he would place in the front showroom alongside other pieces of antique

259

furniture. He was not surprised when one of his men announced the arrival of Steinberg and Wiener who now strode across the floor towards him. More of Laine's men appeared in the warehouse. Laine nodded at them to back off. Wiener watched as the three men left through the door.

'Mr Steinberg, this is an unexpected visit,' Laine said in mock surprise. 'Decided to take up the offer of that drink after all? Please, do come in.'

'Don't play games with me,' Steinberg said angrily. 'You know exactly why we're here.'

'I do?'

'You know you do. The diamonds you gave me are synthetic, Laine. You sold me fake diamonds so I demand my money back.'

He threw a bag down at Laine's feet. Laine looked at it, nudging the bag with his foot as if it were something nasty.

'Fake? You mean as in not real?' Laine smiled then laughed. 'My grandfather stole diamonds from *your* grandfather and all along they were duds. Well can you believe that? Seems like old man Steinberg was a dodgy diamond dealer himself.'

'No, Mr Laine, the stolen diamonds are not in that bag,' Steinberg said pointing down. 'These are Russian fakes that didn't exist in nineteen sixty-five, but you already know this.'

The two men were in a stand-off position with Wiener staying deliberately back so he could deal with any unpleasant behaviour that may arise whilst edging his way towards Laine's office.

'Sorry, Mr Steinberg, I really am confused,' Laine said mockingly. 'The diamonds I sold you were the ones handed to me. I'm no expert so I assumed they were genuine. You yourself did likewise and seemed happy with them.'

He raised his hands with a shrug of his shoulders.

'I only deal in antiques, not gemstones. That's *your* department.'

'We all know *exactly* what you deal in, Laine,' Steinberg growled. 'I want my money back and you can keep that heap of rubbish down there.'

'Now, now, Mr *S,* there's no need to get all huffy on me. No, I'm afraid it's *c'est la vie* – not sale or return. So, if you'll excuse me, I have other business to attend to.'

Steinberg took a step closer then hissed in Laine's face,

'You haven't heard the last of this. You're crossing the wrong man, Laine, and that you may come to regret.'

'Look, Steinberg, if I'd decided to keep the stones, I would've been the loser. You wanted them and I sold them to you. So now you need to take this up with whoever, elsewhere, savvy?'

Laine snapped his fingers indicating for his men to return. As they did, Wiener called out, 'Just stay right where you are, gentleman, and nobody gets hurt.'

They looked across at Wiener who pointed his 9mm Sig at them. One man moved. Wiener spotted the gun in his hand. The room reverberated with the sound of a single gunshot. The man fell to the ground, his kneecap shattered, letting out a scream as he clutched at his knee. Wiener now smiled at them.

'Anyone try that again the next slug goes through the head.'

Visibly shaken by this sudden turn of events, Laine looked at Wiener. He knew the accuracy of the shot fired meant he was no ordinary punk with a gun. He was serious business. The 9mm now pointed at him.

'Get Mr Steinberg his money, Laine,' Wiener ordered. 'Abe, go with him.'

He then addressed Laine's two remaining upright heavies.

'As for you guys, you all face the wall with your hands high and flat against it.' The two remaining men did as he ordered.

In his office, Laine took the money from a large safe then handed it to Steinberg.

'You have my utmost trust so I won't bother counting it,' Steinberg mimicked. He put the banknotes into his own case then picked up the telephone receiver, holding it out towards Laine.

'I think you need to summon medical assistance for your man out there. You don't want him bleeding all over your quality merchandise.'

Laine snatched the phone then slammed it down.

'He can fucking die for all I care, and so will you after this. I ain't no fucking shopkeeper, Steinberg, I have people killed in my business.'

'You okay in there, Abe?' Wiener called out keeping his gun trained on the men facing the wall.

'Everything's fine in here, Ben,' Steinberg replied. He didn't notice Barry Laine open a drawer where he kept his own handgun. As Steinberg turned to leave, Laine looked down in surprise to see the gun no longer in the drawer. He started to pull open other drawers when he heard Wiener call out.

'If you're looking for this little toy, Laine, I have it here.'

Laine hadn't noticed Wiener slip into his office and remove the gun during the confrontation with Steinberg. Steinberg, followed by Laine, stepped back into the warehouse.

'Dinky little thing ain't it?' Wiener said holding up the gun, a Smith and Wesson Chief's Special.

'I'll pop it in the mail for you,' Wiener said. 'Don't want to be accused of stealing your piece.'

Keeping his gun trained on Laine, Wiener backed towards the exit. Steinberg followed.

'Okay, Abe, let's go. Good day, gentlemen.' Wiener closed the door.

'Get the fuck after them,' Laine screamed. 'The bastard's got my money. Don't just stand there, go after them now.'

Laine turned back to his office when his phone rang. He grabbed at the handset. 'What!'

'Steady on, Mr Laine,' a voice said. It was Wiener. 'Just letting you know I've put your little gun in one of the drawers in the showroom, no bullets mind. Happy hunting.'

'If I get hold of that Yid bastard, I'll kill him.' Laine barked. One of his men shrugged as he returned.

'No good, boss, they've gone.'

'I guessed that much, you idiots. Now sort him out,' he ordered, pointing at the man with the wounded knee, 'before he bleeds to death on my Persian rugs.'

***

Pat persuaded Demi to wait for him at the station coffee bar whilst he made his way across town to Rebekah Rosen's office in Churchill Way. Demi now had the key to the locker – just in case. After walking up and down the street a couple of times, Pat ventured inside, failing to notice the car parked near the firm's office with Lennie Randall sitting inside. Lennie was about to visit Rebekah Rosen to discuss his court case. He slid down in the seat watching as Pat entered the building, dialling up Barry Laine at the same time.

'Can I help you, sir?' asked the young female receptionist from behind a desk as Doyle walked in.

'Is it possible to see Mrs Rosen?' he asked.

'Do you have an appointment?'

'No, but I believe she will see me. Tell her it's Pat Doyle, she'll know what it's about.'

'Oh, yes, Mr Doyle. I'll check to see if Mrs Rosen's free,' she said picking up a phone.

Within minutes, Pat found himself in a cramped office on the top floor of the building, files piled high, taking up every available space. The small window looked out onto the street with a Premier Inn opposite. Rebekah Rosen sat behind her desk, black-framed glasses on the end of her nose.

'Is this lot your current workload?' he enquired, amazed at the amount of paperwork in the room.

'They're not all active cases,' she told him. 'Most are dealt with but I simply haven't had the time to file them away as dead.'

'How many *actually* are dead, I wonder?'

'Oh, I'm sure there are a few, Mr Doyle, goes with the territory.'

'Don't suppose that might include Mr Randall by any chance?'

'You know Lennie Randall, Mr Doyle?'

'Please, call me Pat,' he insisted. 'Yes, I've had the pleasure of his company, though he's unlikely to feature on my list of *Come Dine With Me* guests.

Rebekah smiled as she removed her glasses.

'Well, client confidentiality prevents me discussing Mr Randall with you, Mr… um Pat,' she corrected. 'But that's not why you're here.'

'No, I'm here because you wanted us to meet up, remember the phone call?'

'Of course,' Rebekah acknowledged. 'Now if we cut to the chase, it's diamonds we need to discuss, diamonds belonging to my family, stolen from us back in the nineteen sixties.'

'Correct, Mrs Rosen. By a relative of Cardiff's best-known gangster. The infamous Barry Laine, no less.'

'Laine's a problem for you?'

'Is the Pope a Catholic?'

'Well, I know he's not Jewish,' Rebekah responded.

Pat smiled, beginning to warm to the woman, not believing she would set him up with either Laine or Hatchet Lennie.

'Well, Pat, do you have the diamonds with you?'

'Not on me personally, let's just say they're in safe keeping, for now. So tell me, Mrs Rosen, when the diamonds were stolen from your relative, didn't he claim off any insurance?'

The solicitor's face reddened slightly as she replied.

'I don't believe there was any insurance at the time. Anyway, the stones legally belong to my family, now if I believe you are in possession of them, I could simply call the police.'

'I agree, Mrs Rosen, so why haven't you done that already?' He paused. 'But I think we both know the answer?'

'We do?'

'Yes. I read in a copy of a newspaper from nineteen sixty-eight how your family received an insurance pay-out following a protracted court case, as they were never recovered.'

Slipping her glasses back on, she moved some papers on her desk. Pat sensed this to be a nervous reaction to his statement.

'Look,' Pat said, 'I'm not really interested in all that. It's confined to history, so to speak.' He leaned forward in his chair. 'What I want to know is what do *you* want?'

She removed her glasses for the second time rubbing one lens with a small cloth.

'We are prepared to offer a substantial amount of money for the return of the stones.'

'How substantial is *substantial?*' he asked raising his eyebrows.

'A hundred thousand pounds. Substantial enough?'

Pat stood and crossed to the window, looking out at the street below.

'They're worth considerably more. I had them valued closer to a million,' he said without revealing the existence and possible value of the pink diamond.

Pat heard a chair scrape back. He turned to see the solicitor on her feet

'A million,' she gasped.

'Give or take a quid,' Pat said nonchalantly.

'I... I had no idea they're worth that much. In safekeeping you say? I hope they're in an *actual* safe, Pat.'

Rebekah sat down pushing a hand through her hair.

'I suppose now you're expecting a lot more than we're offering?'

'Not so. I'd be prepared to accept your generous offer. I just need to know I won't be double-crossed. It's hard to tell who to trust lately.'

'Yes, that's understandable,' Rebekah said. 'I can, however, give you a guaranteed assurance my father will pay you the full amount. No gimmicks.'

'I'm dealing directly with your father?'

'No, Pat, you'll deal with me, a sort of lawyer-client relationship.'

'Will you charge a fee?' he asked.

'No fee, Pat. No contract, no fee, and no comebacks. Do we have a deal?'

'I'll have to consult my partner, first,' he informed her.

'You have a partner?' Rebekah said, surprised. 'Who is this?'

'The friend I mentioned on the phone,' he reminded her. 'I'll get back to you, how about tomorrow morning?'

'I'm in court first thing. Let's say lunchtime, back here.'

He nodded then made his way to the door.

'Until then,' Pat said closing the door behind him.

***

Lennie sat in his car waiting for Pat to come out of the solicitor's office. After contacting Laine, he was instructed to follow Doyle discreetly, keeping Laine informed of his movements. Laine had ordered a number of his men to drive into the city-centre and wait for further instructions. He wanted Doyle and the girl picked up separately then taken to different locations. If Doyle didn't have the diamonds on him, so be it. He'd get that information from him soon enough.

Laine owned a number of houses around Cardiff, with one house in the south of the city set up with hidden cameras used for secretly filming clients who he could later blackmail. He'd arranged for people to be there when Demi arrived. Three or four of his men would take care of her. He had since lost interest in the woman but he'd still have his fun with her in due course. Doyle would be taken to the warehouse in the city centre – no mistakes this time, and no funny business with fires. He'd get what he wanted then have his body disposed of for good. His mobile phone pinged, interrupting his deliberations.

'Hello, Len, what you got?'

'I've followed them to the station, boss. They're in the coffee bar.'

'Okay,' Laine said, 'I'll send two cars over right now. Pick them up without making a scene. The boys will know where to take them. And this time, Len, make sure they don't jump on another fucking train.'

***

Pat and Demi sat at a table in the far corner of the station coffee shop, wishing they'd gone elsewhere as he recalled their last visit to the place.

'How did it go with the solicitor then?' Demi asked. 'Can we trust her?' She sipped her latté looking cautiously around the station concourse.

'I think Rebekah's genuine enough,' he told her. 'So, yes, we can trust her.'

'Oh, *Rebekah,* is it? My, we are close, and so soon. I hope she's not going to sucker you by fluttering her eyelashes.'

'Demetra,' he intoned. 'Do I detect a hint of jealousy here?'

'Do you hell as like,' she snapped. 'I just don't want to get tucked up after coming this far. Anyway, what's this deal she's offered you?'

He told her about the offer and how he would meet with Rebekah Rosen tomorrow after he'd discussed it with her first. Until then, the diamonds would remain in the station locker.

'One hundred thousand,' Demi said. 'Is that a good deal considering what they're worth?'

'Don't forget there are others besides Barry Laine involved now,' Pat said. 'Look at it this way: we get Laine and the Steinbergs off our backs, plus we'll have a hundred thousand for ourselves. What d'you reckon? Make sense?'

Demi sipped her coffee, giving it some thought.

'Yeah, I guess so,' she agreed. 'Now, I really do need to see my kids, so can we go?'

They made their way out of the station concourse, neither noticing the two cars until they'd pulled up at the kerb alongside them. Two men jumped out of each.

'Excuse me,' one said, quickly flashing some form of ID card. 'We need to speak with you regarding the theft of diamonds.'

Pat and Demi glanced at each other but before they had the chance to speak another of the men stood between them.

'Would you get into the cars, please,' the man with the card said.

'This is that solicitor's doing,' Demi said as they pushed her towards the open door of a black Audi A6.

'Where are you taking us?' Pat asked one of them.

'Just over to the police station, sir,' he said shoving Pat towards the other car. Lennie watched from a distance then reported to Laine that the pickup had gone according to plan.

Thirty-One

In the back of the Audi, Demi looked at one of the two men sitting next to her. She became immediately suspicious of him when he put his hand on her thigh and smiled at her.

'Get your scabby paws off me,' she screamed, pushing his hand away. 'Where are you taking us? You're not police at all, are you? Show me that fucking card again.'

Demi became more agitated as the car travelled towards the Grangetown area of the city, not towards the civic centre. The driver looked back at her.

'You might have a bit of a fight on your hands with that one, pal.' His friend laughed at the remark.

'Nar, she'll soon come round, especially when she starts to enjoy herself.'

Demi's hand went towards the door handle. As the car slowed for traffic lights, she considered jumping out. The man in the back saw her stroking the catch.

'Sorry, darling, child locks. Don't worry, I'm sure you'll enjoy the lads' company. I know they'll enjoy you.'

This time both men laughed together.

They pulled up outside a three-storey house off Penarth Road.

The driver checked no one was about before he pulled Demi from the back seat.

'Get your stinking hands off me, you fucking creeps,' Demi growled, pulling her arm back.

'Just get in the house, bitch or I'll seriously hurt you.'

Demi glared at the man, daring him to do something. He did. Demi didn't see the hand that struck the left side of her face, almost knocking her off balance.

They pushed her through the front door towards the staircase in the hall. Demi felt her face sting from the blow, deciding it was no use resisting.

'Come on, up here,' the driver told her. She followed him up to the next floor then into a room at the front of the house.

Inside the room, a king-size bed took up most of the space. A cabinet with bottles of various brands of spirits stood against a wall. Deep, heavy red curtains covered the windows. Three armchairs and two upright chairs filled the remaining space. Demi scanned the room feeling uneasy at the sight of a camera tripod at the base of the bed. She looked wide-eyed at the two men standing next to her.

'Where are we?' she yelled at them. 'What are you going to do?'

'All in good time,' the driver's companion responded, the larger of her two captives. 'All in good time.'

Demi made a dash for the door but was pulled back into the room by a hand that forced her down into an armchair.

'Now why don't you relax a little, have a drink maybe,' the larger man said, gesturing towards the bottles on the cabinet. The driver held up a bottle of vodka.

'Stick your fucking drink,' she shot back.

It quickly dawned on her what they were planning. This was clearly one of Barry Laine's massage parlours. She'd heard about the things that happened to the women who were brought to places like this. Girls trafficked from eastern Europe, tricked into believing they were taking on respectable jobs only to discover they were to become exploited as sex slaves.

They'd be injected with heroin, gang-raped then put to work as prostitutes for the likes of Laine and other gangsters in the city. Demi felt she was in some kind of nightmare, not wanting to imagine the things they might do to her. She had to get out – but how? There were two of them and no doubt the doors were locked. *Think Demi, think,* she willed herself.

***

The car carrying Pat Doyle pulled up outside the Westgate Street building where Laine waited with Lennie Randall.

'I thought you said we were going to the police station,' Pat said looking out at the building in Westgate Street.

'Yeah, well looks like we've changed our minds,' retorted the small, stocky driver who spoke with a distinct east London accent. They pushed him through the entrance into the showroom area of the premises. The second man followed, locking the doors behind him.

'Mr Laine's waiting for you upstairs, son. He ain't too happy either,' the stocky man chimed. Walking through the warehouse area, Pat caught the redolence of fire damage invading nostrils, as he walked towards where Barry Laine stood in conversation with Lennie.

'Pat,' Laine greeted him mockingly. 'It's so nice to see you again. I take it the boys treated you okay. Did you boys? No rough stuff, I hope.'

Pat glared at Laine.

'What have you done with Demi? Where is she?'

'Demi's fine, being taken good care of. Ain't that right, boys?'

'Sure, guv,' responded the stocky one, 'being taken proper care of as we speak.'

'The man never lies,' Laine said.

Pat moved closer.

'Look, Barry, we both know this is about the diamonds so let's not mess around. I won't let you have them until I see Demi, okay? No Demi, no deal.'

Pat saw Laine nod his head but didn't realise it wasn't an acknowledgment of what he'd proposed. A crushing blow to his collarbone forced him to his knees, excruciating pain making him want to vomit. Laine looked down at Pat retching on the floor.

'Don't play fucking games with me, Doyle,' he hissed through clenched teeth. 'You're in no position to make deals. You just tell me where the stones are, I'll consider letting you live. If you don't, I'll let Lennie here *deal* with you.'

Lennie stepped forward holding the bolt croppers he'd hoped to use earlier. Pat looked up

'Where's Demi?' he stammered. 'Do what you like to me, kill me if you want, but I won't hand them over until I see Demi.'

The next blow to the other shoulder blade almost rendered him unconscious.

Pat lay on the floor, head swimming with nausea.

Is Demi in this building? If he gave up the diamonds, would Laine kill him anyway? Surely, he wouldn't harm Demi. He felt hands grab him under the armpits as the two goons lifted him from the floor and sat him on a hard chair. The room span as he steadied himself from falling back to the floor.

'The diamonds, Doyle,' Laine demanded. 'Where are my diamonds?' Pat shook his head as he looked across at Laine. Seeing Laine nod, he instinctively winced in readiness for the expected blow that came by way of a punch to the face, splitting his lip, he tasted warm blood in his mouth.

'Come on, Pat,' Laine said feigning a reasonable approach. 'How much of this can you take? You're not made for this kind of stuff. Tell me where they are and the boys will ease off.'

Pat touched his mouth with the back of his hand, looking at the blood he had wiped. He felt a swelling in his bottom lip. 'What happens if I tell you where they are?' Pat said. His speech was slurred as if he'd had a dental anaesthetic.

His thoughts bounced off the walls of his mind as he desperately tried to think of a way out of his situation. He didn't believe he could negotiate his way to freedom. Laine would probably kill him regardless.

'Only when I have the stones will I tell you what happens next,' Laine said. 'So, let's go get them, shall we?'

Laine walked to the door as his heavies hauled Pat back to his feet for him to follow. Walking across the warehouse, Laine pointed to the fire-damaged area.

'Your little friend Elroy has to answer for this,' he told him.

Pat wondered what he meant.

'Elroy did this?' he asked Laine.

'Elroy's a dead man,' Laine replied.

Well, that's one thing, Pat thought. *Elroy's alive.* As they walked, Pat formulated an idea. It would only buy some extra time but in that time, he might find a way out of this sorry mess.

Thirty-Two

Demi watched her two captives closely as they talked quietly to each other, occasionally laughing. Each time they laughed they'd look across at her sitting in the chair.

'I need to use the loo,' Demi announced. One of the men looked over.

'So soon? We haven't even started yet.'

'I'll show her where it is,' the other man said, crushing his cigarette into a large glass ashtray. Demi followed him onto the landing.

'It's in there,' he said pointing. 'Oh, by the way, no funny business, just in case that's what you had in mind. I'll be waiting out here, if you aren't out in two minutes, I'll come in and get you.'

Demi went in, sitting on the edge of the bath, not really needing to use the toilet. This was about thinking time. She put her head in her hands, thinking about her children, her parents, and particularly about Pat. She wondered what would happen to him. He would no doubt be told to give up the diamonds. If he didn't, then what? Standing up, she looked in the small mirror, lightly touching the side of her reddened face, still stinging from the blow. Demi wondered how many other frightened women might have looked in this mirror in a similar situation to hers.

Demi then noticed the small window. Standing on the toilet seat, she lifted the latch and pushed. It didn't move. She pushed again but the window appeared stuck fast. Checking around the frame Demi spotted the head of a screw, the reason the window would not budge, not even a fraction.

'Shit,' Demi hissed, getting down from the seat. She flushed the toilet for effect before stepping back outside.

'Thank you,' she softly said to the man still waiting by the door. Demi returned to the room and sat in the same chair. The other man spoke to his companion as he came back in behind Demi.

'Where's the camera?' He pointed to the tri-pod stand.

'Dunno,' the other replied. 'Who had it last?'

'Shit, I bet it's in the other place, now what?' The one who'd shown Demi to the toilet picked up the car keys from the table.

'You keep an eye on her, 'I'll drive across and get it.'

'Yeah, okay but be quick about it, I wanna get started.'

The man left the room. Demi heard him go down the stairs, slamming the front door on his way out.

'Don't worry, darling, he won't be long. The other boys should be here by the time he returns with the camera.'

'Then what happens?' Demi asked in a determined voice. She feigned confidence trying to mask the fear she felt inside.

'Then the fun begins, and guess what, we film it all,' he replied, a grin spreading across his face.

'Film what?' Demi feared the reply.

'The sex of course, what else? You, me, and the boys. Tell you what, when it's my turn, and seeing as I like you, I'll let you choose the position.'

He walked across to the cabinet against the wall, picked up a bottle and waved it at her.

'Care for a drink? Get you in the mood.'

Demi watched as he poured himself a large measure. She recognised the bottle: *Courvoisier* cognac. It reminded her of Christmas as a child; her mother had used the same brand to pour over the Christmas pudding. Suddenly, an idea popped into her head.

'Okay,' Demi agreed, 'I will have a drink,'

'What'll it be?'

'Same as you. Brandy.'

Half filling a tumbler, he brought it across to her. Aping a smile, she took the glass from him.

'Thank you.'

'My pleasure, or at least it will be later,' he said winking.

Demi put the glass to her mouth, taking a small sip of the cognac, almost cringing at the fiery taste; she was not used to drinking spirits. Demi leaned forward to pick up the cigarette packet on the table next to the ashtray.

'Mind if I have one?'

'Sure, help yourself.'

Demi took one of the cigarettes.

'Got a light?' Demi asked holding the cigarette between her fingers.

She put the glass to her mouth again as he picked up a lighter, a Zippo with its distinctive flip top made of high polished chrome, with the *Playboy* rabbit on one side. Flipping the top, he thumbed the wheel. A large yellow flame danced as the flint ignited the wick. He leant across, bringing the flame nearer. Demi held a mouthful of cognac as she put the cigarette to her lips. The man moved closer to her, holding the flame at the tip of the cigarette, not expecting what would happen next. In one deft action Demi sprayed the cognac in a fine mist out of her mouth across the flame of the lighter, at the same time throwing the contents of the glass over him. The spray ignited over the flame.

The man screamed as the rest of the alcohol combusted. Demi leapt from the chair, rushing over to the other bottles of spirits on the cabinet. Grabbing two, she hurled them as he tried to extinguish the inferno by rolling on the floor. Another two bottles followed. Their contents spilled out, the firestorm increasing with the added accelerants flowing from the bottles. The man had become a human fireball as he writhed on the floor screaming, desperately trying to put out the flames.

Demi ran through the door, almost falling down the stairs. She pulled at the Yale lock. A sound at the top of the stairs made her look up where she struggled to make out the shape of the burning man who stood on the top step, skin peeling from his face and hands, barely able to cry out.

'Open, open,' she shouted still fumbling with the lock. 'Please open.'

Tears ran down her smarting face as her heart pounded in her chest. Demi took hold of the lock, put her hand through the letterbox and pulled. Using new-found strength and determination the door opened. She leapt out onto the street desperately looking around, making sure there was no sign of the other man returning. As she started to run towards the main road a taxi passed her.

'Stop!' she screamed. 'Taxi.'

The car braked to a stop.

'Where to, luv?' the Asian driver asked as she slumped onto the rear seat.

'City centre,' she told him. Demi looked back as the cab pulled out into the flow of traffic. Black smoke billowed from the upstairs window of the house.

'Now film that, you bastards.'

***

Wedged between two of Laine's heavies in the rear of the BMW, Pat stared out through the windscreen as they headed for his flat in the bay. Laine turned in the front passenger seat to face him.

'I always get what I want, Doyle. You of all people should know that. All this running around – what's the point? You could never outrun me for long. I'd have caught up with you wherever you went.'

Laine shifted his position to face forward.

'Thing is, Doyle,' he continued looking up at the rear-view mirror, 'I never had you down for the running type. I thought you would have handed over the diamonds from the get-go.'

Pat looked towards his old school friend. Never once did he think the boy he had hung around with all those years ago would now want to kill him.

Pat smirked before he spoke. 'It must have been all those Indiana Jones films I watched.'

His head ached from the beating they'd given him, his lower lip twice its normal size. At least it had stopped bleeding. He didn't know what he was going to do when they arrived at his flat. He'd told Laine the stones were hidden there, that he and Demi had taken them there for safekeeping when they'd arrived back in Cardiff.

He tried to think up a ploy where he could say Elroy knew of the diamonds, and that he had probably taken them elsewhere. Laine's phone rang, breaking the moment. Laine glanced at the caller ID; it was one of the men who'd taken Demi to the Grangetown house.

'What do you want?'

Laine listened and his face reddened when he heard what the man had to say.

'Listen up, you fucking dipstick,' he shouted into the phone. 'Just go after her, get her back. Screw this up once more, you're as good as dead.'

Laine turned towards Lennie.

'She's got away from them. The bitch got away.'

'How'd she manage that?' Lennie responded.

'He doesn't know,' Laine hissed. 'When he got back to the house it was torched with no sign of the woman.'

He slammed a fist into the dashboard.

'Another fucking fire, another one gets away. What the holy shit is going on?'

Pat inwardly sighed with relief. He now had an explanation for Laine when they'd find no diamonds at the flat. He'd say Demi had probably been there and taken them. Except now he didn't know where Demi had gone or what she'd do next. The car pulled up outside the block of flats. Laine turned to face Pat again.

'Right then,' Laine side. 'Let's go in, and believe me, for your sake, this had better be worth it.'

As the taxi pulled up outside Rebekah Rosen's offices, Demi realised she had no money for the fare.

'Wait here,' she told the driver. 'I'll be out in a minute, and then I need to go somewhere else.'

Demi took the front steps two at a time before charging into the reception area.

'I need to see Mrs Rosen,' Demi almost shouted at the young girl behind the desk. 'Tell her it's urgent.'

'Who shall I say is asking for her?'

'Just tell her I'm a friend of Pat Doyle. She'll see me. Now hurry up.'

The girl picked up her phone, spoke then replaced the handset.

'Mrs Rosen will be with you shortly, please, take a seat.'

Demi became agitated, pacing the floor much to the annoyance of the receptionist. As she turned the girl asked,

'Can I get you a coffee?'

'Yes please, white with sugar.'

The girl went through a door behind her desk. Demi turned, making her way up the stairs, looking at the nameplates on the doors. As she reached the top of the stairs, Rebekah Rosen stood outside her office.

'You must be Pat's friend. I was just about to come down. Please come in.'

Demi stepped inside the small room where she launched into a tirade at the solicitor.

'What have they done with Pat? You stitched us up… now, thanks to you, that psycho Laine will kill him. They were going to rape me, you bastard, rape me…' Demi fell back onto a chair, her hands covering her face, shoulders heaving with uncontrollable sobs. She felt a hand on her shoulder;

slowly looking up as tears ran down her cheeks, her eyes met those of the solicitor. Rebekah Rosen was also crying.

'Please believe me,' Rebekah said, 'I had nothing to do with any of this.'

She quietly closed her office door.

'Yes, this firm represents Barry Laine,' Rebekah whispered, 'but that's all.'

Rebekah offered Demi a Kleenex tissue she'd taken from a box on her desk, taking another to wipe her own eyes.

'Where's Pat now? What happened to you both? Please, I'll do all I can to help you.'

Demi hesitated, not sure if she should trust this woman who might still be trying to trick them.

'How do I know I can trust you?' Demi asked. 'How do I know you're not part of this whole thing? That you only want to get the diamonds for Laine?'

'I'm asking you to trust me,' Rebekah said. 'The same way Pat trusted me when we first met. I guess you're the partner he referred to. The one he wanted to consult with about the deal I offered.'

Demi became a little uneasy. Could this be a double bluff?

'What deal?' Demi asked.

'The deal to hand over the stones to my family for a substantial reward,' Rebekah replied. 'You see, they belong to my father, not that bastard, Laine. Pat said he was interested but needed to speak with you first. Do you have the diamonds…?' She broke off from the question. 'I'm sorry. I don't even know your name.'

'It's Demi, and no, I don't have the diamonds,' she lied.

Her mind raced. Demi considered if she handed over the stones Rebekah may not bother to help her. Their predicament would suddenly become none of her business. She had an idea.

'Pat's got them,' Demi said. 'Though more likely Barry Laine, seeing as he took Pat.'

'Do you know where they'd have taken him?' Rebekah asked.

'I was rather hoping you'd know that,' Demi responded.

'Barry Laine has a place over in Westgate Street,' Rebekah said. 'Some type of furniture business. They may have gone there.'

Out on the street they heard the sound of a car horn, the taxi Demi had asked to wait.

'Look,' she told the solicitor, 'I have to go. Can we meet up somewhere?'

Rebekah pondered the question.

'Do you know my father's shop on the High Street, Steinberg's?'

Demi thought for a moment then nodded.

'Meet me there in an hour. My father will be able to help us.'

Demi turned to leave then stopped.

'Oh, by the way,' Demi said, 'I need some money for the taxi. You don't by any chance…?'

Rebekah held up a hand, reached into her handbag and taking out a £20 note.

'Thank you,' Demi said quietly.

'That's okay, I'll put it down to expenses,' she joked.

The two women faced each other, both sensing the chemistry between them. They hugged like long lost sisters.

Back in the taxi, Demi asked the driver to take her to the station.

***

After unlocking the front door, Pat stepped into his flat. Laine went in after him, followed by the others.

'You actually bought this place?' Laine asked looking around. 'I keep rabbits in a bigger place than this.'

Picking up a CD, Laine read the title. *David Bowie: The Man Who Sold the World.* He grunted his dislike of Bowie.

'So, where are the stones?' Laine asked.

Pat picked up a Rolling Stones' CD, *Black and Blue,* handing it over to Laine in a mock gesture of musical friendship. Laine snatched the album from Pat and flicked it across the room.

'Don't fuck about, Doyle I ain't in a jovial mood.'

'I'll go get them,' Pat said. 'They're in a drawer in the bedroom.' Laine nodded at Lennie who followed Pat into the small room. Pat went over to a three-drawer chest, opened the top drawer pulling the contents about, and then did the same with the remaining two. Pretending to act frantically, he pulled out socks, boxer shorts, and ties.

'Got a problem there, pal?' Lennie asked.

'They're not here,' Pat said with raised hands. 'They've gone.'

He turned towards Lennie, head shaking.

'Demi must have been here and taken them. I put them in the top drawer over there.'

Lennie shoved Pat out of his way, Pat stumbled backwards hitting the wall behind him.

'Let me see.' Lennie pulled out each drawer, emptying the contents onto the floor, kicking the scattered items around the room. Laine appeared in the doorway.

'What's going on? Where are my diamonds?' he demanded.

'They're not here,' Pat said. 'I think Demi must have them.'

Laine stepped over to Pat, grabbing him by the throat.

'If you're messing me about, Doyle, I'll have Lennie here drop you off the balcony.'

'Wish I'd bought a ground floor flat now,' he rasped.

Laine's face turned into a scowl as he drove his knee hard into Pat's groin.

'Right,' he ordered his men, 'search the whole place top to bottom. I don't trust this lying bastard one bit.'

Pat sat on his bed, hands between his legs, nausea sweeping through him. He watched helplessly, unable to stop his flat being ransacked as they searched for the diamonds he knew they'd never find.

Thirty-Three

Abraham Steinberg, sitting with Wiener and Rebekah at his home in north Cardiff, listened carefully to Demi as she told him of how she and Pat Doyle came by the diamonds. She started with the cryptic letter written by the undertaker back in 1965, how they'd worked out where the diamonds were hidden, about the night in the cemetery. Fascinated by the story, Steinberg would occasionally interrupt to ask a question. She told him about their trip to London, Rhodes, and Venice and the fake diamonds they had obtained in Rhodes. How Barry Laine had abducted them on their return followed by her lucky escape. Wiener interrupted when Demi told them about the house in Grangetown.

'They were going to sexually assault you while you were under the influence of drugs?'

Wiener looked towards his cousin, contempt etched on his hardened face.

'We're dealing with barbarians, Abe. Total barbarians,' he added.

Steinberg nodded his agreement. He glanced at his daughter next to him, pushing back imagines of such horrors being inflicted upon her. Rebekah spoke next.

'Father, if Barry Laine has the diamonds, do you believe he will let Pat Doyle go?'

'If that were so, my child, Pat Doyle would probably be sitting with us right now.'

'Your father's right, Rebekah,' Wiener said. 'If we do nothing, I don't think we'll see either Pat or the diamonds again.'

'So what do you intend to do then?' Rebekah asked.

Demi looked from Rebekah to Steinberg.

'Will you help, Mr Steinberg? Please.'

Wiener rose from his seat. Demi watched as the imposing figure crossed over to her. Staring at his solid face, she sensed a kindness in his eyes.

'Yes, we will help you as our interest is in the stolen diamonds. We cannot guarantee the safety of Pat Doyle, but hey: we'll do our best.'

Demi moved slightly as a feeling of guilt washed over her, aware of the diamonds in her pocket as they pressed against her leg. She'd collected them from the station before making her way to the jewellery shop. Demi had thought of simply moving them to another left-luggage locker but signs posted around the station concourse informed station users of the impending removal of the locker facilities in the interest of 'security and customer safety'. Demi had decided earlier that handing the stones over to Steinberg was not an option. She needed their help, praying no harm had come to Pat. The longer they left it, the more likely something dreadful would likely happen, something she dared not contemplate.

Rebekah stood next to Demi, lightly placing her hand on her shoulder.

'What about Demi's safety? They may still be looking for her. We can't just let her walk away from here to end up back in one of their brothels.'

'I agree,' Steinberg said. 'You must take her to your house.'

Demi interrupted them.

'No, I'll go to my parent's house. Anyway, I need to see my children.'

'This isn't wise,' Steinberg told her. 'I would prefer it if you only go to your parents when we know it is safe for you to do so. Until then, I must insist you take our advice.'

'My father's right,' Rebekah agreed. 'I'll take you to my house. It's not far from here.'

Demi gazed down at the floor to dwell on their advice. She reluctantly nodded then thanked Steinberg before leaving with Rebekah. Wiener watched them leave waiting until the door closed before speaking.

'Abe, I'll deal with Laine. Leave this to me.'

'What do you intend doing, Ben? No, don't answer that,' he said with his hands raised. 'Just be careful. You are one, they are many.'

'Never been a problem for me before, cousin,' Wiener told him. 'First I need to rest quietly while I contemplate a strategy.'

***

Wiener went to the guestroom to prepare for what lay ahead. Before joining the Mossad, he had trained as a Sayeret Matkal commando. His unit had been dedicated to hostage rescue missions outside of Israel. He later became one of their ruthless assassins. His style of killing, usually late at night, earned him the moniker *Deadly Nightshade*. He was adept in covert operations so taking on Barry Laine and his mob would be, as he saw it, 'a walk in the park'. Sitting quietly, he loaded his Sig Sauer with fifteen rounds. There were three spare magazines for reloading. He examined his commando dagger, presented to him by 45 Commando based at Arbroath after he'd spent three months training with them as a weapons' instructor.

Wiener strapped the dagger in its special sheath to his lower right leg. His ace-in-the-hole. The gun and dagger would be all he'd need.

**

Pat opened his eyes and stared up at a ceiling, his vision blurred as he lay on the wooden floor, trying to ignore the sharp pain that filled his head, his groin, his stomach and ribs. Through laboured breathing, he touched his side and sucked in air.

'Broken rib,' he hissed.

He glanced around, attempting to make out his surroundings. He didn't know where he was but guessed it was back at the furniture warehouse in Westgate Street. Familiar items started to take shape around him, items of furniture. He recognised the smell of burnt wood, from the fire started by Elroy Blake. As he gently raised himself from the floor, he felt a pressure on his neck forcing him back down. Lennie stood over him, his right foot pressed on Pat's throat.

'Where's the girl, Doyle?' Lennie asked. 'Where would she go with the diamonds?'

Pat tried to force a response.

'I… I don't know,' he groaned.

'Wrong answer, Doyle,' Lennie growled as he increased the pressure.

'Ease up, Len,' Laine said. 'Don't want him croaking on us just yet. We never did manage to use the bolt croppers on his friend. Maybe we'll use them on him.'

'Nice one, boss,' Lennie said. A wide grin spread across his face. 'I'll go get them.'

Laine knelt down on one knee, putting his head closer to Pat's contorted face.

'If you tell us where Demi is, I'll make this easy for you,' he whispered in Pat's ear. 'If you persist, Lennie will start cutting you up piece by little piece.'

Lennie returned with the bolt croppers menacingly reciting a nursery rhyme.

'This little piggy went to market, this little piggy stayed home.'

Pat heard a number of men burst into laughter nearby; more of Laine's goons. Pat started to laugh with them.

Laine looked at him with incredulity.

'He's laughing. Why's he laughing, Len?'

'Dunno, boss. Maybe he thinks we ain't serious.'

Lennie leaned over to close the blades of the cutters around the thumb on Pat's left hand.

'He'll soon stop fucking laughing when his thumb pops off.'

'Wait,' Laine placed his hand on Lennie's shoulder. 'I've got another idea.'

Pointing at two of the three men standing nearby, Laine barked an order.

'Pick him up and put him in a chair.'

As they hoisted him to his feet, Pat yelled out in pain. One of the men brought a dining chair over and pressed Pat down onto it. The sudden movement made him feel nauseous. He fell forward.

'Hold him on the chair then,' Laine, snapped. 'Otherwise he'll just fall back to the floor.'

Another man stepped over to help. He held Pat from behind by the shoulders. Laine called to one of them.

'Hey, Bob, come here,' he shouted. 'I need something from you,'

Bob had left Demi with his colleague at the house when he went to find the missing camera. He walked over to Laine who stood in front of Pat.

'What you carrying, Bob?' Laine asked him.

The man pulled out a small Walther P99 semi-automatic pistol.

'Hold it to his head,' he ordered. Bob pressed the pistol to Pat's temple.

'You want to pull that trigger, Bob?' Laine asked. 'You do, don't you? Put a slug clean through his fucking brain, eh?'

Bob grinned as he looked at the others, feeling privileged to be asked to carry out this execution. Pat stared up at the man holding the gun to his temple. Lennie looked confused, feeling cheated out of what would normally be his job.

'No, Bob,' Laine said. 'You don't hold a gun like that, pass it to me and I'll show you.'

Bob's brow furrowed as he removed the gun away from Pat's temple, handing it to his boss. Laine snatched the P99 lifting it to the side of Bob's head, pushing it to the side of his ear.

'See, Bob, you hold it to the side of the head, not the front. Bob nodded. A bead of sweat broke on his forehead as he felt the cold metal of the gun against him. Suddenly, the sound of a sharp crack filled the room. Laine had pulled the trigger, blowing away half of Bob's head. Pat looked on in stunned silence. A mist of red blood drifted in the air. Bone mixed with brain tissue covered his face and front. The two other men stood back, shocked at what they'd just witnessed. Lennie merely smiled. Laine turned to face Pat, still holding the gun.

'The man was a waste of space,' he told him, 'a fucking waste of space. He messed up and paid the price. You see, Doyle, I have a habit of employing idiots. Bob there,' he pointed at the prostrate body on the floor whose fingers still twitched. 'He let me down, him and the other fool let your friend get away. You'd think two grown men could keep hold of a woman in a house, wouldn't you? But no, Bob takes off while the other clown lets the woman burn the place down before getting himself torched.'

Laine paced the floor in front of Pat, who just stared at the smoking gun in his hand, wondering what Laine might do next.

'Take Lennie here,' he pointed to his right-hand man. 'I sent him after you and the woman, and he lets me down. He even tried to double cross me with the diamonds.'

Lennie's eyes widened.

'Look, Barry,' Lennie gasped. 'I never…'

'Shut it, Len,' Laine shouted. 'You insult my intelligence by offering excuses. I know you tried it on so just fucking shut it, okay?'

Laine looked at the other two men.

'Don't just stand there. Get rid of this heap of shit,' Laine said kicking the body on the floor. 'Get some more men here as well. Men I can properly rely on.'

He faced Pat and held the gun to his head. Pat winced, expecting to go the same way as Bob.

'I will give you overnight to reconsider your position, Doyle. If you don't tell me where my diamonds are, I will shoot you. Once in your balls, once in your stomach, once in your chest, finally, after about ten minutes of watching you beg for death, I'll put one in your brain. Then I'll get the girl to return the diamonds to me. Oh, by the way,' he added with a smirk on his face, 'tomorrow we'll be collecting her kids from school. Now ponder on that, eh?'

Thirty-Four

Outside Barry Laine's building, the evening grew darker. A few people made their way along the street, some heading home while others headed for the centre of town, to its bars, restaurants or clubs. On the opposite side of the road, a silver Vauxhall Insignia saloon sat quietly, with its sole occupant inside watching and waiting for the optimum moment to make his move. Lights on inside the premises meant he could see movement. He relaxed in his seat, contemplating how he would deal with the likes of Laine and his cronies.

Wiener examined his sinewy fingers as he opened and closed his fists. He rubbed the knuckles of his right hand against his left palm. Wiener didn't need weapons to kill. He was a master in close combat, known in Hebrew as *Krav Maga, whose proponents were* trained to kill with their hands or anything close by that could be used as a weapon. Wiener recalled the advice of his former mentor during his time with the Special Ops Division, *Metsada,* when he had carried out highly sensitive assassinations for the State of Israel. *Do not be concerned how much damage you cause, do what needs to be done to neutralise your enemy.* Occasionally, Wiener missed his work with the 'Institution', but knew he'd never return despite a recent offer by the new head of Mossad, Meir Dagan.

The large van pulling up outside the entrance doors interrupted his reminisces. Two men climbed out and went straight inside. Wiener figured there had to be a bunch of men inside, including Laine. He also figured they carried guns but were probably rank amateurs in their use. Most second-rate gangsters carried guns, but very few knew how to handle them properly. 'Point and shoot' was about as much as they understood, but they were potentially dangerous all the same. He watched as the two men re-emerged carrying a furled rug between them. A third man joined them and opened the rear doors of the van. They heaved the rug into the back then went back inside the building. Wiener checked his watch – 23:15. Leaving the car, Wiener crossed over to the van. Beneath his black leather jacket, he could feel the bulk of his Sig Sauer in its shoulder holster. A deep side pocket contained three magazines plus a suppressor. The dagger in its sheath was strapped to his right leg.

Wiener opened the rear doors to climb into the back of the van. There was nothing inside but the rug placed there a few minutes earlier. Pressing his foot on the top told him what was inside – a body. *Pat Doyle?*

He unrolled the rug to reveal the body with very little left of its face. He figured it was one of Laine's men. He didn't recall Doyle wearing a shoulder holster, at least. He slipped out of the van and checked the surrounding area before trying the front doors of the building. Locked.

Wiener produced two steel wiggler rakes from a leather wallet and set about the lock. Within minutes the lock sprung and he entered the premises unseen. Standing in the blackness of the showroom area, he allowed his eyes to become accustomed to the dark. He could hear voices from the upper floor. Keeping close to the walls, he made his way to the stairs leading up to the warehouse.

***

Pat Doyle watched the men that surrounded him. Laine sat in his office making phone calls whilst Lennie Randall was examining one of his bright steel axes, running a thumb along the edge of the blade, occasionally looking over to Pat with an expression Pat found unnerving. The other three men sat around a William and Mary oak side table playing cards. A

19th century long-case clock sounded its heavy beat as the pendulum moved in a steady rhythm within its oak case. Pat tried to focus his mind elsewhere by wondering if Barry Laine knew which items were genuine antiques, reproductions or just outright fakes.

An Edwardian-style dressing table stood out as a reproduction as it lacked the worn look of the genuinely older pieces nearby. Pat glanced at the mirror on the dressing table. *What was that?* A movement reflected from the far side of the room. He blinked slowly. This time he saw a man move silently across the back wall. Pat didn't think it was one of Laine's men. Elroy?

He noticed the man drop out of sight. At the same time, Laine stepped from his office. He shouted over at the three card players.

'Hey, watch that table, will you. It's worth more than you lot cost me in wages every month.' He turned to Pat.

'Okay, Doyle, what value do you place on your life, eh? Or the lives of Demi's children?'

Pat felt his breathing quicken. His nostrils flared as he stared at Laine.

'You wouldn't dare harm those children.'

His anger resulted in an excruciating pain.

'If you…' he caught his breath then continued. 'If you do, you're a bigger scumbag than I thought. Only a lowlife would harm a child.'

His voice started to rise despite the pain, directing his rage towards the man in front of him.

'You're a bastard, Laine, a low life bas…'

A blow to the back of his skull cut him short. He slumped forward in the chair, a searing pain shooting through his head.

Lennie stood behind him, stroking the flat side of his steel axe as if it was a cherished pet. Laine crouched down, level with Pat's face.

'You see, Pat, offend me, you offend my friends here.'

Barely conscious from the blow and summoning what little strength he had left, Pat raised his head about an inch from his chest. In a low voice he murmured, 'Bastard.'

***

Wiener watched the whole scene from the back of the room. He needed to choose his moment. He held the Sig Sauer in his right hand, safety catch off, suppressor screwed into the barrel. He could fire off three quick shots that would take care of the card players, sweeping his aim to the left he'd take out the big black guy. Laine he would leave until last. His plan was thwarted when he saw Laine and Lennie Randall walk towards the exit. Laine called back towards Pat.

'We'll be back in the morning, Doyle, with the children. Try anything funny and the boys will wipe the floor with you.'

Laine pointed at his three men who'd resumed their card game.

'Make sure he doesn't burn the fucking place down,' Laine said to them as he went through the door. 'Otherwise you'll all leave in a carpet.'

Wiener re-evaluated the situation. Now only three to take down, maybe without having to fire a single shot, not unless they pulled weapons on him. He crouched, watching. One of the men stood and stretched.

'I need a piss,' he announced to the others.

The man walked towards Wiener in the direction of the male WC. Wiener holstered the Sig then rose to follow him.

Laine's man whistled as he crossed over to a urinal, unzipping his pants, he uttered to himself,

'If those two try and fix the cards, I'll do 'em.'

Waiting until the goon was in mid flow, Wiener took the dagger from its sheath, holding it firmly in his right hand. Grabbing the unsuspecting man around the throat with his left forearm to stifle any scream, he plunged the knife into his victim's lower back. He was assaulted by both the knife wound and strangulation at the same time, and was dead in less than a minute. Wiener took the weight of the body, pulling it back into a cubicle before sitting it on the pan. After closing the cubicle door, he made his way back into the warehouse to resume his position, anticipating his next move. The two remaining men at the card table talked quietly. One shuffled the card pack, occasionally looking towards the toilet expecting their associate to return.

'Is he taking a dump, or something?' one of the two asked. 'He's been in there long enough.'

The second one shouted, 'Come on, Steve, or we'll deal you out.'

Silence.

'Go and see what's keeping him, Dan, I'm down twenty quid here.' Dan rose with a grunt then made his way towards the toilet, calling out as he walked,

'Hey, Steve, you going t'be in there all night, or what?'

He pushed the door, looking around the small space, and then made his way towards the cubicle. Banging on the door, he called out, 'You okay in there, Steve?'

With no response, he stepped back, brow furrowed. Glancing down he spotted a space of about a foot between the bottom of the door and the floor. Dan went down on his hands and knees, peering underneath.

'Shit!' was his last living word as a blow to the back of his head rendered him unconscious. He never felt the knife blade that severed both his trachea and oesophagus, or the blood that pumped from his throat until his heart stopped beating. Wiener decided to leave the body on the floor in a spreading, crimson lake.

Back at the table, the last man wondered what was going on, as he shuffled the cards with occasional glances towards the toilet door. He pushed back his chair rising slowly to his feet.

'Dan. Steve. Where are you?'

He listened but heard nothing other than the steady ticking of a long-case clock.

'Come on, boys,' he called, 'stop fucking about.'

He looked down at Pat. 'You just stay right there, Doyle, move and you're fucking history.'

'I'll keep my eyes on the pot,' Pat quipped.

He watched as the third man walked slowly towards the corner of the warehouse, still calling his associate's names. He reached the door, paused, then gently pushed it open.

'Is this some kind of joke?' he said peering around the door.

In the reflection from the dressing table mirror, Pat watched a form take shape from the shadows and grab the man from behind. Like a macabre voyeur, he watched the man struggle against his captor's vice-like grip before dropping to the floor.

Wiener made his way over to Pat, whose eyes were transfixed on the large man coming towards him.

'Pat Doyle, I'm guessing?'

Pat watched as the stranger put a black handled dagger into a sheath strapped to his leg.

'Yes, yes. And you are?'

Pat began to wonder if the same fate awaited him from this stranger.

'Ben Wiener.' He offered his hand. 'I'm a relative of Mr Steinberg.' They shook hands like old friends.

'Did you just kill those three guys?' he asked.

Wiener looked back towards the corner of the warehouse.

'Let's call it an occupational hazard. Should have been in their job spec when they signed up with Laine.'

He turned to face Pat.

'Anyway, let's get you out of here and seen by a doc. You look in pretty bad shape to me.'

Wiener smiled, and put a hand on Pat's shoulder, guiding him to the exit.

'It's been a long night, Pat, a long and busy night.'

They stepped out onto the street then crossed over to Wiener's car. Pat eased himself into the front seat. A surge of pain made him feel nauseous. As he looked back at the building, he recalled Laine's last words: *I'll be back with the children.* Pat had to act. Fighting the overwhelming desire to close his eyes, he mouthed,

'We… we have to… have to get to the…' and then passed out.

***

Demi and Rebekah prepared to leave Rebekah's home in north Cardiff. Demi had spoken to her parents earlier, telling them she'd collect her children then take them to school.

'Are you sure you don't mind doing this?' she asked Rebekah.

'Of course not, anyway, I promised my father I would take care of you. As soon as they're in school we'll go straight to the hospital to see Pat.'

'Do you think he'll be okay?' Demi asked. 'It's not serious, is it?'

'Not according to Ben,' Rebekah said reassuringly. 'He's been with Pat all night. Sounds like a blow to the head concussed him. The doctor's kept him in as a matter of routine. He should be okay and out of there later today.'

She picked up her car keys. 'Ben also agreed to keep us updated on Pat's progress so don't worry. He's in good hands.'

Demi tried to smile but only managed a quick upturn of her mouth. She felt the weight of the diamonds in her pocket and the same sense of guilt for not revealing she'd had them all along.

'Right then,' Rebekah announced. 'If we go now, we'll hopefully miss the worst of the school-run traffic.'

***

Lennie sat in his BMW outside the small school watching the parents arrive with their children. Some came on foot, others in cars. The man sitting next to him, known as Cockney Harry, asked a question:

'So how d'we know what her kids look like, Len?'

'We don't,' Lennie replied. 'But I know what the grandmother looks like 'cos I met her before. She's the one who'll bring the kids to school. We then feed her a line saying their mother's with us, has been hurt and that we'll take them to her straight away.'

'What if she refuses to go with us, Len? Do we use force? Won't we draw attention to ourselves if she kicks off?'

'Trust me, Harry,' Lennie assured. 'She'll come with us.'

'Shit!' Lennie said as he looked back towards the school gate.

'What is it, Len?' Harry said looking around. Wondering what had happened. 'What's the problem?'

'What the fuck are they doing here?' Lennie said to himself.

'Who's *they*?' Harry said.

Lennie spotted Demi and Rebekah Rosen as they walked towards the school holding the hands of two children between them. Picking up his mobile he pressed a speed dial number for Laine.

'What you got, Leonard?' Laine asked.

'Depends how you look at it, boss,' Lennie said. 'My brief and the woman just showed up with the kids. What d'you want us to do?'

'Your brief? What's she doing there?'

'Dunno, boss.'

'Who's with you, Len?'

'Cockney Harry, I can't get any answer from the others at the warehouse.'

'Okay,' Laine said, 'Never mind about them for now. You get the women and the kids and take them into town. I'll see you there later.'

'What d'you mean? asked. 'You want me to take my brief as well? What's she got to do with any of this?'

'Look, the very fact she's there means she's got *something* to do with it, so yes, the lawyer as well, unless of course you want her to run off saying how you just kidnapped the others.'

***

Barry Laine made his way up the stairs of his city centre business premises. Halfway, he stopped to listen. Why was it so quiet? The only noise he could hear was the sound coming in from the street traffic. He continued slowly to the top where he nudged open the door leading into the warehouse area. He looked straight at the now empty chair Pat Doyle had sat on the night before.

'Hello,' he shouted. 'Boys, where are you?' When it dawned on him that no one was there, he exploded, kicking the wooden chair across the room. He soon discovered the dead bodies of his men, one in the corner, two in the toilet. Hearing a noise, he spun round. There were footsteps on the stairs. Laine pulled his gun, moving behind a large wardrobe. It was a woman's voice.

'Get your fucking hands off of me!' she shouted.

A child cried out, 'Mummy.' Laine waited until they came through the door. Demi, frantic, pulled the two children in close to her. Her young girl cried while the slightly older boy looked around him bewildered.

'It's okay, kids,' Demi reassured them. 'Nothing's going to happen to us.'

Laine stepped out, gun in hand, and walked over towards them, indicating towards Lennie to join him.

'The boys are dead,' he whispered. 'And Doyle isn't here.'

'Dead? But how? D'you think Doyle did this?'

'Don't be stupid, Len,' he almost blurted. 'This is the work of Steinberg's friend. Who else would be capable of this? We have to get them away from here,' Laine nodded towards the women. 'But not the brief,' he continued. 'Lock her in the office, unplug the desk phone and take her mobile.'

Harry waved a small phone in the air. 'Already got it, boss.'

'Where shall I take them – one of the dives?' Lennie asked.

'No,' replied Laine. 'Take them to the taxi office, tell the drivers to tool up. I want them ready for action. That's your patch, Leonard. What weapons you got there?'

'Couple of shotguns, about six handguns, the usual blades.'

'Ammo?'

'Plenty, boss, so what you planning?'

'Not sure yet, Len, but if that big Yid comes back, we'll be ready for him.'

Demi and Rebekah stood together comforting the children. Cockney Harry stood nearby, gun in hand. Chardonnay, Demi's youngest, clung to her mother's leg. Zak tried to act brave but the fear in his eyes revealed otherwise.

'Demi,' Rebekah whispered. 'Don't worry. My father will sort this out.'

'Shut it,' Harry hissed. 'You don't say a word, okay?'

Laine and Lennie looked over.

Demi had a defiant look on her face.

'Sod off, prick.'

'Mummy, please,' her little girl pleaded. 'Please don't shout. I'm frightened.' The child began to cry again.

'It's alright, love,' Demi reassured her daughter, wiping Chardonnay's eyes with a sleeve. 'He's just a nasty little man trying to scare us.'

Harry stepped forward, raising the gun, pointing it at Demi. Both children screamed.

'Harry,' Laine shouted. 'Back off.' He turned to Lennie.

'Go now, I'll join you later. I need to get someone over here to clean up and take care of the bodies.'

Lennie spread his arms out, ushering them towards the door. Demi stood her ground.

'C'mon, love, keep it moving,' Lennie snapped. 'We ain't got all day.'

'I want to speak to him.' Demi said, pointing at Barry Laine. 'This is what you're looking for isn't it? Here, take them and let us go.'

She held out a velvet pouch. Laine took it from her, tipping some of the contents into his hand.

His eyebrows rose. Rebekah looked over. Her face was in a frown. 'Where did they come from?' she asked. Demi ignored the question.

'Demi,' she persisted. 'How long have you had them? I thought…'

'I'm sorry, Rebekah,' Demi interrupted. 'I was going to tell you, honestly, but I needed your help first.'

'At last,' Laine whispered, before looking back at Demi. 'How do I know these are for real? After the last stunt you and Doyle pulled this might be another heap of shit.'

Demi stared at him in stony silence.

'Okay,' Laine said, I'll have them tested. In the meantime, you lot stay with Lennie, if these *are* fake, I'll make you eat them.'

'Oh, they're real enough,' Demi said. 'Now let Rebekah and the children go. I'll stay until you find out the diamonds are genuine. Then I'll let you have the rest.'

She took the remaining four pouches from her pocket.

Laine nodded. 'Maybe.'

With screwed eyes, he looked at Rebekah.

'So where exactly do you fit in to all this? Laine asked, pointing at Rebekah. 'You're Lennie's brief, how come you're with her?' What's the connection?'

'Abraham Steinberg is my father,' Rebekah revealed. 'And the diamonds you have in your grubby hand belong to him.'

Laine smiled at her.

'Right now, my dear, they belong to me.'

'Well, are you going to let them go?' Demi cut in. 'You have the diamonds. My children are frightened. I want them to go home. Please let Rebekah take them home.'

Laine contemplated this new situation. Now he knew that Rebekah Rosen was Steinberg's daughter he had a better idea.

'Lennie will make arrangements for the kids to go home,' he told her, 'but you and the brief stay here for now.' He held his hand out towards her. 'Now give me the rest of the stones before I change my mind about the kids.'

She gave him the remaining four pouches.

Laine turned to Lennie.

'Change of plan. Put the kids in a taxi, then take both the women to the docks office. I'll catch you up later. First, I need to make someone a very attractive offer.'

Thirty-Five

Wiener returned from the hospital with Pat Doyle who sported a dressing to parts of his face and clutched a bottle of painkillers that did little to ease the hurt he suffered. They met with Steinberg to discuss what they should do next.

'How's Demi?' Pat asked immediately on seeing Steinberg.

'Fine, just fine,' Steinberg assured him. 'She's with my daughter. I've tried to contact her but she's not answering her phone.'

His phone trilled in his hand. 'This is probably her now,' Steinberg said.

Taking the call, Steinberg looked up as the colour drained from his face. Pat and Wiener looked on, both realising something was wrong. Steinberg ended the call before facing the men opposite him.

'That was Laine,' he said quietly. 'He says he has the diamonds, Demi, and my daughter. Picked them up when they dropped Demi's children off at the school.'

'Does he have the children as well?' Pat asked.

'He didn't say so,' Steinberg replied.

Wiener stepped over to Steinberg.

'There's something else, isn't there, Abe?'

'Yes. He says he wants a quarter million pounds or I won't see Rebekah again.'

Steinberg dropped his head into his hands.

'What do we do?' The anguish evident in his voice.

'Did he give you any instructions, Abe?' Wiener asked. 'How'd you get the money to him, stuff like that?'

Steinberg lifted his head.

'He said to go to Pat Doyle's flat. Then we will know how serious he is.'

'My flat,' Pat blurted. 'Why my flat? Oh God, I hope he hasn't harmed Demi.'

Wiener headed for the door.

'Let's just go. I'll think of something on the way there.'

***

The three men stood outside the half-opened front door of the flat. Wiener took the Sig from inside his jacket before slipping the safety catch. He touched his lips with a finger then gently pushed open the door. Stepping inside, Wiener moved silently through the flat, checking each room. The bedroom was the last room he looked in. Gripping the Sig with both hands, he lightly pushed the door with his foot.

Wiener moved his head around the doorframe. The contents of a chest of drawers and a wardrobe were strewn across the floor. On the single bed, Wiener noticed a shape covered with a bloodstained duvet. Backing down the hall, Wiener motioned for the others to come into the flat. They stood outside the bedroom with him looking in. When Pat's eyes fell on the bed, he almost leapt across the small space to pull back the duvet. Underneath lay the body of the person who had been so close to him over many years: Elroy Blake. The shattered face of his now dead friend was barely recognisable. Pat's eyes welled with tears as he fell to his knees. Wiener came over to place a hand on Pat's shoulder.

'Who was he?' Wiener asked.

'A… a friend,' Pat replied barely able to speak, 'a close friend who had nothing to do with any of this.'

He knelt there, hating Barry Laine with every inch of his being, mentally vowing to extract revenge.

'Poor guy,' Wiener said. 'They beat him real bad before putting a bullet through his head.'

Wiener had noticed a small entry hole in Elroy's forehead made by a 9mm fired at close range. The exit hole at the back of the skull would be much larger and messier and account for the blood-splattered duvet. Wiener lifted the duvet to recover the body. Pat stood and silently left the room before the three men gathered in the kitchen.

'What do I do?' Pat asked. 'I can't just leave him in there.'

'We sort this mess out first, then call the cops,' Wiener said. 'But not before,' he added.

'How long will all this take?' Pat asked. 'I can't believe Laine did this.'

'Laine has Demi and Rebekah,' Wiener reminded him. 'He wants a quarter million in ransom for Rebekah. We have to go along with this for now. We don't want Demi to be the next victim.'

The thought of this made Pat shudder.

'First, we call Laine, ask what he wants us to do next,' Wiener said. 'We need to find out where they're being held. Once we know that, I'll take care of it.'

Pat shook his head.

'No, let's just call the police and let them deal with it. This has gone far enough.'

'Sure, makes good sense,' Wiener agreed. 'But it would likely complicate matters. We'd all be taken in for questioning. Laine may not find out and think we're stalling. We can't afford the possible consequences of that happening.'

'He's right,' Steinberg said. 'My daughter is being held hostage so I should involve the police. But, no, we must let Ben deal with this. I trust him. You must also trust him.'

'I don't know,' Pat said, 'Demi's children, Laine said he was going to harm them.'

'I think he *was* going to use the children to get to you, Demi and the stones,' Wiener said. 'It looks as though he's got all of them now so he has no further use for the children. If he had them, he would have said so.'

'Okay,' Pat said, 'now what?'

'You know this guy better than us,' Wiener said, 'any idea where he'd have taken them?'

'I don't really know him that well. He has places all over the city, houses, pubs, clubs, the lot.'

Wiener nodded. 'Then we'll wait for his next call – try to draw him out into the open. Until then, I suggest we go back to the shop and wait for that call.'

***

Barry Laine stood in the charity shop beneath the taxi office in Cardiff Bay. Lennie stood next to him. Laine looked around trying to imagine what it was like back in the 1960s when it had been a funeral parlour. Upstairs, the now taxi control room was the place where his grandfather had killed the double-crossing undertaker who had tried to cheat him. Laine smiled to himself. *Good for you, Gramps.*

'This is where it all started, Len. This is where my granddad brought the diamonds after robbing the train, him and my uncle Eddie.'

'Great train robbers, eh, boss?'

'Yeah, and now I finally have the stones.'

He took a velvet pouch of diamonds from a pocket weighing them in his hand. 'Plus a quarter of a million in the bank when Steinberg pays out for his daughter.'

'What about the big guy?' Lennie asked. 'How're we going to deal with him?'

Laine tapped his minder twice on the cheek with the palm of his right hand.

'Up against you, Len, what chance has he got?'

Lennie grinned back at him. He took a steel axe from inside his leather jacket, the overhead light glinting off the polished steel.

'This little baby hasn't tasted blood in a long while,' he told Laine. 'As soon as he shows his ugly mug, I leave this calling card buried in his head.'

'Mind you do, Lennie boy. I want him out of the picture for good. He could complicate my little plan. Remember, whatever you do, Len, like always, it doesn't lead back to me.'

'Hey, boss,' Lennie said. 'Has anything ever come back on you? When I do a job, I leave no trace.'

'I know, Len, but the police have been sniffing around, especially after that bitch torched the house in Grangetown.'

'Yeah, but they put it down to an accident,' Lennie reminded him. 'The body was too badly burnt to make them suspicious of anything.'

'Yeah, but I don't need them prying into my affairs again. So do your job and do it right.'

Taking his phone from a pocket Laine called Steinberg as he made his way back up to the taxi office.

***

In a back room, Demi and Rebekah sat under the watchful eye of Cockney Harry who chain-smoked small cigars. The room had once been the undertaker's bedroom back in the 1960s. A small window let the cigar smoke escape through the gap at the top. The women looked up when Laine entered, holding a phone to his ear. Lennie followed behind. Laine spoke to Steinberg as he crossed the room towards Rebekah; he stopped in front of her then handed over the phone.

'Speak to your father,' Laine said smiling. 'Tell him you're safe and well.' Rebekah took the mobile from him,

'Hello, Daddy, it's me,' Rebekah said calmly. 'Yes, I'm okay. Yes, so is Demi. No, the children went back to Demi's mother. No, they were fine. A little upset, but fine.'

Laine snapped his fingers, indicating for the phone.

'Okay, Steinberg,' Laine said. 'This is what you do. I want the money put in a large holdall. One of my men will pick it up from you. No funny business, as soon as I have the money, I'll let your girl go. Got that?'

He listened as Steinberg spoke then responded,

'Sorry, sir, but the other woman is not part of the deal. She stays with me. You get your daughter back, I keep the diamonds, the money and the woman.'

Demi and Rebekah looked at each other. Laine grinned as he looked down at Demi.

'No', he said into the phone, 'Little Demi owes me big time, she's going to repay in full.'

A long silence followed as Laine listened.

'A generous offer' Laine said after a while. 'One I may seriously consider. You have my number, as soon as the money's ready, give me a call, then I'll give you further instructions.'

Laine laughed as he pocketed the phone. The two women leapt from the chairs, standing together in the centre of the room. Harry stepped forward preventing them making for the door.

Rebekah spoke first.

'What do you mean, Demi stays here?' she demanded. 'You'd better let us both go or else.'

'Or else what?' Laine snapped.

Demi spoke next.

'It's okay, I'll be fine. This low life doesn't scare me one bit,' Demi said venomously.

Laine's face dropped to a sneer. He moved across the room towards them. Rebekah blocked his way. About to push her aside to get at Demi, he stopped short, glaring wide-eyed at Rebekah. A grinning Harry watched, hoping his boss would become violent and start lashing out. He was to be disappointed as Laine simply spoke to the solicitor.

'It would seem your father is willing to pay good money for your friend here,' Laine said indicating towards Demi, 'an extra hundred grand for her safe return. That's on top of the two fifty for you.'

'Okay,' he said to Harry, as he pushed Demi towards him, 'get this bitch out of here. Take her to my place. But before you do,' he snapped his fingers, Lennie handed him a hypodermic syringe, 'give her this. It'll keep her quiet if nothing else.'

Demi had no idea what was in the syringe, but she knew it wouldn't be good news. She struggled fiercely, but it was futile. The full syringe was unloaded into her arm, flooding her system with heroin.

'Me and Len will head for my place. Bring her along as soon as the gear takes hold.'

Within minutes, they were in the BMW heading for Sully.

***

Abraham Steinberg ended the call to Laine, watched by the men who sat in the room with him. He looked across to Pat.

'Can you think of anywhere they might be, Pat? We don't have much time.' Pat rubbed his forehead.

'I'm not sure.' He paused. 'Hang on, there's the taxi office in the Bay, the one over the charity shop. They could have taken them there.'

'Good,' Wiener said. 'At least we have a starting point, always good to have a starting point.'

Picking up the phone, he handed it to Steinberg.

'Abe, give the schmuck a call. Tell him getting the cash together will be difficult. He'll know banks don't just hand over that kind of money at short notice. It'll buy us some valuable time.'

He returned his attention to Pat.

'Right, show me where this taxi place is located. We'll go in my car.'

They drove through sluggish traffic across the city, road works and large-scale construction sites causing near gridlock. Feeling anxious, Pat asked Wiener some questions.

'Are you sure this will work out, Ben? I mean without anyone getting hurt?'

Wiener smiled his reply.

'Oh, people are going to get hurt, I'm afraid. People are going to get hurt real bad. That, I can guarantee.'

Pat shifted in his seat, feeling uneasy with the response to his question. They drove past the statue of the Marquis of Bute.

'What do you do for a living in New York, Ben?'

'I'm retired. Live off a pension and play the markets.'

'That's a form of gambling I tried once, but I lost a lot of money,' Pat told him, 'Got me into a shit load of trouble with a local money lender.'

'Gotta know what you're doing,' Wiener said. 'Often you'll lose but play it right you can make serious money. So what happened for you to lose so much?'

'Ever heard of spread-betting?' Pat asked.

'Sure, it can be a safe way to play the market. Is that what you did?'

'It is, but I lost all my money. Money I didn't have in the first place. I borrowed ten grand from the bank initially only to lose it overnight.'

Wiener glanced at Pat.

'Sorry to hear it, bud. Sounds like you had some dodgy advice.'

'Very dodgy,' Pat confirmed. 'So then I tried again. Only this time I borrowed from a local loan shark. Another two thousand went the same way. Now he's after me, threatening to remove my fingers if I don't repay in a month. When I came across the diamonds, I thought my luck had changed, a sure way out of my financial dilemma.'

'But you didn't figure on Barry Laine, eh?' Wiener said.

'Nope, I thought, sell the stones, pay off my debts, and have money in the bank. Now look at the mess I'm in.'

'We'll sort this out – maybe you'll get a good result.'

Pat thought about this for a moment.

'So, were you a cop then, Ben?'

'Not exactly, I was with the Mossad.'

'The Israeli secret service?' Pat said impressed.

'One and the same.'

'Wow.'

Approaching the charity shop, Pat let Wiener drive past before telling him to pull over.

'It's the place back there. The animal sanctuary shop is where I found the letter, the taxi office is upstairs.'

Ben adjusted the interior mirror letting him see the place without turning around. There were two taxis parked outside.

Stencilled across the front doors was the name *City Cabs*. A man sat behind the wheel of one of the cars. Wiener noticed a doorway alongside the entrance to the charity shop. Someone stepped outside, climbed into one of the taxis and started the engine.

'Are these cab drivers for real or do they serve some other function?' Wiener asked.

'They're Laine's thugs,' Pat said. 'I'm told they use the taxi business as a front for moving drugs around the city, amongst other things. You'll rarely see a fare in one of those cars.'

'Okay,' Wiener said. 'We got two cars, in one, a driver. I'm guessing there are other men in the office. If Demi and Rebekah are inside, there's probably at least three to keep a watch on them.'

Wiener thought for a moment.

'You stay in the car. I'll go across, say I want a ride into town. If they go along with it, I'll take another ride back here. If not, well either way I'll have checked out the place.'

'Won't they recognise you? They've seen you before, haven't they?'

'Yes, but this time I might be the last thing they ever see.'

Outside the taxi office door, Wiener was about to climb the stairs when a man leading a woman blocked his way. She seemed to need his support as she appeared drunk and muttered incoherently as they passed. The man pushed her into the back of one of the cars. Wiener guessed the woman was Demi. Quietly, he made his way to the top of the stairs where he could hear voices from within.

'She went down like a sack of shit when Lennie stuck her with the pin,' a voice said, laughing.

Another voice with a Scottish accent said, 'Wonder what the boss will do to her when he gets to his place?'

'Yeah, lucky bastard. I wouldn't mind a piece of that action sometime.'

'So how long do we keep this *other* lass here?' the Scot said.

'Until we get a call with orders about where to take her,' the other man told him.

Wiener guessed they were discussing Rebekah. He tapped on the door before stepping inside.

'Any chance of a ride into town?' he asked.

The two men in the room looked over to him with surprise. Neither responded. Wiener assessed the layout of the office. The usual radio equipment sat on the desk, but silently – unusual for a taxi business.

'Ride into town?' he repeated.

'There's a taxi on the street,' the Scot said. 'Why don't ye ask him?' The other man moved towards the door.

'Some couple beat me to it,' Wiener said.

'There's two down there, why come up here?'

'I didn't see another one,' Ben lied.

'Be about an hour,' the Scot said abruptly.

'An hour?' Ben feigned astonishment. 'What about the car down there you mentioned?'

'He's spoken for. So like I said, an hour.'

'Jeez, be quicker to walk. See-ya, guys.'

Ben made his way back down to the street. He checked out the man sitting behind the wheel of the taxi parked on the roadside; the other car now gone. They'll use this car to move Rebekah, he guessed.

'Decision time,' he told himself as he crossed back to join Pat.

'They've taken Demi away,' Pat told Wiener with a strained anxiety in his voice.' I saw them put her in a taxi. What do we do now?'

'Yes, I know. To Laine's house, I overheard the guys in the office, so I'm guessing they still have Rebekah over there and she's my priority right now.'

Pat looked crestfallen.

'What about Demi?' he asked. 'She's in serious trouble.'

'I have to take care of Rebekah first, Pat,' Wiener said softly. 'Anyway, I can't risk leaving here in case they move her. Right now she's up there with two guys and those are the odds I like.'

'Yes, I understand, but surely no harm is likely to come to Rebekah, whereas Demi risks being seriously hurt by those bastards.'

'Listen, Pat, I'll do what I can, but first I have to take care of my family.'

Pat made a fist with his right hand, tapping his upper lip.

'Right,' he said, 'my car's parked nearby. I'm going to Laine's place. I need to help Demi.'

'You can't deal with them on your own,' Wiener told him. 'Hell, they'll kill you as well.'

'It's a chance I'm prepared to take,' he insisted.

'I can let you have this.' He offered Pat the Sig.

Pat looked with alarm at the proffered gun.

'I… I wouldn't know what to do with it. I've never fired a gun in my life – except at fairgrounds.'

Wiener smiled. 'You simply point and shoot – same as fairgrounds.'

'I'd rather not,' he said opening the door to get out.

'Well at least take this car,' Wiener said. 'You'll be quicker starting from here.'

Pat turned to look back.

'But won't you need the car if you get Rebekah out of there?'

'That's right, my friend, but I'll be using the one parked outside the building over there. It's a taxi after all.'

Pat pulled up outside the front gates of Barry Laine's imposing house. The electronically controlled gates were locked so he started to walk around the black limestone wall that stood about ten feet high. He continued on, hoping to find another way in. His luck changed when he noticed a gardener's stepladder leaning against a tree up ahead. The pruning work on the ground suggested the job hadn't been finished. The gardener would probably return soon. Moving the steps, Pat set them against the wall and climbed up, just managing to reach the top.

Breathing heavily and hurting from the pain in his ribs, Pat looked onto the grounds of the house from his vantage point. Images flashed through his mind of guards patrolling the grounds with snarling Rottweilers on leashes.

He sat waiting, observing the house and garden that remained quiet without sign of either man or beast.

Pat slid over, hanging down the other side of the wall. He then dropped the last four feet, landing heavily on the damp grass, thankful the soft ground had cushioned his fall. Walking tentatively toward the house, he stopped, aware of being spotted on the wide expanse of the lawn and picking a large Hydrangea shrub for cover. He peered around it, checking the windows for signs of movement. Satisfied it was clear, he crept towards a set of French doors. Pat edged his face from the side to look through the glass. He spotted Barry Laine in the room. Demi, sitting in a chair, stared up at him with eyes glazed from the effects of the drug they'd injected earlier.

He watched as Laine puts his hands on Demi's shoulders, pulling her even closer to him. She moved forward, placed her arms around his neck then raised her head as if to kiss him. Laine leaned forward, eyes closed, ready to receive her inviting mouth.

Suddenly, Demi drove her right knee hard into his groin. Laine cried out as he doubled over. Outside, Pat punched the air. *'Yes!'*

The double-glazed door prevented Pat from hearing what Demi was saying to Laine, who knelt retching on the floor in front of her. Judging by the expression on her face, he guessed she wasn't enquiring after his wellbeing.

The door opened and Lennie stepped in followed by the shorter, yet equally stocky Preston.

Laine managed to recover himself.

'Bitch,' he snarled.

Distracted by the two men who'd entered the room, Demi looked away from Laine, who in that moment swung his hand, hitting Demi on the side of her head. The force of the blow caused her to stagger back. Outside, Pat watched, head spinning with rage. Looking around, he noticed a rockery on the edge of the lawn. He struggled to lift one of the larger stones, his rib feeling like it had punctured a lung as he hurled it at the doors. The glass door shattered into a million pieces.

'Bastard,' he cried out, heading for Laine. When Lennie caught sight of him, he pulled out a 9mm handgun, firing off two shots; one hit Pat in the chest. The other missed him, smashing through the glass of the remaining French door. Pat stopped in his tracks when the bullet penetrated just below the shoulder, face contorted with pain, he looked at where it had torn through his jacket. Staggering back, he fell to the floor.

'Pat,' Demi screamed as she watched him go down. She jumped over and knelt by him, cradling his head in her hands.

'I think he got me,' Pat whispered hoarsely. His eyelids fluttered.

'Don't you dare die on me, Pat Doyle,' she sobbed at him. His eyes closed again as his head rolled to the side.

Demi looked back at Lennie, who still had the gun pointing in their direction.

'You've killed him. You bastards have killed him.'

'Get her out of here,' Laine blasted at the two men in the room. 'Get her out of my fucking sight.' He looked at Lennie, who dragged Demi to her feet.

'Take her to your place, Len. I'll decide what to do with her from there.'

'Get your stinking hands off me,' Demi shouted, spitting at Laine as she passed him.

'You'll pay for this, you miserable, murdering bastards.'

Laine looked down at Pat Doyle lying motionless on the floor.

'Bitch,' he repeated, then followed the others out of the room.

Thirty-Six

Wiener stood on the pavement looking over at the parked car outside the taxi office. The man behind the wheel smoked a cigarette as he repeatedly looked at his wristwatch. Wiener crossed the street to come upon the car. As he came nearer, the driver looked at him suspiciously. Wiener leaned on the roof and lowered his head to speak to the driver.

'Mr Laine told me to meet him here. Am I in the right place?'

'Top of the stairs,' the driver said pointing to the door behind Wiener. 'Who shall I say wants him?'

He picked up a mobile ready to press a speed dial button.

'I'll just go on up.'

Taking the steps three at a time in long strides, Wiener twisted the suppressor onto the Sig. Outside the door, he could hear the ring tone of a mobile phone, the driver outside about to warn of his arrival. Wiener pushed the Sig's safety to off. He waited for a response; the call would distract whoever answered, giving Wiener a better element of surprise. He heard a voice.

'Yeah, what is it?'

Wiener pushed the door with his foot and stepped inside. The man on the phone looked over to see a gun pointing at his head. He didn't hear the muffled thud or feel the 9mm bullet enter his forehead, the hollow point round removing most of his head on impact. Wiener crossed the room to the other door where he pressed against the woodchip-papered wall. The door opened. The Scot stepped into the room, his eyes drawn immediately to the body of his associate. As he leapt over to him, Wiener stepped up from behind, grabbing him around the neck, snapping his cervical vertebrae before dropping him quietly to the floor. *Neutralise your enemy as fast as possible,* he mused. He waited as the taxi driver entered, despatching him the same way as the Scot. Wiener didn't bother to check any of the three men as he knew they were all dead. Instead, he went through to the other room, where he found Rebekah Rosen tied to a chair, her mouth taped to prevent her crying out. He took hold of the tape.

'This may hurt a little,' he said then yanked at the duct tape. Rebekah shrieked as it peeled from her skin. Wiener untied the cord around her hands and ankles then helped her up.

'Ben,' she said, falling into him. He held her as she cried. Rebekah looked into Wiener's face. He could see fear in her expression and felt her tremble in his arms.

'They've taken Demi. Did you see her? Do you know where she is?'

Wiener stroked the side of her face.

'First, we take you home. Check you are safe and well. A doctor will examine you.'

'Ben, I'm okay,' she insisted. 'We have to help Demi. God only knows what they plan to do with her.'

'Yes, I was outside when they put her in the car,' Wiener confirmed. 'I heard them mention Laine's place. They've probably taken her there. Pat's on his way already.'

'My God, what can Pat possibly do by himself? We must hurry,' Rebekah pulled away from Wiener. 'I know where he lives. Come on, Ben.'

'I should take you to your father. You can give me directions to Laine's house on the way.'

'No, Ben, there isn't time. We have to go right away. Where's your car?'

Wiener relented, agreeing to take her with him. Back out on the street he climbed into the Ford Mondeo recently occupied by a man now lying dead with a broken neck. The keys, as he expected, were still in the ignition. Rebekah opened the passenger door, climbing in beside him.

Wiener pulled away from the kerb.

'Where we heading?'

Rebekah gave him directions for the Butetown tunnels that would take them down to Sully. As they sped along the road, they didn't notice Lennie's black BMW as it passed them headed in the opposite direction.

***

Wiener pulled up outside Laine's house where he noticed his own car parked near the entrance. Walking up to the gates he examined their structure – heavy-duty, galvanised wrought iron with decorative scrollwork, probably custom made by a specialist company. Wiener ran his hand lightly down one of the rails. He closely examined the lock and electronic keypad then returned to the car to re-join Rebekah.

'Can you get inside?' she asked, anxiously.

'Sure,' he replied.

Wiener drove slowly forward before stopping with the bonnet just touching the gates. He pressed lightly on the accelerator and the car edged forward, forcing the gates to spring open.

'You've done this before, haven't you?' Rebekah said.

He smiled at her. 'There have been occasions, some harder than others.'

They continued to drive to the front of the house.

'Isn't this dangerous, Ben? They'll see us coming.'

'Something tells me they're not here. No cars on the front drive for a start.' He stopped and climbed out.

Wiener walked around the building. Rebekah followed. He noticed the shards of glass by the French doors. Easing his pace, Wiener slipped the Sig from his jacket pocket and raised his palm, signalling Rebekah to stop. He placed his back against the wall and peeked inside. Small, crystal-like pieces of broken glass glistened on the carpet. It had been smashed from the outside in. Wiener noticed the large boulder on the carpet. *Well that's how he got in*. Wiener spotted Pat lying on the floor at the far side of the room. Satisfied no one else was present, Wiener stepped inside. Rebekah followed behind him and ran over to Pat.

'He's dead. They've killed him and left him here.'

Wiener knelt down next to him placing two fingers on Pat's neck.

'Not quite, but nearly.'

He examined the gunshot wound.

'Probably shot with a round nosed shell, from back there.' He pointed to the room doors. 'Judging by the other shattered door, a second shot missed. Lucky for him.'

'Phone for an ambulance,' Rebekah said.

Wiener had his mobile phone in his hand. From habit, he dialled 911 but still got through to the emergency services. He passed the phone to Rebekah to provide the details of their location. As he did, he was aware someone had entered the room.

Preston. Laine's manservant.

The man held a Purdey side-by-side double barrel shotgun.

Wiener examined the 12-bore hunting weapon pointed at him. In close quarters it would kill him and Rebekah if the man pulled both triggers. He needed to take the initiative to somehow disarm him.

'Stand up, move over by the wall,' Preston ordered. 'Any funny moves and I let go with both barrels.'

Wiener stared back at him, saying nothing. He moved to the wall, drawing the line of fire away from Rebekah.

'You're making a big mistake, my friend,' Wiener said.

'How so? I'm the one with the gun. Now slowly drop your gun to the floor then kick it away.'

Wiener continued to stare at him, silent and motionless.

'Do it now!' Preston shouted, raising the shotgun to his shoulder. Wiener let the Sig slip from his hand. It hit the carpet with a thud. A light breeze blew through the shattered doors, bringing with it the sound of a distant siren.

'My niece just called an ambulance for our friend here. She told them a man needs treatment for a gunshot wound.'

Preston kept the gun pointed straight at him.

'Any mention of guns and the cops are automatically informed,' Wiener said. 'So what you can hear out there is the sound of both ambulance and cops racing here.' Wiener paused. 'Go ahead, shoot. Then take on the Armed Response Unit that will be parked outside in about five minutes.'

Preston lowered the shotgun and looked at Wiener.

'So when they arrive,' he said, 'I'll tell them you did that.' He indicated the Purdey towards Pat Doyle. 'I heard the shot, came down with my gun. Caught you two red-handed.' Wiener figured he was right. The police would buy that line and arrest him.

'You recognise me, don't you?' Rebekah said to Preston. 'I can convince them otherwise. They know this house belongs to Barry Laine. Think about it.'

'She's right,' Wiener confirmed. 'We all need to get out of here, we can continue this debate someplace else or we continue it at the station.'

Wiener took a step forward.

'You have about three minutes, my friend, before this place is surrounded. What's it to be?'

Preston lowered the gun.

'I'm coming with you,' he said holding the shotgun in one hand by the barrel. Wiener took full advantage of the opportunity he'd created. He snatched the gun, turned it then drove the walnut stock into the man's nose. Preston fell to the floor, blood spurting from his smashed face. Wiener stood over him, nudging him with his foot, satisfied the man was unconscious. He looked at the shotgun closely.

'Now there's something you don't often see,' he said after he'd opened the chamber to remove the cartridges.

'Instead of the standard two-and-three-quarter inch chamber this one has a magnum three-inch chamber.'

'Ben, we don't have time to study the dimensions of guns,'

Intrigued, Wiener peered down the barrel of the Purdey.

'I never finished the call to the emergency services,' Rebekah continued. She picked up her mobile from the floor and called again for an ambulance. 'So what were the sirens we heard?' she asked.

'Probably a fire truck,' Wiener said. 'Perfect timing I thought. But our friend here wasn't to know.'

He retrieved his Sig from the floor.

'Well now they *are* on their way,' Rebekah said.

Wiener checked on Pat, who had started to regain consciousness.

'You'll be okay, my friend. Help is on its way. I think the trauma of the gunshot wound caused you to faint. Wounds like this one don't generally knock you out.'

'Demi,' Pat rasped. 'She needs help.'

'Don't you worry about Demi,' Wiener said. 'We're taking care of things. Now I'm sure you'll appreciate we really cannot be found here.'

Pat nodded his understanding.

'There's a bullet lodged in your shoulder. An exit wound would have killed you, so lucky for you it's still in there.'

'Come on,' Rebekah said. 'I can hear more sirens, only this time I don't think it's a fire engine.'

Wiener stood up and looked around the room.

'Damn,' he said loudly.

'What is it?'

'We can't leave him here. We'll have to take him with us.'

'But the ambulance is on its way,' she insisted, 'Pat needs to get to casualty.'

'No, not Pat. Him.' Wiener pointed to the unconscious form of the man who was bleeding profusely from the nose. 'He can tell us where they've taken Demi but we can't wait until he feels better.'

Wiener walked over to Preston, taking hold of him by the back of the collar.

'Time to get up, my little friend.' He pulled Preston to his feet. 'You're coming with us.' The butler started to rouse. Wiener took the Sig from his pocket and pushed the gun into the nape of his neck.

'You drive, Rebekah. I'll take a back seat with our friend here.'

Wiener instructed Rebekah to take a detour down a quiet country road.

'Pull over at the next layby,' he said.

'Why?' She asked. 'Don't tell me you need to pee.'

'No,' he said. 'But I think our friend here wants to relieve himself of something else.' Rebekah gave a puzzled look before she pulled the car over. Wiener hauled Preston from the rear seat, holding him against the car.

'Now, my little buddy,' he hissed in the man's face. 'Some questions for you.'

Wiener pushed the barrel of the Sig into Preston's damaged nose. He screamed out in agony.

'Hollow nose bullet, it'll blow most of your tiny brain away. So, where have they taken Demi?'

Preston shook his head.

'Ah-ah,' Wiener said. 'Now had you said *I don't know* your brain would have been all over this nice car. Let's try again, shall we?' Wiener repeated, only this time louder. 'Where have they taken Demi?'

There was a pause as Preston considered his position. He didn't think the man who held the gun to his head would think twice about killing him.

'They've gone to Lennie's place,' Preston said.

Wiener put his face close up to Preston pushing harder on the Sig. The man screwed his eyes shut tightly.

'And Lennie's place is where exactly?'

Rebekah had heard Wiener's questions.

'Ben, it's okay. I know the address. I've sent letters to him.'

Wiener pulled Preston away from the car and turned him around. He placed the gun to the back of the man's neck.

'Please, no, no,' the man begged. 'I told you what you wanted. Please don't kill me.'

Wiener smiled as he raised the gun then brought the butt down on the man's head. Preston fell, hitting the tarmac, unconscious for the second time that evening.

Thirty-Seven

With the unconscious Preston Taylor deposited safely on the roadside, Wiener drove along the Cardiff road, reaching speeds close to 90mph. Rebekah anxiously held onto her seat as the car took some sharp bends.

'Will he be okay?' she asked, trying to take her mind off the journey. 'He could die back there.'

'He'll be just fine,' he assured her. 'You need to call your father and husband, let them know you're safe and well. Tell your father to send either Michael or Israel to collect you. Then show me where this *schmuck* lives.'

Rebekah spoke with her father. Steinberg agreed to send both his sons to collect her from a warehouse he owned near the river.

Wiener pulled up outside the red brick building and switched off the engine.

'Your brothers will be here shortly,' he said. 'So draw me a map of where this Lennie Randall lives.'

'It's near here,' Rebekah said as she drew directions on a piece of paper. As she finished a car pulled up in front of them – an S Class Mercedes with a registration plate consisting of two letters followed by the figure 1. Steinberg, his two sons and Rebekah's husband, Isaac, climbed out. Rebekah embraced Isaac in the street. Moving away from the cars, Steinberg spoke to Wiener.

'Thank you, my friend. I never doubted you'd get Rebekah back from that *putz*. Come, let us join the others.'

The brothers were hugging their sister when Steinberg senior approached with Wiener. Rebekah pulled away from her younger brother, Israel, and faced Wiener.

'Well, Ben. What will you do now?'

'There's nothing for him to do,' Isaac Rosen interrupted. 'You're safe so we should now inform the police. Let them take care of things from here.'

'Isaac, we still don't have the diamonds,' Steinberg said.

'Then let the police get them back for you,' he retorted. 'This has gone far enough. They kidnapped my wife. I want him arrested and charged.'

A group of chanting young males crossed the river bridge. A street drinker staggered nearby. Isaac Rosen looked around the area.

'What are we doing out here? We should return home immediately.'

He took Rebekah by the hand as he opened the rear door of the Mercedes.

Angrily, she pulled back her hand.

'This is not about the diamonds,' she shouted. 'Stuff the goddamn diamonds.'

The others looked at her, shocked at this sudden outburst.

'This is about Demi,' she continued. 'We have to help Demi. Don't you understand?'

She looked at each of them in turn.

'That gangster Laine has her. He also has the diamonds. Demi had them all along but never told us. She gave them to Laine so he'd let us go. But he only let her children go.'

She turned to Wiener.

'Ben, you promised. You said you would help her.'

'I'll do whatever I can,' he reassured her.

The five of them stood in silence on the roadside. The chanting of the youths faded into the distance. The street drinker continued his journey to nowhere in particular.

Steinberg placed his hand on Wiener's arm.

'What do you intend to do, Ben?'

Ben opened his mouth to reply when Steinberg's mobile rang. Recognising the number, he answered it.

'Yes, Mr Laine. What can I do for you?'

He listened.

'I'm sorry, Mr Laine but that is completely out of the question.'

He listened again.

'Mr Laine,' he continued. 'I have my daughter with me. And you, I understand, have the diamonds. If you want to negotiate the safe release of the girl, you'll need to speak with Mr Doyle, not me.'

He listened again.

'You did what?' he lowered the phone and spoke to Wiener.

'Laine says Doyle is dead, they shot him earlier today.'

Wiener shook his head.

'They must think he's dead, but he was alive when Rebekah and I left him. He should be in hospital by now.'

Steinberg lifted his phone.

'Like I said, Mr Laine, she's not my concern. The diamonds however are another matter. I will be in touch with you about them later. Goodbye.'

He ended the call.

'What did he say about Demi?' Rebekah asked. 'Is she okay?'

'The audacity of the man,' Steinberg said shaking his head. 'He now wants me to pay the quarter million pounds for the safe release of the girl.'

'And if you don't pay?' Rebekah said quietly.

Steinberg averted his eyes from his daughter.

'Well, she demanded. 'What did he say?'

His head fell to his chest. 'That she will be dropped off a boat into the sea.'

'Father,' she blurted. 'I heard you say she's not your concern. Phone him back right away. Tell him you'll pay the money. She *is* your concern. She's all our concern.'

'But he wants a quarter million pounds,' he said. 'The amount he wanted for your return. I can't pay so much money for a stranger.'

Isaac took her arm.

'Your father's right, darling,' he said. 'Maybe Ben can help her, who knows?'

Rebekah tore herself away.

'You heartless bastards,' she screamed, 'you fucking, heartless bastards.'

Rebekah ran across the road towards the embankment. The others could hear her sobbing as she leaned on the river wall. Wiener glanced at Steinberg then followed the distraught Rebekah. He softly approached touching her shoulder. Rebekah turned to face him.

'Ben,' she cried, falling towards him. Wiener held her in his arms.

'Easy, girl,' he soothed. 'Easy.'

Steinberg crossed the road to join Wiener and his daughter. Rebekah still held on to Ben, quietly crying, her head buried in his shoulder. Placing his hand on his daughter's shoulder, he spoke gently.

'Despite the comments of the others,' he told her, 'Despite what I said just then, I am prepared to help your friend. *Our* friend. I will agree to pay Laine the money he demands for the safe return of Demi.'

Rebekah turned to face her father.

'Do you mean it?' she whispered. 'Will you really help Demi?'

Steinberg nodded his agreement. 'Of course.'

'Oh, father,' she put her arms around him. 'Thank you.'

Steinberg held his daughter tightly; he recalled what had happened to her, grateful she was safe and unharmed.

They returned to his car opposite. Rebekah sat in the Mercedes with Isaac, Michael, and Israel. Wiener sat in the Insignia with Steinberg. The engine idled. Inside, the car was warm and the soft glow of the interior panel lights created a comfortable ambience. Wiener examined his 9mm Sig. Steinberg turned the wedding ring on his left hand.

'What should we do next?' Steinberg asked his cousin.

'I agree, it's a considerable sum of money,' Wiener told him. 'It is very noble what you did back there.'

'How could I do otherwise,' he stated. 'My daughter would never have forgiven me.'

He looked over to Wiener.

'I'd never forgive myself. Did you see how upset she became? She feels for this woman. She was showing empathy as well as feeling. Please try to understand my dilemma. I may lose the diamonds as well as the money.'

'But you will have gained the safety and wellbeing of your daughter and the girl. Some things are priceless, my friend.'

'Yes, yes. You are right, but can we be assured Laine will not harm her? That he will return her safely once he receives his money?'

Wiener shook his head recalling similar situations from previous Mossad operations: kidnap, ransom demands, promises not always kept by either side. A truly dirty business – a business he thought he'd left behind.

'Regrettably, there are no such guarantees,' he told Steinberg. 'You must hope and pray for the best.'

'I didn't have you down as a praying man,' Steinberg said. 'I thought you resorted to more earthly methods.'

'In that you are correct, cousin,' Wiener said. 'What I said was *you* must do the praying. I will use those 'more earthly methods' you referred to. Now, phone that *schmuck,* tell him he will have his money. I will personally make the delivery.'

Taking out his phone, Steinberg dialled Barry Laine.

***

Harry and Lennie dumped the listless Demi into an armchair at Lennie Randall's house in Riverside. She pulled her feet up under her legs, resting her head on the arm, grateful for the sleep that overcame her. Barry Laine paced the room, only stopping to look through the large bay window.

'How long before Khalid gets back here?' he shouted at the others. Demi flinched in her drug-induced slumber at the sudden outburst.

'Harry, ring him now, tell him to get a move on,' Laine said, pointing at the Londoner.

Harry got through to a ringing tone. After a few minutes, he ended the call.

'Well,' Laine demanded. 'Please tell me they still have the brief with them.'

'Not sure about that, boss,' Harry said. 'The place is crawling with cops. Someone went in to order a taxi and freaked out when they found three dead bodies.'

'I don't believe this,' Laine said staring up at the ceiling, 'I do not fucking believe this. That Jew bastard has killed six of my men. Six.'

Laine sat on the edge of the bed next to Demi. Spotting the syringe, he picked it up, wondering what the effect of the drug was really like. *Must be good, the shitload of money it's made me over the years.* His rumination was interrupted when the phone in his pocket shrilled its ring tone.

'Shit, who's this now?'

He fumbled inside his pocket for his phone.

'Yes, Steinberg, what can I do for you?'

He listened.

'Is that so? I suggest we discuss this further tomorrow. Then I'll tell you what arrangements I want in place.'

He listened again.

'No harm will come to the woman, unless of course you try any funny business. I also want you to keep that friend of yours away. I've heard about what happened at the taxi office and at my place in town. If I see him, I assure you a lot of harm will be inflicted.'

He paused.

'Good night to you, too, Steinberg.'

He ended the call.

Lennie came back into the room and approached Laine, who was staring down at Demi. 'So what you thinking, boss?'

Laine turned to his minder. 'We go down to the yacht. Frankie will have it ready to sail. Go across to France. Better still, Belgium. The cops are probably looking for me right now. I'm in deep shit from every angle at the moment, so I need to disappear until things cool down.'

Lennie pointed back at the bed. 'Are we taking her with us?'

'Don't be bloody stupid, Len, of course we are. I've just been offered big money for her by Steinberg.'

'You'll get the money then let her go?'

'Not if I can help it,' Laine said. 'Once I have the money, she stays. I haven't fully decided what to do with her yet.'

'Did you bring the stones with you, boss?'

'No. They're in the safe back at my house. You and Harry will take the woman down to the boat. I'll go get the diamonds and meet you later.'

'We came here in the Beamer, boss. We've only got the one motor.'

'Well get Khalid back here. He can take you. I'll take your car.'

Lennie made the call.

Twenty minutes later a horn sounded outside.

'Right, let's go,' Laine said.

***

Demi had heard most of the discussion. She kept her eyes closed, waiting until the two men had left the room. Still feeling muzzy and disorientated, she felt around the bed for the syringe. She pulled her knees up to her chin and stared at the needle in her hand. She physically ached and her skin was cold and clammy. Demi began to tremble, her body craving more heroin.

Thirty-Eight

Wiener pulled up near to Lennie Randall's house. After he'd left the others on Penarth Road, it only took him a few minutes to make the journey. He switched off the car's lights, slid down in the seat and waited. There were lights on inside the house. Wiener noticed movement in one of the windows, the silhouetted shapes of two people. He watched as a car pulled up, a taxi, 'City Cabs' stencilled on the side. The driver got out and went into the house. In the distance, Wiener could hear police sirens. He'd heard them throughout the evening. The front door drew his attention when it opened; light from the hall illuminated the area around the small porch. Khalid, Harry, and Lennie came out.

They checked the street. Lennie turned back inside then pulled Demi out through the door. Wiener could see Demi trying to pull away from the man who had hold of her arm. Her face revealed the pain she suffered. They climbed into the taxi, Demi squashed between Lennie and Harry in the back. The car made a U-turn before heading in the opposite direction.

Barry Laine came through the door. Getting into the BMW, he drove off in the same direction as the taxi. Wiener started the car then eased away from the kerb in pursuit. He followed them as far as a set of traffic lights where the cars in front of him were now side-by-side. The BMW indicated a right turn. The taxi carried on straight across the junction towards Cardiff Bay.

Decision time.

Wiener settled on following Laine. The BMW picked up speed along Penarth Road heading for Sully. Three police cars travelled in the opposite direction towards the city centre with sirens blaring and strobe lights flashing on their rooftops.

At two am there was little traffic on the road apart from the occasional taxi. Wiener stayed well back. They approached another set of lights, with a public house located on the right of the junction. Up ahead, police vehicles with flashing strobe lights blocked the road. The BMW slowed as it approached the junction, and a uniformed officer waved a torch. As Wiener approached, another officer waved him over. The police were armed with Heckler and Koch 9mm sub machine guns. The armed officers swarmed around the BMW.

'Out of the car, now!' an officer ordered, weapon pointed at the driver's door. Laine stepped out with his hands raised.

'Easy, guys,' he said, 'I ain't carrying.'

'Turn around and place your hands on the car.'

Laine spread his arms with his hands placed flat on the roof. Two of the officers swung their weapons around their backs then frisked Laine. Content he was carrying no concealed weapons, they pulled him towards the van, putting him into the rear holding cage. The vehicle took off towards the city. They then approached and asked Wiener a couple of questions regarding his journey before waving him on.

Wiener punched the top of the steering wheel, thinking he'd now lost Laine and the woman. Pulling over, he watched in the rear-view mirror as the remaining officers dismantled the roadblock. *The Mounties got their man.*

***

Khalid pulled up at the first security gate of the Cardiff Bay Yacht Club. Laine's cousin, Frankie Galdini, waited at the gate to let them through. Lennie and Harry, with Demi between them, followed Frankie through a second gate. They made their way along the berth to board the yacht. Frankie eyed Demi over, liking what he saw.

'Keep your hands off,' Lennie warned him. 'She's worth a lot of money to Baz at the moment.'

'I'm only looking,' Frankie insisted.

'Yeah, piss off, Shorty,' Demi hissed at him.

Frankie scowled back at her. At just over five foot four, Frankie had endured taunts about his lack of height throughout his life. Lennie laughed, seeing the look on Frankie's face.

'Feisty little thing, ain't she?' Lennie said.

'Yeah, 'cept she ain't the *littlest* thing here,' Harry quipped.

The two men laughed at Frankie as he made his way inside the Sunseeker Manhattan 50 yacht, popular amongst the criminal fraternity throughout Europe.

They made themselves comfortable in the opulent saloon area with its cherry wood furnishings, cream leather upholstery and white thick-pile carpet. Lennie opened the mirrored, cherry wood cocktail cabinet and poured himself a malt whisky.

'Help yourself, H,' he said raising his glass towards the open cabinet.

'Don't mind if I do,' Harry said, lifting a bottle from inside a holder to examine the label. 'Sure the boss won't mind? Only this is top shelf stuff.'

Demi was sitting on an ivory-coloured leather sofa.

'I need a drink,' she said, voice rasping.

'And I need your body,' Lennie replied. 'Wanna trade?'

She turned her head away.

'There's bottled water in the fridge,' Frankie told them. 'Let her have one of them.'

Lennie nodded. Harry opened the fridge and threw a blue, chilled bottle of *Ty Nant* mineral water at her.

'Suck on that, bitch,' Harry scowled. Demi responded with a middle finger gesture.

'Go easy on her, guys,' Frankie said, feeling sorry for her, despite the comment she'd made earlier. He took the bottle from her unscrewing the cap. 'So how long before Barry gets here?' he asked. 'Only I've booked a time for us to go through the barrage.'

'He won't be long,' Lennie said sipping on his malt whisky. 'He's gone to the house to collect something.'

'Any idea where we're heading? Frankie asked. 'Only he told me to fill her up with diesel.'

'Belgium. Antwerp, I think,' Lennie said. He went to take another sip but paused as the lead crystal glass was just below his chin. 'Hey, Frankie, can you really sail this tub?'

'Sure can. Barry paid for me to have lessons. I passed all the exams, navigation, seamanship, the lot. Passed them all,' he boasted. 'Last year, I took Barry and some bird he was screwing at the time down to the south of France.'

Lennie constantly checked his watch. They'd waited two hours so far. He poured the last of the malt whisky into his glass. Demi dozed on the sofa while Harry flicked through a yachting magazine, his eyebrows rising in feint surprise at the prices of the vessels. Frankie moved over to the sofa. He glanced at the two men then moved closer to Demi, his eyes wandering over her. He was about to speak but was interrupted.

'Hey, Frankie,' Lennie said. 'How'd we get to Belgium from here?'

'Sail around Porthleven,' Frankie explained, 'then up the English Channel. Probably refuel in Poole harbour on the way, then cross the channel to Antwerp.'

Taking a worldwide mooring book from a drawer, he checked the index then flicked through the pages.

'There's a place called Willemdok in Antwerp,' he announced. 'We can arrange to berth there.'

'How long will it take us?' Harry asked, throwing the magazine onto a table next to his empty glass.

'About three days,' Frankie replied. 'Depends on the weather or if we need to refuel in Kent before crossing the Channel. This thing can do about thirty knots an hour in a good sea.' He looked across at Demi. 'Are we all going?' he asked.

'Not all,' Lennie said. His mouth broke into half a smile. 'We're dropping her off on the way.'

'Anchors aweigh,' Harry said laughing, the whisky beginning to slur his words.

***

Barry Laine sat in a small interview room at Cardiff Central Police Station. On the table the standard digital recording machine blinked its blue light. He'd sat in the room for an hour, staring at the door. No one came in. He looked around the room for small or hidden cameras. They had to be watching him.

'I can keep this up for as long as you want,' he shouted at the door. As if on cue the door opened. The two men who entered sat themselves on the chairs opposite Laine. The older of the two spoke first.

'Good evening, Mr Laine. We're sorry to have kept you waiting.'

He smiled as he spoke. 'My name is Chief Inspector Jack Stone and my colleague...' 'Inspector Andy Hamid,' the younger man said nodding. 'Pleased to meet you, Mr Laine.'

Laine stared at them defiantly. A large file the Chief Inspector carried in with him dropped onto the table.

'Cut out the crap will you, just call me Barry. So what the fuck's this all about?'

Hamid removed a piece of A4 paper from inside the file. He made a point of studying it before speaking.

'Earlier this evening we found a man at your home with a gunshot wound. What can you tell us about this?'

'Nothing whatsoever,' Laine barked. 'Now I have a question, I'm entitled to a solicitor, am I not?'

Stone nodded, 'This is only an informal meeting, Mr Laine. You're free to leave if you wish. However, I would advise you to hear us out first. If we decide to arrest you then you'll get your legal representation. Who should we contact?'

'Guy Hilton,' Laine said. 'Of Hilton…'

'We know the firm, Mr Laine,' Stone interrupted.

'Well, until Guy gets here, I'm saying Jack shit.'

Laine sat back in his seat, arms folded, sneering at the two officers.

'What can you tell us about three dead bodies discovered in the vicinity of the premises you own in Westgate Street, Mr Laine?' Stone asked.

Laine, staring up at the ceiling, ignored the question.

'And three more bodies at a taxi office you own in the Docks?' Stone added.

Laine rose from his chair. 'Fuck it, I've had enough of this. Like you said I'm free to leave so…'

'Please, sit down, Mr Laine. Okay, Andy, do the business.'

Andy Hamid placed his hands on the table in front of Laine.

'Barry Laine, I'm arresting you on suspicion of murder. You do not have to say anything but it may harm your defence if you do not mention when questioned something which you later rely on in court. Anything you do say may be given in evidence. Do you understand?'

Laine stared at the younger detective.

'Just let me know when my brief gets here.'

'Sure, Mr Laine, we'll get on to it as soon as we can,' Stone said, rising from his chair. The two detectives left him alone in the room.

'Tossers,' he shouted as the door closed.

***

'Where the hell is he?' Lennie said, checking his watch for the umpteenth time. 'He should have been here hours ago.'

'Relax,' Harry said, sprawled across the leather bench seat. 'He'll be here when he's ready.'

'Sod this,' Lennie retorted. 'Get your arse up to the house, see if everything's okay.'

'He'll be here, Len. Stay cool.'

'Just do as I fucking say, will you,' Lennie screamed at him.

'Okay, okay. I'll go.'

Cockney Harry rose, making a grab for the handrail at the rear of the saloon where three small steps led to the deck area.

'You okay to drive?' Frankie asked him. 'You've had half a bottle of whisky.'

'I'll be fine,' Harry slurred.

Demi watched him leave, relieved Frankie did not go with him and leave her alone with Lennie.

Thirty-Nine

Wiener continued on to Laine's house. Driving though the damaged gates, he carried on to the rear of the property, stopping outside a large garage. He switched off the car's engine. After climbing out, he stood in the dark and silence of the grounds, waiting a few minutes before moving off, contemplating the thought Preston Taylor may have returned to the house. He would not feel altogether comfortable at the wrong end of that Purdey shotgun.

Wiener crept over to the garage to see four cars parked inside through the open doors. He carried on walking towards the house. Heavy black clouds filled the sky, the moon providing some light when it occasionally broke through. In the distance, Wiener heard a rumble of thunder; a storm would be over this area by dawn. He stopped briefly to look at the house; all the rooms were in darkness. He entered through the shattered French doors, his right hand in his jacket pocket gripping the Sig. The only sound was the slow tick of a long-case clock in the hallway.

Wiener entered the study and pulled on a few drawers that were locked. Opening a cabinet door, he discovered a safe and studied its design, wondering if he could crack the combination. He doubted it. It was a freestanding solid steel safe with an electronically controlled, 6mm thick door. He guessed the diamonds were inside. Why else would Laine be heading back here? Walking over to the window, he looked down the front drive leading to the entrance gates, then turned round to make himself comfortable in a leather upholstered chair, placing the Sig on the desk in front of him.

The time ticked by as he listened to the steady rhythm of the clock in the hallway. It chimed the hours and just after the stroke of four, headlamps of an approaching car swept across the room. Wiener watched through the window expecting to see the BMW Laine had been driving earlier, but instead it was one of the taxis from outside the Cardiff Bay taxi office. It pulled up on the gravel drive. Wiener stood back in the darkness watching as the driver clambered out of the car. He recognised him as one of the men who'd brought Demi out of Lennie's house earlier.

Harry reeled towards the door, knocked loudly and called out,

'Barry. You here, boss?'

Taking a phone from his pocket, he fumbled with it as he cursed quietly to himself. Wiener made his way back to the room with the damaged French window. Stepping through, he walked slowly towards the front of the house. He could hear the man speaking into his phone.

'Len, it's me. Yeah, I'm at the house. No, no sign. It's all in darkness.'

Wiener edged closer, his feet making no sound on the gravel beneath him.

The man had stopped speaking and listened.

'No sign of Preston, either,' he said. 'Thing is, there's a car parked on the drive.'

He was about to speak again when he felt the barrel of a gun pressed against his head.

The phone dropped from his hand, clattering at his feet on the gravel. Lennie's faint voice rose up from the ground.

'Harry, Harry, you still there? Who's with you?'

Wiener stepped on the phone, crushing it into the Cotswold stone.

'Who the fuck are you?' Harry asked in a nervous tone.

'I'm your worst nightmare, *schmuck,* and I'm about to add you to the list of Laine's six dead men.'

'Eh?' Harry grunted.

'Your three friends at Laine's warehouse, then three at the taxi office. Do the math. You'll find it comes to six, asshole.' Wiener pressed the gun harder against the man's head.

'Walk over to the car, place your hands flat down on the roof.'

Harry didn't need to be told twice. Wiener opened the passenger side door and pressed the window button, stopping it about six inches from the top.

'Right,' he said, 'slip your hands through.'

He tapped the glass with the Sig to indicate where he wanted the man's hands. Harry put them through the gap. Wiener pressed the button, trapping them in the glass, then frisked him down. Harry was packing and Wiener soon found his Smith and Wesson Chief's Special Air Weight with an aluminium alloy frame and steel barrel. Wiener flicked open the chamber revealing six .357 magnum rounds.

'Nice gun,' he said. Flicking back the chamber, he pocketed the weapon.

Harry began to feel the pain of the glass pressed against his wrists. Wiener brought his face closer to the trapped man. He sensed the reek of stale whisky on the man's breath. Harry struggled, feeling the loss of circulation to his hands. Wiener whispered in the man's ear.

'Okay, *schmuck,* I'm going to ask you three questions. One wrong answer, I blow away the top of your head. Understand?'

'Yes,' Harry groaned as his hands started to discolour.

'First question. What's your name?'

'Harry. Harry Bishop.'

'Good answer. Second question. Who owns this house?'

'Barry Laine. It's Barry's house.'

Harry writhed in pain, moving his feet trying to find a position where the pain might ease. There was no such position.

'Good answer,' Wiener hissed in the man's ear. 'Last question.'

He paused, pushing the Sig hard into the nape of Harry's neck to emphasize his intention.

'Where did you take the girl?'

Harry didn't hesitate with his reply.

'Barry's boat, down the bay. She's there with Lennie and Frankie.'

'She okay?' Wiener asked.

'She's fine. Asleep when I left.'

'Who's Frankie?'

'Barry's cousin, he takes care of the boat. He's going to take us over to France or somewhere but Barry didn't show up. That's why I'm here looking for him.'

'Where's this boat, exactly?'

'You said three questions. Please, let me go,' he pleaded.

354

'I changed my mind,' Wiener said. 'Same deal mind, wrong answer – no head. Now, where exactly is this boat?'

'Cardiff Bay Yacht Club, if you let me go, I'll take you down there.'

Wiener considered the offer. He decided instead to wait in the house, believing the diamonds were in the office safe. Laine would return for them provided the police released him. He was about to press the window button when he heard footsteps on the gravel behind him. Wiener immediately realised his mistake.

He hadn't checked the upstairs rooms. He turned, knowing what to expect.

Preston Taylor stood about twenty feet away holding the same Purdey double-barrel shotgun, pressed into his shoulder aiming straight at Wiener. Harry turned his head, grinning with glee when he saw Preston with the gun.

'Shoot the motherfucker,' Harry cried out. 'Don't just stand there. Pull the fucking trigger.'

Forty

Pat Doyle left the A&E unit at the University Hospital, having discharged himself against the advice of the doctors who'd treated him for fractured ribs and a gunshot wound to the shoulder. He ached throughout his entire body as he walked from the building, past a gathering of patients huddled under a canopy where they smoked cigarettes, still wearing hospital gowns. He'd told the police he worked for Barry Laine, that he'd disturbed a burglar at the house who was armed, who then shot him and left him for dead. The police took a lengthy statement: what did this burglar look like? Was he black, white, short, tall? Did he say anything, if so, did he have an accent? He feigned fatigue and a need to sleep, so they informed him they'd return later to question him again.

Abraham Steinberg had also been in touch with the hospital, leaving details of his home address. Pat headed for Steinberg's house in north Cardiff. In the taxi taking him there, he thought about Demi. Where was she? The pain in his shoulder reminded him of what had happened. Demi came close to being sexually assaulted by Barry Laine. How dare he lay his grubby hands on her? The thought made him seethe with rage. Revenge was what he now wanted. To hurt Laine. What would he do if he had the chance? Pull out his fingernails with pliers, gouge out his eyes, cut off his prick and stuff it in his mouth. He'd read somewhere how American mafia hoods did this to their enemies who messed with their women. He'd also read they'd hung their enemies on meat hooks watching them writhe in an agonisingly slow death.

Yes, that was it, the meat hook. He would skewer Laine on a meat hook.

'What am I thinking?' he said aloud. The driver looked back at him.

'What's that, mate?'

He shook his head, surprised at his own malaise. 'He's turning me into the same monster he is. He's contaminated me. I'm no better than him.' The driver simply shook his head, not bothering to ask what he was talking about.

'Here we are, mate,' the driver said as the car pulled up outside a large house set back off the main road. Steinberg came out through the front door and paid the driver off before taking Pat inside. As he passed through the door Steinberg touched the *mezuzah* on the right-hand doorframe. They went through to the drawing room where Rebekah was waiting and came over to hug Pat. Her husband Isaac shook his hand, followed by Steinberg's two sons.

Pat felt the comfort of the room, warm and dimly lit by lamps placed on various tables, a collection of silverware on top of a long mahogany sideboard, a silver tea service on a salver surrounded by various silver goblets with etched patterns. The centrepiece was a candelabra – a seven-branch *menorah* with a Star of David set in the middle that Pat recognised as one of the oldest symbols of the Jewish faith. Behind the sideboard hung a painting depicting three Jewish elders debating the Torah. His admiration of the artwork was distracted when the door opened. Steinberg's wife, Judith, entered pushing a trolley set with China cups and a coffee service. Pat's gaze moved from one person to the next before asking,

'Where's Ben? I can see he's not here.'

'We're not exactly sure, Pat,' Steinberg said. 'We're waiting to hear from him.'

'And Demi?' he said almost in a whisper. Rebekah spoke next.

'We don't know where they've taken her either. Ben will find her, Pat,' she said, trying to sound reassuring. 'He found me. Ben will bring her back safely. Please, sit down; you've been through a lot.'

Steinberg nodded his agreement. Pat, however, wasn't so convinced. Judith Steinberg poured the coffee. Black and strong, its pungent aroma filled the room. Rebekah handed round a plate of small cakes.

'So what do we do now?' he asked.

'We wait to hear from Ben,' Steinberg said. 'Right now there's nothing else we *can* do.'

They sat in silence, eating cake and sipping coffee. A silence broken by the ring tone from Rebekah's mobile.

The small screen showed Guy Hilton as the caller. Rebekah answered, listening to her employer. Her response was brief.

'I'm sorry, Guy, I can't possibly do that. Not at this hour, not for him.' She ended the call.

'The police have Barry Laine in custody,' she announced. 'He called Guy earlier, asking him to be his legal advisor. Guy wanted me to go with him. Well, you heard my reply.'

Isaac Rosen stood up.

'Why's he been arrested?'

'It's in connection with six dead bodies they found at two of his premises,' she explained.

'Ben.' Steinberg announced.

'I was there when he killed three of them,' Pat said.

'And I was there for the other three,' Rebekah added.

Isaac Rosen shook his head in dismay.

'Abraham, why did you get him involved? He'll land us all in prison. He's committing murder. We are a respectable family. I'm a bloody QC for God's sake. Our lives may be ruined.'

'What choice did I have, Isaac?' Steinberg responded, 'What chance do we stand against the likes of Laine and his… his mob? He's a gangster, a ruthless killer. Only someone like Ben Wiener can deal with the likes of him.'

'You should have involved the police,' Isaac said raising his voice. 'As I'd suggested before all this got out of hand. Those bloody diamonds are not worth this.'

'It's no longer about the diamonds,' Rebekah said to her husband. 'It's about the safety of Demetra Karamanlis, a young, defenceless woman who now relies on us to help her.'

Pat remained quiet in his chair, feeling responsible for everything. This was all down to him. Isaac Rosen glared at his wife.

'We do this for strangers?' he barked.

Rebekah glared right back at him, spitting out her reply.

'Strangers? *Everything* you do is for strangers. Most of your clients are strangers, so don't come that crap with me, Isaac.'

'My clients pay me. It's business,' he shouted back.

'This is business,' she retorted. 'The diamonds belong to my father's business.'

Judith Steinberg came between them.

'Children, please. Stop this at once.' Rebekah looked back at Isaac. 'Demi is in danger. Let Ben sort this out then hopefully it will be the end of the matter.'

'The end of us, more like,' Isaac muttered.

Another phone rang. This time it was Steinberg's mobile.

***

Wiener stared at Preston Taylor, the Purdey pointed straight at him. Wiener stepped closer to Harry, still trapped by his hands in the car window. He quickly realised Wiener's intention.

'No, no.' Harry screamed. 'Don't shoot. Not now.'

Wiener stood right next to Harry.

'Sure, kill us both,' he said to Preston.

Wiener had decided on a gamble. He'd examined the gun earlier. Would Preston have thought to check if it was still loaded? He doubted it. Not the way he was acting – tense and nervous. The barrel of the gun quivered slightly, revealing the man's trepidation. Wiener stood behind Harry and the open car door. If he was wrong, at least he had some protection.

'Go on,' Wiener taunted. 'Give us both barrels. Gun like that should tear us to shreds.'

Harry looked at him in disbelief.

'Are you crazy?' he shouted. 'Tell him to put it down.'

He looked back towards Preston.

'Put the fucking thing down, man. Don't listen to him. He's mad.'

Preston's busted face still hurt. Now he wanted to hurt Wiener. He continued to point the 30-inch barrels straight at the car. The walnut stock pulled tightly into his shoulder ready for the recoil. He squeezed both triggers.

The hammers clicked on two empty barrels. Preston slowly lowered the gun, realising his folly. Wiener stepped back from behind Harry, letting Preston see him place the Sig on the roof of the car. Instantly, Preston took hold of the shotgun by the barrels, ready to beat Wiener around his arrogant, smiling face with it. He stepped purposefully towards Wiener, the now useless shotgun raised over his shoulder, ready to fall like a club. Wiener had taken a calculated gamble. Gunshots would be heard since he'd removed the suppressor from the Sig and his next move required a more silent technique. Preston walked into the trap.

Wiener lowered his hand to remove the commando dagger from the sheath strapped to his leg. Preston continued his approach, raising the gun as if he held a baseball bat. Wiener waited for the optimum moment. The man would need to raise the gun higher before he swung it at his opponent. At that point, he'd be fully exposed. Wiener held the dagger down by his right side. Preston came within three feet, quickening his stride as he raised the gun's stock over his right shoulder. Wiener's hand moved so fast Preston didn't see it happen. The blade entered the celiac plexus, severing the superior mesenteric artery. Preston stopped in his tracks, the Purdey dropping to the ground, throwing up a cloud of dust. Wiener pulled out the dagger, watching as Preston fell to his knees clutching his chest, his eyes bulging as he stared at the blade in Wiener's hand as if he were admiring its quality. Then he started to tear at his shirt, revealing the entry wound. Blood ran down his chest onto the gravel.

Harry couldn't believe what he'd witnessed. He'd seen Preston Taylor in action in the past, seen him take on two men beating them easy. Up against one man, with a gun to use as a club, this wasn't the result he'd expected.

Wiener retrieved the Sig from the car's roof then wiped the dagger on the jacket of the dying man before returning it to its sheath.

'Look, man,' Harry pleaded. 'Let me go and you'll never see me again. I promise.'

Wiener held the Sig to the man's head and pressed the window button. Harry pulled his hands free, shaking them to get the blood to circulate.

'Right,' Wiener said as he opened the back door of the taxi. 'Drag your friend across and put him in here.' Harry didn't hesitate as he dragged the now dead Preston onto the rear seat. Wiener threw the Purdey in after him. He turned to face the house, a deliberate move on his part, deliberate because he knew what would happen next. Harry seized what he saw as an opportunity to make a grab for Wiener – a lethal mistake and the last move he ever made. Wiener drove his left elbow into the man's chest, his fist following up smashing into his nose. Harry staggered back onto the car behind him. Wiener turned, punching his fist into an already shattered nose, this time forcing the nasal bone up into the brain. Harry slid down the side of the car, dead before he hit the ground.

***

Barry Laine stood outside the police station with his solicitor. The clock above the City Hall chimed four. They both looked up at the clock face then checked their own watches in unison, as if doubting its accuracy.

'Thanks for that, Guy,' Laine said holding his hand out for the solicitor to shake. 'You did an excellent job in there.'

'Not a problem, Mr Laine. They don't have enough evidence to charge you with anything at this point. As I see it, you're the victim in all of this. We'll stay with that line unless they come up with any solid evidence. My advice right now is be careful.'

He shook Laine's hand again before walking over to his Jaguar XJ6. Laine headed for Lennie's BMW parked at the back of the building where the police had left it. He screwed the police bail document into a ball, throwing it to the floor in repulsion.

**

Wiener sat in the dark and quiet of Laine's study. A cold breeze blew through the French doors, the distant rumble of thunder still approaching in the dawn sky. The curtain billowed inwards, revealing the space outside and a clear view of the drive. Wiener felt more confident in his belief that Laine would return to the house to collect the diamonds from the safe in the desk. He had three choices: kill Laine as soon as he opens the safe, make Laine take him to the yacht club, or follow him. If he decided to follow, he would need to hide himself in the house first. He rose from the seat to examine the room, deciding that following Laine was the best option.

**

The Sunseeker Manhattan lay securely moored to its berth as it moved on the water with a quiet, gentle motion. In the saloon area, Lennie Randall lay asleep on a leather sofa. Frankie Galdini sat watching one of the inner doors that lead to a cabin bedroom. Inside, on the double bed, Demi lay asleep. She had tried to stay awake, fearful that Lennie would come in and force himself upon her. The craving for heroin lessened along with the easing of the stomach cramps.

She fell into a restless sleep as the city hall clock chimed four, a way off in the distance. She dreamt of Pat Doyle, laid out in a coffin, in the vault where they'd found the diamonds. He looked peaceful as she dropped diamonds around his body. Suddenly she heard a loud crash as the doors slammed shut, enclosing her inside the tomb in complete blackness. Demi suddenly woke, sitting upright. Sweating and trembling, she looked around the small space of the cabin. Outside, she heard the sound of snoring. Her head fell back on the pillow; the torment of the dream still ached in her mind.

Forty-One

Barry Laine pulled onto his drive. He remained in the quiet of the car thinking, *how do I get rid of the Jew?* He was fast losing his men, making him vulnerable. If the other Cardiff gangs discovered this, they'd make their move against him. He called Lennie. It took a few minutes before he answered.

'Lennie, where the fuck have you been?' Laine listened to his half drunk, drowsy minder.

'I'll be with you in about forty minutes,' he told Lennie. 'Have Frankie get the boat ready to sail.'

Laine listened as Lennie explained to him that Harry had gone to the house to try and find him.

'There's no sign of anyone here,' he said quietly. 'How long ago did he leave?'

He listened again.

'Right, you try Harry's mobile, I'll try Preston's then call you back.'

Laine pressed the speed dial for Preston Taylor. An automated voice informed him the person wasn't available and to leave a message. Lennie told him there was no response from Harry's phone either.

Easing the door open, Laine stepped out of the car. In the distance, he heard a siren moving away. A breeze rustled through the trees surrounding the house, and rooks were starting to rouse in the treetops, beginning their early, raucous cry. There were no other sounds.

He took a cautious step towards the house and called out, 'Harry! You here, Harry?'

A movement in a hydrangea bush made him turn. His heart raced, *probably just a fox, or a bird*. Laine stepped up to his front door, letting himself in. Standing motionless in the large hallway, he listened as his eyes scanned for any movement. The long-case clock ticked steadily. Then its mechanism whirred as the Westminster chimes denoted quarter to the hour. 4:45.

He made his way to the study, thick carpet cushioning his careful footsteps. He pushed at the study door with his foot, peering inside the darkened room. The draught from the shattered doors blew past him. Leaning through the doorway, he switched on the lights and glanced around the room, satisfied he was alone. He crossed to his desk and opened the safe. Removing a Beretta 92F pistol, Laine checked its magazine and placed it on the desktop followed by two bundles of £20 notes, totalling £10,000. Finally, a bag containing the five pouches of diamonds. He put the money in the pockets of his jacket. He held the bag in his left hand, the Beretta in his right. Laine took one last look around before heading for the door. As he passed back down the hall, the long-case struck five.

Wiener rose from behind a Chesterfield sofa. He held the Sig Sauer, safety off, suppressor on, ready to fire. After hearing Laine leave the house, he went over to the French doors and waited. The BMW's engine started and it sped off, wheels spinning in the gravel. As it did, Wiener ran back to his car near the garage.

***

Barry Laine pulled up at the first security gate of the Cardiff Bay Yacht Club, unaware of the car that had followed him from Sully.

Wiener watched from a distance as Laine approached the security gate where he tapped out a series of numbers. The electronic gate rolled open and Laine made his way along the mooring to his yacht. Although early, there were a few people about. Wiener noticed another boat owner making his way toward the locked gate.

He reached the gate just in time to catch the man opening from the other side.

'Morning,' Wiener said jovially. He held the gate with his hand to stop it closing. 'I'm with Mr Laine,' he told the man who simply nodded and let him pass. Wiener walked along the mooring passing Laine's yacht, checking out some of the other larger cruisers. Most appeared deserted with no one on board. Wiener climbed aboard a Fairlane Brava and hid out of sight but with a clear view of Laine's boat.

From his observation point he called Steinberg.

Back at the house, Steinberg answered the call and listened. Pat Doyle paced the room, anxious to hear any news of Demi.

'What yacht club are you at, Ben?' Steinberg said into the phone. 'There are two yacht clubs, Cardiff and Cardiff Bay.'

He listened then ended the call.

'Well,' Pat asked. 'Where is he? Did he mention Demi?'

'He's on a boat, watching Laine,' Steinberg told him. 'They have Demi with them but he doesn't know how she is.'

'Do we know which yacht club?' Rebekah asked.

Steinberg nodded.

'Sounds like Cardiff Bay. Ben said it followed the river.'

'He's right, it is the Cardiff Bay club,' Isaac Rosen said. 'I've been there a few times when friends have berthed there.'

'Really?' Rebekah said to her husband. 'And when was this? I know I've never been to any yacht club.'

'Sure you do,' Isaac replied, his voice revealing a trace of hesitancy. 'The Spiegels stopped off there on their way to the south of France,' he continued.

Rebekah frowned at him.

'Are you sure it was the Spiegels you were seeing?' she said, icily. Pat interrupted them.

'I'm going down there. Will someone take me, please?'

'I'm not sure that's a good idea, Pat,' Steinberg said. 'Leave this to Ben. Look what happened to you at Laine's house.'

'Yes, I know,' Pat said, 'but I have to do something.' He looked around at the five people present.

'If you won't take me then I'll go on my own.'

'I'll take you,' Michael Steinberg offered. 'We'll go in my car. I'll drop you off near the yacht club and wait. If things go bad, I'll phone the police.'

Steinberg senior placed his hand on Pat's shoulder as he walked him to the front door.

'Go easy, Pat, I'll try and reach Ben to say you're on your way.'

Standing at the door, they shook hands. Rebekah stepped up to hug him.

'Take care, Pat,' she whispered. 'And don't worry, Demi will be fine.'

Pat looked up and touched the *mezuzah* on the door frame. Steinberg did likewise, saying, 'God go with you.'

Michael had started his car, a silver Maserati Gran Turismo, its 4.7 litre V8 engine purring like an overfed cat. Pat climbed in. As soon as he secured his seatbelt, the car accelerated away reaching 60mph in the 4.9 seconds boasted by the manufacturer.

***

Aboard Laine's yacht, the three men sat in the saloon area. Frankie Galdini had readied the boat to sail: 2500 litres of diesel oil filled the fuel tanks and the two running engines made the boat throb slightly. Laine opened the safe, placing the diamonds and cash inside next to three large bundles of Euros he kept on board for occasional trips to Spain or the south of France. After closing the safe, he poured himself a large measure of cognac, gulping half of it down in one swig.

'Frankie says we're going to Belgium,' Lennie said.

'Maybe,' Laine replied. 'I need to think a few things through.'

Picking up the glass, he finished the remainder of his cognac.

'Looks like Wiener got to Harry and Preston as well,' he continued. 'The police have me in the frame for the boys he killed. Fuck it, Len, we've got to stop this bastard. I want him dead. You got that? Dead!'

Lennie simply nodded.

'Sure, Barry, I keep telling you I'll take care of it. So how long we going to be away?'

'Not *we*, Lennie, boy. You're staying here. I need you to take care of things. Keep on top of the businesses. Otherwise, Osman and the others will walk all over me.'

Laine refilled his glass.

'But the first thing on your list is to kill that damn Jew who's still out there somewhere. You keep telling me you'll do it, so just fucking do it. He's really freaking me out, I want him dead.'

He threw the keys for the BMW at him.

'Remember, the guy's dangerous. He's wiped out eight men already.'

'What about the girl?' Lennie asked indicating towards the bedroom door. 'She going with you, or what?'

Laine rose from his seat, crossing to the bedroom where he unlocked the door and stepped inside. Demi was crouched on the bed, chin on her knees, arms wrapped around her legs. Her tear-streaked face looked at Laine standing in the doorway.

'Yes?' she asked.

'Listen up, bitch. I haven't decided whether to throw you over the side or sell you to a brothel keeper I know in Amsterdam.'

'Whatever,' Demi said in response. The smirk on her face enraged Laine, who slammed and locked the door.

'Right, Lennie, I want you to arrange a meeting with Ali Osman. Get him to see you at the Westgate Street building.'

'No probs, boss. But why do I need to meet Osman? What'll I be saying to him?'

'You won't be saying anything to him, Len, you'll be putting a bullet between his eyes.'

Lennie smiled at the prospect of a killing he knew would enjoy.

'Then do the same with the other Turks,' he continued referring to the Khan Brothers who headed another Cardiff rival gang. 'When I get back, I want all my opposition out of the way.'

'That's not all the opposition, Boss.'

'You mean the Yardies? Don't worry about that lot,' Laine said. 'You can meet with them and we'll come to an arrangement.'

Lennie nodded. Killing the Asian gang leaders would be no problem but the West Indian boys were mostly family to him.

'Now help Frankie untie the boat so we can get away.'

Out on deck the sun rose over the top of the Cardiff Bay barrage. They started to untie the boat in the growing light of dawn, unaware of Wiener who watched them from further down the pier.

Lennie stood back from the Sunseeker as Frankie increased the throttle, the water at the rear of the boat churning and foaming. The boat moved slowly away from its mooring, turning to face the open water. The sound of the engine increased as it picked up speed heading for the barrage. Lennie turned to make his way back to the security gate, oblivious of Wiener's silent footsteps behind him.

***

The Maserati sped along Ferry Road towards the yacht club, slowing as they approached the boat yard of the club before stopping about one hundred metres away. Pat opened the door to get out, wincing in pain as he did.

'I'll wait here for a while,' Michael said. 'How do you plan to get in? The main gate's bound to be locked.'

'I'll think of something,' Pat told him. 'You don't need to wait.'

He looked towards the club's entrance. 'Ben's here somewhere.'

371

'I'll wait all the same. If you need a quick getaway, this is the baby to do it in.'

Pat slapped the roof twice. 'Can't argue with that,' he agreed.

Walking with a slight limp, Pat made his way over to the fence and peered inside the enclosure, hoping to see a familiar sight. There were boats of all makes and sizes around the grounds, some under repair or refitting. In the distance, he could hear the sound of a boat's engine as it moved away. He also heard footsteps. Outside the club's perimeter fence stood the metal hull of a large boat, propped up with heavy timbers. Pat hid behind the hull, crouching down out of sight. Next to the main entrance, Pat recognised first the black BMW and then Lennie, who unlocked the security gate and crossed to the car.

Pat rose to his feet and moved from behind the hull just as Lennie zapped the locks with the car fob. Walking towards him, Pat called out, 'Hey, Lennie, remember me?'

Lennie turned to face Pat, his brow furrowed when he realised who'd called him.

'I thought you were dead. I put a bullet in you.'

'Maybe I am.' Pat replied. 'Maybe I'm a ghost come back to haunt you.' He took a step closer. Lennie pulled the same gun he'd used on him at the house, raising it in line with Pat's chest.

'I don't think you're a ghost, dude,' Lennie said smiling. 'But this time I'll make sure you become one.'

Pat froze in anticipation of what was about to be unleashed, but as Lennie was about to fire another voice called out from behind him.

'I wouldn't do that if I were you.' Lennie spun round. Wiener stood next to the BMW. In his hand he held the Sig, the suppressor pointing straight at Lennie. Lennie raised his weapon as if to fire, so Wiener quickly reached inside the car and switched on the headlamps. Blinded by the intense light, Lennie could no longer see what he was shooting at, as he fired into the bright glare of the car's powerful main beam.

'Shit.' Lennie shouted as he held his left hand in front of his eyes, shielding them from the harsh light.

'I'm still here, Len,' Wiener taunted. 'Why not try again.' Wiener dropped to one knee to get a clear view of Lennie Randall, who had not moved. He gently squeezed the trigger, firing off one carefully-aimed round. Lennie let out a scream as the bullet tore through his kneecap. He fell to the ground in agony, dropping the gun from his hand. Pat ran forward to pick it up as Wiener stepped out of the light. The Sig pointed down at the man writhing on the ground in front of him.

'Oh dear,' Wiener said mockingly. 'That looks painful.' He pressed his foot down on the shattered and bloodied knee. Lennie screamed louder. Wiener crouched down next to him, forcing the muzzled of the Sig against the side of the injured man's head.

'Now then, Lennie,' he whispered, 'I have a question for you. A wrong answer gets your head blown off.'

'Go fuck yourself,' Lennie hissed. Wiener pressed a clenched fist into his knee resulting in a further piecing scream.

'Manners, Lennie. Now here's the question. What's the square root of a hundred and ninety-six?' Silence followed.

'Well?' Wiener asked. 'I do expect an answer.'

'I don't fucking know,' spat Lennie.

'So guess,' Wiener prompted, pressing the Sig harder against Lennie's head. 'Ball park figure.'

'Fifty,' Lennie said looking up at Wiener's face.

'Wrong answer.'

Pat watched, gasping, trying to catch his breath as Lennie Randall's head exploded in front of him. The whole thing brought back the memory of Laine killing one of his own men back in Westgate Street. Wiener straightened up.

'You okay?' he asked.

'Fourteen,' Pat replied in a nervous voice.

'Eh?' Wiener said.

'Fourteen,' Pat repeated. 'The square root of a hundred and ninety-six is fourteen.'

'Yes, I know. Shame *he* didn't,' Wiener said pointing the Sig down at the body. 'He might have walked away from here. Well, hopped probably,' he added. 'Now, come on, help me get him into the car. Oh, you might want to get rid of that thing,' he said pointing at the gun in Pat's hand.

They laid Lennie's body on the back seat of the BMW. Wiener climbed in, then reversed the car into the repair yard.

'Where's Demi?' Pat managed to say, still in shock as Wiener re-joined him.

'On that boat if I'm not mistaken,' Wiener told him, pointing at the Sunseeker crossing the waterway towards the barrage.

Forty-Two

Barry Laine opened the bedroom door and stepped inside. Demi watched him enter as she sat up on the side of the bed.

'Where are we going?'

Laine sat beside her, reaching over to put his hand on her thigh. Demi quickly stood up.

'Get your hands off me,' she blasted, pressing her back against the side of the cabin. Laine laughed at her.

'You saw what happened to Doyle, now either you do as I say or you get the same.'

'Murdering bastard,' she said softly. 'Pat Doyle was twice the man you are.'

'Not anymore,' he said. 'Now when we get away from here you and I are going to get in this bed together. You'll do everything I want, and I'll want the works. So, do as I say and you won't get hurt. Deal?'

Demi nodded once in apparent acquiescence. Laine crossed over to her.

'Good,' he whispered in her ear. 'That's more like it.'

He left, locking the door behind him. Demi stared at the door. Putting her hand in her pocket, she pulled out the pink diamond, staring at it as she turned it between her finger and thumb.

If only Laine knew what she had. What he might do for this.

As she returned the diamond to her pocket an idea came to her. Demi banged hard on the cabin door until Laine returned.

'What the hell d'you want?' he said.

'I want to make a deal with you.'

He stepped into the cabin, closing the door behind him.

'What kind of deal? I don't see you in any position to try and make deals,' he said.

'Just hear me out, okay?'

'Okay,' he agreed. 'So speak.'

Demi sat back on the bed.

'Do you have the diamonds here on this boat?'

'What if I do?'

'Do you have *all* the diamonds is what I'm saying,' she continued.

Laine frowned. 'I have the diamonds. If you're telling me they're not for real…'

'Oh, they're for real,' she interrupted. 'But there's one more and it's one I know you don't have.'

'One more? What are you on about?'

Demi sat rubbing her hands over her knees, looking down at the floor. She told him about the pink diamond and its value. How'd she'd taken it from the rest, hidden it at her parent's home. Laine listened, wondering whether to believe her or not. This could be another of her tricks.

'Why should I believe you?'

'That's up to you, but think about this: what do I know about diamonds? How would I have known its value unless someone had told me?'

He pondered on what she'd said – a diamond worth more than a million. Could he take the chance? He stood up and opened the cabin door.

'Frankie,' he called out. 'Turn the boat around. We're going back in.' Frankie eased back the throttle then came down to the cabin.

'Hey, what do you mean we're going back? I've arranged for us to go through the barrage. If we lose this slot, I'll have to arrange another, it won't be for hours.'

'Just take us back,' Laine snapped. He turned to Demi, still sitting on the bed.

'If you're playing games… trust me, you'll never see your kids again.'

Slamming the door, he went up top with Frankie as they headed back towards the berth. Frankie Galdini carefully manoeuvred the large yacht next to the mooring and secured it to its berth, then phoned to say they no longer required a slot to pass through the barrage.

Laine tried Lennie's mobile but only heard the message prompt. This did not bode well.

***

Pat and Wiener watched as the yacht began to turn back to the club moorings.

'Come on,' Wiener said, going back through the gate.

'What're they doing?' Pat asked.

'Beats me,' Wiener replied. 'Let's just wait and see.'

Pat looked up the road towards where Michael Steinberg had dropped him off earlier. The car and driver were still there, waiting. Pat waved at him and the Maserati moved towards them. Wiener turned to Pat. 'You go with Michael, I'll deal with Laine.'

Pat shook his head.

'No way, Ben. If Demi's on that boat I'm staying with you.'

Wiener thought for a moment. He leaned down on the low roof of the Maserati as Michael buzzed down the window.

'We're okay here, Mike – you go back, tell your father we'll be finished up pretty soon.'

'You sure, Ben? I don't mind staying. I could help if you want me to.'

'You kidding me,' he said facing the sky. 'And have your father to deal with? No, you go back, tell him everything here's kosher.'

Michael gunned the Maserati's powerful engine, a cloud of dust billowing up from its rear wheels as it sped away.

'Nice lad,' Pat commented.

'Nice car,' Wiener added.

***

With the yacht secured to its mooring, Laine told Frankie to sit tight until his return. He tried Lennie's number again, this time leaving a message.

'I don't like this.' He stared intensely at Demi, strongly considering reboarding the yacht with her. He checked his

Beretta was loaded and put it in his pocket, then phoned the taxi office in the dock. Khalid answered.

'I need a car to collect me,' Laine ordered. 'Get down to my boat, and bring some muscle with you.'

'Sure thing, Mr Laine,' Khalid said, 'anything else?'

'Yeah, make sure you're all armed.'

He ended the call.

'Right you, let's go,' he said taking Demi by the arm, yanking her towards the electronic gate.

'We're going straight to your parents to get that diamond. I need to know if it's worth as much as you claim. If it is, I'll let you go.'

'How will you find that out?' she asked. 'The deal is, I give you the stone and you leave me at the house.'

He squeezed her arm, making her wince.

'The deal is whatever I say it is, bitch. I don't trust you one fucking inch. I'll have someone lined up to examine the stone. It's for real, you go. If not, you're coming back with me to the boat.'

***

Wiener watched as they approached the gate. He turned to Pat.

'You stay right here,' he whispered. 'Leave this to me.'

Pat nodded his response, more than happy not to get involved. Wiener made his way around the boats in the yard, keeping a watch on Laine at all times. He noticed that Laine continually glanced at his watch while Demi stood next to him, her hands pushed down into the pocket of her jeans, scraping the ground with her feet. Wiener sensed Laine was waiting for someone to arrive.

A car approached at speed towards Laine and Demi, passing without either seeing it. Wiener saw it though and counted two men inside.

It pulled up at the gate. Laine walked over to the driver.

'Only two of you? Where are the others?'

'There are no others,' Khalid responded. 'But we've got weapons.' He tapped his waistband.

'Great,' Laine muttered. He turned to Demi. 'Get in the car.' Demi climbed into the back and Laine sat beside her. The car turned to head back.

Wiener thought through his options. Either take the BMW with the body of Lennie on the back seat, or try to stop this car. Easy choice to make. All it would take would be a 9mm round in one of the back tyres.

The car swerved out of control before stopping with a screech of brakes. The two in the front jumped out and looked around, senses heightened and on full alert, before examining the wheel. Laine wound down his window.

'What the fuck's happened?' The men checked around the car.

'Must've been a blow out,' Khalid said as he crouched down to take a closer look at the shredded tyre.

'So don't just stand there like a couple of zombies,' Laine ordered. 'Change the damn wheel.'

Khalid opened the boot as the other man pulled out the spare, bouncing it in front of him to check it was fully inflated. Khalid fumbled around in the well then removed the jack and wheel brace. He tapped on the rear window that wound down about five inches.

'Now what?' Laine asked impatiently.

'Be better if you got out, Mr Laine. We need to jack this thing up.'

Laine swore as he opened the door, pulling Demi with him.

Standing on the roadside, Laine watched as the two men started to change the wheel. Demi glanced nervously around, looking at the boats in the nearby repair yard. Khalid soon had the shattered wheel off, passing it to the man who held the spare between his knees. Demi studied the three men, seizing the moment; she pushed Laine as hard as she could and he fell heavily against the car, which in turn fell off the jack. Khalid, crouched next to the wheel, threw himself back as the car crashed to the ground. He collided with Laine, who tripped over him, both men scrambling with each other on the road.

In the chaos, Demi ran towards the boats, hiding beneath one of them. Laine picked himself up and took in the situation. *Another fucking cock-up.* He screamed at his men in fury.

'Go after her, you idiots, bring her back here.'

The two minders took off in pursuit. Demi lay under a propped-up cabin cruiser, trying to control her breathing, feeling sure they'd hear her. She crawled further under the boat. Glancing behind her, she could see the feet of the two men who'd split up to search for her. Khalid's companion approached the boat where Wiener remained, undetected.

Wiener indicated for Pat to remain silent as he removed his dagger from its sheath. The man looking for Demi moved around the stern of the large hull, leaning under the boat in search of his quarry. He never saw the fist that smashed upward into his face, felling him to the ground. Wiener

381

followed him down, pushing the blade into his chest and clamping a hand over the man's mouth to stifle any noises.

Khalid soon found Demi hiding under the hull. He reached out to grab her by the hair.

'Let go!' she shrieked in pain, trying to break free but Khalid's hold was too strong for her.

Pat heard Demi's scream and emerged from his hiding place, rushing across to Khalid who still held on to Demi by her hair.

'Let her go, you bastard.'

Pat threw himself furiously at Khalid who tried to defend himself from the sudden onslaught. Pat pummelled him to the face and stomach, his fists pounding like pistons as he vented a pent-up rage against the man who'd hurt his woman. Demi gasped in disbelief, seeing Pat in front of her, alive – very much alive. She watched him attack a man almost twice his size. Tears ran down her face, her emotions in turmoil daring not to believe what she saw. Khalid quickly took control as Pat began to weaken, the pain from his injuries dulling his effort. Khalid, well over six feet, weighing around 18 stone of pumped-up muscle, grinned as he felt Pat slow down. He caught Pat with a glancing blow. Although it hurt like hell, its lack of connection meant Pat kept going. He tried to jump on Khalid who swivelled on the ball of his left foot, throwing Pat to the floor. From inside his jacket he took out a knife, flicking open the 8-inch blade. He pulled Demi close to him.

'Stay still, darling,' he hissed in her ear as he touched the knife to the side of her neck.

Next to the stricken car, Laine began to panic as he watched what had just taken place. With the Berretta in his hand, he walked back towards the gate, quickening his pace in order to get back onto the yacht. Wiener spotted Laine, now almost running for the gate. He was about to go after him when he noticed Khalid had hold of Demi with a knife to the side of her head.

Pat scrambled to his feet to face the man. Head spinning, he could barely hold himself steady as he struggled for breath. The pain from his ribs burned like a hot poker in his side. He leaned against the hull of the boat with one hand to support himself.

'Le… let her go, scumbag,' Pat grunted, barely able to speak.

'Let her go... take me on instead.'

Khalid laughed at the stupidity of Pat's words. Pat looked straight at him.

'Call yourself a man?' he mocked. Demi shook her head.

'No, Pat,' she pleaded. 'Don't do anything. Please, please, just go.'

Pat shook his head.

'Nah,' he said. 'That ugly gobshite couldn't fight his… his way out of a kid's playground.'

'You little prick,' Khalid snarled back at him. Sweeping Demi's feet from under her, she fell to the ground. Raising the knife, he stepped towards Pat, slicing the air in front of him.

'You're dead meat, son, I'll kill you, then her.'

Wiener walked around a large, propped-up hull coming up behind the man with the knife. Khalid started jabbing the blade at Pat.

'I'll cut you into little pieces,' he hissed. 'You little shit.'

'I wouldn't do that if I were you,' Wiener said loudly.

The man slowly turned to face Wiener. 'Now who the fuck would you be?'

Wiener put his gun away; he didn't need it against a man with a knife. Khalid stepped forward, holding the blade in front of him.

'I hope you know how to use that thing,' Wiener said, his eyes locked on Khalid's. The man stepped closer. Wiener looked around; there were lengths of steel scaffolding tubes lying on the ground. He moved slowly to his right, inching nearer to the tubes. Khalid followed.

'Pat,' Wiener called out. 'Take care of Demi.'

Pat moved across to where Demi lay on the ground, his movement making Khalid glance sideways and away from Wiener, who deftly picked up a short length of scaffolding.

Khalid rushed at him full-on but Wiener calmly thrust the pole forward, hitting him directly in the chest.

Khalid staggered back. With one hand holding the tube, Wiener spread his arms open inviting Khalid to try again. Foolishly, he did. This time, Wiener swung the tube, hitting Khalid to the side of the head as he approached. Khalid staggered sideways and Wiener followed through, bringing the tube down like an axe, hitting his opponent on the crown of the skull, the force of the blow splitting open his head. Khalid collapsed to the ground, twitching, blood oozing from the wound. Wiener knew Khalid would be dead in minutes and threw the pole down on top of the dying man.

Demi held Pat tightly, still unable to believe he was alive.

'I thought they'd killed you,' she kept repeating.

'I'm fine, honestly I'm fine,' Pat assured her. 'Oh, by the way,' he said spotting Wiener, 'this is Ben. He's been helping us.'

Demi lifted her head towards the man stood next to them.

'Hi, Ben,' was all she could manage. Satisfied they were both okay, Wiener made his way to the electronic gate. He could hear the Sunseeker's twin engines increase in power as it once again pulled away from its mooring.

Wiener reached the locked gate. Laine was getting away from him. The yacht picked up speed as it moved across the inner harbour.

Pat came up behind him, wincing in pain. Demi still clung onto him, face streaked with tear tracks.

'Just let him go,' Demi said. 'What can he do now?'

'He can come back, probably will,' Wiener replied. 'I need to end this today.'

He looked around the area where he spotted the steel scaffolding tube he'd used to kill Khalid.

'This should do the trick,' he said to himself, but in earshot of the others. Wiener smashed the tube down with force on the gate's lock. The sound of metal on metal rang out around the perimeter of the yacht club as the lock shattered.

'Jesus, Ben,' Pat hissed. 'You'll have the police here in no time doing that.'

Demi looked up at Pat.

'He's just killed a man back there with that thing and you're worried about a bit of criminal damage?'

Wiener made his way along the jetty, watching as Laine's yacht sped across the water towards the barrage. There was still enough time to sail straight out on the high tide. Pat stood by the broken gate as if afraid to step through until Demi shoved him in the back.

'Come on, slow coach,' she said stepping through behind him.

Wiener checked the area, looking for a means of following the yacht. A number of small speedboats were tied to the jetty, some used as tenders to reach the yachts moored out in the harbour. He jumped down into one of them, a fifteen-foot Plancraft Sigma with a 55 HP outboard motor capable of powering the small craft to 30 knots. One push of the start button fired the motor into life. He noticed a small petrol can towards the stern where the rear seats had been removed; lifting it he could feel it was almost full. He was about to untie the boat when the mooring rope landed next to his feet. Pat jumped down into the craft.

'I'm coming with you,' he announced. 'I've got a score to settle with that bastard out there.'

'Me too,' a voice said from above.

They turned to see Demi scramble into the boat alongside them.

'I think it's better if you both stayed here,' Wiener said.

'He's getting away,' Demi pointed at the yacht as it approached the Barrage that would allow it to pass through onto the open water of the Bristol Channel.

Wiener grabbed the steering wheel and pushed the throttle. The small boat quickly picked up speed, its bow rising up out of the water as it pursued the yacht. With the sudden acceleration, Pat fell back onto Demi. They held on to the side of the speedboat as it leapt into the air then crashed back down, spraying them every time the bow hit the water. Wiener could see the yacht slowing down as it passed through the lock gate. He eased back on the throttle of the small craft and then suddenly increased it again as the yacht cleared the gate. Both boats were now in the open water of the Channel. The yacht moved forward, two 800 HP engines pushing it smoothly through the waves. The sea at its stern churned up into a white foam of bubbles. The little Sigma had no problem keeping up.

Frankie Galdini sat in the white leather pilot seat of the sleek Sunseeker. Sitting opposite, Laine kept looking back at the speedboat in pursuit of them, recognising the occupants.

'How fast can that thing go?' Laine asked his cousin.

'Fast enough.'

'So will they keep up?' Laine took the Berretta 92 semi-automatic from his pocket and checked its magazine.

'Depends how much fuel's in it,' Frankie said. 'But it will run out at some point, and then they'll be stranded out in the Channel. Rather them than me in that thing,' he added.

Laine smiled.

'Good. And this should give them something else to think about,' Laine said holding up the Berretta. He made his way out of the saloon to the rear of the boat where he climbed up to the fly bridge, giving him a better view back towards the pursuing speedboat. He laid down on a large sunbed, took a careful aim then fired off two rounds at the speedboat. One of them hit its mark.

Wiener could see Laine making his way to the top of the Sunseeker. He guessed what was about to happen next. Pat and Demi sat on the floor of the boat as it sped through the water in the wake of the large yacht. The wraparound glass screen suddenly shattered. Pat let out a scream as he clung to his knee. The bullet had passed through the screen, glancing Pat's knee in its trajectory. Wiener turned to face them.

'You okay?' he shouted.

'I've been hit in the leg,' Pat shouted back.

Demi found a box of torn rags and used one to place on the wound. 'I don't think it's serious,' she told Pat as she pressed down on the rag.

'I think it's very bloody serious,' he hissed in pain. 'I've been shot twice in as many days.'

Demi learned forward and kissed him on the forehead.

'Try to be more careful then,' she said smiling.

'How can I if people keep shooting at me?'

Demi opened another box containing teabags, coffee, and a pack of six bottles of *Stella* Beer. 'That'll keep him quiet', she thought to herself.

Just then the boat made a sudden swerve in the water and Demi dropped the bottle as she made a grab for the handrail. Wiener had turned the wheel to avoid another hit as Laine continued to fire at them. He took out his Sig, aimed back at the yacht and fired three successive shots. Even though they hit the yacht, causing some damage, Wiener knew it was a waste of ammo firing blind. He looked behind him and spotted the lager bottle on the floor as it rolled back and forth. Pointing at the petrol can, he shouted at Demi.

'Pass it over,' he indicated towards the red can.

Demi stretched out to grab the can then passed it to Wiener.

'Now sit up here next to me,' he pointed at the other seat. She sat with the petrol can at her feet. Wiener steered the speedboat to the right, away from the yacht. Both boats were approaching Flat Holm, having passed Penarth seafront. Wiener had to act fast, aware of the fuel limitation in the outboard motor.

'How many beer bottles are there?'

'About six I think,' she replied. 'Why? Do you want a drink?'

'Open them and tip the beer out,' he instructed her. 'Then I want you to half-fill them with petrol. D'you understand?'

She nodded.

'Right then, quick as you can.'

He turned to face Pat.

'Have you got your cigarette lighter?'

Pat fished around in his pocket and brought out his Zippo, holding it up for Wiener to see.

'Are we making petrol bombs?' Demi asked.

'That's the idea,' Wiener told her. 'Take a strip of rag and push it into each of them.'

She busied herself pouring petrol through a funnel into three of the now empty beer bottles that Pat held as steady as he could. Petrol splashed over them as the speedboat bounced over the water. Ripping off a strip of material from the rag box, she stuffed a piece into one of the bottles.

'All done,' she shouted.

Wiener nodded as he steered the speedboat to the left, starting to close the gap between them and the yacht. Turning back, he gestured with his hand for Demi to return to the front seat.

'When I say, you take hold of the wheel, keeping her heading straight, understand?'

'I think so,' Demi yelled back.

'We need to get in front of them,' Wiener shouted.

The gap between the two boats closed, Wiener fired two more shots as they closed in, not wanting Laine to have the opportunity to pick them off as they drew level.

'Okay,' he said, indicating for Demi to grab the small steering wheel. Wiener crawled to the rear of the craft where Pat lay bleeding from his knee.

'You okay?' he asked Pat.

'I've had better days,' Pat replied. Wiener held out his hand.

'Lighter.'

***

Barry Laine watched as the speedboat moved away. He fired three more shots from the Berretta but knew they had all missed. Now the speedboat was heading back towards the yacht. Laine smiled as he lay back down on the sunbed and took aim. He fired off three rounds at the boat, this time aiming at the large Mariner outboard motor. One round found its target.

'He's shooting at us again,' Demi screamed, ducking her head.

The speedboat veered to the right as she pulled down on the wheel.

Wiener crouched on the floor next to Pat. He heard the sound of the bullets as one smashed into the outboard. The small craft began to reduce speed as it lost power. Wiener looked up as the yacht increased the distance between them.

'Shit! They're getting away.'

Wiener cut the engine in order to minimise any further damage, the boat came to a stop in the open water, immediately pitching and rolling in the choppy sea.

'At least they've stopped shooting at us,' Demi said.

Wiener looked across the open water at the yacht.

'I'm not so sure,' Wiener announced. 'It's starting to turn.'

***

Barry Laine watched as the small speedboat came to a stop. He made his way back to the saloon where Frankie Galdini had the yacht travelling near its top speed.

'I hit their engine,' Laine said. Frankie tried to look back.

'Should we radio a distress call? A boat like that out here could easily sink.' He looked up at the impending storm, lead-grey rain clouds heading in from the southwest, bringing heavy weather. 'It's going to get rough out here soon,' Frankie said.

'Are you nuts?' Laine shouted. 'I hope the bastards sink and die. In fact, I have an idea to make sure that's exactly what happens. Turn us around.'

'Why? What are we going to do?'

'We're going to smash it to pieces by driving into them.'

Frankie looked at Laine with a furrowed brow.

'Ram them?'

'Yes, fucking ram them. Now turn around, I don't want to hang about here any longer than necessary.'

Frankie reduced speed, steering to make a turn to the port side.

'Make sure we get them side on. I want it to disintegrate when we hit it,' Laine said, almost laughing.

The yacht came about as it started to bear down on the speedboat bobbing in the water.

'What the hell are they doing?' Demi said as she watched the yacht approach them at speed.

'I don't think they're coming to assist us,' Wiener said.

He looked around the boat, starting to pull things about, searching for something, anything. In a stowage locker, he pulled out a metal box.

'I hope this is what I think it is,' he said setting the container down. Wiener opened and removed a bright orange pistol with a black handle.

'What is it?' Demi asked, 'A gun?'

'It's an Orion flare gun,' Wiener said. 'Not something you normally see on modern boats.' He picked up an orange cartridge. 'This is a twelve-gauge flare, it's fired from this,' he said holding up the gun. The yacht was about three hundred metres away, the space between them closing.

'Oh well, here goes.' Wiener took the flare gun, loaded it with a cartridge then aimed it towards the oncoming yacht and pulled the trigger. The flare discharged heading towards the yacht, flying over the top of the craft. He did the same with a second flare, this one exploded on the yacht's roof as it veered to starboard, trying to avoid the attack. Picking up a piece of cloth, Wiener held it under the oil dripping from the outboard motor before pushing it into one of the bottles containing petrol. He turned towards Pat and Demi, handing them a bottle each.

'Okay, Wiener said, 'they'll pass by fairly close giving us our only chance to hit them with these.'

Pat shifted himself to a better position, crying out when he straightened his leg.

'You going to be okay with this?' Wiener asked.

'I'll manage. I take it you'll be setting that rag alight.'

'That's the plan, my friend.' Wiener looked up when he felt rainfall. 'But this won't help things.'

The rain became a torrent.

'Right then, let's do it,' Wiener announced. All three faced the yacht.

'Get ready,' he shouted. 'When I say now, hurl the bottles. Try to aim for the rear of the boat.'

Wiener flicked the top of the Zippo, thumbed the wheel and held the small flame at the tip of the oil-soaked rag, relieved when it started to burn. The large cruiser sped past the stern of the motorboat, missing them by just a few metres.

'NOW!'

As it passed, they hurled the bottles of petrol. Pat's bottle fell short, landing in the sea. Demi's landed squarely on the rear of the yacht. Wiener held back for a few seconds waiting for the burning rag to take hold before he threw his. The bottle sailed through the air directly behind Demi's then landed on the yacht. Nothing happened. There was no sudden explosion of fire.

'Shit,' Wiener shouted, 'The rain must have doused the burning rags.' Demi looked at him 'Now what?'

Wiener dived at the red container, removed another cartridge, loaded the gun and took aim. He needed this to find its mark. If he missed there were only two flares remaining in the box. He fired at the yacht. This time it fell short, landing in the sea.

'Ben,' Demi screamed. 'It's turning back.'

Wiener reloaded, aimed and fired. It found its target, creating a searing white light. The petrol from the bottles ignited as the rear of the yacht burst into flames.

'Yes,' Demi shouted punching the air.

Wiener took out his Sig, firing off a number of rounds at the boat. He lowered the gun, pulling out its now empty magazine, pushed in a full mag and cocked the weapon.

'That should keep them down,' he said.

***

Frankie Galdini spun the steering wheel of the yacht as the flares came at them.

'What the fuck are they?' Laine shouted.

'Flares,' Frankie shouted as one went over, hitting the water.

The second flare hit the saloon roof, the bright light almost blinding them.

'Can you still see them?' Laine said.

'Can't see a damn thing.'

Frankie peered through the screen of the helm station.

'There they are,' he said pointing towards the small craft bobbing in the sea.

He spun the wheel again, realising the yacht had changed direction. The turn failed to hit the small boat.

'Shit, we missed them,' Laine said, looking out of a side window.

As they passed, they heard two crashing noises outside. Laine headed back through the saloon onto the deck. He could smell petrol, and then he noticed a line of white smoke heading directly at them.

'Turn the boat, turn the boat,' he shouted back at Frankie.

The manoeuvre proved too late as the flare struck the yacht, igniting the petrol from the bottles.

'The boat's on fire, get the extinguisher,' Frankie called out.

Laine was about to move when Wiener's gunshots tore into the saloon, shattering some of the windows. Black smoke from the fire began to fill the saloon space. Frankie pointed to the forward hatch.

'It's the only way out. Come on.'

Frankie slowed the yacht then shut down the engine. Laine stood frozen in the saloon. The fire took hold with black smoke increasing as the rubber dinghy attached to the rear began to burn. Turning, he noticed Frankie disappear through the hatch onto the stem of the boat. Laine looked at the Berretta in his hand, not sure how many rounds remained in the magazine. Frankie's head appeared at the open hatch.

'Bloody hell, Barry, you need to get out of there now.'

Laine crossed to the yacht's safe. He removed the bag of diamonds, stuffing them into his jacket pocket. He considered the money but decided against it.

***

Wiener, Pat, and Demi watched as the Sunseeker started to burn. They saw Laine and Galdini climb out to stand on the roof of the forward saloon.

'What are they doing?' Demi asked.

'Going down with the ship, I hope,' Pat replied.

Wiener loaded the last of the cartridges into the Orion pistol.

'This ought to give them something more to think about,' he said firing the pistol.

The flare cut through the two hundred metre distance between the speedboat and the yacht, hitting it square on, exploding into a white light. Wiener found a bottle of engine oil in the stowage locker. He moved to the rear and pulled open the outboard engine's casing to locate the oil filler. He poured in oil then turned to Demi.

'Press the start button next to the wheel,' he told her. 'Let's see if we can get this thing going again.'

Demi found the button. The engine spluttered at first then fired into life. Wiener moved back to the wheel, easing the throttle lever forward. The small boat picked up speed moving swiftly through the water. Wiener headed for the burning Sunseeker.

'Take over here, Demi,' he said, pulling the Sig from his waistband.

Suddenly, there came a loud explosion as the gas canisters from the Sunseeker's galley popped in the heat. The force threw Laine and Frankie into the water as the yacht rocked fiercely. Wiener slowed the speedboat as they approached the two men. Frankie was treading water but Laine floundered, beginning to panic.

'Frankie! Help me,' he cried out. 'I can't swim. Someone help me. Please help me!'

Frankie swan across towards his drowning cousin then stopped to tread water and faced the speedboat. 'Get him out of the water; for God's sake, get him out.' He carried on swimming towards Laine.

'I can't swim either,' Wiener shouted after him. 'And there's no room in this thing for all of us.'

Demi looked at Wiener, then back at the men in the water.

'We have to help them,' she said. 'We can't let him drown.'

Wiener threw a buoyancy jacket into the water but nowhere near Laine. Demi shouted at Wiener as she watched him,

'That's too far away. He'll never get to it.'

'Frankie will,' Wiener told her. 'He's looks like a pretty good swimmer.'

'What about Laine? He can't swim.'

Wiener looked into her face.

'Yeah, shame about that.'

Wiener turned the wheel as he throttled up the engine, heading for the shoreline. Demi didn't know where to look but took one final glance behind as Barry Laine slipped beneath the water. Pat put his arm around her, pulling her into him.

A second explosion from the yacht sent the craft beneath the waves. A cloud of smoke, steam and foam was the only trace left of Barry Laine's beautiful boat.

As the small craft eased its way to the shoreline, they passed a Trent-class lifeboat, launched from Barry Dock in response to the flares seen from the coast. Wiener shouted out as the lifeboat slowed alongside them.

'We tried to help,' he said, pointing to the spot where the yacht had gone down. 'Nothing we could do. There's a man in the water who may need help. We're okay,' he added giving a thumbs-up.

The lifeboat carried on towards Frankie Galdini, who bobbed like a cork in his life jacket, arms waving at his rescuers.

Wiener pushed the throttle, steering the motorboat towards Penarth's pebble shore.

'When we hit the beach we'll go our separate ways,' Wiener said. 'There'll be cops all over the place. You've been hit, so they'll sort out medics for you.' Pat nodded, aware of the injury to his knee that hurt like hell. Demi began to shiver; like the other two, she was wet though from the rain and sea water.

The boat crunched onto the pebble beach. After he and Demi had helped Pat out, Wiener made his way towards the promenade, walking briskly past the pier up the hill towards the town, head down with his hands in his pockets, indistinguishable to anyone who may have noticed him. Within minutes they heard sirens approaching. The police would soon be on the seafront. Pat sat next to Demi on a bench, waiting in the rain, huddled together like a pair of lost souls.

Forty-Three

Demi climbed out of the taxi before helping Pat. He eased himself up, taking the two aluminium elbow crutches from her. They stood together on the pavement opposite Cardiff Castle near Steinberg's jewellery store on High Street. Elroy Blake's funeral had taken place that morning. Most of the city's taxi drivers had attended, including the driver of the taxi who'd just dropped them off.

'He wouldn't take my money,' Pat said looking at the car as it pulled into the busy stream of traffic moving along Castle Street.

'I'm surprised you offered,' Demi said. 'He gave us a lift back, he wasn't looking for a fare.'

'I guess not. Oh well, let's go in and see our friends.'

Demi pushed open the heavy glass door, holding it as Pat hobbled passed. The shop was quiet. A man studied a display of luxury watches under a glass-top counter, looking but unlikely to buy, the cheapest a shade less than £6,000. At another counter, Michael Steinberg showed a young couple a selection of diamond engagement rings, the spotlights picking out the radiance and beauty of the stones as he lay them on the crimson cloth of the tabletop.

Abraham Steinberg stood in the centre of the shop. He raised his hands as Pat and Demi walked in, a smile filling his face. Michael acknowledged them with a small wave. Steinberg kissed Demi lightly on her face then stood back to look at her.

'Such beauty,' he said, taking in her dark eyes, olive coloured skin, brilliant white teeth and long, silky black hair. Pat turned to face her, seeing what Steinberg saw: a woman so stunningly beautiful she stopped you in your tracks.

'How are your children?' Steinberg asked.

'Oh they're fine, thank you. Back in school like nothing ever happened.'

'I'm sorry I wasn't at the funeral today but...'

'That's okay,' Pat interrupted him. 'You never knew Elroy. The flowers your family sent were something else. That was really kind of you.'

Steinberg gave a slight wave of his hand.

'It was the least we could do. He was a good friend of yours, I understand. Did he have any family?'

'Not really,' Pat said. 'There's a son somewhere from a relationship that ended many years ago. No, no family but plenty of friends.'

Steinberg nodded his understanding.

'Is Ben here?' Demi asked looking over Steinberg's shoulder towards the back-office door.

'Alas, no. If I know Ben, he's sitting in a pastry shop somewhere in Manhattan. He did send his apologies but said he felt sure you'd both understand.'

'Perhaps we could go and visit him sometime,' Demi suggested. 'You are able to get in touch with him, aren't you?'

'Indeed,' Steinberg told her. 'I'm sure he'd like that very much. I think he took a liking to you, my dear.'

Demi smiled, as her face flushed.

'How's Rebekah?' Pat asked.

'See for yourself,' Steinberg said indicating towards the shop door.

Turning around, they saw Steinberg's daughter enter the store, her pace quickening when she saw Demi. The two women hugged like long lost friends, both with tears in their eyes.

'Father, why are we standing in the shop?' She took Demi by the hand, pulling her towards the office. 'Come on.'

As they sat together in the wood-panelled room, Pat told how they'd chased after Barry Laine in the small speedboat and how Ben Wiener had used petrol and a flare gun to sink the luxury yacht. He went on to say how Laine had been thrown into the sea and drowned. They both decided not to mention how they could have helped him. How Wiener let him die.

'He deserved to die,' Rebekah said. 'He was responsible for the death of a lot of people. Look what they did to Pat's friend.'

'Yes, people who live by the sword…' Steinberg said solemnly.

'Do we know anything about Frankie Galdini?' Demi asked. 'Will he go to prison?'

'The police are still looking into his involvement,' Rebekah told her. 'But they may not get far. After all, he wasn't really responsible for anything his cousin did. They're laying all the deaths at the feet of Laine and his cronies, particularly Lennie Randall. Gang warfare, that's what they're saying. No mention of Ben, thankfully.'

'What about the diamonds?' Pat asked. 'Will you try to get them back?'

Steinberg shook his head.

'As you know they went down with him. So we have to accept they're lost forever.'

'It was the diamonds that started all this,' Demi said. 'I still can't believe what we've been through.'

Pat took hold of her hand squeezing it lightly. Steinberg pulled open a desk drawer and lifted out a large manila envelope that he dropped on his desk. It landed with a heavy thud.

'I want you both to have this,' he said.

'What is it?' Demi asked.

Steinberg lifted the envelope, tipping banknotes onto the desk.

'It's the reward money for the diamonds. I think you deserve to have it. Ben also mentioned to me about your financial problems, so this should help you get back on your feet.'

Pat let out a low whistle.

'How much is there?'

'Never mind how much is there,' Demi said. 'We can't take your money, Mr Steinberg.'

Pat's face dropped as she said this. 'But Mr Steinberg wants us to have the money, it's the reward…'

'No, Pat,' Demi persisted. 'We cannot take it. Mr Steinberg lost his diamonds. It wouldn't be right.'

Rebekah spoke next.

'My father wants you to have this money, Demi. Think what you both could do with it, especially now Pat's resigned from his job. Go on, take it.'

'Please,' Demi pleaded. 'We really don't want it. Not after all we've been through.'

Demi stood up. Pat was about to speak.

'No, Pat. Not another word.' She held out a hand, helping him to his feet. 'We'll be on our way now. If you get in touch with Ben, please tell him we're grateful for all he did.'

Steinberg returned the money to the desk drawer.

'Well, if you ever change your mind, it'll still be in the bank.'

Demi walked around the desk. 'You've been so kind, Mr Steinberg,' she said then lightly kissed him on the cheek.

Pat shook hands with him and embraced Rebekah.

'You will keep in touch now, won't you,' Rebekah said to them. 'You know where to find us.'

'We'll keep in touch,' Demi assured her as they hugged each other for the second time.

***

Pat gazed down at his latté, slowly stirring the milky coffee. He studied the liquid as it swirled around the long glass. Demi watched him from behind her cappuccino. He wanted to ask her why she'd refused the money, why she'd turned down one hundred thousand pounds, all in tax-free cash. He wanted to ask but instead he put a completely different question to her.

'Why do they serve lattés in glasses, not cups?' He continued to stir, as the metal spoon pinged on the glass. 'The only difference between my coffee and yours is that yours has chocolate sprinkled on top.'

'No,' Demi chirped, 'mine's a cap whilst yours is a latté.'

A foam moustache appeared on her upper lip as she sipped the drink.

Pat shook his head.

'But they're both made with milk. When I was a boy, it was just milky coffees, not lattés and the like. Hell, there's even a flat-white now.'

Demi screwed her face at him.

'You going to drink it or stir it till it evaporates?'

'I'd prefer tea.' He looked over to the counter. 'Do they have tea?'

'Yes, they do, you sulky bugger. D'you want one?'

'Not really. This'll do.'

He lifted the tall glass and sipped.

'Why, Dem?'

'Why what?' she replied.

'You know what I mean. The money.'

'Oh that.'

Demi smiled; Pat's forlorn face amused her. She resisted taking hold of him and kissing him passionately. Instead, she moved from her seat to sit next to him.

'Oh dear, did poor little Pat want to be rich then?' she mimicked.

He turned towards her, a sheepish grin on his face. He wanted to be angry with her, but how could he be angry with such a striking woman?

'No, not rich, Dem – just comfortable. You know? no debts, no loan sharks chasing me, threatening me with knives, that sort of comfortable. Then, after all we've been through, we end up with nothing. No diamonds, no money. Nothing.'

Demi squeezed his hand.

'We don't need the money Pat. We've got…'

'I know, I know,' he interrupted her. 'We've got each other.'

'No,' she said. 'I was going to say we've got this.'

Demi put her hand on the table to reveal the pink diamond between their coffees. Pat's eyebrows rose when he saw the stone.

'Is that… is that? Oh, my God, Demi. Where'd you get it from?'

He could barely contain his excitement as he picked up the diamond.

'This thing's worth a fortune,' he whispered, not wanting the other customers to hear.

'That day I took the diamonds from the station locker,' she told him. 'I removed this one and kept it separate. I figured no one knew about the pink diamond except us. I always knew whatever happened we'd lose the others somehow or other.'

'You crafty little woman, you. That's why you didn't want to take the money. You had this little baby all along.'

Demi nodded.

'We couldn't take Mr Steinberg's money. Not after he'd lost the other diamonds. It just wouldn't have been fair.'

The smile left Pat's face when he considered what Demi had said.

'Is it still fair to keep this from him? Maybe we should return it to him and take the money instead. That would be the honourable thing to do. Wouldn't it?'

Demi looked him in the face for a moment.

'To return it suggests he had it in the first place, which he didn't,' she said softly.

Pat lifted his hand and waved a finger at her.

'No, but his family did, so that's the same thing in my book.'

Demi laughed at him.

'Well, Patrick Doyle, you and I have completely different tastes in books. In *my* book, it's not the same.'

He thought about this for a moment before replying.

'Demetra, from now on, I'm only ever going to read your books.'

They left the station coffee shop arm in arm. Out on the busy street they laughed together as they walked. Pat stopped when he glanced at the paper stand with its headline:

Cardiff Gang-War Ends. Many Dead.

He stopped, pulling Demi closer to him. He kissed her deeply.

'I love you, Demetra Karamanlis. With or without money.'

'I love you too, Patrick Doyle,' she replied. 'Always have, always will.' He was about to kiss her a second time when a voice called out.

'Dr Doyle. We have unfinished business. Please come with us, now.'

Pat looked over at two Asian men who stood by a black Mercedes car – Osman's men.

'Who are they?' Demi asked. 'D'you know them?'

'Unfortunately, I do,' he whispered. 'I owe them money. I think they still want to cut my fingers off.'

'Oh God, not again.'

Demi turned around, looking back towards the station entrance.

'I've got an idea,' she whispered back to him. 'When I say now, follow me.'

The two men watched incredulously as the pair suddenly turned and ran off into the railway concourse, heading for Platform One.

Printed in Great Britain
by Amazon